# THE ALL-AMERICAN

엘

아

메

리

칸

# THE ALL-AMERICAN

*A NOVEL*

## JOE MILAN JR.

**W. W. NORTON & COMPANY**

*Celebrating a Century of Independent Publishing*

For information about permission to reproduce selections from this book, write to Permissions, W. W. Norton & Company, Inc., 500 Fifth Avenue, New York, NY 10110

For information about special discounts for bulk purchases, please contact W. W. Norton Special Sales at specialsales@wwnorton.com or 800-233-4830

Manufacturing by Lake Book Manufacturing
Book design by Chris Welch
Production manager: Lauren Abbate

ISBN 978-1-324-03565-7

W. W. Norton & Company, Inc., 500 Fifth Avenue, New York, N.Y. 10110
www.wwnorton.com

W. W. Norton & Company Ltd., 15 Carlisle Street, London W1D 3BS

1  2  3  4  5  6  7  8  9  0

"어이없다"

Romanization: o-iee-op-da

Pronunciation: [əiːʌpdɒ]

Definition: Stupefied. Dumbfounded. To be subject to absurdity and confusion. From the phrase "어처구니없다," which relates to the situation of trying to mill rice between millstones without a handle.

# PART ONE

## 2000: TIBICUT

# 0

I AM A RUNNING BACK. EVERY MORNING I RUN TIED TO A TIRE. IT BARKS and growls behind me on the trail, all the way through the woods, and up and down the ravine. But this morning, just as we get to the bottom, the tire catches something and yanks so hard the rope snaps and launches me into the stream.

The water is cold and my shirt is drenched and it takes me a moment to get up and slap the goose bumps. I got to stay positive: cold boosts testosterone, clears lactic acid, jump-starts fast-twitch muscle production. This is what Coach Shaw says those mornings before school starts and we're shivering in the weight room next to the broken heater wondering how there could be a zero period.

My body is cold but my thumb is warm.

Blood.

Apply pressure. Breathe. Sit on a mossy log. Think first aid. "Don't be afraid of your blood," like the school counselor said. "It is what you are." What I am is a high school running back. Tomorrow, I have my chance to get out of Tibicut to be a college running back. Uncle Rick couldn't do that. He made this harness and trains me so that I can. And now my ball-cradling hand is bleeding, getting infected, and I'm blinking and breathing through my nose and out my mouth, trying to keep calm, trying not to think of tweakers—looking for a place to smoke some ice—finding my blood-drained body.

I look at the hand. Don't be a pansy, Bucky. It's hardly bleeding, not even a helmet-button's worth. I strip off what's left of the harness and my drenched shirt and wrap my hand.

A squirrel barks up in a tree. I know it shits in this stream.

"Rehearse in your dumb heads," Coach Shaw says. "You actualize what you visualize, so rehearse like a champion and execute." The key to mental rehearsal is to imagine a perfect world without anything else.

I breathe. Close my eyes. Forget the moss, the trees, the gray skies. Don't think how my tire must've caught a knuckle of cedar root or an old brake caliper. Visualize Astroturf, hash marks, hurdling big uglies, bombing down sidelines, running to the end zone, and dancing at the foot of the Stars and Stripes. Blood is nothing.

But I don't get to the end zone. Refs whistle. Kill my play. I'm all alone on the field, stranded by a bad call in my own mental rehearsal.

On the fifty-yard line is a ref who's not a ref but a grinning Asian dude in a gray Members Only jacket and bomber sunglasses. My eyes open as fast as they can.

Grinning Asian dude? I run. Hustle. Flee. Leave the tire down by the stream.

# 1

AT SUNNY MEADOW THERE'S NO SUN AND NO MEADOW, JUST A MOBILE home park buried in the ass of Lion Mountain. We have a view of the 24–7 gas station beside the state route. Sheryl, on the porch, paces and talks on the phone. Sheryl is my mom. I call her Sheryl because she's not my real mother. Just like Uncle Rick isn't really my uncle and Bobby isn't really my brother. Strangers wouldn't mistake me for the rest of the family, they're all white. I'm the only Asian for miles. So, I call her Sheryl like how she calls me Bucky even though that isn't my real name. It's the only name that sounds right.

She paces on the porch with the cordless because she says the house is too stuffy and dark. The laminate wood walls are dark, and ours stink. The cats pissed everywhere. We used to have screens on the windows but the cats slashed them. A cat would spray a pair of shoes or a basketball and Bobby or me would grab the cat and toss it out the window. Sometimes we forgot to check if the screen was in and the cat would cling onto it, clawing and hissing. Now we mostly keep the windows closed to keep the gnats out and Sheryl goes to the porch to call Graham, a six-foot-six soft-hand guy who wears button-down shirts and is always checking his cell phone as if to remind us that he has one and the rest of us don't. Sheryl and Graham are engaged. They're going to move in together in Tacoma, where Graham's got a job as a lawyer and an apartment in a tall building of blue glass and marble and two little girls that adore Sheryl. Here, Sheryl's only got me and Bobby. I'm seventeen and Bobby is eighteen with a GED and both of us are trying to get far away from Sunny Meadow and the single-wide with cat-pissed laminate walls. But when Sheryl sees me coming from the trails she isn't wearing that smile that says she's talking about a future in the city: she looks pale.

First, I think it's because I'm cradling my hand and got no shirt on. But she hollers, "Get in the car." Back into the phone she says, "We'll be there in a minute, just keep talking to him, Jerry." Then she tosses the cordless onto the Lay-Z-Boy that Bobby and me found on the state route.

"We got to go right now." She's pointing at the old Geo missing the passenger side-view mirror. She points at the car whenever we have to rescue a cat.

"I cut my hand," I say.

"Get in the car, there's no time."

"Sheryl, I cut my hand," I say. Sheryl looks at my T-shirt-wrapped hand.

Her mouth opens. Her eyebrows pinch together as if I had just told her I shot the neighbor and here I am half-naked with blood on my hands.

"I fell?" I say. "Into the stream? Must've cut it on a beer bottle?"

"With Rick?"

"No. I was running, you know?"

She hustles me into the house, chanting, "Shit-shit-fucking-shit-shit," the whole time she douses peroxide on my hand. "It's not bad, it's not bad, just a big, stupid, football paper cut." She hates me playing football. She gasps whenever she sees new practice bruises and sweeps a flashlight across my eyes checking for the bruises in my "football head." She doesn't bother to close the cap on the peroxide bottle and goes straight to looping a bandage around my hand, then stops and tells me to do it in the car and starts dragging me out the bathroom, through the living room, until the bandage catches on my American ABBoMbr that I always forget to put away. It yanks me, I yelp, and Sheryl says, "Untangle yourself. Get a shirt. I'll get the car started."

When I get outside with the bandages cradled like a football, I have to sprint to the stop sign, where Sheryl is honking and waiting with the passenger door open.

"The hell is going on?" I say.

She grinds the clutch and just keeps chanting, "Shit-shit-fucking-shit-shit."

We drive out to Uncle Rick's place. It's at the end of a dirt road. If it was paved and had a fancy sign like they do in the suburbs of Tacoma it would be called a cul-de-sac. But here is just one big house and two trailers, three parts of a property that Sheryl and Uncle Rick's mom cut up.

She sold two of the parts and left the third, a trailer with a bowed roof, for Uncle Rick.

We go past the first trailer, Jerry's trailer, and we see Jerry hanging out his window with the phone to his ear and the cord nearly straight: "He's in the backyard!"

Around back, at the edge of the overgrown grass, we see Uncle Rick under the big cedar. He's standing on a purple barstool. He's got a noose around his neck. He's trying to throw the other end of the rope over the large branch hanging low off the tree.

"Rick, what are you doing?" Sheryl shouts.

"Uncle Rick?" I say.

Uncle Rick looks at us like he doesn't know us. Then he says, "That lying son of a bitch." His barstool teeters and Uncle Rick puts his arms out to keep his balance. Then he cups his hands over his mouth: "Jerry, you son-of-a-bitch, I'll haunt your goddamn house."

He has to put his arms out again to keep himself steady on the stool. It's his special stool from the Tibicut Bar and Grill. They closed down a year ago and he broke in a few days later and grabbed his barstool. I asked him how he knew it was his and not just any stool. "There are just some things you got to know about yourself—like the grooves your ass wears down on a stool."

"Rick, get down from there," Sheryl says.

"Sissy, go home," he says.

"You're not thinking right. You're drunk, aren't you?" she says.

"I said go on!"

Sheryl looks over at me as if I will somehow know what to do. I don't know what to do. Who hangs himself? Other people off themselves with a gun or pills. Maybe wait in the driver's seat with the car coughing in the garage, if they got a garage. Other people do these things because they're messed up in the head and suicidal.

But he's tied a noose with the same rope he used to make me the harness to pull the tire around the trails. The one I left down the ravine by the stream. And it's hanging around his neck and down his shirt like a tie.

All I can say is, "Unc?"

"You two get out of here," he says. He keeps trying to throw the line over the branch, but every time he tries, the rope misses or slips and he loses his balance and has to shoot his arms out.

"Rick, you stop this and come down from that stool," Sheryl says.

"Unc," I say, "I broke the harness and Fontinot scouts us tomorrow, and . . . and what are you doing?"

He stops. He looks at me. His cheeks are as red as his beard and I'm surprised he's able to stay level on the stool at all. You wouldn't know it by looking at him now, but in old photos he looked like the Brawny paper towel man. Now coffee and whiskey streak his red beard, and sap and motor oil polka-dot his flannel shirt that's pulled tight over his liver belly. He squints. "What?"

"The harness broke when I was running," I say. It comes out like a confession. It *is* a confession, of something awesome. I hold up my bandaged hand. The bandage is already trailing out a little like a tail. "Fell and cut my hand in the stream."

I think I can see his eyes get glassy. He sniffs, then looks up at the branch and tosses the rope up again and it makes it over. He starts hitching it. I think he means business but I don't know what else to say. One time, Unc said that you know you're finally strong enough when you break the lines that pull you back.

"Aren't you going to come and watch?" I say.

"Buck," Uncle Rick says, "remember your pad level. Leverage comes low from the core. Hip thrusts. Lots of hip thrusts. Now go."

He looks back at Jerry's trailer. "Jerry, you lying sonofabitch! You come and get them out of here or I'll haunt your firstborn!" He finishes the hitch.

"Rick, you're scaring me." Sheryl's voice is calm now and she's got her hands up, walking slowly in an arc toward him, like when you walk toward a scared horse. "Stop this right now."

Uncle Rick tugs on the rope, and suddenly there's the sound of a gunshot or a backfire, and then the branch breaks and falls like a giant green hand, slamming Uncle Rick to the ground. Sheryl screams, I freeze, and Jerry comes running.

After a long moment, someone, maybe it's me, calls out to Uncle Rick. We hear him moaning. With all the branches it's hard to see him. Jerry, Sheryl, and I start breaking the smaller branches off. I can see his red flannel through the branches heaving, pulsing. I don't think I ever saw him cry before. I can't see his face but I know it's flushed and scrunched and he's sobbing. "Fuck me."

Later, the paramedics put Uncle Rick in an ambulance and tell us they're taking him to Wildcat Hospital. We won't get to see him tonight, since this is an attempted suicide and all.

When they're gone, Jerry keeps hugging Sheryl and I walk over to the broken branch. It broke at the trunk. Cedar isn't brittle, isn't supposed to rot like this. Bugs don't like it. But there it is, rotten at the core, little twisty lines like rivers where bugs chomped trails underneath what people could see.

My hand stings. I feel woozy. I sit in the high grass next to the branch. I want to think how sorry I am that I wasn't here sooner, or even figuring that Uncle Rick would want to off himself. But I'm not feeling sad like I ought to. I feel sick and tingly. One of the paramedics had asked me about the hand and Sheryl told him it was nothing. *We'll take care of it.* How will we take care of this? But that isn't even what I'm really thinking about: I keep thinking about the asshole in the Members Only jacket who I haven't seen since I was little enough to disappear in this tall grass, playing hide-and-seek from Uncle Rick and Bobby, by this big cedar that I thought would grow forever, or until someone finally decided it would make good fence posts. That asshole is always wearing sunglasses in the photographs. They're stowed in a dusty shoebox in the back of the closet under another box of mini-helmets I got from vending machines.

That asshole is my bio-father.

# 2

I'M NOT SURE WHAT YOU'RE SUPPOSED TO DO AFTER SOMETHING LIKE that, but the next day is a Monday and I go to school and to football practice. Today is the last time that Larry Fontinot will come to watch us practice. He scouts for some company that talks to colleges and is the only one who ever bothers to watch us. His job is to snag anyone good from the small towns and send them away to a bigger, better place. Twice a year he comes, and when he does we all get jumpy, even Coach Shaw. We can tell he's jumpy because we take a knee in the lumpy grass before the start of practice and he starts waving his rolled-up playbook around and fires into his Mayan speech—how they used to sacrifice the losers to the heathen gods and had celebratory punting matches with sacrificed heads. "That's war, gentlemen. And let me tell you, I've seen war. Guts draped over blasted pickup trucks and godforsaken sands. Remember, the gridiron has no memory. Only performance. Only champions. Only brotherhood. So get ugly. Get mean. That's your only purpose. And if you're not bleeding for your teammates, then your sorry ass will be carried off the field like a corpse."

Bleeding. The cut isn't even staining the bandage but I can feel its sting under my golf glove that I found in a McDonald's bathroom. The glove grips better than any hand, and today I need all the grip I can get.

The only person not nervous is Jimmy Pope. He's a wide receiver who runs a four-five forty-yard dash. He has a bunch of scholarship offers. The last time Larry Fontinot came by, he grabbed Jimmy by the shoulder after practice and gave him his card, telling him to call about his future, then Fontinot waddled off to the parking lot. Jimmy's all right. A real humble guy. But it's hard to talk to him, since whenever he talks I just wait for him to mention scholarships or his star rating or something. He doesn't. But

I guess that's why he's one of the guys with clear skin sitting on tailgates talking to all the girls while I'm walking home alone.

Fontinot sits up in the bleachers with a microwaved burrito in one hand and a pair of binoculars in the other. No camcorder this time. We practice. Cutbacks around cones, pushing sleds, shuttle runs. "Run like they're out for your nuts!" Coach screams. I'm hustling. Showing my speed. Cutting my routes as sharp as an X-Acto knife. I'm not the fastest but I'm an artist. Put me in for punt returns, I sidestep fools for fifteen yards or better. Put me in collapsing holes between the tackles, I slide and fall forward for two yards instead of a loss. I'm that slippery back, a first- and second-down back who sets up the manageable third. Perfect for a scholarship and the opportunity to learn and build my football knowledge into a coaching career so far away from Tibicut that the only thing left of me here is a photo of me in the trophy box by the gym water fountain.

But first Fontinot needs to see how valuable I am: the scrimmage. Fontinot will see me sliding past tackles like a duck in water because my pad level is low and I got all that leverage from hip thrusts.

Everyone says I'll be a doctor or a lawyer, but they haven't seen my grades. Uncle Rick has seen my grades. And he's seen me play. That's why he wants me to play football. That's why I love him. On breaks from pulling stumps for somebody expanding their pasture, Uncle Rick will tell me to take a couple of minutes and run as fast as I can to the far side of the pasture without stepping in any shit.

Eyes closed. Focus. Visualize.

Imagine Fontinot dropping his burrito, standing up on the bleacher, and clapping because he's never seen a bread-and-butter back like me before.

Pump your legs until the whistle. Fall forward.

The ref whistles. It's him again out on the fifty-yard line.

I open my eyes. On the fifty-yard line is only a football tee and a cone.

Up in the bleachers, Fontinot is looking at the far end zone, where the girls' cross-country team warms up and the cheerleaders jump. Usually before practice I'd try to catch a glimpse of Hot Holly, maybe even wave if I feel brave, but the only cheerleaders that ever see me are the gymnast dudes and Chantal, who flips me the bird. She's one of three Asians at our school. Chantal is adopted to a family that's got a boat and a big spread along the water and she's Korean and for once she sees me and doesn't flip me the bird. It's been like that all day, people acting different: at morning weight lifting, guys told me good job after I pumped three hundred on the squat rack, instead of just grunting or hocking a loogie on the floor. In chem, Mrs. Slaughter didn't give me a pink slip after seeing my doodle, in the chem book, of "C" carbon as a curled dick and the two oxygens as its balls. In English, Ms. Griffin, who we call Fake English because she speaks with a fake English accent and is our one-year temp from the "teach the rural poor" program from Portland, didn't ask me to show her my haiku, and skipped over me like I got the flu. It's me and Chantal, the only two Asians, and Fake English doesn't ask me to share my awesome football haiku?

*Sacked quarterback in the N-zone*
*cries like a daisy*
*for safety*

After class Chantal bumps into me and stuffs something in the pocket of my letterman jacket. "What's that about?" I say. She doesn't even slow down, just shoots up the stairs and disappears in the flow of the hallway. It's a note, folded up like an envelope but with a tongue and a little cartoon hand flipping me the bird. So, I guess she already flipped me off once today.

Everyone else is acting different because they already heard about Uncle Rick. And that's just noise for me to stuff in my pockets until later.

The first play of scrimmage: Emmet, our quarterback, throws the ball down the middle, into traffic. The ball wobbles. Suddenly Jimmy swoops in and nabs it one-handed. Fontinot stands, nods. The next play, I get the ball and hand it off to Jimmy on a reverse. He bolts down the sideline for a touchdown while two linebackers and a defensive end plow me into the turf and pop my helmet off. Fontinot golf-claps. It goes like this for a while until Coach pulls Jimmy out and I finally get my chance.

I line up behind Emmet. I hate Emmet. He'll eat a sack rather than toss the rock to me for a checkdown. The ball snaps and Emmet turns, hands me the ball, and there's no hole where there's supposed to be a hole. I back up and already some guys are barreling down on me, and I spin out to the right and hurdle legs and arms, trail behind a tackle, and fall forward for a few yards in the mess. Whistle blows. No high-fives. No "good-jobs." But that doesn't matter. These guys don't get that positive yards off a broken play are gold for a coach. They don't know that because they don't study the game. They didn't learn the playbook the day they got it. They don't realize that the left guard didn't pull quickly enough and that's why there wasn't a gap for me to run through and that's because he's an idiot and probably forgot the play from the huddle to the line. This is what I do: I make something out of nothing. I see the yards of the offensive series—the whole series—not just a single play of Xs and Os. I move the rock forward. That's the mark of an excellent two-down, bread-and-butter back. A Division One back, a three-down D3 back, a thinking running back perfect for schools like Yale that appreciate nuance and excellence beyond the GPA.

Up in the bleachers, Fontinot is gone.

—

After practice I see Jimmy talking to Fontinot in the parking lot by a brand-new green Corvette. I wait for them to finish up, crackle the pebbles under my shoe into the sidewalk, and tap my glossy Barry Sanders folder against my leg to keep me calm.

You're not good enough, I think. You didn't train hard enough. You broke the harness that Uncle Rick made for you and left it and the tire by the stream. Think about the way Uncle Rick teetered on the stool. Think how you had nothing good to say and how his face was lost and burnt and just begging for something or someone to look back at him with a reason to get down from the barstool.

A couple of O-linemen, Darren and Zach, walk past me and gaze at Fontinot and Jimmy.

"You don't think he's giving Jimmy the 'Vette, do you?" Darren asks.

Zach shakes his giant head.

These guys didn't block for me, didn't open up any holes. Fontinot is supposed to be talking to me. He's supposed to be thumbing through my papers, which say my stats, which say I passed my physicals, and which say I passed my classes with a solid 2.57 GPA. "Hey," I say to them, "you guys had to forget how to open a hole today, didn't you?"

"Screw you, Buck," Darren says. "You just don't know how to read a block, man."

"Yeah, man," Zach says. "Maybe you can't see that well."

So, I can't see well? Oh, I know this. I've known this since the first time a kid in the SuperDollar jumped out from behind an aisle with his eyelids pulled to the sides to make little slits while screaming, *Karate Kid!*

"The hell is that supposed to mean?" I say.

"Exactly what I said," Zach says. "It's like you weren't looking or something, you know?"

My fist is clenched and I'm ready. "Go on, I know you want to say it."

"Say what?"

"Say it."

Zach drops his gym bag and I drop mine. Our eyes get wide and still and direct. Darren raises his giant taped hands between us.

"Yo," Darren says. "Yo, Buck, if you want to be pissed, go talk to Fontinot. It's not us, man." He picks up Zach's gym bag and hands it to him. "Come on, man."

By the glittering Corvette, Jimmy and Fontinot are still talking, and Jimmy is nodding in that way that says things are only going to get better. Zach and Darren lumber off toward microwaved Salisbury steaks. A townie future of grub-like children they'd lie to about the time they won 56–0. Jobs they'll never like if they're lucky, speed teeth and drunk tanks if they're not. That is the Tibicut way. Everyone looking out their living room windows and seeing all the paint fading on their walls and the moss eating their lawns and they wheeze, "Oh well," before lumbering off to the kitchen to zap some Stars and Flags fish sticks during the commercial break.

I walk over to the Corvette as Fontinot is getting in. He's telling Jimmy to get his transcripts in on time. I'm going to holler and break things. I'm going to shove my Barry Sanders folder filled with three seasons of bread-and-butter running back stats in his face. But before I can say anything, Fontinot says, "Kid, if I wanted to talk to you, we would've talked." He closes the door and starts the car. Dumb, frozen, I just stand there as the Corvette rumbles out of the parking lot.

"Bucky?" Jimmy says.

Jimmy's next to me. And I feel like the ground is splitting apart.

"You all right, brother? Larry's an asshole, don't listen to him."

Jimmy calls him *Larry*.

I don't look at Jimmy. He would keep trying to make me feel better, I'm sure of it. He's that kind of guy. A good guy from a good family with a good future and a nice house with a gate and a garage and a whole lot of people who like talking to him and being around him.

"What happened to your hand, brother?"

I want to stomp him into the pavement. Take a helmet to his kneecap. Instead, I walk away and don't look back. Jimmy just keeps saying, "Bucky? Bucky? Brother?"

# 3

I CUT THROUGH THE WOODS. THE CROWS AREN'T SQUAWKING AND I SEE a raccoon trotting away with a Cheetos bag in its mouth. At the fork, where the running trails meet, the dirt path is smoothed like a vacuum cleaner over carpet. That's me and my tire, moving all these Doug-fir needles every morning along the crest between ravines. For what?

Then I'm shouting. No words, just an *Ahhiiieee!* that drops to a grunt when I set my Barry Sanders folder on a pillow of fir duff. Then I sledge-hammer my bag into the path and huck my water bottle. It just bounces off one of the cedars and lands back at my feet. Can't even toss a water bottle. So I sit there in my swept dirt. From up here you only see sappy trunks and flaky bark and bent madrones all so brown that you'd swear that they heat up red at night. Everything smells fresh. When the trees aren't creaking in the breeze, you can hear the stream glug. But now, no glug and no breeze. Maybe my tire got into the stream. I should go down there and at least get the harness.

My eyes are burning, but running backs don't cry.

I smell dust in the air. It's going to rain. That's what this is. All the trees are giving me this closed-in feeling, the same feeling I get when our power dies and all the other porch lights and TVs in the neighborhood are still going. I need to go home. I need to be with my VHS of *NFL Films Presents: Born to Run.*

—

The moment I come out of the trail at Sunny Meadow, I hear yelling. Not the kind of yelling that happens over not doing dishes, but the kind of yelling that ends with Deputy Brown from the sheriff's department peeling into our yard with the flashers going.

Bobby and Sheryl are yelling at each other on the porch. Sheryl waves a metal spatula, and Bobby backs away, his McDonald's uniform dusted in brownie mix. Apparently, Sheryl told Bobby to drive over to check on Uncle Rick and he said no. She had been baking. Sheryl never bakes. Bobby has the night shift at the McDonald's in Bremerton and needs to get going soon, but now he'll be late if one of the neighbors calls the sheriff again.

"He's your fucking uncle!" Sheryl shouts.

"I've got work," says Bobby.

"What's more important, your sick uncle or your goddamn job?" says Sheryl.

"You've got a car. Go and see him. I'll see him when I'm free," Bobby says.

"Free? When you're free? He tried to kill himself! You think he'll be there when you're free?"

"Then you go, Sheryl, just go!"

They stop arguing when they notice me. They seem to realize that they're hollering and that the neighbors' dogs are howling.

"I'll go," I blurt. Immediately I think of Uncle Rick teetering with the rope and Uncle Rick asking about Fontinot. I don't want to see Uncle Rick. But already I'm saying, "I'll go and see him."

Sheryl puts the spatula down on the porch table. Bobby starts brushing the brownie mix off his clothes.

"That's sweet, Bucky," Sheryl says. "Now, Bobby, go with Bucky and see your uncle."

Sheryl doesn't want to go to the hospital because Uncle Rick will be threatening to skin the staff and turn them into hats. They'd have noticed his woodsy body odor that comes of living wild off the land and pints of whiskey spilt on his beard. It's enough for me to get embarrassed. And ever since Graham and the glass apartment building, Sheryl has been trying to bring back morning breakfast. She's been trying to get us to call her *Mom*. She probably can't go because of Graham, or his kids, or something. Me and Bobby are second string. I'm sort of adopted, abandoned by one of Sheryl's ex-husbands. Bobby was abandoned by a different ex-husband. Uncle Rick joked that Sunny Meadow was a like a church stoop.

Bobby needs to work the CheapO Lube during the day and McDonald's at night and hates them both. Sheryl works at the 24-7 and I work during vacations. Usually, I help Uncle Rick bale hay, chop wood, build fences, that kind of thing. The whole time he's telling me about how counter plays work out of I-formations, how to keep pumping my legs until the whistle blows.

But Fontinot won't talk to me. My grades suck and this family gets EBT cards with the car ferry to Seattle printed on them. There's no walking on to a college team for me. There's no going to college or maybe even graduating high school for me. I failed.

Maybe Uncle Rick already knew. Maybe that's why he hasn't been around on the porch smoking cigarettes and searching the help-wanted when I get home from practice.

I go inside and drop off my stuff, then Sheryl hands me a pan of burnt brownies. "Brownies. Didn't go well. Give them to Rick."

"You won't see him, so you send him burnt brownies?" Bobby says.

She ignores Bobby. She sees my cut hand holding the pan and she leans in to examine it. Then tells me to wait a moment. She comes back with some cut cream and rubs it on my cut. "Tell Rick," she says, "that I'll be around tomorrow with some better brownies."

"Tomorrow, tomorrow, tomorrow, Sheryl, it wouldn't be tomorrow if it was Graham," Bobby says.

Sheryl eyes Bobby. This is the moment that brings the sheriff: she'll snatch the spatula, start screaming and swinging and the dogs will be howling and the neighbors will be watching from their windows with their Rainier or Olympia beers sweating in one hand and a phone dialing in the other and they'll all say into the phone, *They're at it again.* Sometimes, when she's serious, she gets the broom. One time she got a cat-mauled window screen and started thwacking us with that.

But this time Sheryl takes a deep breath and says, "Quit calling me Sheryl. I'm your mother." Then she walks off to her room and slams the door.

Bobby and I stand stupid and stunned.

Another first.

I wonder if Sheryl wishes that Uncle Rick was gone, maybe me and Bobby too. She loves us, I know. But sometimes—it's just one of those things, like Puget Sound in summer. It looks warm and deep, but when you jump in you knock your ass on the rocks and the water is freezing. Sheryl tries. But since Graham drove up in his SUV to the 24–7 and asked her where the nearest Old Spaghetti House was so that he could take her there, she seems to try less. Bobby says Graham is the future and we're just trash by the door. I say benchwarmers.

After I think I hear her crying in her bedroom I tell Bobby, "Sometimes you can be a real piece of shit."

"Shut up, Buck," Bobby says. "Let's go."

I bump into the screen door with the brownies. The brownies rattle.

# 4

BOBBY DRIVES AND SMOKES AND THE WIND BUFFS OUR EARS. "DON'T TRY and make me talk to him," he shouts. The truck doesn't have a stereo, but Bobby's got an Alice in Chains CD rattling in the gap where the stereo would go. We wouldn't be able to hear it anyway: the truck is loud, shakes so hard your teeth chatter. Sometimes I imagine its bolts rattling loose under me. But I never make fun of Bobby's truck. I make fun of his mouse arms. I make fun of how he can't hit a barn door with a shotgun or draw back on a hunting bow. But his Yota is off-limits. Besides, I don't have a car and Bobby worked hard changing oil and draining fries. It was missing a wheel and a bed fender when he got it. But each month he worked. Now it runs. Changing brake pads and peeling the T and O decals off the tailgate so it could transform from TOYOTA to YOTA was my contribution.

"Can't wait to get out of here," Bobby shouts, "working Humvees and tanks rather than shit-eating pickups. SEAL Team Six, baby. You listening? I'll be like Rambo, with a wrench."

"Rambo didn't have mouse arms," I say, "or a wrench."

"Unc's being an asshole," he says. "A selfish douche-nugget. Playing on our feelings and shit—no, I'm not going to see him."

"You have to," I say.

"No, I don't," he says. "I have to go to work. That's what I have to do. I'm a grown man. I don't have to see him if I don't want to. You don't either. You can just hang out in the McD's parking lot and do push-ups or whatever until my shift ends. Maybe you can cross the road and piss on the Skippers drive-through microphone."

We sway to avoid another pothole. Every time Bobby avoids a pothole, he ends up hitting another. The rearview mirror falls off and the passenger door needs to be locked to stay closed. Neglect gouged these roads. But beside the road is all trees and green. Tibicut is far out. So far out they don't bother to put in streetlights.

Uncle Rick is at Wildcat Hospital, miles away in Bremerton. Bobby works in Bremerton. Tibicut people who have jobs work in Bremerton. Tibicut doesn't have jobs. It has a SuperDollar where there used to be a main street. It has an abandoned sawmill where kids go to party until they puke on rusted log chains. There's a crater left by an exploding meth lab next to the town's mossy welcome sign that also congratulated the girls' Little League team for winning the division championship in '77. There are two kinds of Tibicut townies: the stranded, and the rich. All the kids plot an escape plan.

Chantal's family is rich. Her letter is still in my jacket. Right before Chantal started flipping me off we used to sit together at the lunch table. We used to talk. Then one day I said a thing in a way I shouldn't have. I knew it was bad and all I could do was bail from the table and head straight for the hallway. She caught up with me and shoved me into some lockers.

"What the hell?" she said.

I shrugged.

She shrugged and made a googly dumb face at me.

"Why do you care so much about this Korean stuff?" I said.

"Because it matters," she said.

"Whatever."

"*Whatever?*"

"Yeah, well, you go off and tell everyone how you *chinky-chink, love you long time.*"

That's when she slapped me. Then she flipped me the bird. Her black hair, thick like a horse's mane, swung and flicked like chains as she stormed away.

In the hallways we always pass on the far sides of the hall, no eye contact and plenty of blond and brown and red hair to get in the way. But on the sideline with her poms, when she sees me, she flips me the bird. I've seen her birthmark just under the ruffle of her cheerleader skirt: the color of redwood shaped like a bowie knife. If I look at cheerleaders, I usually look for Hot Holly. I don't want to think about Chantal, never did. But after she walked off, hair whipping, the knife stuck me. Every time I have to shake my head really hard to think about Hot Holly instead.

But now I get a letter from her.

Maybe it says she forgives me and wants to meet up and bang in the back of her Buick or something. Or maybe it's just a pity letter for a loser like me, with an uncle like mine, and an escape plan that's gone off in a green Corvette.

How I'm gonna tell Unc?

A pothole breaks loose a chunk of brownie. It tastes sweet, sandy, and sour, like chocolate and baking soda.

"You think Uncle Rick was really trying to off himself?" Bobby says.

"He had a noose around his neck," I say.

"Why not eat a pistol?"

"I don't know. Why do it at all?"

We juke a pothole. He flicks his cigarette out the window. "What an ass-hole. He wasn't trying to off himself, probably just trying to motivate you."

"Motivate?"

"You know, like your stupid tire. Motivate you for what's-his-face to draft you to college or whatever."

"He had a noose around his neck. The branch broke."

"Maybe he ran out of whiskey. You never miss the water until the well runs dry."

We pass the gas station with the clean bathrooms and the bait shop that sells moonshine out the back. Our first ride in the Yota was to the bait shop for banana brandy. You go up to the counter and say that you fish with tube worms and the guy with the eye patch and the POW MIA vest will tell you to go out back and will sell you a milk gallon or a Coke bottle worth of 'shine.

I would rather do push-ups in the parking lot or my chem homework than tell Uncle Rick that Fontinot doesn't want anything to do with me.

Bobby doesn't say nothing, not until we pass Toy's Topless, the only strip club—and speed trap—in the county. "Give me some brownie," he says.

I chip off a piece and hand it to him. At the stoplight I hear it crunching in his mouth over the whine of the timing belt. From here you can see the gray hulks of the Navy shipyard. They look dangerous, huge. But up close, rust bleeds from between the panels of their hulls. They will be cut up and piled in big sheets just behind the fence. A lot of people just call it the scrapyard, since they haven't built a ship in fifty years. But they have jobs, scrapping.

"Uncle Rick is just in a bad way," I say. "We got to go see him. Don't you think that Unc needs us now, just to shoot the shit and stuff?"

"It's cruel here," Bobby says. "Moss grows on your soul." He shakes a cigarette out of the pack and tosses the wrapper out the window. "You ain't going to find our dumb asses under a falling branch, right? You, a football-playing doctor and shit, and I'll be motherfucking Rambo."

I munch on more brownie, wonder if baking soda is poisonous, feel Chantal's letter in my pocket.

What do you say to someone that wants to off himself? *Don't? I need you because now I'm a disappointment to you and me?*

Bobby will know what to say. He says he won't go, but he will. He gets really positive when he talks to Uncle Rick. He looks calm. He knows what to do.

Once the hospital is in view I ask Bobby, "So what are you going to say to him?"

"Not going to see him," Bobby says.

"Knock it off, you have to."

"Don't want to talk to him. I'll drop you off but I ain't seeing him. You can't make me."

He's serious. At the stop sign he looks me in the eye. Bobby has a hard time looking eyeball-to-eyeball, but when he does, his eyes open so wide you'd think he's gone crazy. Dead eyes. I'll-drape-you-in-chains-and-drop-you-to-the-bottom-of-Puget-Sound eyes. It's the only thing that makes me think Bobby—wimpy mouse arms, can't shoot a damn or do thirty push-ups—Elcock could survive in the Army. I figure those eyes are from his bio-father, who is locked up at Cedar Creek for killing a guy who took his parking spot. If I push too hard or dead-arm him, he'll take his cigarette and burn me.

We pull around a corner to drive up the last woody hill to the hospital when we hit this pothole full of water and it splashes up into the engine block and on the battery and the alternator and every exposed electrical thing in there and the engine coughs and dies and we roll a moment until Bobby pulls us over to the curb. From the top of the hill, water streams down the road like from a spring.

Bobby is already reaching behind his seat for rags.

"You might as well come up and see him. It's going to take you at least an hour before you'll get it to turn over."

He tosses the rags on the dash. They're already wet. He looks at me. He's planning to burn me.

"They'll have dry towels," I say.

# 5

YOU'D THINK THAT A KNOCKED-OUT FIRE HYDRANT WOULD SPOUT water straight up like they do in cartoons. But by the time we get up to it on top of the hill, it is just bubbling out, flooding the hedges, pooling a parking lot, spewing a stream that traces the curb all the way down the hill. In the dry half of the parking lot, there's a crowd of smokers in hospital gowns. But no one is looking at the busted fire hydrant lying like a fallen soldier in the road; everyone is looking across the road at Affordable Al's Asian Auto. There's a pickup stuck halfway through the big display window.

We join the crowd behind a couple of guys with long beards who lean against their IV poles.

"Shiiit, who'd rob a car dealership?" says the taller guy.

"This ain't no robbing. He's got hostages," says the shorter guy as he lights a new cigarette off the cherry of the old one. "Someone is banging someone's wife."

"What's going on?" Bobby says, then lights his own cigarette.

Taller beard looks at Bobby, then at the pan of brownies in my hands. Then he points his cigarette at the fire hydrant, then at the remnants of a truck bumper and a trail of plastic and paint and oil and tread marks leading to the pickup. Its tailgate dangling off to one side. The truck bed looks crunched like a beer can. "Someone's holding up Affordable Al's," he says.

"Ain't a holdup," the shorter beard says. "That guy isn't in any hurry to leave. Figure Al had it coming for a while."

"Them fucking commercials," taller beard says.

Security guys with cop mustaches start telling people to head back into the hospital. But nobody moves because just then three soft-looking salesmen in sport coats run out the side door of the dealership and toward us. Even the security guys stop talking and turn to look at the soft guys jogging and all their fat jiggling. A fourth tubby guy stumbles out the side door but he falls to the ground. He rolls onto his back. He's got a pistol—a Smith & Wesson .500 Magnum, chrome, a hogleg, just like the ones you'd see on the cover of *Hunting Tools*. It's so big in the small tubby guy's hand that it looks like a joke. He's pointing it back at the swinging side door and he's screaming, "I'll kill you! I'll kill you!" Then out comes Uncle Rick, in his hospital gown, carrying a Costco-sized bottle of bourbon. He takes a drink and bows to the short fallen tubby guy and Uncle Rick points at the top of his head like he's showing the guy the spots where he's going bald.

The tubby man pulls the trigger.

Now, you'd think that at a distance of forty yards we wouldn't be able to see that, but we could because the guy yanked on the trigger—one-handed—like a man that doesn't own a gun. He did it a couple of times and finally Uncle Rick says something—that to us is just mutters—walks over, takes the gun from the guy, and slaps him across the face. Then Uncle Rick points the gun up with both hands in the air and squeezes the trigger and we hear that thing boom like a cannon. Unc looks at the pistol. He's never had anything that expensive, I bet. He holds out his hand, pulls the guy up, and says something to him we can't catch. The guy has got swamp pits right through his sport coat. But he nods and they go back into the dealership, Unc following the guy in, like none of it is a thing.

"Was that Uncle Rick?" I say.

"Yeah, that's Unc," Bobby says. He tosses his cigarette on the ground and lights another. His hands are shaking.

"Cops are gonna come," I say.

"I know," Bobby says.

"It won't be Deputy Brown either," I say.

"He's got a pistol," he says, then stops. What he doesn't say is that Unc can shoot. I've seen him take a revolver and shoot five flying crows with six bullets, like pointing at them with his index finger: bam, bam, bam, click, bam, bam. They all dropped. One bullet was bad and didn't fire. Bad percussion cap.

Bobby tosses his cigarette. "I'm going in there. Coming?"

There's a hum from the smokers, of affairs and insurance and bets. The soft guys from the dealership are next to us, behind a van, wheezing and coughing into their cell phones, "I love you."

Bobby doesn't wait for me, he just walks. He's rounding the hedge to the street before I start trotting after him, keeping the brownies ahead of me.

"Look at these two dumb motherfuckers," one smoker says. "Going to give the gunman some brownies."

"Go get'm, Jackie Chan!" someone else shouts.

We're halfway across the road when a security guard starts shouting, "Hey, you two, stop! Now! Cops will arrest you!"

But we keep going, passing the rows of clean cars and into the dealership.

# 6

BOBBY AND I GO THROUGH THE SAME DOOR THAT UNC AND THE TUBBY guy went through. Bobby pulls the door open slowly without any sound, not even a hinge groaning. Maybe it does groan but I don't hear anything because I can hear Unc's voice, raspy, like someone fresh from thrashing in the water.

"It's that moment when you know there's no tree of microphones waiting for you," Unc is saying, "and there's no way for you to fix that shitty leak in the corner of the bathroom. You know the kind, a black cloud of mold blooming in the corner. For long time you just watch that son of a bitch blossoming from the shower to the mirror and you can't do anything about it without help and there's no help coming. Quit eyeing the pistol," Unc says.

"Keep it," the tubby guy says. "I'll even give you a box of shells. Just let me go."

"No."

"I won't press charges. I'll give you the gun. Won't charge you for the truck, just let me go."

"Bullets," Unc says. "Shells are for shotguns, artillery, not pistols."

"What do you want? I got nothing else."

"People can't talk anymore, can't listen," Unc says. "Why did you leave the safety on?"

"I don't know. I didn't want to shoot you," tubby says.

"You wanted to shoot me."

"I was mad. I was worried about my job. I'm sorry. Just let me go."

"You'll get to go."

"Really?"

"But you're going to listen," Unc says. "You didn't know because you got money to buy things you don't even know how to use. You know how to clean this? Have you ever chewed on something you hunted? Bet not. You're another one of those assholes that sees a spotted owl on the TV and makes rules and protests and kills the lumber yards to save a fucking owl that you wouldn't even be able to tell from any other fucking owl if you saw it out on your lawn gutting your little shit-eating dog. Probably can't even change the oil in your own truck."

"Unc," Bobby shouts.

The hogleg goes off. We drop to the floor. The brownies rattle against the pan. The dealership smells plasticky, like the toy aisle of the SuperDollar. I've never been in a dealership or a new car, and I've never been shot at before. I check my arms, scan my legs, no leaks.

Bobby searches himself too. No leaks. We can hear tubby guy sobbing.

"Goddamn it! Don't shoot!" Bobby shouts. "It's us, Bucky and Bobby."

"Bobby?" Unc shouts.

"Yes!" Bobby shouts.

"Go away," Unc shouts. "I'm busy."

We're beside this little green coupe with so much tire shine that it glares lines on the carpet. It even lightens the hallway. Bobby's foot bangs the pan of brownies. "Dipshit," Bobby says, "say something."

"I'm here," I say. I don't want to be. "Bucky."

"What?" Unc shouts.

"Just let me go," the other guy shouts.

"It's us! Don't shoot," Bobby says.

We round the corner and through the first open door and we see Unc seated at a desk in his hospital gown. Tubby guy sits across from him in a sweaty sports coat. It's as if this were Unc's desk with the Bridgestone coffee mug and he was selling tubby guy a car. It could be Unc's desk, since it's got a big bottle of Jack and a pistol. There's dust in the air.

Bobby tries to say something but he just coughs.

Then we all are quiet. Injury-time-out quiet. Bobby and me in the doorway, me holding brownies, the salesman looking sweaty and wheezing, Unc sniffing and staring at the bottle of Jack he's gripping like it's trying to run off, everybody like that until the salesman clears his throat and says, "Are those brownies?"

"Yeah," I say. "Sheryl made them."

"Sissy can't bake," Unc says.

I put down the brownies on the desk. Everyone stares at them.

"Meet Ronald," Unc says. The guy in the sport coat nods to us, then stands and holds out his hand. We shake. Our hands are all sweaty. He sits back down and we're all silent again.

There is a big bullet hole in the ceiling panel and sirens out beyond the windows of the showroom. Police are coming.

I should be the one holding up a car dealership. It's not like I got anything going: no ball, no girlfriend, nothing.

Ronald takes a bit of broken brownie and taps it against the table.

"We came to take you home," Bobby says.

"I ran a ten-thousand-dollar truck through the front of a dealership," Unc says.

"Twenty-five," Ronald says. "Not that it matters."

Unc sips the whiskey and nods. He taps the pistol against the bottle. "I thought I wanted to be a body, but I got a miracle, a safety. Now I know that I just want someone to know what it's like to be—and feel—like shit."

Unc looks over at me like he's just now recognizing me. "Did Fontinot talk to you?"

Sirens are echoing in from outside. Everyone is looking at me.

"No," I say.

"Figured as much," Unc says.

"All right, let's go," Bobby says. "They'll be plenty of people to talk to outside."

"What do you mean," I say, "you figured?"

"Shut up, Buck," Bobby says.

"Longest of long shots," Unc says, "metrics aren't right."

"Metrics?" I say. "You had me pulling a tire."

"Gave you a job. A man crumbles to nothing without a job," he says, then laughs. "I was nothing until there was a safety that said I'm something." He sips whiskey. His white chapped lips pucker while his red beard bobs as he gulps. "I'm not a body. Now I just want people to listen."

"Metrics?" I say.

"Ronald wants to go," Bobby says, "don't you, Ronald?"

"Yes," Ronald says. "I'm listening."

"I feel better," Unc says. "I'm not a body."

My metrics, wrong? Wrong? Now everyone shifts in their chairs getting ready to walk out. Unc looks relieved. Unc told me I had a chance, when I didn't. Told me I could be somebody, and now, not. And everyone is looking at Unc and he looks light and happy and here I am feeling this tidal wave, a typhoon of smoking, churning oil shooting out from deep in my stomach and spouting up my spine into my skull. They all are acting like my being nothing but bad metrics is no thing. Like everyone knew but me. Like I'm this harmless limp curl of cigarette smoke who carts around pans of shit brownies. Unc and Ronald stand like the meeting is over and we're all going out to Sizzler.

The typhoon rushes into my bad-metric arms, over inadequate elbows, and into my fists like a pair of broken doors caught in bad-metric tornado winds that fling them right into Unc's big dumb head, his dumb red beard, his filthy BO that wants Ronald and everybody to listen to him, this asshole who crashes trucks and takes other people's guns like it ain't no thing, like none of this matters because everyone needs a job, just to keep sweating and pulling and not thinking because we're just big bad-metric bags of nothing.

My body is moving. Squared hips built with hip thrusts and hills, built with the pull of tires and pain and mud and work and sweaty Ts and bloodied hands and I'm tackling Unc and we're falling and crashing into a bookcase and sharp pointy things are dropping on us and people are shouting, screaming. I'm screaming. I'm punching and grabbing with my no-good metrics. Hurting this man, with the kind of grind that only a two-down-bread-and-butter running back can do.

The hogleg goes off like thunder in an oil drum.

*1*

THE BREMERTON COPS, POSTED AT THE DOORS, RUSHED IN WITH GUNS
drawn and shouting like they do on TV. But they didn't find anyone with
guns drawn. They just found me rolling on the floor of the office clubbing
Unc with my fists. If I heard them shouting, I didn't care. As far as I can
remember, I didn't hear them warning they'll shoot or tase, or any of the
things that cops say when they see a brawl on the floor, a car salesman
wailing in a corner, and a mouse-arm kid in a McD's uniform screaming,
"I'm a friendly!"

Every time I hit Unc squarely with my fist, I yelled, "Tire!"

I'm sure they told me to stop. Police have to. Deputy Brown used to sleep
or pass out in his car in front of the Tibicut Bar and Grill on his off days
after his wife ran off with a sailor. He would shout, "Stop!" to anyone stum-
bling out too late and trying to start their car. He made them sleep it off
long enough before driving home. Unc said that's why the bar shut down:
Deputy Brown's wife ran off, so he wanted everyone else to suffer.

But I was blind and deaf. The only thing I knew at the moment were my
shouts, "Tire! Tire!" burning bright with hot hands smacking Unc until a
crackle of the Taser froze my joints and had me shaking and chattering so
bad my teeth are still ringing with it.

The hogleg hit nobody.

After that, cops pulled us out, tossed us in different cop cars. My head
rattled against a window and everything tingled, buzzed like Sawzalls.

Cops put me in a room with walls of what looks like ceiling tiles that
have yellow blotches. Maybe at one time the tiles had been up in the ceiling
under dripping pipes? Maybe someone threw coffee at another or someone
spat on the walls? Had someone, refusing to confess, been tossed against
the walls and their acne popped?

The room smells moldy and the light buzzes. In the corner is a camera with a red light. The table is bolted to the floor. I'm cuffed to it and the cuff chafes my wrist. My metal chair wobbles. I wait a long time.

I can't play football, so maybe this is what I'll become: arrested and mug-shotted. I could start jacking 24–7s and McDonald's and run down roads with a wheelbarrow full of copper, racing tweakers to stay fit.

The door opens and two guys in suits come in. One uncuffs me and takes the chair beside me, while the other stands across from me and leans against the wall.

"My name is Detective Kerensky," says the cop sitting next to me. "This is Detective Burns. What is your name?"

"Everyone calls me Bucky," I say.

"What about the name on the student ID?" Kerensky says.

"Nobody can pronounce that name," I say.

"Humor us," he says.

I say it. It limps out broken and wounded. I can't remember the last time I said my paper name.

"That is a hard name to say," Kerensky says. "I have the same problem; everyone calls me 'Karen-skee,' not 'Kerin-skee.' They don't sound the same, don't look the same. It's the plight of immigrants, isn't it?"

"I guess," I say.

He asks me how I like school.

"You play football?" Kerensky says. "Never would've guessed, figured you'd be too smart for football."

Then they ask me what happened. I tell them.

"So, let's start at the beginning again," says Kerensky. "I'm curious, can you tell me how to say your name again? It bothers me when people mistake my name, like I'm sure it bothers you."

It sounds worse the second time.

"Be-ung-huck, right?" Kerensky says.

"Close enough," I say.

"So the guy that held up the dealership," he says, "Uncle Rick?"

"Yes, but he wasn't holding it up," I say. "He was freaking out. Trying to off himself." It hurts so bad as soon as I say it, right between the sternum and pec.

"Whatever he was doing, he was doing it with a *gun*, right?" he says. "Holding a hostage?"

It sounds so serious. *Hostage. A holdup.* The way they say *gun*, the emphasis on *it*, is as if it were a demon or widow-maker, makes me realize this is serious to these guys. Their faces are all grave like we've killed somebody. It was bad, yeah, but would people be so serious if Uncle Rick had beaten everything up with a baseball bat? If it had been at the old Tibicut Bar and Grill? If he had owned the dealership and fired everybody on Christmas Eve?

"Where did he get the gun?" Kerensky says.

"From the guy, the big guy."

"The hostage," he says, "gave the gun to your uncle Rick?"

"Yeah," I say.

"Mr. Stone?" he says.

"You know, the tubby guy," I say.

"The overweight man, Mr. Stone, you saw him give Rick the gun?" he says.

"Yeah," I say, "after he tried to shoot Unc in the head, but didn't know about the safety."

"You saw this?"

"Everyone saw that."

"So how do you know that Rick didn't bring the gun with him?" he says.

"It's not his," I say. "I know just about all of Unc's guns," I say. "Even the ARs are beat-up. He's never had anything as fancy as that."

The two detectives pass a look. I start to feel like I did something more wrong than roll around on the floor with Unc.

"Are you guys part of an organization? Militia, gun groups, anything like that?" he says.

"No, we don't have money for that," I say.

"How many guns does your uncle have?" he says.

"I'm not sure," I say. "A lot. I guess Uncle Rick spends his money on guns. I only have a .22."

"We don't have a record of you owning a gun," he says. "In fact, we don't have any records on you."

"I got the .22 for my birthday," I say.

"From who?" he says.

"A guy Sheryl was dating," I say. "I don't remember his name."

There's a knock on the door. A policeman hands Detective Burns a folder. He opens it and holds up the photo of me, Uncle Rick, and Bobby in front of a Christmas tree with a whole bunch of guns laid out on the floor. I've got my .22 in my hands.

"Yeah, that's it," I say.

"You keep calling him Uncle," says Kerensky. "Are you related?"

"No, not really," I say.

"Not really?" he says. "Like an uncle once removed or something?"

"No. He's Sheryl's brother," I say. "Sheryl Monroe?"

"So, Sheryl Monroe adopted you?" he says.

"Not really. She's my stepmom," I say.

"Where's Dad?" he says.

I shrug.

"Mom?"

"I don't know," I say. "My bio-mom died when I was little and my bio-father ran off after leaving me with Sheryl. That's all I know."

"What about this other guy, Robert Elcock?"

"Bobby? He's my stepbrother. Different father, different mother, ditched like me."

"Where is his father and mother?"

"His father is locked up at Cedar Creek. His mother OD'd."

Detective Burns, leaning against the wall, clears his throat. He is still flipping through whatever is in the file folder. "Sounds like"—he clears his throat again—"Ms. Monroe's got a regular church stoop."

"Never mind him. Burns is just old and cranky," Kerensky says.

"What does this have to do with Uncle Rick?" I say.

"We're just talking," Kerensky says.

We've been *just talking* for a long while. I have no idea what time it is, but I'm getting hungry and tired and want to go home. There's this tingling, humming, where my bones meet.

"Can I go home now?" I say.

"Just a few more questions, Bucky," Kerensky says. "When did you become a citizen?"

"What do you mean?" I say.

"When did you become an American citizen?"

"I guess when Sheryl married my bio-father."

"Okay," Kerensky says. "So you and Bobby go to the dealership to meet Uncle Rick."

"No, like I said, Bobby and I were going to the hospital to give him brownies and check on him. The truck stalled because of all the water in the potholes."

I tell them the story again. They nod. Detective Burns asks me all the same questions again about the pistol, tubby guy, and where and when something happened, where was I born, how do I feel about the Pledge of Allegiance, do I know what sarin gas is, am I Christian, am I a Muslim, am I aware of any human smuggling or drug smuggling or prostitution rings.

I get tired. Can I leave? Am I under arrest?

*Just a few more questions.*

When they finally leave they tell me to stay. I ask them again, "Am I under arrest?"

"We don't know what you are, just yet," Kerensky says. "Just sit tight and someone will be by to take you home in a bit. Once we have this all sorted."

And I wait.

Punching Unc was wrong. He didn't know what he was saying. He's a man trying to off himself.

And I wait.

But what if he was right? What if everybody, Unc and Sheryl, Coach Shaw and the lineman, Chantal, what if everybody knew my metrics were wrong but me? What if it never was about how hard I yanked the tire up the hill or studied the game, but just metrics?

—

After a really long while, a cop pops his head in, checks the corners, then tells me, "Come with me."

The visiting room is empty except for one table with Graham, Sheryl, and some guy in a suit. Sheryl runs over to me after the cop uncuffs me and hugs me tight. It must be morning; I can smell Sheryl's shampoo. Graham's got a polo on, not even a button-down.

"Hey, next time," the cop says, "wait for him to come to the table."

Graham approaches the cop and shakes his hand. "Thanks, Dave."

"Don't mention it," Officer Dave says. "Seriously. Everyone is in a piss-ing match upstairs over whatever is going on with your kid. But, I don't know. A kid has got to see their parents. Shouldn't be questioned with-out them."

"You okay, Bucky?" Sheryl says. "Did they hurt you?"

"They tased me," I say.

"They tased you?" Sheryl says.

"Yeah," Officer Dave says. "Tasing kids ain't right. I'm old school. I sub-due with batons."

"No shit, it ain't right. We should tase you assholes," Sheryl says. "Then sue you."

"Hey, now," Officer Dave says, "you're getting to talk to the kid here and now. This ain't normal procedure, okay? You'll need to wrap this up quickly." He pats me on the shoulder, like when someone says *good boy*.

"I'm sorry for fighting with Unc," I say.

"We'll get to that," Graham says. "But are you okay?"

"He got tased, Graham," Sheryl says. "My kids are in jail getting tased."

Sheryl leads me to the table and sits me across from the other guy, who has horn-rimmed glasses, short hair, a shirt and tie, completely clean. He looks like a guy on a yard sign running for office.

"This," Graham says, "is a friend. An old friend from my backpacking days in Asia. We used to drink together and—"

"Jesus, Graham, we don't have time for this," Sheryl says.

"My fingers still tingle," I say.

"Bucky, we'll get those assholes later," Sheryl says. "But right now I need you to be really quiet and listen to this man, Dick Cooke, he's your lawyer."

"Richard," Graham's friend says. "Don't call me Dick. And those that tased you were city cops."

"Dick, I mean Richard, is your lawyer," Sheryl says.

"Why do I need a lawyer?" I say to Graham. "Wouldn't you be my lawyer?"

"Richard is a friend," Graham says.

"A very good friend," Richard the lawyer says. His voice sounds flat, drawn-out. There are bags under his eyes.

"He does immigration law and criminal law. I do real estate law," Graham says.

*Immigration.* I think of people looking happily up from the deck of a steamer at the Statue of Liberty.

"Mr. Yi?" Richard the lawyer says. "Would you like me to be your lawyer?"

They're all looking at me. My elbows hum and tingle so bad they itch.

"That's you, Bucky," Sheryl says.

"Yeah," I say, "sure, why do I need a lawyer? Don't you cost a lot of money?"

"I do," Richard the lawyer says, looking at Graham. "But I owe Graham. And I hate abusive police. So this is on the house."

I nod.

"Tomorrow they're going to charge you with resisting arrest, if we're lucky," Richard says.

"I'm sorry," I say. "But I stopped Unc from doing something really bad. This can't be that bad. People fight and—"

"Bucky, let Richard finish," Sheryl says.

"But I didn't do nothing," I say. "They tase me and now *I'm* in trouble?"

"Bucky—" Sheryl says with a high, arching tone I've never heard from her before. It's the sound of mothers snapping at their children.

"Look," Richard says, taking out his business card and sliding it across the table. "You need to memorize this phone number. If something happens, you need to find a way to contact me. Also, memorize the email address."

"Memorize?" I say.

"This is serious," he says. "If you get charged, you're lucky. If not, it might be a long time before we can talk."

Sheryl sucks in one of her deep calming breaths.

"That little hostage stunt you're involved in made the rounds," Richard says. "Went through all the police systems, including the FBI's new one. I think you came up on immigration's unknowns list. They would love to prove how good the system is by sending you away. I have to ask you, do you know when you became a citizen of the United States?"

I look at Sheryl. She's pie-eyed.

"When I got here?" I say.

"Do you have a copy of any of the papers?" he says to Graham.

"Like I said, I sent it all in when we got married," Sheryl says. "They have it all."

"Mr. Yi, do you know where you were born?" Richard says.

"He was born in Korea," Sheryl says.

"I'm talking to my client," Richard says. "We don't have much time."

"Korea," I said.

"But there are two Koreas. Which one? Which city?" he says.

"I don't know, the good one?" I say.

"They have all that information," Sheryl says.

"This is what I was talking about," Richard says to Graham. "Your girlfriend lost his documents. We don't even know if he's North Korean or South. And we have no proof he's American."

"Fiancée," Graham says.

"I met his father in South Korea," Sheryl says.

"You were in South Korea?" I say.

"Look," Richard says to me, "we don't have your documents yet. And because this was a hostage situation, and their hope of foiling some evil terrorism plot, I don't know what they're going to do with you. My gut says they're going to take you away to somewhere we won't be able to talk like we should. I think that's why the immigration feds are upstairs."

Everything is quiet. Sheryl's tearing up and reaches for my hand. Graham rubs her shoulder.

"Terrorism?" I say.

"Unfortunately, I think that's what's going on. It's the only thing that makes sense," Richard says.

"When can I go home?" I say. "I left my tire in the stream."

"I think their point will be, they are going to send you home," Richard says.

"The truth is," Sheryl says, then stops as a door opens behind us.

"Memorize the number," Richard says before the cops come in and take me.

# 8

THEY DRIVE ME TO THE IMMIGRANT DETENTION CENTER. THEY TELL ME and five other guys to strip naked and put all of our stuff in big clear bags. I clutch the card. The whole way over, in the van, I repeat the numbers.

*2-0-6-5-5-5-6-4-3-0.*

They search us. Tell us to bend over and touch our toes while they spread and look in between our cheeks. We stand back up and a guard sees the card. "Sir," he says, "everything must go in the bag."

"It's a card. It's my lawyer's phone number," I say.

"Sir, if you don't comply, you will be forced to comply," he says, and rests his hand on his Taser.

I'm scared and naked and cold and still feel the hum in my arm and my nuts crawled way up in me and I'm embarrassed more than I've ever been. Not because of some needle-dick joke. This is different. Everyone's got Tasers, sprays, and, somewhere, guns.

*2-0-6-5-5-5-6-4-3-0.*

I hand him the card.

They give us pale blue shirts and sweatpants. They give us clear plastic bags with towels and a roll of toilet paper. A guard says they've run out of toothbrushes but should get some tomorrow.

They send us into a large warehouse with a high ceiling where there are giant fans and giant lamps and glints of spiderwebs floating in the drafts. It has concrete floors and chain-link fences separating sections, with a line of porta-potties. They line us five new guys by a gate.

There's a woman with a dark blue uniform. She says welcome to Seatac Temporary Immigration Detention Center. Also known as STIDC, pronounced "steedick." She tells us about our daily routine, when we eat, when we can go to the blacktop outside, the different times they do count, talk and talk and talk. Then she starts saying these things in bad Spanish. I can't speak Spanish but I can tell she can't either.

*2-0-6-5-5-5-6-4-3-0.*

I can't do math but I'm okay at memorizing numbers because digits correspond with football plays. For example, a *Power I 206 blast* would have three running backs behind the quarterback, (power I) and 206 would mean that the "2" back (the tailback) would be running without lead blockers (0) through the "6" hole which is an even number, which means to the right. This is a misdirection play, which is great when the defense isn't disciplined and is stuck in the habit of going one way and not the other.

If I think like this, mentally rehearse the plays, I can remember Richard's number. I think of the opening series of a game, a playoff game. Power blast, a deep toss to Jimmy, an option—

"You will listen when I talk!" The lady is in front of me. She has taken a long stride back and has got her hand on her belt of reloads and handcuffs and pistol and Taser and she looks ready to attack. "Comply! Cumplir!"

"Okay," I say. I put my hands up. "I'm listening."

"Good," she says. "Enter the cage." She walks us into the cage, where there's only men. I'm thinking pocket passes, blasts, and options. *2-0-6-5-5-5-6-4-3-0.*

"This is your bed," she says by one of the kind of mats Bobby used to lay out on the ground to work underneath the Yota. "You are Bed Forty-Two," she says.

"Bed forty-two," I say.

"At all times, when somebody asks your designation, you will comply and state your name," she says. "What is your name?"

"Bucky," I say.

She shakes her head.

"In bed forty-two?"

"*Bed Forty-Two* is the only designation that matters," she says. "Only complete sentences, please."

I'm in a warehouse being told my name is *Bed*. That isn't a complete sentence either, even I know that.

*2-0-6-5-5-5-6-4-3-0.*

I have to tell Richard the lawyer, I'm at Seatac's steel-dick. Help. People who can't make complete sentences are holding me. They call me *Bed*.

Is Richard even a good lawyer? He was dressed like the lawyers Sheryl watches on *Ally McBeal*. But besides being dressed like a lawyer and owing Graham, I know nothing about the person who can save me, get me home.

They show us the porta-potties. They show us the shower and the trough that serves as our sink. "Toothbrushes will be in tomorrow," the guard says. "Don't ask for hot water, we're not getting it." Then she points to the far wall by the guard box where there are three pay phones. Two are missing receivers, their metal cords point toward the floor like the tails of something hunted, skinned, and hung. "During your daily recreation time, you can use the phone in the middle," says the guard. "The other two, illegal aliens like yourselves vandalized. Therefore the consequence is that all of you now must share the one operating phone."

There's got to be forty or fifty of us in this cell of chain-link, not including the other chain-link with women and children, all to use one pay phone. *2-0-6-5-5-5-6-4-3-0.*

"Any questions?" the guard asks.

"Why am I here?" I ask.

"What is your designation?" she asks.

"Bucky," I say.

"No, your designation," she says, "your bed."

"Okay, Bed Forty-Two, but I don't belong here. When can I go home?"

"Bed Forty-Two must make a complete sentence," she says, "using his designation."

"Bed Forty-Two wants to know when he can go home?" I say.

"Good sentence," she says, then looks to the other five new guys, each of them a shade of brown like how everyone behind the chain-link is a shade of brown. "Do any of you have a real question?"

"I'm seventeen, why aren't I with the kids?" I ask. On the other side of the chain-link is the fence where the women and kids are sitting on mats like they use in PE and they're watching us like we know something they don't. "I'm an American. I say the Pledge of Allegiance. When can I go home?"

The guard blinks.

"Bed Forty-Two wonders," I say.

She gets in my face. "As long as it takes to get you out of here," she says, her spittle hitting me, "Bed Forty-Two."

A few hours later, I use my first rec time to use the phone. There are only a few guys lined up to use it, the same ones I came in with who didn't get toothbrushes. They dial, listen, and hang up. They're quick. When it's my turn, it asks for coins. I don't have any coins. I dial collect. It says, *restricted number.* I dial again. Same thing. It won't let me use collect, and they took all our coins when they bagged our stuff.

The guys who used the phone before me are huddled together.

"Hey," one of them says, "phone work for you?"

I shake my head. They nod. "Same."

"Bed Forty-Two, I know nothing about phones," a guard says when I ask him why all the phone numbers are restricted. "I just guard you illegals."

# 9

AT SOME POINT IN THE TWO AND A HALF WEEKS IT TAKES RICHARD THE lawyer to find me at steedick, I begin to refer to myself in the third person: Bed Forty-Two hears other men fart in their sleep. Bed Forty-Two shakes chain-link fence until guards rest their hands on Tasers. Bed Forty-Two picks at terrible lunch of nuked frozen veg, refried beans, peanut-butter sandwiches and tiny expired pints of milk. Bed Forty-Two suspects that Cama Cuarenta y Uno stole his toilet paper, and swears that the Mylar blankets give rashes. However, he can only feel places that itch, can't see any rashes.

Richard the lawyer is well dressed and stern-looking with his horned-rimmed glasses. He sits across from Bed Forty-Two at a large cafeteria table, the same kind the school uses for lunch. He tells Bed Forty-Two how hard it has been to find Bed Forty-Two. His long crane-like neck sticks out from his collar. When he swallows, his collar button peeks above his tie knot. He asks why Bed Forty-Two didn't call.

Does he have any fucking idea what Bed Forty-Two has been through? Because the last two and a half weeks have been like those dark moments in a dogpile, where the sun gets shut out by the weight of three-hundred-pound linemen shouting, *Motherfucker*. But dogpiles, even on the goal line, last maybe a minute or two. And at the bottom, below the stink of armpits and cheap deodorant, mud and turf, time stretches and twists with the groans of guys and plastic and foam. But you know why you're there: You want the ball. You need to find and take and keep the ball. You bleed for the ball. Things are simple and long and every shot of cleat or hand-wrench of your face mask doesn't matter because you know why you are there. Without the ball, you're just being crunched by twenty-one assholes.

Why is Bed Forty-Two here?

The phones don't work, Bed Forty-Two tells Richard the lawyer.

Richard says that's against the law. They're required to do this and that and this.

Here, your eyes burn because you can't sleep. Things happen and you're not sure when they happened. Whens and whys don't get answered. Time is made by guards who order inmates named *Bed* to stand next to their mats for count. There are six counts a day, four regular and two random. One before each time the inmates eat their beans and mixed veg. One count after rec time outside on a pad of oil-stained asphalt. During count, the inmates named *Bed* count off like on a school trip.

"Bed Seventeen."

"Bed Thirty-Six."

"I am Forty-Two." Guards don't move until Bed Forty-Two correctly says, "I am *Bed Forty-Two*." Most say their Bed numbers in Spanish. (Cama Cuarenta y Uno is Bed Forty-One, who has a mustache that reminds Bed Forty-Two of Super Mario.)

All Beds lay on mats and under Mylar blankets that crinkle and make sharp corners. Bed Forty-Two doesn't sleep. Can't sleep. Even when the big lights that blast pale fluorescent white shut off and the orangey lights stay on signaling sleep time, Bed Forty-Two wonders whether they're lying about it being nighttime. There are noises: lights buzz, guard boots thump, Mylar crinkles, men sniffle and babies cry and someone snores and another farts and walls creak like they're crumbling. And it smells. The worn pleather mat smells like sweat and tires. The porta-potties leaked their chemicals and shit on the floor twice in two and a half weeks.

And then here's Richard the lawyer.

Bed Forty-Two leans in, tells the lawyer across the table, "And yet, the phones don't work."

Richard leans back from Bed Forty-Two. No toothbrush has given Bed Forty-Two scorching breath. Bed Forty-Two smells funky from mouth to ass. If Cama Cuarenta y Uno didn't take his toilet paper, he hopes it was one of the fathers who stay really close to the fence and watch their wives and children behind the other chain-link-fenced cell, and who save their battered bananas to pass along through the gaps during rec time.

"Okay, okay, we'll bring this up with the judge," Richard says, "at your hearing. Besides, I think we got a good case here. They're clearing the charges for Bobby. Your uncle looks like he is going to take a plea, and we got copies of your immigration documents." He pushes the papers across the table. "The problem was that they returned it to the wrong address and the check bounced. But those were circumstances outside of your control, and . . ."

He keeps talking. He keeps thinking that there's a comeback. But there's no two-minute offense where Joe Montana drives the team down the field to hit Dwight Clark in the back of the end zone.

"Too late," Bed Forty-Two says, "already had my hearing."

One day or night, the guards took Bed Forty-Two to a small room with a TV and a camera. On the TV someone who was dressed up like Judge Judy told Bed Forty-Two that he was in violation of something and something and that Bed Forty-Two would be deported. When the judge asked if Bed Forty-Two understood, he said, "No, I don't. Everyone calls me Bucky. I'm American."

She told Bed Forty-Two that his name was not Bucky. He was inmate something-number-number—aka Bed Forty-Two—at steedick. Bed Forty-Two was an alien, deceptive in his paperwork. He was By-ong-huk Yee, a name she apologized for not knowing how to pronounce. There is no Bucky.

They showed Bed Forty-Two the same paperwork that Richard has on the table. His birthday. His age. His citizenship. Each of the things he thought he knew, the papers say he didn't. These people say Bed Forty-Two is older than Bobby. Bed Forty-Two is nineteen. His birthday is in spring, not winter.

Bed Forty-Two is a foreign body, whose ground zero was somewhere in South Korea, where his name would not be Bed Forty-Two, but Beyonghak Yi. Or *Yee*. Or *Lee*. Or *Why-ee*.

"I was worried that they would do that," Richard says. "They're trying to send you out of the country before we can appeal. They're treating you like a terrorist. We'll fight it."

"Can I see Sheryl?" I say.

"I only found you a few hours ago. She'll be here tomorrow, I'm sure," he says. "I brought a letter for you from her, and a couple of others from myself and one of your friends. I've been carrying them around for when I found you. The guards have them and you'll get them as soon as they are finished examining them. Those letters are very important. They outline what you'll need to do if they send you away before we can stop them."

"What's going to happen?"

"Honestly? I don't know. But we'll stop them."

Bed Forty-Two gets teary. Bed Forty-Two can't remember when he last got teary, because a teary football player was one that either won the Super Bowl or no longer could play football.

"We're trying," he says. "Listen, Sheryl is a very determined woman. She and I, and Graham, will figure out a way to get you back. You just need to pull yourself together. Be noble. Like a warrior, a samurai. That's in your blood, tough guy. Remember that and hold tight. Focus on a better future. Got it? Do you remember my number?"

"2-0-6-5-5-5-6-4-3-0."

"Right," he says. "Hang tough, we'll figure this out."

Then Richard the lawyer is gone. Probably driving a Corvette. Maybe even barking the tires and racing Fontinot. Maybe Hot Holly is in the passenger seat next to Fontinot, her hair flickering like a flag.

Bed Forty-Two picks the scabs raw from his knuckles. Keeps them bleeding like the day he hit Unc in the dealership. Sheryl would hate to see Bed Forty-Two's hands like this. Would dab peroxide with a cloth like she always did. She'd say that football is just a game, why hurt yourself over a game? I love it, Bed Forty-Two would say. And she would nod. Because anything can happen in America. Barry Sanders got good because as a kid he played ball on asphalt. No pads, no soft green turf. He didn't want to get tackled. He learned to blast and twist through those slivers of light that are touchdowns waiting to happen.

So Bed Forty-Two jukes and powers through O-lines in his head, again and again, remembering Richard the lawyer's number. Bed Forty-Two does sets of sixty push-ups, and switches to crunches during the hours that the guards say to sleep and the hours the guards say it's day. A thousand push-ups and two thousand crunches are the goal but Bed Forty-Two loses count. Bed Forty-Two has moments of make-believe, like when he was little and played with sticks in the woods with Bobby and other kids from

Sunny Meadow re-creating WWII and Bed Forty-Two played the enemy. In these moments he knows this will pass because he believes in America and believes in football.

Bed Forty-Two will find a way to walk on at some shitty community college.

His name is Bucky.

He wills it to happen.

His will sees nothing more bad happening because nothing seems real until that very night, after Richard the lawyer had left, after three roll calls and he is breathing stink and dozing between sets of sit-ups when a guard nudges him awake with a Maglite. He's led out of the cages with three Chinese guys and handed the letters that Richard had brought and a plastic bag of Bed Forty-Two's stuff he came in with. "Get out of your blues," the guards say. Then they all walk out into the parking lot, in the rain, into a van with barred windows.

They drive but he can't see outside until the door slides open and he's at the airport. "You're going back home," the guard tells Bed Forty-Two.

# 10

## SHERYL'S LETTER

*Dear Bucky,*

*If you're reading this, then I'm so sorry. I don't know what else to say. I love you. You know that. I don't know how we all got here. Dick says that you might get deported before I get a chance to see you again, so I'm writing this. He says your father and I did something wrong with your paperwork. But he means I screwed up. I never checked, never thought your father wouldn't do it right.*

*This is my fault.*

*I was in love and didn't think of things like I should have. Your father had this way about him. His English was good. He went to some big time school in Korea and he just did all the paperwork and all I had to do was sign. And you were so small and so cute and I just wanted it all his way.*

*Your father made me feel whole after Bobby's father. And I got betrayed, again.*

*I should've known better.*

*You never asked but I went to college for a year. Never graduated. Failed classes. Bunches of loans. I did go abroad for a semester and that's how I met your father. I met him in Korea. I met him drinking with friends and he asked me to be his partner in a game of pool. He was one of the few people I got along with, one of the few people that didn't treat me like shit because I was a woman or grew up poor. Korea was poor. Women treated like shit. But he was married and I knew better.*

When I came back I dropped out of school to help my parents out and got a job at a diner where the SuperDollar is now.

He found me later. Brought you. We got married. Then he left. I thought something happened to him. I did. Filed police reports and everything. He was just gone. Later, I learned that some sorry men do you the favor of disappearing.

I don't want you thinking that I'm anything but thankful to have you as my son. You're my son. I cleaned your snot and underwear and your cuts.

Graham trusts him and he's working for free but I don't understand why he can't find you. How could they send you away for a mistake your sorry father, and I, made?

We'll fix this soon.

Find Kim Tae Hee. She was the daughter of the host family I stayed with. She's got to be thirty-six or -seven now. They had a hostel which is like a hotel but for poor traveling people. She's good. Her family speaks English. All you need to say is that Sheryl Monroe says, "You owe me because of Itaewon," and she'll help you. If she pretends not to know what you're saying tell her that I was the blondie that got her out of that terrible bar on "the hill." Her address was Woldekeom-ro, Seongsan Dong, Mapo-Gu, Seoul, South Korea. I can't find a phone number. But people in Korea are very helpful.

We'll figure things out. I think your father is in Korea. He used to sell clothes. I think he only came to America to give you a better life than he had. I met him in Seoul but he was from some town way south. He went by "DJ" for Dong Jun.

Play pool. You might be good at it. He was.

I don't know what else I can tell you that would help.

I hope you never see this. We will get you back. Stay strong. God bless and be nice to yourself. You try too hard sometimes.

Your mom,

Sheryl Monroe

# 11

ALL THE PASSENGERS ARE ALREADY LOADED WHEN THEY FINALLY BRING
the three Chinese guys and me on the plane. We're handcuffed. We walk
up the aisle, a guard in front and a guard behind us. We pass little girls
and boys, businessmen and -women and Asians, so many Asians, and they
all eye us as we go past them to a middle aisle in the back next to the
bathrooms.

We are the bad guys.

One of the guards uncuffs us, then sits next to me. He pulls a magazine
from the seat pocket in front of him and starts flipping through like this
ain't no thing.

I've never been on a plane.

*The doors are now closed,* says the captain over the intercom, *please turn
off all electronic equipment.*

"Hey," I say to the guard. "Hey, you got to get me off this plane."

The guard says nothing.

"I don't belong here. This is a huge mistake. I'm a running back."

The guard rolls up his magazine and then points it at me. "Kid, this is a
long flight. I've been doing this long enough and I've already heard so many
excuses that I don't care. The order says you belong here on this plane. So,
that's that. I'm going to read this magazine and you're going to be quiet and
we're going to have a nice flight and I'll watch you get off the plane and into
Korea without incident. Got it?"

A dude flight attendant is next to us. "Excuse me, you need to buckle
your seat belts."

"Right," the guard says, and buckles.

I'm about to buckle when a thought strikes. "What happens if I don't?"

Dude puffs up like a barnyard rooster. "FAA rules say every passenger must buckle up before we can take off."

"Buckle up," the guard says.

I do nothing.

"If you resist, we will have to remove you," dude flight attendant says, then stops, realizing something.

I stuff the buckles under me. "Remove me," I say. "Douche-nugget," I add for effect.

"Kid," the guard says to me, then turns to the dude: "Give us a minute."

"I need to see him buckle in," the dude says.

The Chinese guys are watching us.

"Give us a minute," the guard says. The attendant eyes him, eyes his police badge, then me, and finally marches back down the aisle to a phone.

"Kid," the guard says, "you're how old?"

"Seventeen to nineteen," I say, "depending on who you ask."

"You need to buckle up."

"No," I say.

"There are two ways this can go, the hard way or the soft. I'm in no mood for any bullshit."

"You heard the stewardess, FAA rules," I say.

"You're going home."

"That's what I want, to go home, to Tibicut."

"That ain't happening."

"FAA rules," I say.

"If you force my hand, this will get very ugly, very quickly, and you're not going to like it and you will still have to go back to your country."

"This is my country."

He points at the paper in my shirt pocket, the one that says *Order for Removal*.

"I'm not buckling up," I say.

"You think you're a tough guy, don't you?"

"I'm not buckling up."

He stares. I can see his eyes tracing the outline of my delts, my pecs. He's weighing me. He's calculating like a D-coordinator what kind of play I'm trying for.

"I just want to stay home," I say. "Nothing personal, but you're taking me from home, from my family, from school, from everything." I don't intend this but suddenly things are getting glassy, melty. I snort hard to keep from bawling.

He sees this and something softens in his shoulders. "Kid, I don't know you, but I don't want to hurt you. I can't help you. I can only hurt you if you don't comply, and you will still go on this plane out of here." He takes a breath and looks down the aisle. "What I can do, if you buckle up and this plane takes off, and only if you do it without any more games, is get some-one to talk to you."

I'm smashing my lips because if I don't, I'll cry.

"How about that? There's a woman here on the plane that can talk to you."

"About what?"

"Korea. She's a marshal, like me, but for Korea. She might be able to help you."

"Help me stay home?"

"Maybe help you get back, I don't know. But you need to buckle up, let this plane go."

The guy is clean-cut like policemen always are, but he's got this soft look about him, cheeks too chubby. He's older and there are little white hairs peppering the black. Maybe it's the glassy eyes, but he's looking at me. Not at my forehead or past my shoulder, but right in the eyes without that chal-lenge, like a teammate. Taking me seriously.

"She's right down there," he says, "just a few rows off." He points down the row.

My eyes are locked in on him. I can't move them. As far as I can tell he's being straight with me. So, I buckle up. The attendant comes by and sees my buckle and keeps going and I think I hear the Chinese guys sigh beside me but I don't look or care, just look straight ahead at the phone in the back of the headrest in front of me. No matter how much I blink, the phone seems fuzzy, like a dream rather than something real that I could unhook and call Sheryl, call Bobby, call Uncle.

What would I even say if I could call them?

*Unc, did you mean it? Did you ever think I could make it?*

*Bobby, did you know?*

The lights go out. The plane moves and the engines give off this hum like far-off blenders. I must've been on a plane before, that's how I got here. We take off, my ass clenches, and I keep looking at the phone and wonder how the hell you could call from a plane when you're far out over all that water.

In my *Order for Removal of Korean National Beonghak Yii*, they misspelled *Yi*. I think maybe that's a loophole. There's a thin gap in the print running down the length of the paper. Their printer must be running out of ink.

Beonghak, the name I can't pronounce, printed on all my report cards and on my learner's permit. But that has nothing to do with me. It's like the name of the town is just a name, doesn't tell you anything about it. *Tibicut* means "try really hard" in an Indian language. Is that what Tibicut does, try hard? We don't even pronounce or spell the name right: it's supposed to be *Taybisu*, according to Coach Shaw. People screwed it up somehow when writing it down.

The plane keeps climbing. My ears pop like going up a mountain. The captain comes back on the intercom and tells us that we're leveled off at thirty-five thousand feet and he says he's going to turn off the seat belt sign, but we shouldn't get up unless we have to.

"All right," the cop says, "you stay right here."

He goes down the aisle and talks to a woman. I can't hear what he says over the engines and chatter that's in other languages. Some I think is Korean. He's gone awhile, like the woman doesn't want to come over. Then she stands up. She's Asian. The guard sits in her seat and she comes and sits next to me in the cop's seat. She puts a book in the seat pocket and looks over at me. Says nothing. Just holds out her hand and I give her my *Order for Removal* and she looks over it, too quickly to read, and hands it back.

"What's your story?" she says.

"I'm getting wrongly deported."

She gives a loud laugh. "You guys hear that?" she says to the Chinese guys next to me. Then she says something in another language. They say something back and keep talking until she puts her hand up and shakes her head for them to stop. Then she looks back at me, waiting for me to say something.

I blink. "I only speak American."

She laughs. She shakes her head and digs out her book and starts flipping through it like she's looking for her spot. The book isn't in English but in some language that has got all these letters that look severe and barbed.

Then she just reads. Ignoring me.

"Hey, I don't belong on this plane," I say.

She licks her finger, flips a page.

"They say my paperwork was screwed up," I say. "The check bounced. My bio-father got married to Sheryl, my stepmom, and then he bailed. My uncle tried to off himself and I lost my cool and beat him up while he was holding up Affordable Al's. You know Affordable Al? *Al knows Asian Autos?*"

"I don't know Al," she says.

"I lived my whole life in America. That's all I know. I'm not Korean, don't speak Korean, don't eat dog or anything. I love football."

"I don't eat dog," she says.

"You know what I mean."

"The United States," she says.

"What?"

"North America has a lot of nations. Americans always seem to forget that."

"Look, can you help me?"

"No." Then she says something in another language.

"Aren't you a cop or something? Protect and serve? Help me."

"That paper says that you're an illegal alien."

"I'm no alien."

"Yii isn't Smith. It isn't even a D'shawn."

"That isn't my name."

"The paper says otherwise," she says, then flips another page.

The woman's hair is tied back, thick like Chantal's. For all I know, she's fresh from college. One of the Chinese guys leans over and says something that gets her to close her book and say something so vicious that it gets him to stop smiling and to stop leaning.

"What did he say?" I ask.

"Ask him," she says.

"What the fuck?" I say. "Why did you agree to sit here if you aren't going to say something to me? Help? Are you even a cop?"

She gives a grunt, an *ah*-like sound, a yes.

The lights go out. She leans the seat back and closes her eyes.

"Lady," I say.

"I have the authority to have you gagged quiet," she says without opening her eyes. "In our country, that's what cops can do. So don't disturb my sleep."

It's not long before she snorts and shifts her head on the pillow. The plane shudders and all the plastic groans and rattles.

I know I shouldn't have said that thing about eating dog. That's ignorant, the kind of thing that would rile me if I heard it from someone at school. Should've asked for her name. Should've been cool and collected and calmly walked her through it all. But maybe she doesn't know anything. Might not even be a cop. Just another two-face like the cop who traded seats with her to get away from me, to get me to comply, and now this plane is going and humming across the Pacific. To Korea.

Foreigners hate Americans and burn American flags. They will dogpile me in their mobs. They'll kill me because I'm American but America tells me I'm not.

I smell shit coming from the bathroom. I'm buckled in, trapped, in the dark, with stink. I can smell it on my breath. I can smell it coming from my pits. It's like I never left steedick.

Breathe. Breathe. Breathe.

I'm breaking down. Gonna cry like those kids on Pee Wee football teams that lose.

What would Barry Sanders do?

What would Coach Shaw say?

Coach would say rehearse good outcomes in your dumb head.

Barry Sanders would run for a hundred yards and the Lions would still lose. Score touchdowns and simply hand the ball off to the ref with courtesy and dignity.

I tell myself: Have some fucking dignity.

You're an American. You are—were—a running back, and if you ever hope to be one again you must have dignity. This is just a small hiccup. America is the greatest nation on earth. It will not forget you.

But they're punting me. And now I'm thinking about Hot Holly, how I never even once talked to her. I'm thinking about Jenifer Pain, who I made out with behind the band room before junior high football practice. It was on the down low and we never let anyone know because she was a band geek and I was a baller and no one would understand and one day she got caught giving Emmet a handy in an empty chemistry room. Emmet, now our quarterback. She moved schools after that. She never returned any of my calls when I was just going to say sorry that I didn't ask her to be my girlfriend.

Breathe. Regroup and push the pile forward. Always fall forward.

I remember the times that teachers got mad at me for marking *other* for race on state tests. They got madder when I filled in *running back* for *other*. There was that time in the locker room during tryouts when some dipshit new kid told me that Chinamen don't know football and I smacked and stuffed him halfway into a locker before Jimmy and some other starters pulled me off him saying he'd never be first string.

All these bad memories, make me feel guilty. Like I ought to apologize.

I smell shit again.

But it's not the plane.

It's me, imprinted in my pores. Reeking repulsive concrete and mildew and the sharp bite of something like rotten cheese or that gunk you find pooling in the dark, stagnant parts of the ravine.

And there he is again between the cedars instead of the fifty-yard line. My bio-father, grinning under his sunglasses, wearing that tan Members Only jacket.

Lights on.

I must've fallen asleep.

Flight attendants hand out little yellow cards and white slips written in Korean. One leaves a pair in the back seat pocket for the sleeping marshal next to me.

The plane lands. The marshal wakes and grumbles. She starts filling out the paper. The captain makes an announcement in Korean and then in English: *Welcome to Korea. The temperature is fifteen degrees Celsius, or fifty-nine degrees Fahrenheit. Set your watches sixteen hours ahead, the date is . . .*

"It's funny," the woman says, "you wake up in a different place, a different time, maybe you're also a different person."

She signs her little yellow paper with the flair of signing a game ball, then looks over at me.

"Did you fill yours out yet?" she asks.

"No," I say. "I don't know how to fill them out."

"You don't?" she says.

"It's in Korean."

"Forms like these always say the same thing," she says. "Are you bringing in stuff you shouldn't? Where are you staying? Are you a criminal or plan to be one?" She points at a column of boxes. "Just mark these boxes all the way down and you'll be fine."

"I'm Bucky," I say. I hold out my hand to shake. She eyes my hand like no one has shaken her hand before, then she shakes it. "Call me Janie," she says. Then I start marking the forms.

"Different time, different place, different people," she says, and laughs. "You really don't speak any Korean?"

"Like I said, I belong in America . . . I mean the U.S."

She *hmms*. Like only now she's believing me. "Have you got a lawyer?"

"Yeah."

"Listen to your lawyer. And find your dad. That'll help."

"How do I do that?"

She laughs. "That's for you to figure out, kid. But my guess is you go to a government office. Good luck to you."

Then she gets off the plane with everyone else, except me and the Chinese guys and the guards. Once everyone is gone and the cleaners board the plane, the clean-cut guard says, "You three stay right there"—he points at the three Chinese guys. "Kid"—he points at me—"you come with me."

# PART TWO
## ROOTS AND SOUP

# 12

## LETTER FROM RICHARD

*Bucky,*

*If you are sent back to Korea, these are the things you need to do:*

*1) Don't panic.*

*2) You need to ascertain the status of your citizenship in South Korea. When you arrive in South Korea you will likely be held by immigration for an extended period of time while they figure out your situation. Try to get copies of the paperwork.*

*3) Get a phone card.*

*4) Call +1 (206) 555-6430, leave a message if I don't pick up.*

*5) Have fun. If you play your cards right, you will be able to think of this as a short vacation.*

*Best,*

*Richard*

# 13

THERE ARE SO MANY PEOPLE WITH BAGS ON WHEELS. LINES ON THE floor lead us to big signs with English letters: FOREIGNERS, and another with big Korean letters and small English, KOREAN NATIONALS.

"You go in that line," the cop tells me, and points at the NATIONALS line.

The hallways are big and there are signs for toilets away from immigration. I heard somewhere, maybe in Fake English's class, that airports are neutral territory and some guy in France refused to go through immigration and there was nothing that the government could do. So he lived off McDonald's for years in the terminal. I think of running for it. Hiding out in the airport, maybe climbing into the gut of an airplane with the luggage for a ride back to America.

"Kid," the cop says, "that's your line."

"Is there no other way? That lady you had me talking to didn't tell me shit."

"My job is to make sure you go in that line. If there's another way back, it's through there."

The line has all of these Asians, businessmen dressed in sport coats and black slacks. I line up behind them. The guard stands off to the side to watch and make sure I go.

People hand their passports to the officers stationed inside these glass boxes, who flip through each passport, hold it up and compare the picture to the person in front of them, hand the passport back, and wave them through. No one smiles. No one says a word. This line moves faster than the lines at SuperDollar. When it's my turn, I look back and the guard is by the far post, watching me. I hand my *Order for Removal* over to the officer. Maybe the immigration officer will bring me to a back room where they

tase me and then put me on a plane back to America—*Return to Sender,*
motherfucker.

Maybe they'll see my misspelled name and tell me to wait in the terminal by a McDonald's while they sort it out with the U.S. That's when
the American government will figure out the mistake they made and then
Richard can bring me home.

The immigration officer scans the paper, types on his keyboard, looks at
his screen. He takes a deep breath.

It's coming. Taser. Burning flags. Something.

He says something flat, monotone.

I shake my head.

He says it again. I ask, "English?"

He points to the big sign hanging over the hallways leading out. 한국에
오신 것을 환영 합니다. Under it says, in little English letters, WELCOME
TO KOREA.

I look for the cop from the plane, but he is already gone. The officer in
the box bangs on the glass and motions for me to get a move on.

Then I'm at baggage claim. All these people are waiting at conveyor belts
for bags. I've only got a ziplock in my hand that's got my letters, a wallet
with twenty bucks, and some brownie crumbs in my pockets.

I go to the guards waiting by the exit, thinking maybe they'll pull me
into a back room and send me packing back to America. They just grab my
skinny yellow-and-white forms from the plane and wave me through.

Outside is a scrum of people like nothing I've ever seen. A mob. Black
hair, tan skin, high cheekbones everywhere. I try to step back, it's too much,
but people behind me surge, bumping, pushing me forward. Where there
aren't people are tall aluminum columns with giant TVs showing people
dancing around fried chicken buckets. Phones ring and chirp. From kiosks,
women in pastel uniforms shout, kids squeal, and shoes rumble against the
floor like floodwaters hurdling walls. It smells of perfume and hair gel and
cigarette smoke and things I've never smelled before.

Between a trash can and an aluminum column, I try to breathe. Everything is hazy. The air feels so thin, and gulping does nothing; I think I'm
going to drop. Things get simple. I weave through the bodies, take all the

tunnels I can until I reach a pocket where I can look up and see signs for the bathroom. I hustle there. Go into the first open stall and lock it behind me. I sit on an odd-looking toilet with my pants still on. The air is all piss and farts and bleach but with the door closed I can breathe, through the nose and out the mouth. Foulness in and out. I shut my eyes and visualize. My swept trails and the sounds of trees swaying in the breeze. That's the place I know. There is a place I ran, seas of trees where I could hold my head up high and breathe.

I need to make things factual. Make a trail to run forward.

Fact: I'm far away from home.

Fact: I'm alive and not in jail.

Fact: No one is coming to tase me.

Sway for a moment like the trees. Be serene as trees.

I nearly fall off the toilet, have to catch myself by pushing off this handle off to the side of the toilet and accidentally press the big button. A woman's voice speaks in Korean, and the next thing I know, the toilet is squirting my ass, my pants, from a little handle sticking up from the toilet seat.

This all breaks whatever was clamped down on my throat and now I'm breathing and thinking clearly, swatting my ass like that will help me dry. I need to get out of here. Sheryl gave me an address. I need to go to that address.

I dig out my letters from the plastic bag. They had been opened and read by the assholes in steedick. There's one from Sheryl, another from Richard the lawyer. The third is the one from Chantal that I haven't read. In the bag too is the other letter Chantal wrote me that I had kept in my pocket from the day this all started, the one with the middle finger she drew.

Acid churns up my chest. Keep things factual. Focused. I stuff Chantal's letters back into the bag. There'll be time for that, but not now.

I keep Sheryl's letter in hand. With a wet ass and a light head, this is all I can do. Find a way to that address. Fact.

# 14

THE TAXI DRIVER GETS ME TO SEOUL AS THE SUN DROPS. HAZE SMOKES the air, and smoke trails from the driver's window as he burns one cigarette after another. Off the highway, he seems to cuss at the traffic lights. At one light he rubs the head of a green fat Buddha glued to the dash. At another he thumbs through some prayer beads, grunts, then pulls the car onto the sidewalk and cuts the corner. People scurry to buildings and lampposts while he honks and scrapes the muffler on the curb. He waves his hand out the window to cut into traffic. I can't watch.

Back at the airport, a woman with a red flying-saucer-shaped hat had helped me get the taxi. I pointed to the address in Sheryl's letter, and she smiled and shook her head and got a woman on the phone who talked so fast it took me a minute to realize she was speaking English. "HowcanI-helpyou?" "Couldyourepeatthat?" She called her coworker her "colleague." But the two of them figured out where I was trying to go, took my cash, and exchanged it with these green and blue bills and coins. Then saucer-hat argued with the taxi driver who was squatting at the curb, sipping something from a skinny can and smoking, until he finally agreed to get me on the road to Seoul.

Now my ass lifts over every hill. The seat belt—I'm wearing a seat belt, for once—groans with the corners. But he gets me to the Sunshine Flower Hostel and coughs and laughs to get me to open my eyes and give him his money.

The door ain't even shut when he peels out with all kinds of smoke trailing behind him, barking tires, grinding gears, drifting over the centerline.

Korea is a stuffed country. The only way to see sky is to look right up. In every other direction are walls of low buildings so close in, people have got to hear assholes in the next building fart. Signs jut and hang off the walls and corners. Black moss streaks the signs and in between the bricks. But it isn't like any moss I've ever seen, more like dust or mud. An old woman at a red cart sells some kind of donut ball. A bunch of suits with briefcases and cell phones jammed to their ears crowd the sidewalks with women and teenagers and kids who all seem to have phones jammed to their heads or in their hands in front of them like compasses.

Inside the Sunshine Flower Hostel, a girl with purple hair is playing with her cell phone at the front desk. Purple like bubble gum grape. In Tibicut the only dyed hair I saw was blond. But she's pretty. Got a black sweater with rainbow bands across her chest. She looks up from her phone.

Girls always know when you're looking at them, thinking stuff.

I walk up and she says something.

No, not something, she says something like, "Anyanghaseo."

That is how you say *Hello*. Got to be *Hello*. She says some other stuff but this was *Hello*.

"Do you," I say, "speak English?"

"Oh hi," she says. She puts down the phone and sits up. "How many nights?"

"Um, a lot."

"Room?" she says. "A private room with its own bathroom is sam-man-won a night."

"Huh?"

"Oh, um . . ." She looks up at the ceiling, counting. "Thirty thousand won . . . like, forty dollars."

"Look—"

"Bunks are"—she counts—"a lot cheaper, like fifteen bucks."

"I'm looking for Kim—just a second." I take out Sheryl's letter. "Kim Tae Hee."

She laughs.

"Seriously," I say.

She keeps laughing.

"What's so funny?"

She points to a poster above a bookshelf with a bunch of DVDs. A model with dyed orange hair looks like she's cooling her neck by rubbing a sweating green bottle against it. "That's Kim Tae-hee," she says.

"Is this the right address?" I show her the address in Sheryl's letter.

"Kind of," she says. "No one uses this kind of address style anymore. But that's Kim Tae-hee."

"You sure? Does your family own this, or—"

"Is this a pickup line?"

"What? No, I just . . ."

She's giving me the you-fucked-up eye. But how could I have fucked up? I need help, and a place to sleep and figure shit out. This is where I'm supposed to go. A streetlight outside comes on and drops light through the window.

"My stepmom said that her friend's family owned this place. Your mom isn't named something like Kim—"

"No, sorry," she says. She picks up her phone.

"Are bunks comfortable?" I say.

"They're bunks."

I say okay. What else can I do? I put what money I have left on the table. It's a brown paper, a couple of blue papers, and some shiny-looking quarters. It doesn't look like much because it isn't much.

"That isn't enough," she says.

We both stare at the shriveled bills on the table next to her Hello Kitty solar-powered bobblehead. Her phone vibrates.

"I—can I please use your phone?" I say.

That wasn't the right thing to say. She scoots back.

"No," she says. "Sorry," she says. "I don't know you," she says.

"Okay," my mouth says. *Run*, my legs say with a twitch. "Thanks," my mouth says. Legs walk me back outside and around the corner.

Outside, dark comes from every direction like how the car honks bounce off walls in every direction, near and far. I recognize none of the makes of cars on the road or parked on the side. A truck named *Bongo*. A car called *S/M*. Ha! That means kinky sex! I know cars and I don't know S/M except for the kinky sex! With whips! Whips!

Fact: Plan has gone to shit.

Fact: Sheryl was wrong. But Sheryl is sharp. She rips Band-Aids off and always remembers to put bottle caps back on and to put stuff back in the fridge. Up-front and honest. Yet these things don't seem to be true anymore.

Facts: Got no way to get my four thousand calories of real food to keep my muscle mass. No money. No place to sleep, no language, no map, and no plan. Every single thing has gone completely to shit.

Question: Did Sheryl lie? Did she just want to keep this yellow boy running, like Uncle Rick did?

Then I cry. I've never cried like this before, snot dripping and spit stringing from my lips. I'm going to die here. I'm going to die without ever getting a blow job, a parking ticket, or an All-American selection. I'm never going to walk out on a shitty job or even drink in a bar lying about how I got league MVP or a 56–0 win over those tweaker-baby Bremerton kids.

I bawl until my cheeks are flushed like a fire in a mobile home, until some schoolgirls in green blazers and green checkered skirts and absurdly large socks that lip over their shoes like flaps on a bulldog watch me from the bus stop. Probably thinking, What a strange man with great delts and a wet ass shaped like a baboon's.

Across the street a taxi stops and a couple of white guys get out and go down the stairwell. The sign above says COMMUNES LONELY HEARTS PUB.

I go down the stairs and push through the saloon doors. Walls painted black between curling music posters stained nicotine-yellow. Behind the bar, rows of vinyl records packed tight like book pages. Dust clings to liquor bottles. Guys play chess in a corner. A guy and a girl clack pool balls and sip beer. The two guys from the taxi mount stools at the bar.

A Korean guy with white hair pours drinks and talks English to the white guys. The white guys got accents. They say, *Pints.* The older white guy with graying hair points and says, *Oi.* He's pointing at me and saying, *Oi.*

"Oi, you a'ight?"

The other guy and the bartender look at me too.

"I don't know," I say. "Got nowhere to go."

"Well, his missus done kicked him out," he says, pointing at his skinny friend with the brown hair, "and rightly so."

"That's uncalled-for," the friend says.

"You're a wanker and ought to apologize to her. He"—pointing at the bartender—"had nowhere to go and opened this fine establishment, which is now our local. So you're in good company. Here, have a pint."

—

This is Simon. He's English. His English is different from Fake English's. He says, *Oi.* He says, *Bullocks.* He's got graying hair and a potbelly.

This is Scottish Mark, who's different from English Mark, Irish Mark, and some other Marks. He is skinny and younger than everyone else and has lost his girlfriend, who everyone calls his *missus.*

This is Hyunshik. This is his bar. He smokes and drinks and quizzes his customers about the songs he plays on the turntable. *Who's the bassist?*

"Sting," says Simon. "Only a numpty wouldn't know that."

Simon and Scottish Mark teach flight attendants at something called a hak-won. "A tutorial," Scottish Mark says, "on the language skills stewardesses would need in first class."

A few weeks back, Scottish Mark necked with one of his students at Club Monkey.

"I didn't approve then," Simon says.

"You didn't say anything either," Scottish Mark says, "did ya?"

"Drummer?" Hyunshik calls out to the room.

"Mickey Jones," says one of the guys playing chess.

"Well, look what happened to you," Simon says to Mark.

A few hours ago Mark's girlfriend heaved his clothes, his books, DVDs, and pots and pans and plants and ashtrays out the window, all the parts of his material life raining down on his 150cc scooter. "I just want to find the cock that told her," Mark says. "I need a shot. Hyunshik, four shots. Whatever foul whiskey you keep in the well."

"Only good whiskey here," Hyunshik says, changes the record, drops the needle.

Cassettes, CDs, radio, those are the things music I know comes from, never a record player. Now the speakers pop as the needle rides the spinning plastic.

"*Nashville Skyline*," the chess players shout with the first strum of the guitars.

Hyunshik lines the shots on the bar. Mark passes them around.

"To wankers," Mark salutes, and we all shoot, and it tastes horrible and burns right down my chest to the hot lead of my stomach.

"So, our dear American," Simon says. "What's your name? What's your story of woe?"

"Bucky, I guess."

"You guess?" Simon says. "Do you suppose it's as good of a name as any other?"

"Everyone calls me Bucky."

Mark laughs. "Now, that's the most American name I've ever heard."

"And your tale of woe?" Simon says.

"I don't know," I say. I mean it too. Maybe it's the alcohol. I'm not much of a drinker, because it saps your legs and adds soft weight. The three of them stare. "I was going to play football."

"American football," Simon says.

"Is there any other kind?" I say.

They all laugh.

"What's so funny?" I say.

"We'll explain later," Simon says. "Go on."

"I was going to play football, but I didn't get scouted. So, I don't know. One moment I'm doing that, then the next I'm being put on a plane to Korea. Everyone says I'm from here, so here I am. Broke. Just here. Trying to figure shit out."

The three of them are nodding in that way that drunks do when they're reliving something in their heads. They're all somber.

"You're in the right place," Simon says.

"Mate," Scottish Mark says, "you're just another refugee."

"I don't know about that," I say.

"You are," Scottish Mark says. "Everyone here is, except Hyunshik. He's just an arse."

"Fuck off," Hyunshik says.

"To refugees," Simon says.

We drink.

———

The saloon doors swing and the girl with the purple hair walks in. Mark and Simon say, *Hello, my lovely*, and *Hello, Miss Purple*. She stops, squints at me. Says, "Well, hello again," before she sits at the bar on the other side of Mark and Simon.

My face burns with a heat cold water couldn't stop.

My petty crumpled cash drops on the bar and I mumble, "This is all I got. I'm sorry if it isn't enough to pay for what I drank, but I haven't got anything. Thanks." I'm about to start bounding up the stairs when Hyunshik says stop.

"You can lift heavy things, right?" he says.

"Yeah, I guess," I say. "I deadlift three-fifty."

All three guys look over to the girl with the purple hair.

"I don't know," she says. "I guess it's like a hundred and fifty-something kilograms."

"About a hundred and fifty-nine kilos," says one of the chess players.

"Always the bloody accountant, Winning," Simon says.

"So?" I say.

Hyunshik takes me up to the back flight of very narrow stairs, past a pair of bathrooms, to a back door and an alley. There is a half-sized clear-door refrigerator. "Can you bring this down the stairs to the bar?" he says.

The refrigerator teeters easily. It's light. "Yeah."

"Bring it down. Do that, I'll pay," he says. "Good?"

Do this? Yes, I can do this. The refrigerator is bottom-heavy. It tips easily over my shoulder and I fireman-carry it down the stairs, only once bumping the wall by the corner when I turn. Everyone down in the bar watches me carrying the refrigerator until it's snugly in the corner with another clear-doored fridge. Then Hyunshik has me stack kegs and boxes of liquor, carry a man out that I hadn't noticed passed out on a back couch and toss him into a taxi.

The night swells with English and Welsh and Scots and Kiwis and Irish and Northern Irish and Aussies and Canadians, Kenyans, South Africans, and Koreans who speak English, then the night drifts to quiet while I carry things and stumble bodies up the stairs and into taxis.

At the end of the night, Simon, Scottish Mark, and the girl with the purple hair are still at the bar. They hand me another beer. Hyunshik hands me a wad of Korean won. They give me a name, because, *Every bloke needs a good moniker.* They call me Bucky the Hulk.

Hyunshik starts turning off lights and Mark and Simon stumble into taxis. I ask the girl with purple hair if there are still bunks over at the hostel.

"Haesoo," she says.

"I don't speak Korean."

"Instead of just saying, 'Hey,' use my name," she says. "Like normal people."

I don't get it.

"Haesoo is my name," she says. "It's easy to remember. Think, *Hey, Sue.* You know, you look so Korean, but you're totally not."

"Yeah, well, I guess I am."

"Lots of gyopos come through here can't speak either."

"Gyopo?"

"Foreigner Koreans," she says. "Let's get you a bunk. I need to go to sleep."

She leads me back to the hostel and gets me a key to a locker for the bag I don't have. She takes some cash and tells me to grab any bunk without a body in the men's bunk room. She says good night and leaves.

I get a top bunk and stare up at the ceiling.

I'm alive. I'm a *gyopo.* There's a single word for what I am.

Good feeling slides out, and in comes a headache. All that beer.

All night guys snore and fart, and one guy laughs in his sleep. They are travelers, traveling. They have stuff with them to put in their lockers.

# 15

I WAKE UP AND PRETEND TO SLEEP UNTIL ALL THE GUYS ARE OUT OF THE bunk room and the hostel lobby gets quiet. When an old lady comes to take the sheets, I leave.

Outside, everything feels like I'm looking through the wrong end of a scope. My hands move, pass blue bills to the woman selling donut rolls on the sidewalk like I watched the snot-snorting kids do. Inside the rolls is mashed sweet potato. I wander. The big roads have the honking traffic I've only seen on TV.

The sidewalks are no better, cracked and bumpy, people elbowing, people rushing the gaps, feet shuffling the mass of people forward. Even short shriveled grandmas and grandpas hustle. I bump more people here in ten minutes than all the people that have ever lived in Tibicut. The air chokes with breath and car exhaust and smells from carts and whatever is steaming from the muffler tips sticking out of the buildings on each floor into the alleys. Cafés and cell phone shops blast music into the crowd from big hanging speakers.

I can't breathe.

Then I see the stairwell to Communes. I get out of the crowd, pretend to read handbills taped and nailed to the black walls leading to the dark bar below.

—

Hyunshik comes and stops a second at the top of the stairway and grabs the mail. He looks down the stairwell, says something stern. I say, "It's me, Bucky the Hulk."

"Oh," he says.

He puts me to work.

—

Someone left a notebook in the bathroom. Brand-new. Still in plastic wrap, which is the first time I see a notebook in plastic wrap. I take it back to the hostel at the end of the night. New things smell different.

—

The only time I don't feel stuck and nervous is when I talk to Haesoo.

—

Outside is like being in a closet in the day and a pinball machine at night.

I wait for Hyunshik in the stairway to the bar, in the dark, while the birds perch on rails and old nails sticking out from the handbills. They bob their heads with gray, hazy daylight behind them. They're eyeballing me. Waiting for me to do something. I go deeper down the stairwell. It's the only place I feel I can breathe.

Hours pass. I should think about getting home but all I can think about are trick plays. Fake punts. Fumblerooskis. Statue of liberty. All are about misdirection, *Look over here*, while the ball is really going over there.

—

Something is in the corner of my eye, but it's gone when I look over. In the alleys it has got to be stray cats. But what about in the bar?

—

A full keg weighs 72.8 kilograms, which is like 161 pounds. I line the backroom wall five kegs deep and three kegs high, which is like deadlifting 161 pounds five times, then doing ten power cleans. And that's not even taking each keg off the truck, carrying it downstairs on my hip so my knees don't knock it on the way down. If I was really studding it, I'd carry one on each shoulder, which would be 322 pounds coming down the stairs. But I'm no stud.

Thousand-yard rushers don't have bad metrics. But truth be told, our division is weak. Being tough would get you a thousand yards. I'm more than tough; I know plays backward and forward. I can tell the difference between a linebacker cheating up or faking his assignment. If he's faking, his hands rest on thigh pads. If they're out in front of him, that means he's going north and south. My transparent eyeballs can see through the bullshit. These transparent eyeballs soaked in knowledge from a shitty league, a shitty team, learned to see the creases and how to earn.

But they caught no tells from Sheryl.

—

I buy running shoes, clothes. Haesoo helps. She shows me the way down to this stream of cattails winged by grass with a line of trees, a rubberized running track, and a bicycle blacktop. Haesoo tells me it is like a bike highway that links all the little streams to the big river that can take you anywhere in the city. Every kilometer are these workout spots with pull-up bars, and body weight machines so you can twist and work your interior abs.

Here, I can breathe.

—

Some places sell kimbap: veg and meat on a thin bed of rice rolled up in seaweed the circumference of a bicycle hand pump. The seaweed doesn't taste good but most legit workout meals don't either. Kimbap is cheap, like fifty cents a roll. Then I go to Communes. Lift stuff and move stuff and hang around the bar and drink beer with Simon, Mark, and Haesoo and all of these people who speak English and teach English.

—

A Canadian woman rides the subway thirty minutes to get here. "It's my local," she says. I've never been on a subway.

"I don't blame you," she says. "Here people die in subway fires. One time, this train stops between stations, catches fire. All these Koreans just fucking stood there and died because they waited for someone to tell them what to do."

"What were they supposed to do?" I ask.

"Not fucking burn to death, underground, in a subway car. Break a window out or something. Show some fucking sense. Save yourself. We would. A bunch of Canadians would've saved themselves."

"Have you ever saved yourself from a fire?" I ask.

She looks at me a long moment, then puts her hand up in my face, gives off this deer huff sound, and walks off.

—

In the bar people make a very clear distinction: *We* speak English. *They* learn English. *They* are strict and *we* are not. *They* wear uniforms based on their age and *we* don't. *We* think for ourselves and *they* follow "groupthink." And so on.

*I* am in *we* but look like *them*. No one has said anything about that, yet.

—

Runners coming the other direction only see me as another runner coming on their left, just part of the landscape.

But when I open my mouth is when they see me. Cashiers give me a look like, *Why are you fucking with me?* My heart thumps. Some don't deal with me and just wave their hands saying, "No, no, no," like I'm begging for change. Other turn their heads to the next in line, like I'll disappear, which I usually do.

This is when I feel the gap around my heart. This is what Emmet, our quarterback, must feel like when the pocket breaks and every big man comes for big hits like falling trees. This is fear. The great pass is only possible by accepting what's going to hurt. Target A is covered. Target B fell down, and here they come.

—

There are five different Marks that hang out at Communes: Scottish, Irish, English, gay, and angry. On trivia night, the Marks form a team and beat everyone. The shady guy in the corner who always wears black tracksuits is called Mr. Kim, even though a lot of people have the name Kim. GI Dan is in the U.S. Army, and hides in the stockroom with the kegs when the MPs come by looking in after curfew.

I'm Hulk. The first night I was Bucky the Hulk, but now everyone just calls me Hulk, except for Haesoo, who calls me B&H. Everybody has a nickname.

Winning, the Scottish chess player, says I look nothing like a B&H.

—

Canadian Craig, who is always getting into fights over the pool table, comes up to Simon, me, and a couple of Marks at the bar. He says, "The Lone Ranger is at the bar. A cowboy walks into the bar and says, 'Who's got the big white horse?'

" 'That's my horse,' the Lone Ranger says, 'Silver.'

"The guy says, 'It looks like shit. Didn't you cool him off after you rode him?' The Lone Ranger tells Tonto to go cool off his horse. Tonto goes out and starts running circles around the horse. Later another cowboy walks in and says, 'Who owns that big white horse out there?'

"The Lone Ranger says, 'That's my horse, Silver.'

"The guy says, 'You left your engine running!' "

Everybody laughs.

Then Canadian Craig says, "How do you know a Korean broke into your house?"

"How?" says Angry Mark.

Canadian Craig chalks his pool cue. "Your computer is working, your homework is done, and the dog is missing." He smiles, and the guys laugh, and he goes back to the pool table.

I laugh too. I'm supposed to. But suddenly something feels different.

—

*Work ethic is the start*
*of everything,*
*49ers Coach Bill Walsh said.*
*I work.*
*What starts?*

—

Why haikus? That ain't even Korean.

—

One guy hears me say, *In America you'd never hear of anyone playing pro soccer.* He comes over, tells me that the first thing wrong with Americans is they call the beautiful game *soccer.* "It's football. Or footie." The second thing wrong with Americans is that their daft decisions affect the whole world. It isn't right that Americans can call football *soccer* and expect the rest of the world to change their minds. He has to hear *soccer* on every shit channel that's full of American shows. Third thing, other countries should be able to vote in American elections so they wouldn't elect so many stupid and evil leaders that affect their countries too.

GI Dan hears that last part and says that is a bunch of commie horseshit.

—

Mr. Kim wears tracksuits, smokes Seven Stars cigarettes, and runs a hi-fi music store around the corner that also sells knockoff fancy suits. He doesn't seem to blink. When he plays darts he wins. He helps people with Korean paperwork, including Hyunshik. But people don't like talking to him. Sometimes when I'm clearing tables I get this tingling, like when a linebacker eyes me, and I look over and see Mr. Kim watching me.

At the end of the night there's only me, Haesoo, and Hyunshik, and I ask what's Mr. Kim's deal.

"He's just weird," Haesoo says before Hyunshik says something sharp in Korean, and then asks me who the guitarist is on the record.

Later, I walk Haesoo a couple blocks to her apartment. She says it's nice to be walked by a guy that looks like he can lift small cars. Maybe she likes me and we'll make out or something by the front door and then trip over each other up the stairs to her apartment.

When we get to the front door to the complex, she squares up to me. "Mr. Kim is a defector," she says, like I'm supposed to know what that means.

"Like off the *Enterprise* in *Star Trek*? A shield?"

She takes and minute and looks back at the sleeping guard in the apartment guard box. All nice apartments have guards in boxes.

"No, like from North Korea."

"Oh," I say. The only thing I know about North Korea is that they're bad and everyone always asked me if I was from there or the South.

"I think they executed his family after he came. The loneliest man I've ever met." She gives a sigh that melts me.

"I'm lonely," I say.

"What?" she says, and takes a step back. "Are you hitting on me again?"

"I got deported. From America," I blurt. "I need to go home."

"Oh," she says.

Then I tell her everything, can't stop myself. As soon as I finish, she says she's so sorry but she needs some sleep. Then she's gone.

# 16

## CHANTAL'S LETTER

AFTER SPILLING MY GUTS TO HAESOO, I CAN'T SLEEP. I SHOULD BE DOING something to get home, but I just can't. Then I'm thinking about Chantal. I dig out the first of Chantal's letters. The one with the middle finger. I read it with the streetlight coming in through the window.

> *Dear Bucky,*
>
> *I don't hate you because you were mean to me or because you embarrassed me or because you act like a meathead trauma victim. I hate you because you're the only person I can hate.*
>
> *So I have to smile all the time. Not just for Cheer, but all THE TIME. When I don't, everyone asks me what's wrong. Nothing's wrong, but other people get all anxious that if I'm not smiling then something isn't right. Like I'm plotting. Other people don't always have to smile.*
>
> *That's why it feels so good to flip you off. And because you're an asshole for freaking out like a meathead trauma victim, no one asks me why I flip you off. Not even the teachers.*
>
> *But here's the problem: because we haven't made up to be civil and all of that, we can't talk. And I really need to talk to you.*
>
> *No, I don't like you.*
>
> *I DO NOT LIKE YOU.*
>
> *You're a nice guy . . . Well, no, you're an asshole. But nice butt. But your buzz cut makes your head look like a cantaloupe and really the problem*

*with you is I would never mess around with a meathead trauma victim. And you get this creepy look on your face sometimes. Are you zoning out or staring at my chest? It's gross.*

*I can feel you doing it when you sit behind me. Don't even have to look back at you. Quit that. I don't think you're actually a creep but all the girls will think you are because of that.*

*Anyway, I really need to talk to you because you're the only one that could possibly get what's going on with my life. You're going to pay attention because I'm the only person that can get why you're such a weirdo.*

*You want to play football at some good meathead program. I want to go to Yale. I have a perfect GPA, good SATs. I applied for early acceptance. An alumnus, a Japanese man with an accent, living in a big house on Mercer Island, some doctor at the University medical center, interviewed me and said that he could not recommend me because what kind of well-rounded person can't say their own name?*

*I said what do you mean?*

*He says, "You know what I mean. Your Korean name. Your real name."*

*I say it. He looks at me and says something in Japanese or Korean or something. I took French and read books in Latin. How the hell am I supposed to be able to speak an Asian language?*

*So, he says this thing, and looks at me, and I say, "Sorry?"*

*"What do you know about Korea?"*

*I know that they're on a peninsula. That there were three kingdoms that lasted a long time until they became one kingdom that was called Joseon, that lasted 600 years as a puppet state to China and hated the rest of the world. It was nicknamed the "turtle kingdom," until the Japanese colonized and opened it up. I know that after World War Two the North Koreans tried to turn the whole Korea communist with help of the Russians and Chinese until the US saved the South. I know Korea is third world and that I was saved by the H adoption group. I've eaten kimchi from the Chinese grocery store in the International District of Seattle. I've seen hanboks and have several masks. I plan to travel to Korea after graduation and volunteer for an aid group and tour and learn about my roots.*

*The alumnus just stared at me. "I cannot recommend you," he says. "And therefore you will be denied."*

*He had a pair of Spanish swords above his fireplace. Should have impaled him like a conquistador.*

*I was so mad but my parents said nothing the whole way home. None of my friends say anything either, until today, Holly tells me that I should be happy that I got an interview, that no one else from our school would've gotten that. She means it like I didn't deserve it.*

*Don't you get tired of how people ask you where you're from like you're from under the sea?*

*I heard about your uncle. Is he okay? Are you okay? You're like zoned out and scribbling into your book and everyone is just acting like they're not watching, but they are, because, you know.*

*I was thinking that I ought to try talking to you again, but you're so broody and pissed I thought I ought to write you, so that's this.*

*You're not a complete asshole, okay? You just act like one. I know that inside you're different. So if you'd like to talk or just write, you know, do it.*

*Chantal*

*(Bora)*

*PS: Do you know how to say, Bora? I've also seen it written as Bola. Is it supposed to sound like Ebola, the disease? Or like Bora Bora? What's your Korean name?*

Chantal's letter makes me feel odd, more than the missed chance to mess around. Sure, back there we could make out and hold hands in the halls, but I could also go in a SuperDollar and buy eggs and the cashier would just say, "What's up, Buck?" Life is happening there, not here.

I need to get back.

I'm about to open her other letter, the one that Richard the lawyer brought with him, but I stop myself. I want to give myself something special to hang on to, like replaying touchdown tape.

# 11

MY EYES POP OPEN AND IT'S MORNING. NOT NEARLY LUNCH, BUT REAL morning. The bunk room is empty because everyone is in the dining room at the long table talking and clanging metal bowls. Korea loves little metal bowls for drinking water and for rice and soup that all have this bell-like ring when spoons hit them.

Two weeks here, and I've never had the free breakfast.

Everyone at the table speaks Korean except for one couple who look Korean but speak English. I sit next to them and say hi and I ask them what we're eating.

"Roots and soup," the guy says. "Love Korean food but in the end it's mostly roots and soup. Especially the cheap stuff."

"Seaweed is good for your hair," the woman says. "That's what my mother tells me."

They're Korean Americans, gyopos, from Los Angeles, traveling around Korea for their honeymoon and practicing their Korean. "Connecting with our roots and soup," the guy says, and laughs.

He's a dentist and she's finishing pharmacy school.

I lie, tell them I'm doing school. Just taking a break.

"Gap years save lives," the guy says.

"Figuring out what to do with your life is really important," she says.

The others glance up at us, noticing our English. At night, when Scottish Mark, or Simon, or anyone else takes me in a taxi to a McDonald's or to a street vendor selling terrible mini-pizzas, I see same glances, the same lean over the table one person makes toward the other to whisper. What are they saying about us?

The couple don't notice. They ask me if I've done a temple stay. They're going to some mountain near the east coast with a famous temple where the air is supposed to be better and the monks claim that they have a wild bear family living nearby.

"I'm not sure you want to be near bears," I say.

"You don't get it," they tell me. They are special bears with white Ts on their chests. And outside the DMZ, they don't exist. And they exist only because the North and the South leave this one wild valley alone because they can point guns at each other from the tops of hills. "They're like unicorns, saved by a never-ending war."

Have I been on a DMZ tour? they ask. How about the clubs in Hongdae? Seoul tower with all those trails on Namsan? Dongdaemun Market? Gwanghwamun?

No, I say. I just got here. Been hanging out with the locals.

One of the Korean-speaking Korean guys takes his tray back to the rubber tub they set out for dishes and hocks a loogie into the trash can.

"There's so much to see and only two weeks to see it," she tells me. "Only two weeks to really get to know our roots."

"And soup," he says.

They laugh together like people do on TV. They say nice to meet you and synchronize their watches before going to their respective bathrooms.

A few more spoonfuls of soup and I miss protein powder and boiled eggs.

—

Sheryl doesn't stop crying when I call. Between sobs she asks if I know what time it is.

"I don't," I say.

"It's late," she says, "and only bad news comes this late."

"I'm alive."

She still sobs. I hear Bobby asking, "Is it him? Is that him?" and Sheryl mumbles and then passes the phone and Bobby's voice comes through so far and distant but close like we're talking through the wall between our rooms.

"Bucky, you douche nugget," Bobby says. "We thought they took you to a goo-lag or something."

No goo-lag. I have been here for two weeks and don't write home, don't call, don't do nothing to get back to Sunny Meadow. I've just been here, being here. I don't tell him that, though.

"You got a job at a bar?" Bobby says.

"I had twenty bucks and a toothbrush. What was I supposed to do?"

"No, shithead," he says, "I'm not clowning you. I'm impressed."

Sheryl is still sobbing. She must be drunk. She only sobs long when she's really drunk.

"Aren't you supposed to be in the Army already?" I say.

"Delayed. We need to get some money. Government sent a bill."

"A bill for what?"

"Fifteen hundred dollars for your plane ticket."

"They deport me and we're supposed to pay?"

"Yeah, it's fucked—" he says.

"Will you quit fucking cussing!" I hear Sheryl say, and then the phone passes hands. "Bucky, I'm so glad you're okay, and don't worry about the plane ticket. We'll figure it out. You need to call Dick. He's your lawyer. Call him."

Before we hang up Sheryl says she loves me. I say I love her. Love is not a thing we say, but now it's a thing. Like any of this is normal.

Richard's card is all bent and the corners are fluffy.

# 18

ROSEY GRIER, PART OF THE 1960S L.A. RAMS' "FEARSOME FOURSOME" defensive line, used to knit on airplanes to get over his fear of flying. He wrote a book, *Rosey Grier's Needlepoint for Men*. Coach Shaw used to bring it to practice. He'd bang on the hardcover and say that real defensive players are so ferocious, so ugly, that they can do whatever they want without fear.

Dress in a tutu.

Cry at a Disney movie.

"You know why?" he'd shout, and then bang the book against a guy's helmet, or clap it up against a guy's ear hole if he wasn't paying attention. "Because these are uber-men. They make ferocious men look like children. They know how to break your knees with the shift of their weight. They're tough enough to say they like movies that make them cry. You make fun of a man like that, you will know fear."

At first Rosey doesn't look particularly ferocious with a needle and thread on the cover. But when your eyes rise and see the way that he looks right into the camera, you shudder. Those are some I-eat-running-backs eyes.

There's a woman next to me working on a scarf. I wonder if she can shift her weight and level a man so hard that he cries and hides. There's a grandmother with a back bent like her life has been hauling kegs. She's wiping dust from a fake plant. She scowls like it's a habit.

Haesoo dropped me off, here, at the "dong office," which is like a neighborhood city hall. I can never tell Bobby. He'd ask how long did I have to sit in the dong office or how many dongs I had to look at.

Here they can verify whether I'm a citizen, see what paperwork my bio-father filed about me. Verify if I actually match the info the Americans

THE ALL-AMERICAN    87

put on my *Order for Removal*, because they may have marked me as the wrong person.

"So you're saying I might not even be this guy?" I said.

"Maybe," Richard said on the phone. "But really we just need to establish what paperwork there is on you in Korea."

This is step one in Richard's plan to get me back to America. When I finally got ahold of him, he told me the same plan that had been on the letter: Find out my status, get the paperwork saying I left as a child, and then report back to Richard for step two, more paperwork.

The security guard gives me a number. And I wait until my number gets displayed on the big ticker and I'm sitting in front of this guy with a pencil tie and dark bags under his eyes. He squints. There's a snake plant on one side of his cubicle and a cactus on the other. "Hi," I say, "English?"

The man smiles, chuckles.

"I don't speak Korean," I say, and dig out my *Order for Removal* and put it on his desk. "Can you help me? Does someone speak English?"

The man smiles and waves his hands. "No, no, no, no."

"Phone?" I motion to the phone on the desk. "Can you call someone? English?"

He smiles and waves his hand. "No-no, no-no." He stands and walks to the back room.

The clock says I wait ten minutes. Fifteen.

The leaf-wiping woman gets seen and leaves.

The knitting woman gets seen and leaves.

At twenty minutes, I stand up and scan the counter and the other cubicles. I can't see him anywhere. In the next cubicle is a woman helping an old man who keeps turning his head to hear what she's saying.

"Sorry to interrupt," I say, "but . . ."

She smiles and motions gracefully for me to sit back down. I sit. I wait. I could've knitted a jersey by the time the guy comes back and sits down in front of me. He's smiling and I wonder if he was watching me from the CCTV, hoping that I'd just leave. The phone rings and he picks it up and hands it to me.

"Hello?" I say.

A guy's mousy voice responds, "Hello?"

"Hi," I say, "this is really weird, I know, but I need to find out the status of my citizenship. I've got some paperwork from the U.S. I imagine you need some information about my father and stuff, right?"

"Hello?" mousy voice says.

"Can you hear me?" I say.

"Yes. That man is not my father."

"No, no, I need to find out my citizen status. My biological parents were Korean."

"The man in front of you cannot speak English," he says.

"Yes, I know. Now, can you tell him I'm looking for—"

"I'm sorry. The colleague who handles foreigners is not in today. You must come back tomorrow."

"I'm not a foreigner. Can you help me? You know, translate over the phone?"

"I am very sorry. Have a good day."

The line goes dead and the guy in front of me is waving with both hands and saying, "No, no," with a big smile. He stands, still smiling, and motions me to the door.

"Call him back," I say. I point at the phone.

The man stops smiling, keeps flipping his hands toward the door, motioning me to leave.

"No," I say. I point at the phone. I'm not leaving.

The man picks up my *Order for Removal* and holds it out for me in one hand and motions to the door with the other.

I shake my head, point to the phone. "Call him," I say.

He stops. He straightens up. He sneers and says something I'm sure translates to, *Get the fuck out.*

"No," I say.

He starts shouting and throws my *Order for Removal* right at my face. Like I'm some dog.

Then I'm yelling. I yank the phone out of the wall and fling it past his head. Then the cactus, the snake plant, and a stapler all go past his head and the man is no longer shouting but red and frozen.

It's like watching slow-mo game footage. Like there, projected on the wall, is all the rage breaking against the desk of some dong with a skinny tie. A wave, a surge crashing past the rocks, is heading straight on through to his smiling face to rip him out to sea.

There's commentary on the footage. Hulk has seen faces like this government man's. It's people like him who have sent Hulk here. They smile and say yes or no and maybe they cage Hulk and deport Hulk, and now they pretend they can't help Hulk because he's foreign. Because he's nothing but a stray.

Hulk pushes over the desk and it takes part of the cubical wall where the woman and the old man are. The woman is screaming. The old man is laughing.

"He has known fights," Rosey Grier's voice chimes in like pregame analysis. "But that was many years ago, before football found the way to work out most of his anger on the field. To be ugly. To show his ugliness in places where it doesn't pay to be pretty. This is not the way to salvation. To be fearsome, one must acknowledge fear as a fact like the strength of a cross-stitch. Only then can you obtain true ugliness and true horror-inspiring awe to be part of the Fearsome Foursome!"

I hear Michael Jackson's "Don't Stop 'Til You Get Enough."

This is the moment Coach would press pause and the center of the frame would be snowed and bent. He'd ask, *What do we see? What happened? Why?*

Lights go out. There's no projector. No Michael Jackson. Just some heavy thuds.

Red blooms over everything.

## 19

MY BIO-FATHER HAD A BLACK LEATHER SUITCASE WITH GOLD TUMBLE locks that always popped at 000 000. GI Dan has the same kind, with his name stenciled on the side of it.

# 20

I'M CUFFED TO A LOOP SET IN THE BENCH AND MY FINGERTIPS ARE INKED. My wrist chafes and my jeans stick to my skin and my pockets are empty and my shirt stinks and my head pounds with those needle points under my eyebrows that tell me I had a concussion.

There's a woman dressed in a suit leaning against the wall on the opposite bench. Maybe she's a detective. She just strolled into the hallway, eyeballed me, then posted up against the wall and started smoking a skinny cigarette. Everyone here smokes.

"So tell me," she finally asks, "do you feel better?"

"I feel like shit," I say.

"Yeah," she says, and takes a drag. She looks familiar. But it's hard to tell, since all I see right now is the V her jaw forms under her chin as she blows smoke up at the ceiling. "The guy who beat you up is retiring soon and asked to get out from behind a desk. Bored. He used to smack around demonstrators. In fact, he's out in the break room right now, telling how it all happened. I left after he said he that you tried to roundhouse-kick him."

I rub my head. In America they just would've put me in a hold or tased me. Getting clobbered in the head, I guess, is the Korean way of dealing with problems. What's next? Fingers crushed with pliers? Caning my calves?

The woman looks blankly, or maybe she's looking at the smoke. I know her somehow. If she's looking at me, she's waiting for me to say something. Even if she isn't looking at me she's waiting for me to say something.

"Can I get some aspirin?" I say.

"Nope," she says, and takes a drag.

"You speak good English."

"So do you," she says, and smirks. "But you really don't speak Korean at all."

"How do you know?"

She drops her cigarette into a skinny Coke can on the floor. There's a glint of spittle at the corner of her mouth. "You couldn't read the customs form and couldn't talk to anyone at the office."

She's the woman from the plane. The one who talked about different times and places but wouldn't tell me a goddamn thing about how to get back home. She's taller than I thought, taking up space like she owns it.

She says her name but it's something I can't pronounce, or maybe I just can't hear, because there's this feeling in my body like I'm swinging toward a ravine that dives deep into rock.

I say her name. She sucks air through her teeth.

"Just call me, Janie"—she laughs—"Rocket."

"Janie Rocket," I say.

"See, at least you can say that."

"I just want to go home," I say.

"Start at the beginning," she says. "How does a Korean boy like you end up in a place like this?" She taps her heel against the cinder-block wall.

The off-white walls, like the jail, like steedick, like study hall, tell me I ought to lie. But lie how? How do you lie right when you don't know what is right?

At Communes, I just say I'm *here for my roots*.

Janie watches me as I tell the story about Sheryl and Richard and Graham, how I miss my VHS of *Born to Run*, which all comes out like the last bits of pus from an exploding zit. She lights a cigarette and watches me, then the cigarette, then the ceiling. When I've run out of breath and things to say, she coughs and lights another.

"So," she says, "you haven't talked to your father, no communication or anything all these years?"

"Who are you?" I say.

"I'm Janie and your best chance to get out of here," she says. "So?"

"No. I haven't talked to him since he left."

"You're sure he's here?"

"I hope he's dead," I say, rubbing my head. But it occurs to me that if he's dead, then I never get to find out why he left.

"Are you trying to meet with him?" she says.

"No. I just need to find the paperwork to help me to go back to America."

Janie looks at me a long while. "We are all looking for something, aren't we?"

"Are you a detective?" I say. "Can you get me out of here, get me an ID card?"

"You watch college football?" she asks. "How are my Bruins doing?"

"They're a middle-of-the-road team, with an outside chance to win a bowl game," I say.

She nods. "Can't watch the games from here, I guess I should be glad." She leaves.

I lie back on the bench. Above, light tubes flicker.

Why did I Hulk out?

Targets fight nastier because they're cornered. But I wasn't a target at the dong office. I was getting passed around, ignored. In football, you can't hit players who are defenseless. Or away from the play. What does it matter if he thinks I'm a dog, throws my papers in my face?

Sheryl would be ashamed to see me here. She'd say I was "acting like some thug."

Could end up in a jail worse than steedick.

Janie comes back and uncuffs me. "You might not think you're lucky, but you are. They aren't pressing charges."

"Why?" I say.

"Well, looking at the tapes, it gets fuzzy who provoked whom. Really, the guy shouldn't have thrown the papers at you." She sighs. "Besides, the damages are all covered from your wallet," she says, "not that I could prove that."

"You gave them my wallet?"

"No, they are *returning* your wallet."

"You guys took my money?"

"Beyonghak, you assaulted that man," she says. "Really, the problem here is that you, Beyonghak, need to figure out who you are." She stands me up, and walks me out to the desks in the front.

*Beyonghak*, she said.

*Bee-young-hawk.*

*Beyounghawk.*

My name. She said it correctly. I say it to myself. The sounds are marbles rolling around in my mouth. *Bee-young. Young-hawk.* Bounce the lips and flea-flick the tongue: *Byeong-hawk.*

"Yi Beyonghak," Janie says to the desk man.

That's my name. The man says it slowly to his computer monitor. Starve the *aw*, cut the *all* with a *k. Beyong-hak. Beyong-hak. Beyong-hak.*

I sign some forms. The desk guy grunts and shakes his head. Janie and he say some things, then he just waves us off. Janie says I'm free.

Then I'm out in the parking lot. It's night. Maybe morning. I look out onto the dark streets and there's so few cars, so few people. A few apartments have lights on. All the buildings look so tall and the sky above so cloudy, you feel boxed in.

I missed my shift at Communes. Do I still have a job? My wallet is empty.

"Want a ride?" Janie says.

She's wearing a bomber jacket and a bandanna now.

"Oh, you don't have to do that—I just . . ." I want the ride, but somehow I feel that would make me even more helpless.

Janie walks into the dark beside the police station and a moment later an expensive-looking motorcycle cranks to life. She rolls it into the streetlight. It has a sidecar, old but restored.

"Sure?" Janie says. "Got room."

We weave through the tight alleys and side roads. She doesn't need any directions, not like I could give them. When we stop at the hostel I step out and everything tingles. There are a couple of guys squatting on the curb, smoking and drinking out of a green bottle. Janie kills the engine.

"Beyonghak—"

I slap my leg. The tingling won't go away.

"Yi Beyonghak from Yeosu. U.S. immigration was right, you're Korean. You're in the system. I found your hojeok."

"Yeah, my hojeok," I say. Like I know what a hojeok is.

She takes an envelope out of her jacket. "Family registry. You're on it."

I reach for it. She pulls it back. "Don't screw this up, Beyonghak. Don't fight the wrong people." She hands it to me and I hold the envelope in my hands. It feels hot and steamy in the cold.

"Tomorrow, give this to a taxi driver." She hands me her business card. It's just says *Janie R.* No numbers, no address. On the back is only a little bit of Korean printed and a whole lot written by hand. "That'll get you to a dong office that speaks English."

I want to tear the envelope open but I stop myself. I breathe. "Are my parents alive?"

"It doesn't work like that. When you open it, you'll see. I would offer to help but that's well beyond my duties." She starts the engine. "The registry was filed in Giwon. Way south." Then she waves and rides off down the alley, motor roaring, smoke and exhaust curling in the light.

# 21

FIRST OUT, MY *ORDER FOR REMOVAL.*

Next, just a bunch of printouts tied together with rough string.

No connect-the-dots, links in the chain, lines and branches of names and history drooping from a family tree, it's just a bunch of square boxes. Korean. A few numbers—dates? Bland and boxy and as boring as a history test. Just a printout.

At the bottom there are two boxes of Korean highlighted. I guess one is me.

Someone knocks on the bathroom door. I say, "Busy," but someone jiggles the doorknob.

"It's busy," I holler. This is my only private place, why won't they leave me alone?

But the doorknob keeps rattling and finally the latch gives and a guy stumbles in, reeking of beer and barbecue, and throws up in the sink.

I'm out on the stairs and Haesoo raises her head from the desk.

"Toilet or sink?" she says.

Behind me he chucks again.

"Sink," I say.

She sits up and rubs her eyes, checks her cell phone, and looks at me. "You're sober. You weren't at Communes. When the night shift guy asked me to fill in, I thought something happened."

"I got arrested and released."

She smiles. "Ah, that's cute."

I blush, I think. There's a moan from the bathroom. Somewhere outside the hostel a bottle crashes and guys laugh. She goes to the window and fires some sharp words.

"Assholes," she says. "Some guys in Busan get a few days off and come up here to get wasted and make a mess. They could just stay there and get wasted and make a mess on the beach."

"Busan is south, right?" I say.

There are grumbles outside. "They better not be peeing," she says, then goes back to the window and changes her tone: less threatening and more matter-of-fact. And she stands there with her arms crossed in a motherly way. There's a stool by the computer and I sit and realize I've still got this paper in my hand, my family tree. Answers to questions I didn't even know I had. Not just bio-father or bio-mother, it's pages and pages, everything tied together with string.

I've got roots.

Uncle Rick worked as a gold miner in Alaska, digging in muddy ground with bulldozers and loading the buckets into this giant washing machine with filter carpets that picked out all these little flakes of gold. You don't find nuggets, he said, but flake after flake that you melt together to get rich.

Maybe there's enough flakes of Korean in my head to make some sense of this tree. Maybe my bio-parents taught me how to read but forgot to teach me how to speak. One character looks like a cracked box. Another, an ant by an overturned bucket, or maybe a radial tire. Another looks like a scythe next to a pool stick.

My eyes are jerky-dry and my head hurts when Haesoo snaps her fingers in front of the paper. She's got a mop.

"B&H?" she says. "It's late, you know."

"Yeah."

"I thought only Koreans sleep with their eyes open. You know—pretend to be paying attention in class but sleeping."

"I wasn't sleeping. I don't think."

"You have been looking at that for like thirty minutes. Those drunk guys came and went. You did not even move. That was pro."

"I was just, well, trying to read this." I show her the paper.

"A hojeok. You're looking for your family?" she says.

"Something like that."

"But you can't read," she says.

"I can't read this," I say.

"That can be a problem," she says.

"You can read it," I say, and give her the biggest smile I can.

"You know, I have a problem too." She points up the flight of stairs to the bathroom. The door is open and I can just make out a limp arm holding on to the edge of the toilet bowl.

"Is he dead?" I ask.

"His friends wouldn't clean him up or throw him in his bunk. But you're B&H. You wouldn't have any problems throwing him in his bunk and cleaning up the bathroom, would you?"

"And you'll help me out with the paper?"

"I already helped you with a place to sleep. Since we're friends—"

"You'll help me out with the paper."

She gives me a big smile and tilts her head a bit to the side. She leans forward on the desk and I think she's going to kiss me. "Over there is the bucket," she says, and hands me the mop.

The smell in the bathroom feels like an awl against my temples, even after taking an aspirin. I strip the man to his underwear and carry him into the bunk room. Haesoo tells me his bunk is a top bunk, but I drop the drunk on the floor and give him a pillow. Haesoo tells me to put the clothes in a bucket and I ask why bother and she just shakes her head. "You weren't raised right, were you?" she says, and I just go ahead and do it. I wipe and scrub and cough and clean the bathroom. Flies dive-bomb me and cling to the rubber gloves. I work. Behind the toilet. Under the mirror. From under the little trash can to the doorknob. The guy had thrown up everywhere.

After an hour, I'm done with the bathroom, and I rinse and hang the guy's clothes up on some rusting nails hammered in the grout between the wall tiles. I step out of the bathroom and look down at the lobby. She's asleep at the desk.

I step over the snoring drunk and I climb the ladder to my bunk. Already the sky is turning blue in the window.

If the snoring, passed-out, stripped-to-his-underwear guy on the floor was my bio-father, I'd ask him: *Do I have grandparents? Cousins? Family stories about how somebody ran off with someone else's wife or lost the farm in a card game?* When he finished, I'd tell him every bad thing that happened to me because he left. Then I'd kick him. After that, I don't know. What do you do with family?

## 22

THE ID PLACE LOOKS THE SAME AS THE DONG PLACE BUT I'VE GOT A DIF-
ferent guy with a different skinny tie clicking on the computer. When I ask
if he speaks English he does this sigh and slouch where his shoulders drop
like the folding wings of the *Top Gun* plane. "Yes," he says. Then he looks at
his computer. He clacks the keyboard. I think what he must've been like in
high school. Stuffed in lockers, I'd bet.

"Yes, I said," he says. "What do you need?"

I've got my family tree and place it on the desk between us. He peers
down at it and then up at me. He leans back.

"What do you want?" he says. "I speak English; I do not read minds."

"What is my citizenship?"

"I don't know," he says. "Is that yours?"

"Yes."

"So you're Korean. Congratulations."

"Can you look me up?"

"What do you need? What form exactly do you need?"

"Info on my citizenship."

He leans forward, motions me to lean in too. "You see all these people
waiting? That guy looks like he delivers chicken. That guy looks like he installs
cable internet. To be here, they have to take the day off. Probably without pay.
Now here you are, another gyopo who can't speak, can't tell me what they
need, while all these poor people have to wait. Don't waste time. Care."

"I care," I say.

"Let's try this from the beginning again. What. Do. You. Need?"

*To shove douchebag*
*into a locker.*

*A barrel.*
*A tar pit.*
*To chain him*
*under a shitting horse*
*in a leaky barn.*

I don't hulk out. He's a defenseless player in a game he doesn't even know.

"I need the paperwork regarding my citizenship status," I say. "ID. Birth certificate. I need anything from when I left as a child, because right now I'm trying to go back to my fucking country." I put the *Order for Removal* on the table. "You want one less gyopo here? Help me figure out exactly when I left and if my father is still here."

He looks at the *Order for Removal*, taps his pen against the table like how Uncle Rick used to tap ash into a tray.

"What was your crime?" he asks.

"Tried to stop someone from killing himself. And a bounced check on my immigration paperwork."

Douchebag pencil tie leans back, does this nod thing that means he will say sorry.

Instead, he cracks his hands and thumbs through my family tree. Haesoo read the tree and told me my people are from way down south. Must've had land or something years ago, because the tree goes back. Like five hundred years. The landless don't have registries like that. The yangbans, the old aristocrats, had records that go further back. My family was middle-of-the-road, probably fished, because everyone down there fished.

"What about my mom?" I asked.

"She's there," Haesoo said.

"How did she die?"

"It doesn't say. Usually the hojeok only says who is in the family and who is head of it. A father or son. Birthday. That kind of stuff." She stopped to help the sheepish Busan drunks to check out. Then she took her glasses off her face and looked at me. "How do you not know what happened to your own mother?"

"I lost my family," I said.

Pencil tie types on his computer. He clicks and types and then the printer starts to work. He smiles.

"Happy birthday, Mr. Yi. Today is your birthday."

"The registry says today isn't my birthday."

"They used the lunar calendar on the registry, but today is your birthday on the solar."

"How old am I?"

"You're ninety."

"I'm not ninety."

He sighs. "Nine-*teen*."

This is not supposed to be my birthday. But then again, every few weeks that seems to change. Maybe next time I'll be twenty-one, older than Bobby.

"You should get some mee-ok-gook," he says slowly. "You know, mee-ok-gook? Birthday seaweed soup? Across the street is a place you can get some, then go do your physical next door."

"Physical?"

He pulls one of the papers from the pile on the printer tray. "You have one week to do your physical for military service. Usually men schedule it later, when they know where they're going to college, but you did not complete the paperwork on time."

The printer finishes and he hands me the pile of papers. He fills out a pink slip and paper-clips it to the top of the file and hands it to me.

"Downstairs, get your photo taken and then get your ID. The next paperwork is for a passport. Next, give this paperwork to the Giwon office to get your birth certificate. This last paper is your information to give the physical people. Eat some mee-ok-gook, then do your physical."

"Does this mean I have to go to the military?"

"All Korean men must do military service."

"Even me? I'm going back to the U.S., you know, once this stuff is straightened out."

"All Korean men must do military service." He points at the paperwork. "You are Korean. You are registered. You are notified to do your service. Happy birthday. Do your physical."

He leans to one side and calls out to the crowd something I figure means, *Next*.

"Bucky, I wouldn't worry about that," Richard says on the phone. "We're doing everything we need to do." With an ID, a birth certificate, plus the documents that Richard has, I can go back to the U.S. Back to Tibicut.

I will start wind-sprinting in the morning. I will finish school and walk on to a community college team and get a scholarship, because I'll work harder than anyone, ever. And I'll make out with Chantal, maybe Hot Holly too, maybe even get laid.

Things are looking up. I'm working my way home.

# 23

"GIWON IS HERE." HAESOO POINTS TO A BLANK GREEN SPOT ON THE COM-
puter screen. "Way, way down south."

"How do I get down there?" I say.

"How much money do you have?"

I shrug. I've got a wad of green bills that has been growing in my locker since I started working for Hyunshik. It's mostly green bills, which are like ten thousand won each. Like ten bucks a bill. Maybe I got a couple hundred bucks? Whatever it is ain't much. There might come a time that I have to sleep in the park under a lean-to, spending days plucking and gutting pigeons to roast.

She laughs. "You're really something else. You got sam man won? Thirty?"

I nod.

"I mean you have it, not that you're going to rob someone or something."

"I've got it," I say.

She eyes me for a moment and smiles. "Train," she says. "The cheap train. It'll stop everywhere you don't need to go and it'll take you a day, maybe two, but you'll get there cheap." She laughs again. "Wish I was going with you. Looking for your family sounds like fun."

"I'm not looking for my family," I say.

This is the part when she's supposed to pry. She supposed to ask, *Then what are you looking for?* And I'm supposed to react in a huff and spill my guts.

"Whatever," she says. "If they're anything like my family, you'll be sorry you found them."

Maybe there's a rule not to pry, here in Korea when you speak English.

She blows some purple hair from her face. She's pretty. Even with black-
ening circles under her eyes, she looks happy. Maybe it's not happy, but I
feel happier looking at her. I've never had that feeling before. I look up at
the clock to stop myself from saying something stupid.

"I'll take you there," she says.

"Where?"

"The train station."

—

After stacking three kegs and four boxes, I ask Hyunshik if he has time
to talk. He says bow three times. Okay, I say, and I bow. "Not like that,
dummy," he says. I've got to go to the floor, on the knees, and hip-hinge my
forehead down to the concrete.

"Why?" I say.

"You miss work, asshole."

I do it, three times. Feels a bit like a burpee.

"I got arrested," I say. "Fighting."

Hyunshik nods.

"I need a few days to go south."

"I don't know you. You not employee, understand?" he says. "How
many days?"

—

In the subway, people charge the car doors like popping through the two
hole. My first time on the subway, and Haesoo and I hold on to rings hanging above us, crowded and pressed up together. I think about speeds of
trains and open spaces. I don't want to get a stubby with Haesoo pressed
right up against me like this. At the station, while we waited for the train,
an old blind guy parted the crowd by thwacking legs with his stick. He had
this stereo playing a kind of music I've never heard before, like a whistling
duck with a guitar backup. I kind of liked it. He hit me in the shins as he
passed by. He had this collection box with coins and blue bills taped to the
stereo he carried around his neck. I wonder if he hits everyone who doesn't
give him money.

—

Seoul Station is big. Very clean. I look around, and there's glass and escalators and a long wall of tellers, and more mobs. Flowing toward doors, out of doors, up and down stairs, and all the feet and voices clacking together like rain thumping tin roofs and birds scattering under it. The mob stuffs the air with breath. Haesoo tells me to go up to the teller and to buy a ticket to Giwon.

"What do you mean?" I say.

"You hoboing the trains?" she says.

"Hobo the trains? Where do you learn this stuff?" I say.

She folds her arms. "You have to buy a ticket."

But I don't speak Korean. "But couldn't you," I say, "you know . . ."

"Just go up and tell them where you want to go, and say juseyo."

"Juseyo."

"Please."

"Look, can't you just help me out, I mean—"

That's when she grabs my ear. When I was growing up, Sheryl never grabbed ears. She did smack me a couple of times with a wiper blade for throwing the cats, but she never grabbed my ear. "Go get a ticket," she says. "I'll see you when you get back." She lets go and storms off into the current of black-suited people.

At the ticket windows, the agents shout and the customers shout back. I think of steedick. America. Immigration people in the FOREIGNER line at the airport. How I can't say anything others can understand. I get in line. Plan what I'm going to say.

Anyang haseo, "Hello."

I'm going to Giwon.

Anyang haseo. Giwon, juseyo.

It's my turn. I freeze. Blank. What if the ticket-window woman doesn't understand me? What if all the people behind me laugh and push me out of the way, then take my money and call the police to beat me for fun?

The woman looks up at me from behind the glass and motions me to come. "Giwon, juseyo," I blurt. She looks at the computer and shakes her head. "Giwon?" I say, and she shakes her head and says a bunch of things that I think means, *I see you sweating and looking suspicious, the cops are on their way to tase you.*

She raises a finger. "One," she says in English. "Busan." Then she raises two fingers. "Two, Giwon. Okay?"

Nod, you idiot. Nod.

I nod.

Once I have the tickets in my hand, an old woman elbows me in the ribs and pushes herself to the ticket window. I did it. I got a ticket. Without help. I want to thank Haesoo, maybe take her in my arms like they do in the movies and stick my tongue in her mouth, tell her how I'm the kind of guy who does wind sprints in the morning.

But I don't see her anywhere, just the tide of black hair.

# 24

ALL DAY AND ALL NIGHT I LISTEN TO THE TRAIN'S WHEELS BEATING THE track. It's definitely the slow train. Once the train stops in a tunnel and I think the engine has dropped a rod and we will have to huff it. After half an hour the train starts moving again. I don't talk to anyone and no one talks to each other. I live off the vending machines in between the cars and stare out the window. When the car is empty I do wall sits. I sleep a lot. I dream of hearts beating. When I wake I hear the wheels pounding the gaps between the rails.

—

If I could be honest with myself, I would admit that I can't cope with loneliness. Every moment that this train car stays completely empty except me, without any old guys rattling newspapers, depressed people looking out the window, munching on chips, I think that the world would be no different if I offed myself.

If I'm being honest with myself, I love football because you can't play by yourself and even the assholes on your team are still in some way part of you. Maybe a douchebag—ought to be shoved into a burning car rolling off a cliff's edge—part of you, but still a part.

—

TV OUT THE WINDOW: a game where you create a movie based on what you see out the window. A tweaker carting copper. A deer munching leaves. Some guy burning trash, and an old VW bug for sale. You make up a story about how the tweaker is bringing the VW back to life to assemble with other cars like Transformers to fight the evil deer. You keep telling the story until someone says, "Boring."

I used to play that with Bobby. We learned it from Unc.

There are no tweakers out these windows. Lots of trees on hills. Lots of small, terraced farms growing rice and apples. I've never seen rice grow. Looks like flooded lawns.

—

I think about how my bio-mother might have died. Was she going to the pharmacy to get me something? Was my bio-father with her? How I see her in my mind is this bloody mess melted into the steering wheel and dash, her long black hair carpeting it, a crown of twisted metal studded with sparkling glass.

When I think of my bio-father, I think only of his stupid jacket and his stupid aviator glasses.

—

A train attendant shakes me awake. Busan, she says, with a bunch of other words. Busan is where I transfer. I wander the station looking confused until a nice station worker with a raspy laugh looks at my ticket. Then he calls some people on his walkie-talkie and guides me to the right train. I say thank you and he grunts.

—

I hope Sheryl and Bobby are doing okay.

—

Now we're on the coast, threading through stone passes and pine hills on one side and miles of mudflats on the other. The mud seems to go out forever and it's smooth like pudding skin. Then there are these little stranded islands of rock. Like jagged peanut chunks sticking out of a candy bar. Trees grow on them. Green grows everywhere in this part of Korea, cracking the rocks, clinging to cliffs, carpeting hills.

It's nothing like ashy gray Seoul. Very pretty. A Tibicut.

—

The brakes scream and the train slows and the windows rattle and suddenly from around the hill there's this little town of concrete boxes growing out of the foot of the mountain. The blue roofs sag. It looks poor, like the kind of place you wouldn't admit being from.

The train stops at a lone platform. In small letters on the big station sign I see in English, GIWON.

Down the road dusty men hurry to catch a bus and a group of old women with giant visors weed a garden in an abandoned lot. In the corner of the lot a kitchen sink leans against a stack of tires. A two-stroke pull-along tractor creeps by, hauling a bed of radishes, and all around and down each path are houses with blue tiles and blue tarps in places to keep the rain out.

Maybe one of those doors is my father's door. I try to imagine banging on a door and a startled old man opening it.

*Hi, Dad,* I'd say.

Actually, one of these doors *could* be his.

At the center of town is a tall, official-looking, clean, glass-windowed building with big Korean gold lettering over the front door. The little lettering on the door says CITY HALL.

There's a big policeman guarding the ticket machines. He looks like he knows how to handle himself. He asks people, I guess, what they're doing there and gives them a ticket. When it's my turn I try to smile at him and not look at his billy club.

"Anyang haseo, I don't speak Korean. Does anyone speak English?" I say.

The policeman looks at me. He says something.

I'm sweating. Are we going to rumble? "English?" I say. His hand moves quickly, and before I can run, he gives me a ticket and a smile and motions me to sit. My number is called immediately, and I go to an old guy at the end of the counter who is staring at the clock on the far wall. I hand him the family registry and my crisp new ID.

"Anyang haseo. Do you speak English?"

He looks at me, then the registry, then the ID. He leans back and wipes his mouth and digs out a pack of cigarettes. He lights a cigarette, shakes his head and mutters, and picks up the phone and starts talking. His voice is rough. He gives me the receiver.

"Hi?" a woman says.

"Hello?" I say. "I'm here to get my birth certificate. And an address for my father."

My *father*? That leaps out of me before I can contain it. It's true. I do want to see him. "I got this family registry," I say, "it says the certificate is here. And, well, if you guys got my father's address or something, that would be cool."

"Stop, stop." She takes a deep breath. "Birth certificate and whose address? Can you speak hankook-ah?"

"Birth certificate and my father's address. His name is—well, I don't speak Korean. It's here on the family registry."

The old guy behind the desk is already thumbing through the papers of my family registry.

"I think he lives somewhere near here," I say.

"Why do you need his address?" she asks.

"Because I don't have it."

"What is your name?"

"Yi-Bee-young-hawk," I say. "Beyonghak Yi."

The woman's breath scrapes the phone. "Give the man at the counter your identification and the phone."

The old guy puts out his cigarette and takes the phone. With a deep breath through his teeth, he starts typing on the keyboard. He squints and runs his finger along the monitor. He shakes his head and turns away from me and says something with a level tone into the phone. Then he hands it back to me.

"I'm sorry, he's dead," she says.

"What?"

"Dead. Yi Dong-jun, living at Giwon, missing for sixteen years. Therefore, dead."

I feel a tingling in my arms. I wait for her to say something, but it's silent over the line.

"Where is he?" I say.

"Dead."

"I understand that, but you said missing?"

"Missing too long. Therefore, dead."

"So, where is his body?"

"Dead."

"Does he have a grave or something?"

"We have last address. My colleague will write it down. Very sorry. Please change me to my colleague," she says.

The man gives me a weak smile of sympathy, pats my hand, and says something I take for condolences. He talks to the woman on the phone and hands me a brochure with a little smiling girl hugging a puppy.

Then he digs out his cigarette pack. It's empty. He mutters, crumples it up, and throws it in the trash.

# 25

THE FIRST TIME I SHOT A BIRD, I WAS TEN. WE WERE OUT BACK, BOBBY, me, and the kid who lived down a few trailers who never wore a shirt in summer. I think his name was Daniel but I'm not sure. We all just called him Skin. All of us had already shot guns with Uncle Rick, but Sheryl wouldn't let us have any for ourselves yet. So, after a couple of months digging up stumps for a farmer not far from where we lived, we saved enough money to get a couple of air-pump BB guns.

We shot cans. Then we shot crabapples off trees. Bobby couldn't hit nothing. He'd complain that it was the gun and we'd switch and he'd still miss. Just like when we were out with Uncle Rick shooting real guns, Bobby always pulled the trigger, never squeezed.

One day, after Bobby got angry and stormed off, it was just me and Skin. Skin was a good shot and we started playing horse with targets farther and farther out until it came to a pair of robins picking the ground just at the line where the grass and the woods met.

"Think you can get a robin?" I said.

Skin got on one knee, pumped the BB gun, and aimed. He shot, and the BB dropped in the grass. The birds kept pecking at the ground.

"Too far," he said. "Could do it with my grandpa's .22."

I got on a knee and pumped the gun. I knew Skin was right; it was too far. But I just wanted to prove it could be done. I wanted to be better than Skin. So, instead of aiming, I grabbed a rock and threw it way past the robins into the bushes. They took off and flew toward us and I shot one right in the chest. When you shoot a bird with a BB, it doesn't just drop, it tumbles. We could hear it thump the ground, roll, and beat its wings as it gave off this airy kind of squawk.

I put it out with the butt of the BB gun. And we stood there for a minute, amazed. I wasn't sure if I was supposed to be proud or ashamed.

"Show-off," Skin said. "I never ate robin before."

"Me neither," I said.

But when I brought the robin back, Sheryl wasn't proud of me and told me to deal with the nasty thing outside. I didn't eat it and I threw it in the bushes for the cats. Uncle Rick just shook his head the next time he saw me, and Bobby didn't talk to me for a couple of days because he knew he couldn't hit a robin in the air.

I felt no pride and no shame. It just happened. Later, when assholes started shooting up schools, people kept talking about how the killers loved killing animals and playing *Doom*. I didn't know anything about playing *Doom*, but I liked hunting and shooting with Uncle Rick. I wondered if there was something wrong with me, something cold.

Now I'm in a taxi, and in the same way I wasn't sure how to feel about that robin, I'm not sure what I'm supposed to feel about my father. A little voice tells me to go back to the train, I've already got my birth certificate, what I came for, why go looking for ghosts?

The undercarriage scrapes the change in the road, the line between the paved town and the dirt countryside. We pass some farmland that's covered in rows and rows of black vinyl and clear greenhouses, little naked ground, lots of plastic.

We stop at the foot of a hill not far from town. A dirt path winds into the thick of the woods. The driver points up the path. I pay him and the taxi leaves, kicking up dust.

The path up is rutty and overgrown. Patches of sun break through the canopy. Looking into the brush, you can still see where someone hacked the forest back to make way for a truck. A few birds I don't recognize caw above. The woods are quieter here. As if everything wild just ran.

At the top of the hill, just past a couple of persimmon trees and a pile of hubcaps, is a clearing and the teeth of ruined walls: a collapsed house. Through the doorway there's rubble of blue roof tiles. The window frames are rotted and plaster flakes fill the gaps in the grass. Everything sun-baked. Nothing intact.

A breeze whistles through the house. Out past a rusted car, behind a pair of rusting refrigerators and a pile of rust-spotted tin cans and broken glass, are cages. Many, many cages. I step on a plastic bowl and nearly trip on a spike in the ground. This I've seen before. I know rust-flaking metal and weeds and broken things that used to be special and new and pricey. Just like I know somewhere nearby, maybe in the woods, or in a run-down barn, there's a pile of pallets with stakes and links to build a wall around a pit of dirt that smells of piss and blood and sweat.

So, my bio-father liked dog fights.

Win any money?

Lose so much you had to ditch me?

I kick a half-buried plastic jug. I'm not mad, but somehow, as if some-one is watching me, I act this way to play along. It is an old feeling. Deep. It sticks down your throat and under your chest and vacuums everything you've got.

Where is he? Where's his grave? All I find is rust and trash between the stalks of grass. I try to imagine a man living here. It doesn't feel right, like one of those abandoned chicken shacks that traps a bunch of water in its foundation, so far out in the woods you just can't figure out why anyone would bother to put something up.

I think of the robin again. How the cats fought that night in the bushes and how a couple of strays never returned.

"They run off. That's what strays do," Sheryl used to say, looking out the window above the sink, smoking a Mustang Cool. "They don't want noth-ing to do with anything but for a meal. When they find it somewhere else, they go. They just go."

I go back down the path, not bothering to look back or into the brush or up into the trees, because there's nothing to learn that I don't already know. Bio-Father is dead and gone.

It's a long walk back to town. And after the plastic-covered farmland, the houses with bad tile roofs and cracked walls and empty lots with little gardens and empty lots with kids kicking around soccer balls screaming with the goals and dancing like touchdown dances and the houses crum-bled and gutted for their wire and pipes and anything still good and usable and after the corner where you see the only nice new thing in the town, the city hall and a gas station across from it with a convenience store, and you notice that instead of Pennzoil T-shirts, these people got different kind of freebie shirts. A man squatting by his tractor, smoking, has a Buffalo Bills shirt. It reads SUPER BOWL CHAMPIONS.

The Bills never won a Super Bowl. It's a fake.

Giwon is broke and sad and tired, and the people say whatever it is in Korean that means, *Oh well.* If I had grown up here I would be just as broke, trying to get out. Maybe playing soccer. I bet every kid in Giwon has an escape plan. Would my metrics be right for soccer?

Tibicut is way over there and Giwon is here, but it feels like you could go over the hill and be right on top of Lion Mountain and see Sunny Meadow in the crack of its ass.

# 26

## CHANTAL'S LETTER #2

Bucky,

I saw Bobby when he came to clean out your locker. You're lucky. Going to Korea? That's so ballsy! I heard that you got thrown in jail or something, but that didn't sound like you.

You're going to go and find out about who you really are, what we really are. I don't know if I'm brave enough to go to Korea after graduation like I planned to. My parents tell me to wait until after college, but then I'll be getting a job and just doing the whole life thing. Who just does it, like you're doing?

If a meathead like you can do it, then I can too. You inspired me to just do it.

I'll see you there.

No, don't go thinking that I like you. I don't.

You better learn how to say your name, learn some Korean. Quit being such a dumb meathead.

Chantal

# 27

BACK ON THE TRAIN, I READ CHANTAL'S LETTER, AND THAT'S WHAT I get? I'm not sure what I was supposed to get, but if you write to a dude getting deported, shouldn't he at least get a nudie or something? What did Bobby tell Chantal? How did he already know that I was going to Korea? Did he tell her I was coming over here for a vacation?

Didn't the dealership thing make the news?

Would she really come here?

---

"You're like a dog that meows," a man's voice says. "You're not one of them. Never will be."

It's in Korean but I'm thinking it in English.

"You listening? Or did you bash your head too many times against all those dumb white monkeys?"

I sit up in the dark. The only lights on are the ones lining the walkway. People snore. The people behind me are sleeping with their mouths hung open.

"We were writing poetry when they were still flinging shit at each other in the trees. They've only been bathing regularly for a hundred years."

Across the aisle there is a man with his head swung back and pointed right up at the ceiling, face covered by a baseball cap. His skin looks ashy even in the orange streetlights that we pass that make it through the blind on the window. "You can do great things there, if you just stop meowing," he says into his cap.

He's in these white robes like what kung-fu guys wear.

"I'll just go to sleep if you're not going to say anything," he says, in

Korean, but, somehow, I know. Just like I know that voice, but I don't know where from.

"Who are you?" I say.

"Who are you?" he says.

"Not funny."

"I got lots of names."

"Are you my bio-father? You a ghost?"

"Quit meowing, or I'll run for it."

"I'm not meowing."

"You aren't listening either. There's something you've got to know or else you'll never get home."

"What do I need to know?"

"Tell me you'll listen."

"Okay."

"Tell me, or I'll go back to sleep and we'll never ever talk again."

"Okay, I'll listen."

"Are you listening?"

"I said I would, asshat."

The guy starts snoring that fake snore you do in class when class really sucks.

"Sorry," I say. "What do I need to know?"

"Meow, meow, meow; meow, meow; meow-meow, me-ow. Meow. Meow."

"Okay, I'm like doubly, totally fucking sorry, man. Good enough?"

"Listen carefully."

The brakes squeal. The wheels beat. The train car groans as we take a bend. I say nothing. Under the cap I imagine the man's face, and all I can think of is Mr. Kim, the North Korean who's always eyeing me at the bar.

"Good," he says, "listen. I used to take clothes up from Busan, this cheap Chinese stuff, fresh off a ship, and get these reject labels shipped from a cousin working in a Japanese factory. I'd take it all up to Seoul, take the tags off the shirts, put the Japanese labels on the Chinese shirts, and sell them as Japanese-made, mid-quality shirts at the market. Would make a killing. But the thing is, those labels, I have no idea where *they* really came from. Columbia? Thailand? Mexico? Now, the thing you need to know is—"

Lights come on and my eyes open. Across the aisle isn't Mr. Kim, but a businessman in a suit without a baseball cap, on the phone, with one hand cupped over it and his mouth. People are groaning awake. I raise the blind, and it's still dark.

I can't hear anything the man says into the phone.

# 28

EVEN AFTER GETTING BACK TO SEOUL STATION, TAKING THE SUBWAY back to the hostel and walking through the doors and into the bunk room and locking up my backpack, even after showering and dressing in clean clothes and saying hi to Haesoo and she coming up and hugging me, and letting go and me telling her that everything was great and I'll tell her more at the bar later, after moving kegs, moving mops, sweeping stairs, dusting bottles, and a long night of stuffing drunks in taxis and breathing cigarette smoke and drinks and me telling Simon and Mark about going south, after closing the doors and going back to the hostel and climbing up the ladder to my bunk and closing my itchy eyes and trying to go to sleep and even after I figure out what time I need to call Richard the lawyer to figure out what's next, I smell stingy-sweat, everywhere.

It takes forever for Richard to get on the phone. Takes a few more moments before he remembers who I am. Like my situation is nothing, easy. "Great," he says. "We'll have you on a plane in a jiffy."

After we hang up, I feel mad. Then not. If he's not worried, if this is nothing, then that must mean I'm heading home. It's just a formality. Like putting in the benchwarmers for the fourth quarter because you're up by thirty-five and you know you won't lose.

I can smell the trees already.

—

It takes twenty minutes of waiting in line before I can get to the window of the U.S. Embassy, where a Korean woman asks me why I'm here.

"I'm here to go back to America," I say.

"Are you a citizen?"

"Sort of."

"Yes or no."

"Yes."

"Where's your passport?"

"That's the problem, I'll need a new one."

It goes like that for a while until she finally points to another line that doubles back on itself by a pair of porta-potties. They look like the ones in steedick. In fact, these are the first porta-potties I've seen since steedick.

—

I hand my documents over. I tell the guy behind the bulletproof glass what happened and that there is probably something from my *lawyer*—I say that loud and slow like how people here speak Korean louder and slower at me thinking that is how to make me understand it—in their email saying that they ought to get me out of Korea. Get me back to America. Get me back in time to figure out how to walk on for a community college team.

The guy looks at the screen. Asks a guy named Bill to come and look at something on the screen.

Bill comes and leans over the guy's shoulder like the words he's reading don't make sense, like it's a bomb threat or news that the Cleveland Browns won the Super Bowl.

Bill looks at me. Picks up my documents, flips through the pages, and squints like suddenly things are going to change.

"Bring him out back," Bill says.

*Out back* sounds bad.

Bill goes to a Marine in fatigues who's sitting off to the side of a desk. He looks over at me and stands up. Maybe to tase me. Or to pistol-whip me and then kick the shit out of me *out back*.

"Hey?" the guy behind the glass is saying. "Hey, go over to the door at the end of the hall, past the bathrooms. Bill is going to take care of your case now."

"Am I in trouble?" I say.

The guy looks blank, tired, fed up. "Just go to the door at the end of the hall, past the bathrooms. Bill is going to handle your case."

Do I run? Do I try for the bomb doors? There are all these cameras and Marines in fatigues with nine-millimeter Glocks in Velcro holsters, but do I run?

No. My legs just pull me along, obedient to the English spoken to me. Everything is tunneled to the door at the end of the hall that opens, and the Marine from out back stands holding it open.

"I'm going to walk you out back," he says. "Protocol."

"Okay," I say.

"You lift?"

"Like dead lifts?" I hate it as soon as I say *dead*. "Yeah."

"Cool. You're bigger than any Rock Marine I've seen."

*Out back* turns out to be a windowless office with Bill sitting at a computer monitor and clacking on his keyboard. He's got a hula girl on a spring on his desk. I've only seen those in reruns of *Hawaii Five-O*.

"So, Beyonghak, you're a long way from home," Bill says, pushing up his glasses higher on his nose like old people always do. When the printer starts he looks over at me. "I want to apologize to you."

Here it comes. Marine is going to pistol-whip me.

"I don't know how it happened, or why, but you shouldn't have been sent out here. Your lawyer did a good job of proving your name isn't the one on the deportation order and that the bounced check wasn't necessarily . . . Are you okay?"

I am not okay. My eyes are washy and I'm biting my lip hard enough so that I don't break down.

"Yeah," I say. "I'm okay. I thought you all were going to pistol-whip me."

"Why?" Bill says with all the gasp of movie-speak.

"You guys aren't going to tase me, right?"

The Marine behind me clears his throat. "No tasers here."

"Why would we tase you?" Bill says. "What did you do?"

"Nothing."

"Do you know of a threat?" the Marine says. "Is there a reason why we should subdue you?"

"No, I just, don't know. Bad things keep happening."

"Kid," Bill says, "we're sending you back to America."

"You sure?"

"Well, yeah. It'll take us a few days, but I think so." The printer stops and he puts the stack of papers in the desk space in front of me. "I've never repatriated one of you before. I don't know anyone who has. In fact, I'm not really sure what forms to fill out, but I figure we start with these and go from there."

"There are more like me?"

"I can't really go into that."

"Like how many?"

He flips through my docs and puts them off to the side. "You're not going to need any of that anymore. You'll get a nice blue temporary passport, don't you worry."

"How can there be more people like me?"

"Listen, you're going back. Be happy."

There's tension in his voice, a warning. *Don't pry. Don't question. Just be happy. Breathe. Don't worry. Be happy.*

I nod.

And we get to work signing forms. Then I'm back out on the street with a paper that says *Temporary Documents of Immigration.* Easy as that.

Everything made up because of some black ink on paper.

—

Seoul is getting colder. Out the bunk window, people's breath smolders out through their scarves. People are always on the street here. Even when I toss dudes into cabs at four in the morning there are people walking, no, hurrying. They hurry with these stares three yards ahead of them and only slow down when they stare down at their phones. Sometimes I imagine that there are these invisible strings that connect phones, like lures to some far-off poles, and that people staring down at their phones are being reeled in.

I get to go back to America. I can breathe again, even if it's the breath you can see in the morning. I'm wind-sprinting, again. Getting ready to really train. Bill at the embassy has been talking with Richard the lawyer. They think I'll be on a plane in a few days. I haven't told anyone at the bar. But Haesoo says I look relieved. Just breathing, I say. Which is true. Holding breath is one of those things that the body can do without realizing it. Even while breathing those whimsy shallow breaths. In between plays, you got to exhale all and inhale all so that you get that oxygen back down in your legs.

When I blow my nose, the snot in the toilet paper—what Koreans use for tissues—is gray or black. Not sure if it's the air or the smoke from the bar.

—

Others? Like me?

—

Haesoo must run stairs. Her butt has got this perky ledge and when she drops off a barstool and adjusts her jeans, all I can do is watch it. She catches me with my mop in my hand staring at her instead of the spilled bottle of Hite in the corner. She says to me, "B&H, don't you dare."

Sorry. That's what I'm supposed to say, and make my eyes mark out the territory of the spill, the shards of glass. Instead I go up to her. "You know, I think you're pretty. I like you."

Brave. This wave of courage is coming up to me because now I get to go home. I don't have to stay here forever, don't have to stare down at stains.

She squints at me, checks her phone, then walks out the saloon doors.

Two different Marks at the bar laugh at me. Winning throws a crumpled receipt. Simon comes out the bathroom and is relayed my lame pickup attempt. They all agree that it was a "schoolboy error."

"Treat them mean, keep them keen," Hyunshik tells me before handing me another bucket. "Someone puked in alley, on door. Clean up."

By the time I finish cleaning the street pizza that hit the door, Haesoo is back at the bar with another woman, and there's a ring of guys around them.

"There he is," Simon says.

They all look back at me with a bucket in one hand and a plastic-bristled broom in the other. Scottish Mark moves out of the way.

It's Chantal.

# 29

CHANTAL IS AT THE BAR WITH HAESOO, BOTH GRINNING LIKE THEY'RE sharing secrets, while the rest of the guys circle like flies because here was a new girl, young and pretty and Korean but speaking English like a native. I feel a tight rope of fear yank me out of there. All I can say to Chantal is, "Hi." Flat.

Her smile relaxes and she's realizing something. "Hi?" she says at the same time Haesoo bursts out laughing as one of the Marks whispers something in her ear and GI Dan shouts for "shots" from Hyunshik.

I bolt to the kitchen and behind the kegs to put the bucket and the broom in the corner. Each time I lean the broom up against the wall and turn my back, it scrapes the wall and crashes to the floor. After the third time, I leave it.

This is my miserable fucking adventure. Why is she here? She's got good grades. Her parents have a boat and she'll go to some good college to be a lawyer or something. No one would deport her.

Tipping over a three-high stack of kegs would make a great big bang. I want to do it so bad. Bang! It would feel great, but then everyone would look at me and ask what the hell is my problem. What could I say? *Piss off, Chantal? This is my miserable bar?*

What really bothers me is that seeing her here bothers me. I get to go home. What do I care that Chantal is here to ruin everything? She'll be here a week and will be saying *piss off* and *anyang* in no time. She's already friends with Haesoo—how soon before she tells her everything I've ever said? Everything I ever did? About how I'm from Sunny Meadow and I'm poor and nothing but a running back?

There's something dropping in my stomach like a kettlebell dipping a trampoline, dropping right down the center through my ass and legs and through the cracked tile floor, burying itself so deep that would take a backhoe to claw it out.

I should go out there. Find out why she's here, how she found me. I should want to laugh with her, touch her, hug her, shuttle her out into the alley and make out, feel the whip of her hair against my arms, like how it could've been, all these things to see if she's real, if any of this has been real. Do people miss me? Did you miss me and regret not getting with me?

I want her gone, but I don't want her to leave.

I just want her alone, me and her, not all these people around us.

I go out behind the bar and she and Haesoo are dancing by the chess-board with a pair of Marks. No, that's not dancing.

Haesoo might be dancing, swinging her arms and listing side to side like it's cool. Chantal is bumping up against English Mark. They're grinding. We haven't seen each other in like two months and I step in the back for a moment to drop off a shitty bucket and broom and she's out here grinding?

Simon leans in and braces himself against the edge of the bar. "She's from America," he says, stabbing the ice in his glass with a straw. "You Americans always seem so easy."

The rest of the night I clean corners and carry drunks. I watch her get smashed and dance and not look at me, like I'm nothing, until she's puking into a trash can in the women's bathroom. I'm cutting lemons behind the bar. Haesoo asks me to carry Chantal back to the hostel. Chantal's staying in the Penthouse. I try not to care. I take a shot of whiskey when Hyunshik isn't looking. "Kiss me," I say to Haesoo. "Or at least let me take you out for a kimbap sometime."

Haesoo leans in over the bar. Booze flames off her breath. Here it comes. Here it comes. I have to lean down because she's short. Here it comes.

Oh no, she's going for the ear. Maybe she'll tell me to take her some-where more private.

"Quit hitting on me. Every time you do, I think we won't be friends. You and I, only friends. Keep liking me and you're going to be miserable."

She hops off the barstool and starts dancing with GI Dan and English Mark. Simon salutes me with his drink.

I go up the stairs, and Chantal is sitting on the floor and leaning up against the stall door. Her hair looks wind-whipped. She rolls her head to one side and looks up at me.

"I'm so drunk," she says.

"Let's go. I'm taking you to the hostel," I say.

"I fucking hate you."

I try to grab her arm.

"Don't touch me," she says.

"Haesoo said—"

"You stupid, secretive, meathead fucking, stupid-stupid shithead! We don't know each other! You antisocial, meathead, dipstick shit-nugget, head."

I try to grab her arm again. She slaps my thigh. Then she tries to hammer her fist into my crotch but she just hits the other thigh.

"You're the moronest friend ever," she says. "*Hi?* Fly all the way here, and *hi?*"

"Let's get you to the hostel."

"Fuck your hostel!"

Hyunshik and Haesoo round the corner. Hyunshik says some Korean to Haesoo and then leaves. Chantal's chin is on her chest. Her neck will hurt in the morning. I'm ready to leave her, empty some ashtrays. But Haesoo squats down. "Chantal," she says, "wake up. This is B&H. He's a really good guy. Very strong. We call him Hulk. He's going to give you a piggyback ride to the hostel, okay?"

Chantal rolls her head up and looks at her, then at me. "A really good guy?" she says.

"Yeah," Haesoo says.

Chantal gives this big dumb drunk smile, then says, "I'm Chantal. From Tibicut. You know Tibicut? No one knows Tibicut."

"C'mon, let's get you going," Haesoo says.

She nods. And we get her on my back. Then I carry her out of the bar and out onto the street. Her body is hot and heavy, like a Molotov ready to burst into flame. We're past the bus stop when her drool seeps through my shirt to my shoulder.

"I didn't come because of you," she says.

"Yeah, you did," I say.

"Put me down."

I stop. She's wobbly on her feet and she leans against a wall leading to an alley. She dry-heaves. Says fuck. Says, "I think I'm dying." Then she leans back against the wall. "It's like a merry-go-round." She takes a few big breaths. "Spin, spin, spin." She smiles at me, then starts tipping.

I climb three flights to get her to her room. She's up in the penthouse. Up here is nice. There are no bunks, no farting dudes, but instead there are windows with views of hills and big skyscrapers. I put her on the nice futon rolled out on the floor. Her hair brushes my neck and there we are on the floor, so close we can look at each other's pores. Her eyes are open and still.

"You fucker," she says, like I'm not there, like the words are all marbles. "Kiss me," she says.

Her hair is everywhere, like I'm looking down at her in water. Then we're kissing, and it tastes of Long Islands and vomit and it's wet.

Next thing I know, all I feel is her breathing and all the tension goes out of her mouth. She snorts. She's asleep.

Suddenly I feel like a thief in the room. I got to get out. There's an energy drink, a Pocari Sweat, on the nice table. I put that next to her, along with the nice trash can, then I'm out, closing the door behind me.

# 30

THEN I'M BACK AT COMMUNES. I'M ANGRY, STEWING, AND CONFUSED. Chantal comes here, grinds English Mark, tells me I'm shit, then after I carry her all the way up the stairs we kiss. Then she sleeps and snores? That's it? I'm angry and horny and having to breathe at the top of the stairs and tell myself none of this matters. I'm getting to go home. It doesn't matter why Chantal is here.

It's late and the bar is nearly empty. Winning, the chess player, and Simon are talking to Hyunshik at the bar. Haesoo is playing pool with GI Dan and a beautiful fresh-off-the-plane British girl with long red hair down to her butt. There's another white American girl who works at a kiddie English academy and is cute but only comes out when she's so hammered she only slurs and rests her head on her forearm on the bar or a table.

What makes white girls beautiful in Korea is being thin, Simon tells me.

"Hulk," Winning says to me, "remember one thing: Only refugees come teaching in Korea. Economic refugees. Social refugees and the others."

"What do you mean by *others*?" I say.

"People who have to hide." He nods toward the beautiful British girl. She takes her time bent over the pool table racking the pool balls.

"Don't stare," he says.

I see her do a little dance with the pool triangle, like it's framing her face. She takes a shot and licks the rim of her shot glass at Haesoo and GI Dan. "That one," Winning says, "is too pretty to be here unless there's something seriously wrong."

"I wouldn't mind some wrong," Simon says.

Do I count as an other?

Hyunshik tells me I'm done for the night and hands me a wad of cash and asks me if I'd like a drink. Just then the British girl bumps into me. She's googly-eyed. She's drunk. "You play pool?"

She's got low-cut jeans and a low-cut long tee and I have to try really hard not to stare. "Not really," I say.

"He does," Simon says.

"A real hustler," Winning says.

"I need a partner," she says.

Over by the table GI Dan and Haesoo say, "We need a fourth." The American girl is still resting her head on the chessboard table.

So I play. I've never played pool before. The British girl and I hammer the balls hard enough to pop off the table. We lose. Haesoo giggles and GI Dan says things in her ear making me think of hitting him until he buys us shots of whiskey. The British girl drinks and bumps me with her butt and bends over the table to line up the shots. She closes one eye as if she's working out all the geometry, tongue slightly out the corner of her mouth like she's tasting the curls of smoke from the ashtray. We all take a shot each time we do sink a ball. By the time we're finished, my cheeks are burning and GI Dan and Haesoo are talking in the corner, when the British girl asks me if I feel like dancing. I'm afraid to say yes and to say no. But I don't decide, she grabs my hand and we're up and out the stairs and she's holding her American friend's hand too, who shot up awake like the nap made her sober. They're skipping.

"Monkey time!" the American girl is screaming down the street, while groups of Korean girls and guys look over at us. "Ain't this something?" British girl says. "It's so bright! So many lights! It's like we're in a video game!"

We end up at Club Monkey. They stamp our hands with glow-in-the-dark ink. Inside is packed and cigarette smoke hazes everything. We pass lockers. We shuffle through trash on the floor, then we're in this large room with giant projectors showing some old Korean film, and lasers beam through the smoke. Light the only thing you can look at in the hot mass of people, pushing and pulsing with the downbeats. I'm grinding with the British girl, her friend lost to the mass, and then we're making out and she's kneading my butt, my arms, like I'm dough. I'm drunk. She puts my hand on her butt and she's licking my ear and grabbing my junk.

No girl has ever grabbed my junk.

She says in my ear, "I like you," then she bites, and it hurts but she's rubbing me through my jeans and I'm scared I'm going to burst my pants and then she leans back and smiles at me and says, "Tell me you like me."

"Hell, yeah!" I say.

Then she seems to remember something. Her hand is gone from my crotch. "Where's Becca?"

She looks around. She's looking for her friend and I'm thinking, Oh no, oh no.

"Pick me up," she says.

"What?"

"Lift me up," she commands.

I lift her up, her chest right in my face, and I can feel her squealing even though I can't hear her through the bump of bass. She puts her hand on top of my head like it's a fence post and pulls my ear to turn her. Then she pats my head telling me she wants down.

"I think I see her." Then she leads me through the crowd. We find Rebecca by the bar, surrounded by three hip-hop Korean dudes trying to impress her with their dance moves. "Wait here," British girl says, and cuts through the guys and leans over to talk to Rebecca.

I feel dizzy. I'm going to have sex. This is how it happens. She's going to lead me somewhere and it's going to be excellent. But, somehow, it doesn't feel so excellent. Something's off. Something tingles on the back of my neck. Maybe everyone can see how stoked I am and that I'm scared.

Below a bank of laser lights cutting smoke at the bar, I see the defector North Korean Mr. Kim in his black tracksuit. He's watching me. Really watching, not that kind that someone looks at you until you catch them: he stares through the body. I'm looking his way and he's looking at me and neither of us breaks the gaze. I go to him.

"Hulk," he says.

I shout over the music, "Why are you eyeballing me?" I'm surprised with how up front I am. It must be the drinks.

He drags on his cigarette. He blinks, naturally, and keeps looking at me like I'm nothing.

"Cigarette?" He pushes over his pack of Seven Stars.

"Smoking is disgusting," I say.

He nods to the British girl and Rebecca, who both have cigarettes now and are laughing loud enough for me to hear them. The three guys are having a full-blown dance battle in a space that has opened in front of the girls.

"Would you just stop eyeballing me?" I say to Mr. Kim.

"I see you. So, I look," he says in this way, dripping with a Korean accent sharp as a whistle. But his voice carries through the thumps of the music. He's thin, but carries himself like a cocky free safety who always gets running starts to dust off runners. He's wearing a silly black tracksuit.

"Stop looking at me, okay?" I shout.

"No," he says.

"No?" I can feel myself getting angry. I've got five inches and at least forty pounds on this guy. Does he know five-finger death grips or something? But I've got only a little bit more time before I'm home. Why get in trouble before I'm out? Maybe I'm being an asshat and don't even know it.

"Maybe we got off on the wrong foot. I'm Hulk." I hold out my big weight-lifting mitts, ready to wrench his tiny hands. But he just looks at me. It cuts.

"Bow," he says. "I'm elder."

"I'm not Korean," I say keeping my hand out.

He puts out his cigarette in the ashtray. He smiles. He shakes my hand. His grip is sturdy, callused, like a man who's swung sledgehammers.

Then I feel British girl behind me, her hands grasping around my waist. She bites my ear and pinches my stomach like a bee sting and says, "Let's get out of here." I look back into her green eyes and they melt any anger I had. She takes my hand, starts pulling me back through the crowd, and I look back and Mr. Kim isn't looking my way, just lighting another cigarette, holding out his lighter and watching it longer than someone ought to, until British girl pulls me far enough through the crowd that I can't see him anymore.

Right in front of the club British girl fires her tongue down my throat so far I think she's trying to lick the hot ball of nerves by my tonsils. She does it again waiting for the cab. In the taxi, she hands the driver a paper, hops on my lap, and says, "It's afternoon in Brighton, you know? Greenwich mean time. Wild? We're so far ahead, it's the future! A neon electro-future so completely different, don't you think? And so dangerous! Just think, a few miles away there's all these North Koreans with ancient, hidden cannons pointed right at us!" She makes pistol hands in the air and starts chuckling. "Boom-boom-boom!"

The driver is grinning in the rearview mirror. Instead of thinking about what's the best way to unhook a bra when we get to her place, I start thinking about Mr. Kim. He's North Korean—maybe a spy. Funny thing is that if he didn't have the tracksuit, he'd look like every other middle-age guy here. Thin, stoic, then quick to laugh when drunk and cheeks beet-red.

Bras have three to five hooks, at least that was what Bobby used to tell me.

Long ago, when Chantal and I talked normally to each other, when everyone said we needed to be together and she and the cheerleaders sat with me at the lunch table, I used to get nervous like this. Now she's back. Probably puking in a trash can. We kissed. She came looking for me—or for her roots and soup.

When we get to the alley, British girl bolts out of the car and shakes her shoulders, sways and staggers her hips right out front of the taxi's headlights. The driver looks back at me, still grinning, and says something fatherly and reassuring to me after I hand him his cash. I can only nod.

We go into the alley. A tall building from the next block lights the way with neon signs. I ask her name. She sloppy-kisses me and gnaws my lower lip. She says, "No names," between her teeth.

At the door to her building she tells me, "No peeking," while trying to read another paper in her hand. She presses the code and the door whooshes open. Then we're up two flights of stairs and through her door and the lights are out except for a little dome night-light overhead that flickers and ticks like a stopwatch banging away hard enough to break glass.

She bites my neck. I kiss her ear. I am in a girl's room, a studio apartment, in the dark, making out with a hottie, hotter than Hot Holly, my nose deep into her long red hair smelling of cheap shampoo and cigarettes. We're pressed up against the wall and she's undoing my belt. My hands feel the back of her bra. There's no hook. She rips my belt out and I hear the buckle rattle on the floor and she's back biting my lips when she pushes off me. "Wait!" she says.

"What?" I say, scared that this is all about to go wrong. She's changed her mind. She's got a boyfriend coming through. She's got three days to live and I've been infected with Ebola.

She shuffles across the room, kicking papers and stuff on the floor between the furniture looming from the faint light through the window—a bunk bed, a desk, chairs, and a table with a radio. The room is small. She goes to the table, turns on Christmas lights tacked to the wall, and starts Oasis's "Champagne Supernova" on the CD player. Then she sits in a chair and crosses her legs. She's got my belt in her hand.

"Strip for me," she says, "like a show."

I take off my shirt.

"Not like that," she says. "Mysteriously, sexily. You know, dance for me."

I don't know how to dance. But I know how to bounce my pecs. I smile at her.

She whips the ground with my belt. "Close your eyes. Dance."

I sway my hips and my pants drop and I'm in my briefs. I've lost muscle mass. Don't blow this. She's not judging your size.

"No," she says, and whips the floor again. "Dance for me."

There's only one dance I know, it's a Deion Sanders touchdown dance. Galloping like a cowboy. But slower, trying to match the song. It's already starting over with waves crashing. It's on repeat.

I hear her giggling, but not mocking, I don't think. "Yes, come closer," she says. And I go closer, thrusting my hips and my tented underwear. My breath is hot and my sweat smells of alcohol. She stands up. Her finger traces my neck down to my crotch. She kisses me, then steps back.

"Take your cock out."

I reach down.

"Don't stop dancing."

I'm swaying, and I take it out and I'm dancing with my cock out and all I feel is air.

"Stroke yourself."

I'm worried my hands are too big and it'll make me look small. But I can't say that.

She whips the floor again. "Be free. Stroke. Like I'm not here."

I stroke, slowly, and dance, doing what I can to make myself bigger than I really am.

"Let me help you," she says, and I feel her hand around my cock. "Don't even have to go looking for it." She holds it tighter than I ever would. Then she pushes me onto the bunk bed and I feel her tongue and teeth around me and oh my god it's happening! Her hands are clawing my ribs and then I'm scared that I'm going to blow, that I'm not going to do this right. But I put my head back on the field of play, grinding out those yards, breathing for patience and coolness so I don't go too quickly and miss my touchdown. She stops. My eyes open. She's on top of me, naked. Her white skin reflects green, red, and blue from the lights. Her pink nipples are wide like sand dollars. Her hair drops down and I can't see her face.

"Your knob's clean, right?" she says.

"I'm a virgin," I say too quickly.

I hear her laugh, then she leans back and there it is. I'm in her! She's warm! The sheets are smooth as mud and the bed creaks like sticks. What if she isn't clean? But she's moving and I'm there looking up at her neck and her hair swaying with her breasts and the ribs of the bunk above her. Then she puts my hand up to her throat and she tightens it like she wants me to choke her.

"Tighter, you fucking Muppet!" she screams. And I do as I'm told. Our naked bodies clap together. She slaps my calf so hard it sings. Slap! This time it cuts my shin and rattles like a buckle.

It is a buckle.

I let go of her throat.

"What are you doing?" I yell.

She slaps me and leans forward and smothers me with her breasts. She whips me and tells me to *shut up and earn it, virgin.*

I buck, but she's got her heels under my thighs and isn't letting go.

She presses her nails into my scalp and my cheeks. This is a game, I tell myself. This is cool. I'm getting laid. She leans back and my hands go for her throat, when she knocks away my hand and pushes off me and rolls over onto her back. "Lick my neck, virgin," she tells me.

"Bounce your pecs, virgin," she says.

"Suck my thumb, virgin," she says.

I do what she says. I do what she says when I'm in her and not. She chokes me and whips me and we do this in the bed and on the floor and long enough for a neighbor to bang on the wall for us to shut up. When it's over, when she asks me if I died, my head is throbbing and there's blood spotting the sheets. The belt buckle cut me. There are welts on my skin and the sickness of our sweat and our stink and alcohol seeps from our breaths and the sky through the window is turning from battered blue to bleeding red, and that's when she runs her nails over the sleekness of my abs, licks a cut on my leg, and smiles. "You're all better now, virgin. Time to go home. Can you put the sheets in the washer? Rebecca ought to be back any minute."

Trash flickers like flags stuck in the crags of light poles. I limp. It's Sunday. Pigeons coo. Buses pull away as I get to the big road and are trailing diesel exhaust. The breeze bites. Far off, the sun is up behind clouds and tall buildings. There are scabs on my arms and on my legs rubbing against my pants. Maybe I'm bleeding. I laugh. I'm no virgin. But there's another thing. Its pitch is sharp and throbbing with beats of blood in my temples. It pops into my head and down my throat until I'm gagging and chucking guts into a trash can. And suddenly I get scared. Some random hottie just whipped me, bled me. Did I even like it?

I don't even know her name. That kind of thing can't happen back home. There are no randos. Chantal wouldn't have whipped me. I always thought that I'd sleep with her, like some preordained thing. Like water is wet. But instead I wade through aches to the subway station. Billboards show Kim Tae-hee, smiling with a sweating bottle of soju. She was supposed to be Sheryl's friend who would help me. Sweat drips off my head, reeking of something stronger than alcohol.

# 31

I'M THROUGH THE DOOR BEFORE ROOTS AND SOUP AND GO STRAIGHT
for the shower. I'm peppered with scabs. I scrub around them, trying to get
the smell off my skin, out of my hair, trying to disinfect, to get clean. There's
a scar in the webbing between my thumb and my index finger. It's from the
stream when my harness broke. It's lighter than the rest, like a gap in sun-
tan. On the bunk, sipping water doesn't stop the thumping in my head, the
stinging in my body. I listen to guys roll out of bed and grunt and fart and
go to breakfast and back. I can't sleep. I get in my sweats and I'm about to
head out for a run when Chantal comes down the stairs. "We need to talk,"
she says, then stops. "Did you get in a fight?"

"You're welcome," I say, and walk out the door.

She follows me. "Hey, we need to talk."

I start jogging. She starts jogging. It all hurts so bad I think I'm going to
throw up. When we get down to the stream I start running. She's still tail-
ing me. Cramps start. But I sprint hard, really hard, until I pass the pull-up
bars and a pair of strolling policemen and go into a public bathroom that's
cold and has got flies buzzing and those toilet bowls in the floor. I go into a
stall, try to catch my breath.

She comes in right after me, into the men's room, and starts banging on
the door.

I don't want to talk. I want to go back to America.

"I feel like shit and you make me run," she says.

"Go away."

"Asshole, we need to talk."

"Go away."

"I'm not here for you. I thought if you could go to Korea, why couldn't
I? Everything got weird after you left. Like somehow I should be gone too.

Did you get my letter? I talked to Bobby about getting the letter to you and to tell you that I was coming to Korea to study. He gave me the hostel's address, your address. There's a language school nearby, for people like us, Bucky. And, I just needed to get out. I wanted to be near someone I knew here, who gets it."

"Gets what?" I say. "I got deported. I work at a bar. What's there to get?"

"Asian temptress bullshit. Guys wanting me to say, *Love you, sucky-sucky long time.*"

"You're smart," I say. "Why not go to college away from me?"

She bangs on the door. The latch rattles and pounds my headache.

"I got off the plane," she says, "and no one looked at me. I got to the hostel and had lunch with Haesoo, it was so comfortable. She taught me how to say my name correctly. Like breathing for the first time. I had kimchi and it was good. I didn't tell her I knew you."

"Go away."

She bumps the door with her body this time. All the stall walls shudder.

"What is your problem?" she says. "You're the one that kissed me."

I open the door. She's all flushed, her hair falling out of her hair band. She's eyeballing me hard.

"What?" she says. "You thought I wouldn't remember, *Hulk*?"

"You wanted me to," I say.

"And you didn't?"

"I don't know."

"Why are you making this so hard? Did you get my letters? Don't you get that I'm the one that knows, like really knows, you?"

"What do you know? Go away." I slam the door and latch it.

There are other voices coming in from the track. Men's voices. They're getting louder.

"You stupid meathead! Open this door and say sorry! Open this door and talk to me!"

She's banging on the door, hard. The stall feels smaller, like it's collapsing in on itself.

"Fuck off!" I say.

"I will knock down this fucking door!"

And she does. She shoulders the door, the latch pops, the door smacks the wall, and the wall cracks off its braces. The wall collapses into the next stall.

Chantal has got saucers for eyes.

A couple of dudes are shouting from the doorway. Chantal turns and screams at them, then at me, then she does this scream-sob thing before she starts smacking me with both her hands, and the next thing I know, a pair of cops are pulling us apart.

—

My first thought is that British girl reported me and the cops finding me with Chantal in the men's room makes me look like a real bad character. But the way the cops lead us by the arm, not with cuffs, tells me that this is only about Chantal wrecking the bathroom.

Only one of the cops speaks any sort of English. It's hesitant, like stuttering. But his tone sounds flat and serious, like cops everywhere, it seems.

—

While we wait at the station, it occurs to me that the thing about Chantal that bothers me so much is how she wants to be here. As if someone who waves pom-poms belongs somewhere other than Tibicut.

She thinks Koreans want her here.

They don't want her here. Deep down, she doesn't want to be here either. There is a reason people immigrate to America. It's not because it's a vacation. It's because it is so bad back home. In America they can be free. People come to Korea for a visit, like a state park. No one wants to live in a state park. No one wants to eat kimchi every day. Look at stupid paperwork like the stuff they shoved in front of us on clipboards with Korean and tiny little English under it in parentheses. Who wants to live in a place where the only green fields you see are rice paddies, baseball diamonds, and soccer fields? No football. No bio-father. No gravestone.

Chantal's leaning the back of her head against the wall. That's the way people sit in the dark. Alone. She flew here, knowing only one asshole, and he's still an asshole when he sees her, and they kiss and everything gets weirder. I want to hold her now, say sorry, and let her cry into my shoulder.

"My name is Beyonghak," I say. "Bee-young-hawk. Beyonghak."
She looks at me.

"That's how to say my name. I'm not sure about yours. My bio-father is dead. I'm not sad about it. I just want to go back, play football. Some community college ought to let me do that. In Tibicut, people know me, know what a running back is."

"Bucky," she says. "I'm so sorry about your dad."

"Fuck him," I say.

She's looking at me in that way only people worth a damn can. Dead center. It melts me something wicked and I have to looked down at my clipboard and all the stupid little boxes on the paperwork because I think I'm going to say something really stupid and scary.

"Did you find any other family?"

"No."

"You've been here weeks, right?"

"About six weeks."

"Did you look?"

"Not really."

"And you've been just hanging out in that bar?"

"Did you come here for me?" I say.

"No," she says. "I came for me, to learn Korean, figure out some stuff before college. Like how to say my name."

"Korea isn't gonna hide that townie stank."

"I bet you haven't been anywhere outside that bar the whole time you've been here."

"Whatever."

She scoffs.

"I so have," I say. "I went to the countryside. Looks like shit country, like everywhere. Found out Bio-Father is dead. I got—" I almost say that I got laid, but suddenly figure that's not a good idea. "Got a job. I've seen enough of Korea."

She doesn't say anything. I look over to her. Her eyes are still dead center on me.

"It sucks your father is gone and that you feel like you shouldn't give a shit," she says. "It sucks that you got here the way you did, but come on.

Really, six weeks? You're here and you have such a chance to learn what you are, speak the language of our people, you know. Figure out who you really are. You act like some meathead, but you write haikus. You read that stupid football stuff while everyone else is screwing around in the lunchroom. You are not like them.

"When you left," she says, taking a long deep breath, "when you got removed, I had this moment at practice. I looked around and I'm like, I don't want to be with these bitches. I don't want to be some fetish for those assholes asking me if they could get some Chinese. And that college interview made me feel so rotten, like I was dirt, some dumb fraud, so ignorant about everything I am."

She talks too much. I don't want to listen.

"Be-young-hawk?" she says. "You really think that's the way to say your name? Can you say hello? Can you say, *Hello, my name is Bee-young hawk?* I bet you can't."

"That's great, *Chantal*. You just go and learn Korean and be Korean and whatever else you want."

She stares. What I'm supposed to do is hold steady, but instead I look around, think maybe I can go to another room or something. Maybe I ought to throw the water cooler at a cop and get jailed.

"You're a shit friend," she says.

"We're not friends."

"Trust me, I'm the closest thing to a friend you've ever had. The football team is a bunch of losers trying so hard to be *manly* for each other that they're afraid their own shadows are gay. Did any of those losers write you? I bet not. Because they don't get it. I do."

"I'm going back, like, really soon," I say. "The embassy is giving me a passport and everything."

"You don't think about who you are? Who we are? You think you can run away and be one of them?" She's leaning forward now. "You think you're *Bucky*?"

"Whatever." I lean my head back against the wall. There's another welt or scratch or something on the top of my head.

"Listen to me," she says. "Are you listening?"

The welt has got to be the size of an Oreo.

"Come with me to the language school," she says. "That's what you really want, deep down, isn't it? To get what it means to be us, to know what we really are? I can get your tuition paid. My parents would pay. They heard what happened to you."

She wants me to be her little study buddy? She comes all the way here, wants to be boyfriend and girlfriend or something, then tells me that what I really want to do is to go to school, here, to learn Korean?

"Tomorrow we'll go to the school together, okay? You'll meet everyone, then get started."

Why does everyone get to tell me what to do?

"You kiss me," I say, "and you're telling me that you're here to learn Korean?"

"I was drunk, and you kissed me," she says.

Just like how British girl told me what to do, just like how Haesoo tells me what to do, just like how cops and the teachers and the lawyers and the guards and Hyunshik, how everyone gets to tell me what I want and what I want to do because they are better than me, now Chantal is going to pay, no, her *parents* are going to pay for what everyone tells me that I really want to do: be Korean. I never wanted that.

"Working at that bar isn't you," she says, "and football isn't either, because you know there's no NFL for you. But you are Korean, *Beyonghak.*"

Chantal, pretty bowie knife Chantal, thinks I'm cute but too dumb to even know what I want. That I'm too dumb to realize all this shit was actually good for me because what I want doesn't match what everyone else thinks.

Now I'm mad. I know the moment of a punt return, when you cross a line, and almost all the blockers are behind you and you see a path to the end zone. The football gods have blessed you.

"Is Jimmy Pope a loser?" I say.

"What?" she says.

"All football players are just meathead losers, right? Jimmy gets to go to school and ball. I bet you fucked Jimmy Pope. I bet you fucked him long time."

Chantal sideswipes my head with the clipboard so fast it cuts me, and even she's shocked, holding up the clipboard like it is about to jump out and swipe someone else's head.

A policewoman comes shouting and points at me and down at my paperwork. I feel the cut bead with blood. Then she tells Chantal, "Come."

Chantal gets up. "You're worse than them," she seethes at me. She's got tears in her eyes. "You're just a fucking rotten banana. Go back, townie trash. Go back." The policewoman takes her around the corner and I wait a long time for Chantal's hand to appear and flip me the middle finger. Her hand never comes.

—

They make me pay a hundred thousand won, like a hundred bucks. I'm pretty sure they let Chantal out first, I don't see her on my way out of the station. I decide to finish my workout along the stream. By the time I get back, Haesoo is at the front desk of the hostel and asks me if something happened.

"I fell," I say.

"No," she tells me. "Chantal checked out."

## 32

I MOVE KEGS, SWAB FLOORS, AND SCRUB DISHES. HYUNSHIK DOESN'T even give so much as a glance when he sees the scratches on my face. Sunday is slow and I try my best to stay in the back. Chantal's name is Bora, like some island out in the Caribbean? Is it pronounced *Bo-la* like Ebola?

—

Simon and Winning show up. They play chess. When they see me, they chuckle.

"Schoolboy error, mate," Simon says.

—

At the embassy, Bill gives me a lot of forms. After I sign them all, Bill says, "You're flying tomorrow." He hands me a blue passport. They spelled my name right. It's only good for one month.

"After a month what happens?" I ask.

"I guess," he says, "you go to a hearing? There they reverse the decision and we give you a permanent one? I've never done this before. Ask your lawyer."

—

On the phone, Sheryl again says she loves me. Bobby is gone to the Army and Unc is at Cedar Creek Penitentiary. Sheryl will be moving in with Graham soon and I just picture being in the living room all alone with a bunch of fucking cats.

I can't get Richard on the phone.

—

People pack into the bar so tight I forget that I'm leaving. Haesoo is playing pool again with GI Dan. I'm wiping tables thinking about telling her that I'm leaving for good, but she's smiling and laughing at stupid things GI Dan says. That's when British girl comes up behind me, grabs my belt, and whispers, "You're helping me with some homework tonight."

She's got a long tee on again and her hair up and she's already swaying through people to the pool table. It's dark, but I can't believe there's not a mark on her neck. Like nothing happened. Like I'm the only one who bled.

I go back and wipe the bar. She's playing a game of Cutthroat with Haesoo and GI Dan at the pool table.

"You working?" Hyunshik says. "Cut lemons and work. Stop staring to customers."

—

I get through the night, wiping tables, sweeping glass. During a lull, I go out to the alley to empty the trash and get some air. At the end of one side of the alley, two figures cut shadows out of the streetlight. A man and a woman, forehead to forehead, almost leaning into each other like two sides of a skewed archway, the man's side hunched to meet the uplifting woman. Their voices are murmurs and calm and happy and their hands rest on each other's hips. The vision of it stops me. I don't know why. Then I realize who it is: Haesoo and GI Dan. But their hands aren't tracing each other's lines, their teeth aren't biting each other. Something serious has been said, and suddenly I hear a sob from Dan, his shoulders shake, but they don't move or break. The sob echoes. It comes at me, by the dumpster, holding a trash bag of lemon rinds and cigarette ash. It comes like some three-hundred-pound lineman and knocks me back at the point where ribs meet breastbone and hurts something wicked and I drop the trash and I turn right out the other way to the main drag with neon signs and the drunk crowds of the night.

*Neon signs buzz and rattle*
*like an old chain saw idling*

*tired and toothless*
*after its last deep cut*
*before being tossed to the trash heap*

I find a place to breathe by the taxi stand, on a bench behind a noodle stall. Pop my knuckles and breathe in through the nose and out through the mouth to oxygenate my blood and calm me down. I need to do this because everything is boiling in me now. Haesoo loves GI Dan. Chantal hates me. British girl scares me.

In and out, breathe.

My fingers start to tingle from how hard I'm popping my fingers and holding them down.

Tomorrow, I get to go home, where football fields wait for me to try out and make a team and achieve dreams. I'll forget all of this, whimpering on some bench behind a noodle stall. I got to finish my shitty shift at my shitty job and collect my cash and go. Hulk up. Help Hyunshik close, say my goodbyes, and tell everyone I'm fine and that I won't be back and have got places to go where I'll know how hot it'll be in the afternoon by the smell of the morning fog. Thanks for all the beer.

I'm back in the bar five minutes, sweeping up glass, when British girl grabs my ass and whispers in my ear, "You're taking too long, and the natives are restless. Next time?"

She winks, then hurries up the stairs, hand in hand with an Asian U.S. Army guy with a barbed-wire tattoo around his neck.

# 33

BOBBY USED TO ASK, *WHAT'S FLYING LIKE? WAS IT LIKE GOING OVER A HILL too fast on a four-wheeler? Was it like falling?* For a while, he wanted to be a pilot. I wanted to be a garbageman. This was before football. Garbagemen got to work late at night and there would be all this cool stuff you could salvage. I didn't remember flying.

Sometimes we would be out in the yard or by one of the ponds that had little moss islands, and we would look up at the jet trails cutting the sky.

"Think it's hard to fly a plane?" he asked. "I'll fly a plane."

In dreams I'm never on a plane. Just bobbing in the ocean, in the dark, after a crash, holding on to a rough cushion. Penalty flags of fire flicker on the waves. Sometimes shark fins sweep around the fire. No people. Just me and sharks and fire floating in the dark.

I dream more in Korea than I did my whole life in Tibicut.

When Bill shook my hand at the ticket counter, he said the airline had upgraded me to business. The counter ladies asked if that was okay. I said sure, thinking that they would put me back by the bathrooms where people shout on the phones attached to the backs of headrests and farts leak out of the bathroom.

Instead, I'm in a big seat that is almost as comfortable as the Lay-Z-Boy that Bobby and I nabbed from off the side of the road. TV in the headrest ahead of me. There's a guy who looks like a Korean Mr. Belvedere with a bottle of wine and a towel over his arm, and a lady who just came by with a basket of steaming towels. I'm not sure what the steaming towels are for. Wiping the crust out of my eyes and ears?

That's what brought me back to the dream: steaming towels.

Out the window, way below us on the pavement, is a guy with giant glow sticks hanging out. If community college fails, I can do that. After we land I could ask the airport people if they're looking for anybody, just in case. The airport is near Tacoma. That's where Sheryl and Graham will be. Unc is way out in the Cedar Creek Pen, and Bobby is gone, and Chantal is here and gone, and I'm wondering what exactly did everybody in Tibicut hear about me?

How would I even get a ride up to a community college? Where am I going to stay? What is it, any of it, going to be like after we land?

A guy bumps my arm with his briefcase, black with gold tumble locks. A gray Members Only jacket. From behind I think I see the gold rims of aviator glasses.

I swear it's my bio-father.

"Hey, Dong-jun? DJ?"

I stand, and the other passengers seated in business class turn their heads from their books and newspapers and wine and look back. He doesn't.

"Hey, DJ? Bio-Father?" I say.

Everyone, even Mr. Belvedere, is looking back at me.

The man turns too. It's not my bio-father. Just another middle-age dude wearing clothes a generation out of style.

Someone taps my shoulder. A very pretty flight attendant, with a sing-song voice, asks me a question in Korean.

"Sorry," I say. I'm always saying sorry. "I thought he was someone else." Everyone is watching us. "Sorry, everyone," I say, and sit back down.

"Oh, um, you sit in this seat, correct?" she says.

"Sorry, I thought he was someone else, that's all."

She looks up at the seat number and back down at me.

This seat is too comfortable. I knew it. Caused a little scene, and now everyone knows that I don't belong in the nice chair but in the back by the bathroom. "You guys put me here."

"Oh, I'm very sorry. Come with me, please." She smiles before I can get angry.

Just beyond the bridge from the plane to the building are two soldiers. Maybe SWAT. They're in all black, bulletproof vests, and have MP5s slung over their shoulders. The soldiers are big too, bigger than me. Lots of vanity curls. Lots of steroids. They have sunglass and smug smiles until they really see me—probably the only other guy in the terminal that can squat 350—and then they pose a little taller.

An older policeman-looking guy with a liver belly is talking to the ladies at the desk by the gate. He looks back at me. He barks some Korean and takes a few steps toward me.

"They put me in that seat," I say, "and I thought that guy looked familiar. A mistake. That's it."

He clears his throat. Grins. Barks some more. He's pissed—not the boiling-over kind, but the kind of an assistant coach trying to impress something on you. I look over to the desk ladies, hoping for help. They moved me to business, not me.

"Ask them," I say, pointing to the desk. "Just ask them." But the officer goes silent like he's going to stare me down. The women at the desk all look away, like they're ashamed, like this is a shakedown.

My first thought is that somebody spotted me as a good target. But a shakedown for what? I've got a couple hundred bucks and a temporary passport saying I'm American. I have rights, again. I don't need to listen to or take this shit from anybody. I've got a lawyer.

The policeman hollers.

"It's just a goddamn seat!" I shout, and suddenly he grabs for my arms and I swat him away. The guys with the MP5s are pointing their short barrels at me. Standard on a MP5 is a moon-curl thirty-round clip that empties in less than a count to three. I put my hands up, speak calmly.

"Hey," I say to the women at the desk, who are still looking away like this isn't happening. "I really need some help here." The women don't move, don't even look my way. The policeman forces me down on my knees, hands behind my head, and cuffs me.

"I know you all can speak English," I holler. "Can you at least tell the police that I'll move seats?"

The women don't bother looking back, but there is one mousy voice that says, "You're in trouble."

"For what?" I call out. "For what?"

No one responds. The soldiers give each other a little smirk. They lead me through a crowd of people watching, whispering, and taking photos with their cameras.

—

In the past three months, I've been arrested three times. Ha! I'm a criminal.

—

The police office is in the basement. It's small, got a few moldy-looking cubicles. Liver belly's got a photo of two chubby children with fat folds around their wrists eating ice cream. My metal chair is missing a foot and keeps teetering. The officer keeps his eyes on me, occasionally shaking his head. The beefy guys with guns are breathing loud behind me. Roid wheeze. We wait.

Finally, an office worker—another douchey pencil-tied guy—drops off a yellow folder. Liver belly opens it and there's copies of my Korean documents, just like the ones I left at the U.S. Embassy, and a copy of what looks like a print of my family registry. The officer thumbs through my passport and then the other printouts. Then he speaks, in Korean, calmly.

"I don't speak Korean." I look back at the beef brothers. "Do either of you tools speak English?"

The officer taps his fingers. He stands up. Everything is quiet. So quiet. Having people yell at me, I can handle. But quiet is something else. I strain to hear people outside the glass doors but I don't hear anyone. I don't hear planes taking off or flying by.

How deep do you have to be to not hear planes at an airport?

The phone rings and liver belly picks it up. He hands me the receiver.

"Do you speak Korean?" says a man with a slow thick voice. He sounds pleasant.

"Um, no," I say.

"My colleague thinks you are lying," he says.

"Look, the flight attendants changed my seat. I didn't do nothing. Just going home. And that guy I stopped on the plane, I thought I knew him. But I don't. I have nothing to do with him."

"Hmm. You speak Korean, yes?"

"I don't speak Korean. I really don't speak Korean," I say.

"Hmm. Okay," he says.

"Okay," I say, and there's silence on the line. "Can I go now?"

"You in trouble. Big trouble," he says.

"Okay?" I say.

"One moment, please." I can hear him flipping pages in a book.

"Like I said," I say, "the airline moved me. The U.S. Embassy is sending me home. That's it."

"Fugitive!" the man says, triumphant.

"What?"

"Fugitive. *F-u-g-i-t-i-v-e.* You know?"

"Yeah, but—"

"You run away from military service."

"I'm just going home."

"You are Yi Beyonghak, yes?"

"Yeah."

"Your father is Yi Dong-jun?"

I have to think. "Yeah, but—"

"You do not register for military service. You flying to USA. No return flight. You are fu-gi-tive. Fugitive! Like movie, but guilty."

"I'm an American."

"You are Korean."

I'm bobbing in the dark. "This is a mistake. I mean, come on, I'm American. Just let me go, please."

"You are Korean citizen."

"But I got papers. Papers. Call the embassy!"

"America do not matter. You are born in Korea. You are Korean, did not surrender citizenship before ninety, and told to register. Now you run. Fugitive."

I feel like I'm sinking. "What's going to happen?"

The man sighs. "You go to military or jail for many years. Then military service."

"I don't speak Korean, didn't grow up Korean; I just want to play football. Let me go back home to America."

"You really don't speak Korean?"

"No."

He coughs, then says, "Let me talk to my colleague."

They argue. Liver belly raises his voice, presses the phone so hard against his head that his ear goes red. Through the phone, I can hear the other man raising his voice. A calm loud voice. All the Korean washes around me like a TV left on in a room to remind you that you're not alone when you really are. Then someone says something that can't be taken back and the shouting stops. Liver belly looks past me to the men in black. I look back at them but I can't read anything from their dumb faces. The calm guy must've won. He is on my side. They're going to let me go.

Liver belly sucks air through his teeth and offers me the phone.

"You only have one choice," the calm voice on the phone says, "you go to jail or Army."

Ha! I say. Ha! HA!

"What's so funny?" he says.

I can't stop laughing.

"You're laughing at the Army?"

I keep laughing because I know that Richard can't do nothing even if he answered the phone. I laugh because there are no choices. What I want doesn't matter because I was there on the plane, so close to home, hours from home with its rocky beaches and moss-swamped lawns, from play actions and bootlegs, from some future that now can't be.

I keep laughing as the beef brothers lead me down hallways and out to a parking lot and as they shove me onto a bus with some other guys who all look up at me, then away. That makes me laugh harder. I laugh because everything is a big dead-arm bruise that hurts but makes you laugh instead of cry. They cuff me to the bus seat and say the thing that I'm sure means they think I'm fucked in the head, and I laugh and laugh and laugh.

# PART THREE

## BE ALL YOU CAN BE

# 34

A DUDE IN FATIGUES IS BEHIND THE CAGE DOOR UP AT THE FRONT OF the bus. Has got a shotgun, a Remington Model 870. Combat shotgun. Old school. He can clear this bus out with those eight shells in thirty seconds.

Ha! That's a funny thought. Get killed on a bus in Korea from a shotgun with MADE IN THE USA stamped on the side.

The squatting sun rakes the mudflats.

Forever ago, in the weight room, Coach Shaw framed a big cartoon of a frog with its two hands reaching out from a pelican's bill and wringing the pelican's neck with, *Never give up said the frog to the pelican,* written under it in Sharpie.

Never give up? Why would he say that to the pelican? I never thought of that before.

I feel nothing except itching under my scabs.

"My reason for retirement is simple," Barry Sanders said in his prime. "I am more keen to leave the game than I want to stay there."

When you have no feeling, what is left to play for?

The bus pulls off the road and into an old beat-up gas station and rest stop. Mr. Shotgun shouts some stuff and everyone else stands up. I guess I'm the only one cuffed on this bus. He opens the cage door and they all file out, along with the bus driver. Mr. Shotgun waits for all of them to leave before he walks up the aisle to me.

"Need to piss?" he says.

"Sure," I say. East out the window are hills and woods. West of us is the ocean. If I run, I ought to run east and die among trees.

Outside, the other guys form a line to the bathroom, while I stand by the bus with Mr. Shotgun. They only glance, don't have the conviction to stare. I'm the bad character.

If I run for the hills, Mr. Shotgun could blast me. Running for it would be enough reason for him to shoot, I figure. If he's good with his pattern, it would pepper my spine, get into my lungs, and I'd be dead and gone in no time.

This useless blank thing I feel is actually hot and heavy like rocks from dying fire. It is knowing that I'm dying.

Maybe I ought to run west instead. If Mr. Shotgun is bad with his pattern and I still got enough in my legs, I'll run for the ocean. Dive in. Catch the riptide and churn and tumble in the dark until I'm drowned.

Die alone. That's what Uncle Rick got wrong. He did it within sight of others. There are just some things you ought to know about yourself.

"Mr. Shotgun," I say.

"Shut it," he says.

"Do you really speak English?" I say.

He's behind me. "No, I don't." He bumps me in the ribs with the shotgun stock. "So, shut up and wait your turn to piss."

"You sound British."

He bumps me again. Harder. Treat them mean, keep them keen.

"Listen," I say, "I'm going to run for the ocean. I'm going to kill myself. What are you going to do about it?"

I hear what to my ears sounds like the clicking of the safety. "You're going to the Army. It's not a death sentence. Quit moaning."

"I'm not moaning; I'm suicidal."

"You're not suicidal."

If people hear that you're suicidal they're supposed to listen to you, give you their full attention, let you know that your suffering really matters. "You don't know that."

"You're just," Mr. Shotgun says, "another wanker dealing with a world full of bullocks."

One of the guys coming out of the bathroom looks toward the hills. Mr. Shotgun shouts at him and the guy looks down at his feet and starts back for the bus. Mr. Shotgun nudges me and the next thing I know I'm in the bathroom, struggling because of the cuffs to get my thumb and pinkie to work in just the right way to unzip my fly.

I should be running for the ocean, feeling the burn of shot in my back while lukewarm life seeps out of my useless unwanted body. But instead I'm trying to get my dick out and this all seems ridiculously hard when it shouldn't be. How will I get it back in my pants if I'm struggling to get it out? Can't die with my dick out.

On the windowsill above the urinals there's a half-white, half-tan cat watching me.

It would be funny, walk out of here with my dick flopping around. "Hey, Mr. Shotgun, can you put my penis back in my pants?"

Maybe they would kick me out of the Army before I even start for being gay! Maybe I can write them a haiku about my penis flopping around! Because I'm gay! Send my gay ass back to America!

What would I do in America?

Nothing. Because I'm dead.

"Who says you're dead?" a familiar voice says, in Korean, but somehow I understand.

I look down.

Penis doesn't say anything. Just keeps peeing.

"Will you look at me when I talk to you? Meow?"

I look up at the windowsill. The cat's looking at me.

"Why do you want to be dead?" the cat meows in something like Korean that somehow I can understand. It sounds like Mr. Kim.

"Meow," the cat says. "This is the greatest opportunity you've ever had. When I was selling clothes, price was dictated on perception, not quality. However, you couldn't call rags fancy and get away with it for too long."

"I'll run into the sea," I say. Or die with my back shotgun-made into hamburger meat. "I don't give a fuck."

"Perception is key. Meow?" the cat says, and jumps down onto the urinal next to me and then on the floor. It sits.

"What you need," the cat says, "is to do what you are told. Be told what to want, what to do, to be, to find. This will lead you to opportunity: Be completely you in the present. Change those tags. Buy cheap from China and sell high with tags saying they're made in Japan. Iron on a fancy slogan. That's how you win the shell game. Believe that they're one hundred percent cotton and they will be. That's the way to profit."

Yes. This is what I want: To be told what I want. What to do. What to be. From cats. From people. From countries.

"Come on!" Mr. Shotgun yells, sending the cat leaping onto a urinal and out the window.

Back on the bus my head goes empty. The sun goes down and no one speaks. The windows rattle. The mudflats stretch. The engine struggles against the grades of the hills.

Everything gets really simple: There is no football. No over there. No nothing. There is only the present. Outside is dark. Stars glimmer, shine, and twinkle like light off pom-poms.

Now things feel good. Everything before is gone. Everything ahead is gone.

These roads have no streetlights. Only the headlights pointing forward mark out the lines for the next curve in the road and the trees you would crash into if you took your own path.

# 35

THE SUN'S NOT EVEN RISEN WHEN WE PULL UP TO A WHITE ARCH IN spotlights with a bunch of Korean, and then NOONSAN ARMY BASE in English. The letters have black moss stains dripping down.

*Arches frown.*
*Letters cry black streaks.*
*Be all you can be.*

They take us off the bus. One soldier—an officer?—walks down the line with a clipboard, stops in front of each of us, and asks a question in Korean. *What's your name?*

Yes. That's what it has got to be.

*Eedum?* he asks. That's, "Name?"

He kicks my shin. He barks in Korean and squares up on me like skinny guys always do, like how drill sergeants always do in the movies.

"My name is," I say, and point at myself, "Beyonghak Yi."

It's quiet again.

All eyes locked on me.

I feel proud. He asked me a question and I had an answer, in Korean. Language has got to be like learning sideline signals for plays. I'm not just a body. I am a body that can be asked its name in another language and respond. A body with a name.

The man looks up from his clipboard. He smiles. Then he says something soft and sincere. Then he raises his hand toward me, almost like he is going to tap me on the head and say, *Good boy.* Instead, there's a loud *thwack* that I hear before I feel.

He flicked his middle finger against my forehead. It stings and I take a step back. Soldiers laugh at me and the officer calmly marks something on his clipboard and moves on. Before I can even think, another soldier is yelling and pushing us toward a table where they box clothes, wallets, watches, everything we brought with us. I smell smoke. Things are burning.

—

They buzz my head too close. They give paper tests I can't take because it's all in Korean except for math, which I hate because I suck at it. Whenever math teachers handed back grades to me, they'd stink-eye me like I was kidding.

Sheryl said I needed to get good grades in math. "Math is money, Bucky. It's the language spoken around the world. If aliens come, we'll be talking to them with math." Sheryl used to sit down and try to help me with my math homework. She was good at it. I guess that's why she didn't mind being a cashier at the 24–7.

—

After the tests and medical exams, they line us up in four rows and five lines on a wet field and Mr. Shotgun appears out of nowhere and pulls me aside.

"You are Ee sodae," Mr. Shotgun says.

"What did you call me?" I say.

"Listen, you stupid twit, this trolly isn't slowing down for some wanker who can't speak Korean. You're in Ee sodae. That means second platoon. This row is your platoon. Your number is Twenty-Two. Ee-Ship-Ee. Understood?"

We do jumping jacks. We run. The last line of the day leads to one of a group of Twinkie-shaped buildings, where they divide us into squads—I guess—and walk us into these small rooms with knee-high-lifted floors on both sides of a concrete path leading to the outer door. They sit us at the edge of the lifted floors. The soldier who has been yelling at us is there talking to us softly. He shows us footlockers that are against the walls, each of which has our bedding to lay out on the raised floor. This is where we'll sleep. No beds. Just linoleum and concrete and this thick, beat-up blanket. No one speaks when we pull out the bedding, arrange the sheets. Then we put it all back again and repeat. They have us practice this for an hour before we finally get to lie down. Silence. The steel rafters above looks like the ribs of a whale.

Lights out.

Someone sniffles in the dark. No one says a word. The silence is so perfect we can hear tiny whistles of breeze filling the gaps that should've been caulked and plugged.

## 36

I DON'T REALLY SLEEP BUT THERE'S THIS MOMENT WHEN I CLOSE MY eyes and there are cats in the living room of the trailer. They meow.

—

Hana, doo, set, is how you count push-ups, one, two, three.

"Algesseumnida!" and "Neh!" is the answer to all questions. Army movies taught me that these mean yes.

So far, boot camp is like spring camp for football. But no one is bleeding or throwing up. Just a lot of yelling and running and doing high knees in place. That stuff is easy. But I haven't seen Mr. Shotgun and I don't understand a single thing anyone is saying.

—

We sew white tags into our greens. I am 2-22. Why does everyone but me get to say what my name is?

—

A wonsan pok-gyeok is a punishment yoga position where you put the top of your head in the mud, or on a helmet, and your hands behind your back, legs straight, ass in the air, and make your body a tipped-over L.

Some guys wail. I don't. I'm in shape and I can monkey see, monkey do better than most.

When we wonsan, I think about what I could've said to Chantal.

—

The second day is almost over when two soldiers—officers, I think—meet us at the dirt lot after we're done flipping logs. They call our numbers and we each get a small sheet of paper. For a second I swear I see English, but it's Korean. Everyone walks toward the buildings, and I follow because that's what you do when you have no idea where you're supposed to go. And I am okay until the crowd splits up into different buildings, leaving me outside and lost.

There's another guy by the corner of a building looking toward the barbed-wire fence and the thick pines behind it. He's got a big head, cartoonish. He looks back at me through these thick-rimmed glasses and I run to him and start pointing at the paper in my hand and shrugging my shoulders.

"Come," he says. He points at his paper, then at mine. "Same, same."

"What?"

"We are same," he says. "We are doomed."

He sleeps on the far side of the barracks. I saw him scribbling in a little notebook last night, as if it would blow up and he needed to hurry. He's number four, I think.

"You speak English," I say.

"Very small." We start walking.

"Chong Junho," he says. He emphasizes *Jun*. "But here, Sa, number four."

"How did you know I didn't speak Korean?"

"You cannot say numbers right."

"I'm—"

Four raises a finger up to his lips as we enter a large room filled with what must be a hundred guys, all sitting on the floor. There's a skinny sergeant standing on a table in front, yelling.

For an hour the skinny sergeant barks, preaches, shakes his fists like he's snapping goose necks. He squints when he stops and we say our Algesseumnida. My legs fall asleep. I'm still not used to sitting on the floor. What is this man saying? Is it about Mayans playing soccer with the heads of fallen enemies, like how Coach Shaw used to tell us? But with each Algesseumnida! everyone seems to dig it—except Four.

When it's over, we separate into squads and march around in circles in the rain. The rain is cold but it's nice to see Four assigned to my squad. At least one person I can talk to. After an hour we go to the mess hall. Today, people are talking.

"How did you learn English?" I ask Four.

"School." Four looks around to see if anyone is watching. "Computer games. I like Western computer games."

"Cool."

"No. Not cool. Very not cool." He slurps soup.

"So, what was that guy talking about at that meeting?" I say.

"What guy?" he says.

"The sergeant."

"Surgeon?"

"The guy, you know, the guy—the guy who was speaking." I nod toward the preacher-sergeant, who is eating alone, standing with a bowl in his hand in the far corner of the mess, chewing deliberately. He pans his head like a floor fan.

"Ah, Joong-sa," Four says solemnly. "He's Joong-sa, leader?"

"Okay. Our sergeant. What did he say?"

"Terrible. He say we real soldiers of Army. Two months later we go to DMZ."

"DMZ? Like the border-with-North-Korea DMZ?"

"I wanted computer tech. Not DMZ."

"Us?"

Four takes a bite of kimchi and pushes his tray away. "Shit-terrible. No computers. Many guns. Many bears. Very shit-terrible."

After dinner, in the dark, with tiny shovels in our hands, our squad takes turns filling sandbags with mud and running them up the hill and piling them on the top. I am running up the hill when suddenly my sandbag bursts. I look down and want to retie it but the skinny sergeant is already marching up, pitching forward, voice booming. He comes face-to-face with me, yelling and spraying spittle.

"Algesseumnida!" I say, then I get down to do some push-ups. He grabs me by the neck and pulls me up and leads me off the hill. He's talking really quietly. Then he stops, and the only thing I can hear is the rain hitting mud.

"I don't understand. I don't speak Korean," I say.

The skinny sergeant cocks his head. He looks around as if maybe there is someone behind him, then he turns back to me.

Coach Shaw told us that in the Army, you must look men in the eye. Even when you screw up and don't know how you did it. So I look at the sergeant and say again, "I don't speak Korean, douche nugget."

He looks around again, all smiles. Everyone stops and watches us. The sergeant yells, and everything starts again, and then he kicks me behind the knee and I drop to the ground.

"Wonsan pok-gyeok!" he yells.

The sergeant grabs me by the neck and pushes the top of my head into the mud. Then he grabs my belt and pulls my butt high.

Then the sergeant calls over one of his minions, a lower-rank sergeant, I guess, to keep an eye on me while he marches off in a hurry toward the buildings. After what feels like twenty minutes, my hamstrings burn, my back shakes. I try to put my hands to the ground but each time I do, the minion forces my arms back to their original position. I hold on. My legs and back begin to crumple and I feel like wailing. When I start falling down to my knees, the minion pulls me back into position. The rain falls heavier.

I try to think of something happy and fluffy, like sleeping between pillows and drinking warm milk. Think of refreshing showers and ice baths sucking out the lactic burns in your hamstrings that now pull like two cords slowly cracking and splaying and separating in terrible smoky friction, and think of all those fucking knives of cramps and rubber hammer heads of cramps. Feel that shaking, quivering.

A sandbag just broke. I didn't break it. Isn't the Army supposed to be a band of brothers? But all I feel like is an asshole with a number.

At the end of lunch, Sixteen had gone up to the sergeant and said something really quiet, and the sergeant knocked over the guy's tray onto the floor and made him do a wonsan with his head in a bunch of greens right there on the mess floor while the rest stepped around him.

Steedick all over again.

Behind me, through my legs, I see the sergeant come out of the building with the offices and march back to us. His skinny face scowls on his skinny neck on his skinny body, marching on his matchstick legs. He gets to the squad and starts yelling.

A lone mousy voice responds. Minion pulls me up and I see Four coming. "Stupid and me, team," Four, aka Sa, says.

For the rest of the day we are together. And every time I'm slow making a turn in formation or don't get all the mud into a sandbag, Four and I have our heads in the mud. The sergeant keeps a bead on us. By the time we're done and the sun comes out, we've got mud-cast hats.

—

Up in the guard towers, along the fence, the guards have rifles. Are they loaded?

—

A door opens and GI Dan sweeps in and says, "There's been a big mistake, where's the American?"

I say, "Right here."

"Where is the American?" GI Dan repeats, and he starts kicking the mats. "American?"

The guys on the mats looks up at him blurry-eyed and just shake their heads and lie back down on their pillows. I keep calling, but GI Dan just throws up his hands and storms out.

My eyes open.

Just dark and snores.

Stupid dream.

—

We march, dig, yell. I get my head buried in dirt. They only give us seven rounds and watch us load the clips. I think of shooting the sergeant because he's a dick. Downrange they've got these photos of guys who look like Mr. Kim. Then again, those photos could be any of us.

I shoot six into Mr. Kim—one into his ribs, four at his throat, and one right above his left eye. The sights are off and with another clip I could set them, but I'm still able to put one in a crow that was flying way above the target. It bursts into feathers and a mist of blood and gristle.

Everyone is silent and watching the feathers twirling down, and the sergeant looks at me with that kind of shock that says he's never seen that before. Then he snatches my rifle and has me do a long wonsan while everyone else gets another clip. It doesn't matter. Only two others can even group their shots. They haven't figured yet that bullets drop in arcs, like arrows from a bow, not straight lines.

—

We're in a classroom looking at a pamphlet with these little cartoons that have very calm-looking soldiers using tourniquets on themselves, and the sergeant up front is telling us something.

"Sa," I ask, "what's he saying?"

Sa shushes me.

I point at the cartoon guy who is wrapping himself with a bandage that looks like a small pillow.

"Not important, not helpful to you," he says.

Using a compass, tying different knots—ever since I went the wrong direction while we were dribbling soccer balls on the parade ground with rifles above our heads, Sa has been like that. I think he's sick of wonsans.

"C'mon, Sa," I say, "it's first aid."

"Why you not speak Korea? Stupid. Terrible stupid."

—

Sa taught me that the old I've-got-your-nose trick that everyone plays with kids is the same as the middle finger, in Korean.

—

The sergeant figures wonsans aren't working for me. He ups the ante: everyone in the squad has to do wonsans whenever anyone—usually me—makes a mistake. Before, they just snickered. I'm too big for them to pick on like they do to a small dark kid, Sam-Ship-Oh—Thirty-Five. They whip him with towels when he leaves the shower and tip over his cup at dinner. Now they glare at Sa and me.

—

Four days in, we come back to the barracks, and my mat and Sa's mat are wet and stink of piss. And the bastards are all smiles—even Thirty-Five.

I'm about to stomp over and foot Thirty-Five and stuff the little asshole into a trash can, then the anger stops. Thirty-Five is looking away, but he's tensed in that way people do before a hit. I've seen guys like him get bullied my whole life, and I never did a thing. Is this what it is like to get whipped with a towel? To walk lightly, hug the corners, struggle for a pull-up, get all the abuse?

Why did I only want to break the little guy?

*Because you're a meathead.* That's what Chantal would say.

I'm not a meathead.

—

At lunch they serve this off-brand Spam, so fatty it glistens. I don't eat this kind of thing, but now I bite it, and it's so good. Like Lit'l Smokies. I can enjoy this like Lit'l Smokies and not be ashamed, no one eyeballing me like I'm not a real baller. I suck on it and put it under my cheek like the old guys do with snuff, and it feels so good.

—

Emmitt Smith wore number twenty-two.

—

In the office, sitting on his desk, Mr. Shotgun smiles when I come into the room. "You're a wanker, Twenty-Two," he says. "Do you know that?"

He points at the diamond on his collar. Mr. Shotgun is a lieutenant. "Walk back through that doorway and salute your superior."

I walk back through the doorway and salute. It's early and dark and the windows are fogged. The sergeant dragged me out of bed and brought me to a hallway and pointed to the only open door with the light on. And here I am.

He sips from a steaming paper cup.

"You've got two problems, Twenty-Two," he says. "Do you know what they are?"

"No, sir," I say.

He scoots over a bit on the desk. There's a stack of notebooks and books tied together in a bundle. "You became my problem. Because you truly don't speak any Korean. The sergeants know for certain now that you're not playing some game."

"You're going to teach me Korean?" I say.

"Your second problem," he says, then sips from his paper cup. "Today is payday."

"Payday," I say.

"Yes," he says.

"Why is that a problem?"

"I wouldn't know. You're the criminal here. Care to explain this?" He holds up a letter in which there's some boxes and numbers and things highlighted.

He hands it to me. Its Korean looks threatening. There are numbers in red, big numbers, with a big minus sign.

"I don't get it," I say.

"Debt," he says, "the debt collectors found you, Twenty-Two. And you owe a lot of coin."

"I don't own anything. I don't have debt."

"Your family, numpty."

"I don't have any family."

"Twenty-Two, why are you here?" he says. "And don't give me that hollow bovine look, why are you here in my Army?"

"Because," I say, "I'm unlucky?"

"You're here because you're fulfilling your duty as a man, a Korean man. You owe this money because you are fulfilling your duty as the head of your family."

He sips. He looks smug, like he's conquered something, until his smile drops. "Oh dear," he says. "You really have no idea what I'm talking about, do you?"

I shake my head no.

"Impressive," he says. "This means you need to have a chat with your pa. Are you listening to me? Your family has been racking up debt. Now their creditors found you. And our dear government sees it fit that you shall pay. And by the looks of it, pay for a very long time. My Army might never get rid of you. But first: Let's get started with some Korean. What we have here is a gem, straight from the Yanks."

He hands me a faded snot-green paperback. The corners are fluffy, rat-chewed.

KOREAN

**BASIC COURSE**
Volume 1

This work was compiled and published with the support of the Office of Education, Department of Health, Education and Welfare, United States of America.

**B. NAM PARK**
**FOREIGN SERVICE INSTITUTE**
WASHINGTON, D.C.
**1968**

DEPARTMENT OF STATE

# 31

MEN ARE SWEAT, STINK, AND SCARS. THEY RUB THEIR CALLUSES AND contemplate pain as they stare off into the wilderness. Men scramble through the limbs of a dogpile. Men stand with power and demonstrate honor, and die in artillery-made moonscapes, telling their brothers to *give 'em hell.*

However, looking up at the ribs of the barracks at night, snores to the left and farts to the right, Twenty-Two thinks that all may be wrong.

Hana: Bio-Asshole-Father is not dead.

Doo: Twenty-Two knew that all along but never admitted it.

Set: Lieutenant Shotgun said that the Army will garnish Twenty-Two's wages for his two years of military service. Then Twenty-Two has to pay off the debt or stay in the Army.

Net: Twenty-Two will pay the debt of a father who abandoned him.

Dasut: What man has Twenty-Two met that was like a man is supposed to be?

Yasut: What kind of man is just a number?

—

In the mornings, I parrot whatever Lieutenant Shotgun tells me to repeat in Korean. He says my pronunciations sounds like farts in water. But I'm sounding better, I think. Lieutenant Shotgun calls me Ee-Ship-Ee, Twenty-Two. Now everyone else calls me Kojangi.

Whatever that means.

—

There are two systems of numbers in Korean. When you count, you're supposed to say hana, doo, set, net. When you talk about formal things, or big numbers, you say ill, ee, sam, sa. I guess it's the difference between one, once, and first?

—

The only mail I get are debt letters. I ask Sa to look at them and tell me what they are about. He looks, squeezes his eyebrows together, and searches for words in his big head.

"Debt," he says.

"What else? Like from who?"

"Bank. *I-N-D-K*." He points at the logo from the bank that's called *INDK Bank*, which is written in English at the top.

"But what is all this stuff?" I'm pointing at the stuff beside the big red numbers.

"Debt for . . . industry?"

"What else?"

"I don't know, Kojangi," he says. "You are big debt."

I need help. But I don't know who can help me. No one even knows I'm here.

—

I am the whipping post, the one picked on. Stuff taken and ruined, cocks painted on my cheeks with shoe polish while I'm asleep.

The Army is supposed to be a like a sports team. At the beginning of the season, everyone hates each other but cling together for survival until the moment of adversity, then there's the heart-to-heart and a *wow, we're not so different after all.*

Heart-to-hearts are hard when all you can say is, "Hi," and all you get is, "Kojangi." When I asked Lieutenant Shotgun, he laughed. Told me to get back to work studying Korean. He still says my pronunciation is "shite." He makes me do the alphabet, aloud, which sounds like this:

Basic Syllable Chart

| 1 | 2 | 3 | 4 | 5 | 6 | 7 | 8 | 9 | 10 | 11 | 12 | 13 | 14 | 15 | 16 | 17 | 18 | 19 | 20 |
|---|---|---|---|---|---|---|---|---|----|----|----|----|----|----|----|----|----|----|----|
| a | ka | kka | kha | na | ta | tta | tha | la | ma | pa | ppa | pha | sa | ssa | ca | cca | cha | ha | ang |
| ə | kə | kkə | khə | nə | tə | ttə | thə | lə | mə | pə | ppə | phə | sə | ssə | cə | ccə | chə | hə | əng |
| o | ko | kko | kho | no | to | tto | tho | lo | mo | po | ppo | pho | so | sso | co | cco | cho | ho | ong |
| u | ku | kku | khu | nu | tu | ttu | thu | lu | mu | pu | ppu | phu | su | ssu | cu | ccu | chu | hu | ung |
| ɨ | kɨ | kkɨ | khɨ | nɨ | tɨ | ttɨ | thɨ | lɨ | mɨ | pɨ | ppɨ | phɨ | sɨ | ssɨ | cɨ | ccɨ | chɨ | hɨ | ɨng |
| i | ki | kki | khi | ni | ti | tti | thi | li | mi | pi | ppi | phi | si | ssi | ci | cci | chi | hi | ing |
| e | ke | kke | khe | ne | te | tte | the | le | me | pe | ppe | phe | se | sse | ce | cce | che | he | eng |
| æ | kæ | kkæ | khæ | næ | tæ | ttæ | thæ | læ | mæ | pæ | ppæ | phæ | sæ | ssæ | cæ | ccæ | chæ | hæ | æng |
| ya | kya | kkya | khya | nya | tya | ttya | thya | lya | mya | pya | ppya | phya | sya | ssya | cya | ccya | chya | hya | yang |
| yə | kyə | kkyə | khyə | nyə | tyə | ttyə | thyə | lyə | myə | pyə | ppyə | phyə | syə | ssyə | cyə | ccyə | chyə | hyə | yəng |
| yo | kyo | kkyo | khyo | nyo | tyo | ttyo | thyo | lyo | myo | pyo | ppyo | phyo | syo | ssyo | cyo | ccyo | chyo | hyo | yong |
| yu | kyu | kkyu | khyu | nyu | tyu | ttyu | thyu | lyu | myu | pyu | ppyu | phyu | syu | ssyu | cyu | ccyu | chyu | hyu | yung |
| ye | kye | kkye | khye | nye | tye | ttye | thye | lye | mye | pye | ppye | phye | sye | ssye | cye | ccye | chye | hye | yeng |
| yæ | kyæ | kkyæ | khyæ | nyæ | tyæ | ttyæ | thyæ | lyæ | myæ | pyæ | ppyæ | phyæ | syæ | ssyæ | cyæ | ccyæ | chyæ | hyæ | yæng |
| wa | kwa | kkwa | khwa | nwa | twa | ttwa | thwa | lwa | mwa | pwa | ppwa | phwa | swa | sswa | cwa | ccwa | chwa | hwa | wang |
| wə | kwə | kkwə | khwə | nwə | twə | ttwə | thwə | lwə | mwə | pwə | ppwə | phwə | swə | sswə | cwə | ccwə | chwə | hwə | wəng |
| wi | kwi | kkwi | khwi | nwi | twi | ttwi | thwi | lwi | mwi | pwi | ppwi | phwi | swi | sswi | cwi | ccwi | chwi | hwi | wing |
| we | kwe | kkwe | khwe | nwe | twe | ttwe | thwe | lwe | mwe | pwe | ppwe | phwe | swe | sswe | cwe | ccwe | chwe | hwe | weng |

These sounds match with the Korean letters, like this:

KOREAN BASIC COURSE

| 1 | 2 | 3 | 4 | 5 | 6 | 7 | 8 | 9 | 10 | 11 | 12 | 13 | 14 | 15 | 16 | 17 | 18 | 19 | 20 |
|---|---|---|---|---|---|---|---|---|----|----|----|----|----|----|----|----|----|----|----|
| 아 | 가 | 까 | 카 | 나 | 다 | 따 | 타 | 라 | 마 | 바 | 빠 | 파 | 사 | 싸 | 자 | 짜 | 차 | 하 | 앙 |
| 어 | 거 | 꺼 | 커 | 너 | 더 | 떠 | 터 | 러 | 머 | 버 | 뻐 | 퍼 | 서 | 써 | 저 | 쩌 | 처 | 허 | 엉 |
| 오 | 고 | 꼬 | 코 | 노 | 도 | 또 | 토 | 로 | 모 | 보 | 뽀 | 포 | 소 | 쏘 | 조 | 쪼 | 초 | 호 | 옹 |
| 우 | 구 | 꾸 | 쿠 | 누 | 두 | 뚜 | 투 | 루 | 무 | 부 | 뿌 | 푸 | 수 | 쑤 | 주 | 쭈 | 추 | 후 | 웅 |
| 으 | 그 | 끄 | 크 | 느 | 드 | 뜨 | 트 | 르 | 므 | 브 | 쁘 | 프 | 스 | 쓰 | 즈 | 쯔 | 츠 | 흐 | 응 |
| 이 | 기 | 끼 | 키 | 니 | 디 | 띠 | 티 | 리 | 미 | 비 | 삐 | 피 | 시 | 씨 | 지 | 찌 | 치 | 히 | 잉 |
| 에 | 게 | 께 | 케 | 네 | 데 | 떼 | 테 | 레 | 메 | 베 | 뻬 | 페 | 세 | 쎄 | 제 | 쩨 | 체 | 헤 | 엥 |
| 애 | 개 | 깨 | 캐 | 내 | 대 | 때 | 태 | 래 | 매 | 배 | 빼 | 패 | 새 | 쌔 | 재 | 째 | 채 | 해 | 앵 |
| 야 | 갸 | 꺄 | 캬 | 냐 | 댜 | 땨 | 탸 | 랴 | 먀 | 뱌 | 뺘 | 퍄 | 샤 | 쌰 | 쟈 | 쨔 | 챠 | 햐 | 양 |
| 여 | 겨 | 껴 | 켜 | 녀 | 뎌 | 뗘 | 텨 | 려 | 며 | 벼 | 뼈 | 펴 | 셔 | 쎠 | 져 | 쪄 | 쳐 | 혀 | 영 |
| 요 | 교 | 꾜 | 쿄 | 뇨 | 됴 | 뚀 | 툐 | 료 | 묘 | 뵤 | 뾰 | 표 | 쇼 | 쑈 | 죠 | 쬬 | 쵸 | 효 | 용 |
| 유 | 규 | 뀨 | 큐 | 뉴 | 듀 | 뜌 | 튜 | 류 | 뮤 | 뷰 | 쀼 | 퓨 | 슈 | 쓔 | 쥬 | 쮸 | 츄 | 휴 | 융 |
| 예 | 계 | 꼐 | 켸 | 녜 | 뎨 | 뗴 | 톄 | 례 | 몌 | 볘 | 뼤 | 폐 | 셰 | 쎼 | 졔 | 쪠 | 쳬 | 혜 | 옝 |
| 얘 | 걔 | 꺠 | 컈 | 냬 | 댸 | 떄 | 턔 | 럐 | 먜 | 뱨 | 뺴 | 퍠 | 섀 | 썌 | 쟤 | 쨰 | 챼 | 햬 | 얭 |
| 와 | 과 | 꽈 | 콰 | 놔 | 돠 | 똬 | 톼 | 롸 | 뫄 | 봐 | 뽜 | 퐈 | 솨 | 쏴 | 좌 | 쫘 | 촤 | 화 | 왕 |
| 워 | 궈 | 꿔 | 쿼 | 눠 | 둬 | 뚸 | 퉈 | 뤄 | 뭐 | 붜 | 뿨 | 풔 | 숴 | 쒀 | 줘 | 쭤 | 춰 | 훠 | 웡 |
| 위 | 귀 | 뀌 | 퀴 | 뉘 | 뒤 | 뛰 | 튀 | 뤼 | 뮈 | 뷔 | 쀠 | 퓌 | 쉬 | 쒸 | 쥐 | 쮜 | 취 | 휘 | 윙 |
| 의 | 괴 | 꾀 | 쾨 | 뇌 | 되 | 뙤 | 퇴 | 뢰 | 뫼 | 뵈 | 뾔 | 푀 | 쇠 | 쐬 | 죄 | 쬐 | 최 | 회 | 읭 |
| 왜 | 괘 | 꽤 | 쾌 | 놰 | 돼 | 뙈 | 퇘 | 뢔 | 뫠 | 봬 | 뽸 | 퐤 | 쇄 | 쐐 | 좨 | 쫴 | 쵀 | 홰 | 왱 |

"*A*," Lieutenant Shogun says, "sounds like *ah* like when you piss. It is written in Hangul like . . ." and he points to the 아 character. "Now, when you combine your *a* to a consonant like *k*—which sounds more like the *g* in *God*—they go together to make a new character looking like this." He points to the 가 character in the book. "Get it? The consonant fills the hole of the vowel. Simple."

I don't get it. It's not simple. But I don't say anything.

"Just repeat after me, you Muppet," he says.

"Ah," he says.

"*A*," I say.

"No, *ah. Ah.* With your mouth open. *AH!*"

"Ah," I say.

"Easy, right? All your mouth-breathing finally helps," he says. "Now let's go across to the next sound. *Gah.*"

"Ka," I say.

"Are you trying to be difficult?" he says.

"No." I point to the *ka* in the book. "It's *ka.*"

He points to the 가 character. Then he points at the *ka*. "Do you think these are perfectly the same? Because they're not. They're similar but not the same. Repeat after me, 가."

"가," I say.

"There's hope for you Kojangi. Now, 까," he says, which sounds like the start of *caught.*

"까," I say.

"Now copy those two characters into your notebook," he says. "One hundred times, and say them out loud."

—

Sa translated Kojangi as "Nose-aholic," which makes no sense. A nickname? Like Shorty? Third Nipple? Unibrow?

My nose isn't big. Heart-to-hearts are hard when I'm the guy in the corner, the reject.

Others have it worse. Last week, some guy from another company was found duct-taped naked to the flagpole. Thirty-Five seems to fight daily around the bathroom. I see him with these bruises around his shirt collar like the ones I got from British girl.

Sa sometimes has the same bruises. He doesn't say anything about them. He just scratches in his notebook and stares off into the distance in that it-is-what-it-is sort of way.

I don't know what this is anymore.

Got to keep my eyes only in front of me.

—

We have hand-to-hand practice. I get the guy who I'm pretty sure cut the holes in my socks. My boot slips and stomps his ankle. Repeatedly. He grunts, grits his teeth, doesn't do anything.

I don't feel any better either.

—

When I'm not looking, they strike.

—

Every window has bars. Every fence has barbed-wire coils running along their tops and along their base.

Staying in my lane isn't working. There's nowhere to run to. There's no one to talk to except Sa. I need people to like me.

—

Nobody is allowed to call home. Because no one likes me, I can't borrow money to pay for stamps to write Sheryl and ask Richard the lawyer to bust me out. So I steal two stamps from Thirty-Five's locker. My letter is pitiful.

> *Sheryl,*
> *I got taken into the Korean Army. Help.*
> *Love,*
> *Bucky*

*Bucky* feels weird as soon as I write it, weirder than *love*. Not that Twenty-Two or Kojangi are better, but Bucky just doesn't seem right. I want to tell her that Bio-Father is alive and racking up the bills and that I'm broke and that everything is shit.

But how much help could Sheryl even be?

—

"만" romanization: *man*
Pronunciation: US [máːn].
Definition 1: just, fully, only.
Definition 2: 10,000.
Definition 3: Gulf.

—

We wake and yell and march and yell and wonsan and yell and do push-ups in the mud. When we get to the mess hall I realize everything is quieter. Different. I load up my tray with roots and soup and sit next to Sa. He's alone, eating with his bulbous head hanging over his tray. If he dressed up as Charlie Brown he could get in a boxing ring with another dude dressed up like Mickey Mouse and make some money boxing at the county fair. Maybe I could skim off the top to pay my bio-asshole-father's debt.

Ha!

I think of this stuff instead of the quiet voices plotting against me. "Blah blah blah, Kojangi, blah blah blah." Snicker, snicker. I don't need any Korean to know that tone. But today the tone is different, serious.

I sit down and take a bite of root. "Om shik maht adan gayo?" How is the food? I ask Sa.

"Eum-shik kwuenchan seubnika? Stupid." He pumps his legs and that shakes the table. "Eum. No Om."

"You're a shit teacher," I say.

"Ee-Ship-Ee namoo byungshin ya."

*Ee-Ship-Ee* means *Twenty-Two*. *Namoo* means "very," *byungshin ya* means "is shitty idiot." So, Sa just said, "Twenty-Two is very shitty-idiot."

Or, written in Korean: "이십이 너무 병신 야."

We slurp and chomp with our mouths open. The hum grows. Forty days behind me, and I'm not able to correctly ask, *How is the food?* Not even a clue to the talk ping-ponging around me. What if I spend the next two years having to wipe shoe polish off my cheeks and still can't speak?

Someone clears their throat and spits, "Gundae sliga."

Then I hear it again, "Blah blah blah, Gundae sliga."

And again, from the other end of the table, "Gundae sliga! Blah blah blah! DMZ blah blah blah."

I turn to Sa, who stares hopelessly into his empty bowl.

"What is Gundae sliga?" I say.

"Soccer," Sa says. "Army soccer."

"Why is everyone talking about it?"

"It is very important. Our team versus another. Very important. Sergeants love it. Gambling. Lots of money. And choices. Where we go. West Sea DMZ, East Sea DMZ, islands. We will lose. We will go to East Sea DMZ and bears eat us. Terrible, crazy-terrible."

I look at all the black buzzed heads in the mess hall.

"Wow. Bears," I say.

A guy a few tables away jumps up on the table and flexes his biceps. He is a big guy with veins popping everywhere, a gym rat. Yet he looks functional, like a boxer. He's the only other one in camp who's got legs as big as mine and a legit six-pack. He starts beating his chest, talking shit. Talking shit has the same tone in every language. Guys applaud and hoot before the sergeants come and slap him in the back of the head and get him to the floor between the tables, wonsaning. But the look on his face says it all, he is cool. He has friends to tell that wonsans are nothing.

"Did you play soccer in school?" I ask Sa.

Sa looks up from stabbing some withered kimchi with a chopstick. There's the sound of something heavy dropping in the kitchen. He flinches.

"No," he says.

"I played a little bit in school. Goalie. I used to be pretty good. But my real sport was football."

It was true. A couple of times during gym class I played goalie. I was good.

"So?"

"We aren't going to lose."

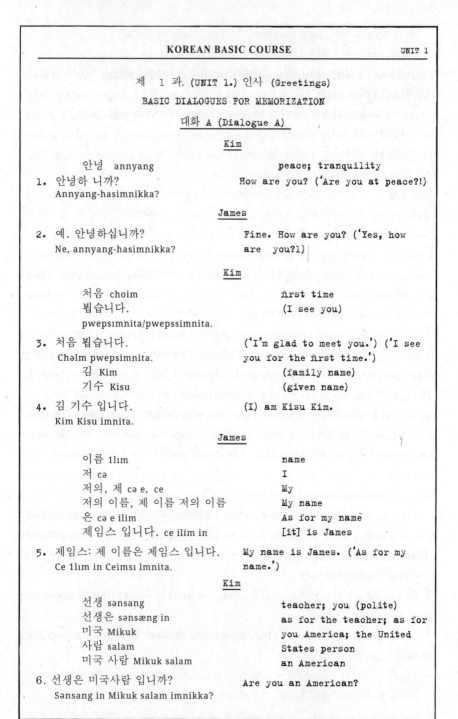

제 1 과. (UNIT 1.) 인사 (Greetings)

BASIC DIALOGUES FOR MEMORIZATION

대화 A (Dialogue A)

### Kim

안녕 annyang                         peace; tranquility

1. 안녕하 니까?                       How are you? ('Are you at peace?!)
   Annyang-hasimnikka?

### James

2. 예. 안녕하십니까?                   Fine. How are you? ('Yes, how
   Ne, annyang-hasimnikka?            are you?l)

### Kim

처음 choim                           first time
뵙습니다.                             (I see you)
pwepsımnita/pwepssimnita.

3. 처음 뵙습니다.                      ('I'm glad to meet you.') ('I see
   Chəlm pwepsimnita.                 you for the first time.')
   김 Kim                             (family name)
   기수 Kisu                          (given name)

4. 김 기수 입니다.                     (I) am Kisu Kim.
   Kim Kisu imnita.

### James

이름 1lım                            name
저 cə                                I
저의, 제 cə e, ce                     My
저의 이름, 제 이름 저의 이름          My name
은 cə e ilim                         As for my name
제임스 입니다. ce ilim in             [it] is James

5. 제임스: 제 이름은 제임스 입니다.    My name is James. ('As for my
   Ce 1lım in Ceimsı lmnita.          name.')

### Kim

선생 sənsang                         teacher; you (polite)
선생은 sənsæng in                    as for the teacher; as for
미국 Mikuk                           you America; the United
사람 salam                           States person
미국 사람 Mikuk salam                an American

6. 선생은 미국사람 입니까?             Are you an American?
   Sənsang in Mikuk salam imnikka?

—

Every time I see Kim in *Korean Basic Course*, I think of Mr. Kim, smoking, looking through me. I have to say his part in a deeper voice than when I speak James's part. It makes Lieutenant Shotgun laugh. He has me repeat the dialogue one hundred times. Then he has me copy it five times in Korean and has me write it five times from memory, repeating the phrase out loud, as he slurps hot drinks out of little paper cups and watches.

—

From the top of a hill I can see down to the parade grounds where my squad practices. They look small and gawky, like little guys in Sega. They collide, pass, miss, and chase the ball into a ditch. The sergeant on the field rubs his head with his knuckles.

Up here the wind blows and it is cold and sharp. The sergeant's chubby minion is on the hill with us. His stomach jumps when he barks. Sa and I aren't practicing. We are the cast-offs digging a hole at the top of the hill. The hole crumbles in on itself with each scoop.

Those clowns on the field can't play any sort of ball. You could tell before any of them even got near a ball, a bunch of wimpy, skinny, and soft guys who spent their time behind computers, cell phones, cable TV. They whine and heave trying to do ten good push-ups. Yet the sergeant still went with them rather than me.

I plunge the shovel into the dirt and feel pain gun through my back and legs—leftovers from wonsans both Sa and I had to do after Sa translated what I wanted him to say to the fat man. "Tell this fat-ass clown I want on the team. I can play ball."

Sa must have translated exactly that, because the next thing I knew we were wonsaning.

The fat man barks at us. Sa looks over, Eeyore-like. "Kojangi, we stop dig. We fill again, byungshin."

On the field the squad dribbles and stumbles like drunk giraffes.

"Sa, you don't want to go to the East DMZ, right?"

Sa thinks a moment. "Bears will eat Kojangi."

"You'd like that, wouldn't you?"

"Yes." He shovels more dirt back into the hole. "People talk to Sa then."

A scream echoes from below. A little man in front of the goal rolls on the ground clenching his leg as a small crowd gathers around him. The sergeant is yelling. He has lost his hat. His bald head is turning red and shining in the cold sun. "Sa, if I was on the team, just maybe you'd understand how good I really am and we could—"

"Lose?"

"Win," I say. "You have to explain to the sergeant that I can really help us win."

"No."

After we fill the hole, the fat man barks at us to dig it up again.

"Quit being an ass clown and let me help the team."

"Americans all stupid like Kojangi? Sergeants no like you—no like me. Team no like we. I say to them, I no say to them, you play, you no play, no matter. No trust, no like, no play."

Shoveling hurts. Being the whipping post hurts more. I am here and tell myself every morning that it's going to get better, like one of those empowering tapes you can always find at Goodwill. Feel like taking a boot and shoving it down a guy's throat? Take a breath, learn a word. There is only the present. Stay in the lane. I've got a little notebook that I use with Lieutenant Shotgun and Sa late at night to learn Korean with all kinds of words I forget or can't say right. Yesterday, I learned the word *doeng*, 똥, after finding my hat in the toilet floating alongside a turd.

But this—this I know deep down in the bucket of my soul: I can play ball. Any kind of ball. Better than these guys. They don't care how well I shoot or move through the woods with a compass. People care about sports. Sports earn respect. We all know who the ballers are in school. No one knows the kid with glasses who gets straight A's.

Below, on the field, the bald sergeant is chasing and whacking a guy on the head with his clipboard. The others keep playing against themselves, poorly. If I want to survive this whole thing, I need to play. This is my chance.

The handle of Sa's shovel loses a bolt and separates from the blade. He sighs. We get on the ground and I find it and hand it to him.

"Please," I say, "just talk to them. I really need this."

Down on the field is another yelp, and then the anger of a sergeant's voice. Sa puts the bolt back in and faces me. I have a sudden terrifying image of Sa stabbing me with the shovel.

"No," he says, and impales the ground. "I hate wonsan pok-gyeok."

—

This barracks always has the smell of sweaty guys with atomic socks but tonight it's worse with the menthol sports rub. At 2100, when our hour of "free time" begins, no one glares at me. Instead they check their bandages and trade roles of paper tape.

I get up and walk by bodies until I reach Sa. He's staring up at the rafters as if he can see stars.

"Sa, you gonna come and help me?" I say.

Sa raises his fist and puts his thumb between his index and middle fingers.

"Yeah, well, screw you too."

I pass the office the sergeants are never in and go to the smoking room. I knock on the door and someone grunts. It is a lounge with leather couches and a glass-topped coffee table. The room is dim, and the sergeant—the bald, skinny, scowling one—is gazing up at a chalkboard on wheels. He is fixed on the X's and O's.

"Joong-sa nim, um, anyang hashimnika?" Mr. Sergeant, hello.

I can see the veins at his temples. He blinks. He grunts.

"Okay, jeh ga"—I point at myself—"want to play Gundae sliga." I mime kicking a ball.

The sergeant blinks.

I look up at the chalkboard. I point to the O in front of the goal and at myself. "Je ga, goalkeeper hesimida." I did goalkeeping. I put my hands up in the air ready to catch a ball. "In high school, jeh ga." In high school, me.

The sergeant stares at the chalkboard and then at me. He sucks air through his teeth and shakes his head. Then he nods and puts his cigarette out.

"So, Gundae sliga"—I point at myself—"jeh ga?" Me?

The sergeant nods. "Yeah, yeah," he says, and leads me by the arm and leaves me out in the hall and closes the door.

Sa is writing in his little notebook again when I get back. I see a drawing of a house on fire before he notices me and closes the notebook.

"I'm playing," I say.

Sa looks at me.

"I'm playing," I repeat.

"We will lose," he says.

—

We march, shoot, train, scramble, wander, wonsan, search, fire, duck, hide, seek, climb, fall, dig, dig, dig, fill, fill, fall, wonsan, throw, punch, aim, fall, hit, read, wrap, cut, load, load, load, algesseumnida!, unload, pull, pin, push-up, sit-up, squat, jump, wonsan, and practice soccer.

—

The day of the game comes and the ceiling beams look redder. All night I kept waking up in mid-terror like I was being chased by a linebacker with a chain saw. I open my eyes. No pee on my blanket. I check a pocket mirror, no shoe polish on my cheeks. I can't remember the dream. I usually remember my dreams.

Since I began practicing with the team, I haven't talked to Sa, and that means I haven't talked to anyone except to Lieutenant Shotgun. At the same time no one bothers me. No snickering, no Kojangi, nothing. While Sa dug holes and filled them back up on top of the hill, I faked knowing how to play goalie, which wasn't all that hard. Just tiring. Like all my football reps worked the wrong muscles for soccer. But I can use my hands. After a couple of days I block most of the kicks. I'm going to win. I can feel it.

Everyone seems a bit jumpy. As the game gets closer, people stop snoring, and you can just hear them worrying. This game is a big deal. Bears or no bears. And for me, it's even bigger than that.

Win, I told myself before I went to sleep. Win.

I'm still telling myself that when we get to the field. Goals made of PVC and nylon rope are up, and there is a group of sergeants from different squads talking and passing a helmet. It looks like they're making bets.

I grab at a tuft of stray grass and grind it up in my hands and smell it like I used to before a game. It smells sharp and raw. It has never known fertilizer.

Our sergeant, the skinny bald scowling one, comes over and starts picking the starters. He chooses the tall lanky guy—who is always coughing—to be goalie. Not me.

The guys in my squad take their shirts off and warm up. The entire camp gathers, the old women who work in the kitchen, officers, and watchtower guards all sitting on an embankment that protects the buildings from the rain runoff.

We are skins and they are shirts, and within the first minute of kickoff, the shirts score. It is bad. The crowd wails as this one guy on the shirts, a guy all muscles and veins, steals the ball from our guy and bolts down and throttles the ball past our coughing lanky goalie as if he had been caught squatting on the toilet.

I feel a nudge and I see Sa. "No, this is nothing," I say. "I'm going to play. We're going to win."

Then we hear the impact. A boom. We look over and don't see the ball until it ricochets off the head of our lanky goalie. Fortunately, it goes up and over the goal. The goalie stands there motionless, as if shot, then tumbles over. The crowd loves it. An officer playing referee whistles and the medics come out.

"Kojangi." I feel the sergeant's iron grip on my biceps. "Go."

Alone in front of the goal, feeling the breeze against my buzzed scalp, I watch my team talking in a huddle at midfield. They look back at me. We are all unsure. After the ball is thrown into play the dust kicks up and swirls around everybody and it's just shadows. I hear kicks, yelps, then a figure erupts from the dust with the ball, the muscleman who knocked out the last goalie. I recognize him, the gym rat. He is in full sprint. He charges toward me and looks down for a moment at the ball and then booms it. I get in front and the ball punches me in the gut. I hold on. After a breath I look up and see the gym rat pointing at me with wide crazy eyes.

"I'm gonna get serious now, yo!" he says, like he's from L.A. or something. "Real serious."

I cough. How did I not know that this guy from the other company could speak English?

Thirty seconds later, I'm diving for another shot from the gym rat. This one barrels down on me like a Cadillac on a stray cat. But the ball doesn't go in. I get up and look at my fellow skins, hoping for a nod or something. Everyone is already in position waiting for the ball. Sharp pains shoot through my ribs, and my ears ring. The gym rat is pointing at me again.

"Bring it, douche nugget," I say, and hulk up and flex my biceps with the ball in one hand like I own this, because I do. He's not the only one who's done some reps. This is who I am: an athlete. I compete to win.

I can be the hero. I can take the pain. The crowd starts chanting, "Ko-jang-i, Ko-jang-i."

It goes like this for a long while: the gym rat keeps breaking away and shooting, and I keep diving and blocking. Finally, when the wind starts kicking up the dust, and I'm doing what I can to blink it out of my eyes, a shirt finally manages to pass gym rat the ball over all the skins and gym rat catches me on the wrong foot and whooshes it into the net. He's somersaulting until the referees call offsides. The gym rat blows up. He shoves the closest person to him, which happens to be our little Thirty-Five. But Thirty-Five has had enough of that kind of thing, so he takes a swing at the gym rat. Suddenly there's mosh pit of buzzed heads in the middle of the field, even some people from the crowd charge out onto the field to join in. After the sergeants pull everyone apart, guys are spitting blood and setting noses.

Then the whistle blows for the half, it is still one–nothing. I'm trying hard not to limp. There are these little cuts leaving tracks of blood through the dust pasted on my skin. Blood ain't nothing anymore, but I still need to lie in the grass. The sergeant yells until his skin is crab-red. Everyone is bruised and busted. The sergeant gives us new instructions for the second half. He nods at Thirty-Five and the guys pat him on the back. The sergeant nods at me. Some of the guys help me up from the ground. They smirk with approval. My plan is working.

The second half starts as a riot in the dust. Guys are full-on tackling and sliding for the ball. And for the first time the game is being played past midfield in the shirts' territory. The gym rat is bent over in a wonsan on the sideline, a penalty for the shoving incident. Without him, the shirts are paper. But still it isn't until the seventy-fifth minute when short dark Thirty-Five scores a goal. He runs, sucking his thumb, which is weird, and other guys chase and high-five him. I just hold on to the goalpost. My victory is coming.

But, what if he's the hero? What if I'm back to where I started and I wake up to find a turd in my hat?

In the eightieth minute the wind really kicks up and sand gets in everyone's eyes and teeth and ears. The score is still one–all. The sergeants are yelling and waving their arms. Everyone is gassed. They guys are flailing at the ball any chance they get, puking on the sideline, and keeping going. This is to save our lives from the bears. I start spacing out, until there's a scream and a whistle to carry off the injured. When the shirts break through and shoot, I fall in front of the ball to save the goal. At the eighty-fifth minute, just before injury time, I have visions of saving the game during a shootout. My moment is coming. I will be the hero.

In injury time, after a shirt limps off the field, there is a cheer from the embankment. It is hard to see through the dust. This is what it feels like to be in the Sahara. Out of the dust and chaos the gym rat blows through with the ball. He had been allowed back in. He weaves and zags and dances toward me. I move forward and make myself as big as I can, as if standing tall in front of a charging bear. Then I hear the report of him kicking the ball. I throw myself toward it. The ball hits my arms and my arms hit my head and I crash on the ground and slide. The ball pops right back to the gym rat. He kicks it again.

It swooshes into the net and the whistle blows and people scream and the game is over.

It begins to rain. They're fighting again. I just lie there listening to the shouts and the raindrops pattering the ground. Nobody bothers to come and stand me up. Nobody comes to kick me. I am alone. Rain kicks up the dust and rain will slap it down again and I know this will all turn to mud.

Far away, there's a tire stuck in the mud. Probably still strapped to the harness I left because I wasn't good enough.

Even in the language I speak, sports, I can't speak the words to get my body into the right positions to win. Metrics all wrong.

Deported and deported and deported until I'm finally so far off I'm at the hilltops watching booby-trapped valleys and bracing for shoe-polished cheeks and piss-filled canteens.

"I said"—Sa's round head blocks the light from the clouds above—"we lose. One guy very good. Pro."

"You didn't say that," I sit up and look over to the guys at midfield shoving each other in the rain. "It's never going to get better, is it?"

"Maybe we okay."

"How?" We watch the MPs running by with their batons in hand toward the brawl.

"Maybe," Sa says, "bears not eat Kojangi. We all lost."

"What exactly does *Kojangi* mean?" I say.

"Nose-aholic."

"No, Sa. Really, what does it really mean?"

"Big nose."

We watch the MPs wail on guys.

"My nose isn't big," I say.

"Ugly foreign bastard. Foreigner fucker. That is Kojangi."

The rain gets heavier. The field is melting to mud. Everything hurts, everything throbs. Cracked and battered like some old dead stump. Sa takes off his glasses and wipes the lenses on his shirt and sucks air through his teeth. I try brushing myself off a little.

"My name is Beyonghak," I say clearly. "If you ever call me Kojangi again I will beat you until you can't see. Tell all the other ass-clowns the same. I am only Beyonghak. Okay?"

Sa looks way off toward the fences, the barbed wire, the pine forest. Takes a manly sniff.

"Okay?" I say.

"You not only one they hate."

There is a low voice behind us clearing his throat. We turn and see our skinny sergeant.

Sa jumps on the ground to get into a wonsan and I do the same. But the sergeant stops us. He smiles. He says something quiet and quick and then smiles one of those fatherly smiles you see on TV. He helps Sa up and gives a nod and a pat on the shoulder and does the same to me. Then he walks toward mob with a baton in hand.

I'm stunned. I feel fuzzy inside and I can't help but smiling.

"What did he say?" I say.

Sa shakes his head. "He say we real Korean soldiers now. Our team, real soldiers, Kojangi."

Beyond the fences, a soft-looking fog grows from the pines, hiding the trails we run. Past that are rice paddies with old beaten-up houses with ragged tractors and towns with nice shiny new neon and cell phones and cable TV. I've got an excited-sick feeling in my gut about what is beyond that.

"Don't call me Kojangi," I say.

"You call me clown-ass. I call you Kojangi. Fair."

"No, it's not. I get to choose what people can call me."

"There are worse things than Kojangi."

복무 합니다                               [he] serves (in the military)

9. 한국의 젊은 청년 들은 (누구나) 다       Does every Korean young man have to
serve in the military?
군 대에 복무 해야 하나요?

최 장군

만 이십세                                 (full) 20 years old

군                                        armed forces

(군 에) 입대합니다                         [he] joins the armed forces

군 대 복무                                military service

의무                                      duty

10. 에, 그럽지요. 남자는 만 20세가 되면     Yes.  Every man has a duty to enter and
serve in the armed forces when he
다 군 에 입대해서 군 대 복무 할 의무 가 있지요.   becomes 20 years of age.

부르스

복무 기간                                 period of (military) service

11. 대개 복무 기간은 얼마 동안인가요?       What is the usual length of service?

최 장군

육군                                      Army

징병                                      the draft; conscription

소집                                      summon; conscription

소집합니다                                [they] summon

제대                                      discharge

제대합니다                                [he] gets discharged from the
service

12. 육군 에 징병으로 소집되어 가면          If drafted, one can get discharged
after two years of service.
2년 후 에 제대할 수 있읍니다.

해군                                      Navy

해병대                                    Marine Corps

공군                                      Air Force

지원병

volunteer (soldier)

13. 그러나, 해군 이나 해병대, 또는 공군 에

But if one goes into the Navy, Marine
Corps or Air Force as a volunteer, he
usually serves for 3 years.

지원병으로 들어 가면 만 3년 동안

복무 하는 것이 보통 이지요.

부.르스

사병

enlisted men

장교

officer (in the military)

사관 학교

military academy

14. 사병으로 가지 않고 처음부터 장교로 가는

Isn't there any way one can go in as
an officer from the beginning without
going in as an enlisted man? I mean,
without graduating from the military
academy.

길은 없나요? 정식 사관 학교를 졸업하지

않고 말입니다.

최 장군

대학 재학중

while in college

후보(새)

(officer) candidate

합격했읍니다

[he] passed exams

훈련/훌 연/

training

훈련을 받습니다

[he] gets training

15. 물론, 사관 학교를 나 오지 않고도 장교가

Of course, you can become an officer
without going through the military
academy, but if you want to be an
officer, you have to take and pass an
officer candidacy exam during or after
college. Later, you must receive
training.

될 수 있읍니다만 장교가 되려면 대학

재학 중 이나 졸업 후에 장교 후보생 시험을

써서 합격한 후에 훈련을 받어야 되지요.

# 38

LIEUTENANT SHOTGUN GIVES ME A PAPER OF HALF A DIALOGUE:
*Hi, my name is Twenty-Two. I am an enlisted man. What is your name?*
*How are you?*
*Nice to meet you too. I am in the Army. How about you?*
*Have you seen any Communists around?*
*Have a great day!*
"Translate this into Korean," Lieutenant Shotgun says. "You have five minutes."

After five minutes, I hand it back written in Korean. Lieutenant Shotgun looks at it a long time and then stands up and gives a nod that's almost a bow. "You might've learned something. Not enough, but something."

—

The day we graduate boot camp, they give us new greens with our names in gold. Mine reads 이 병학. Under the Korean it reads, "YI BEYONG HAK." Then we march around in the mud a few times while some officers at the podium give speeches.

When it's over, we file into a church and pray. They hand around boxes of Choco Pies, which are like Moon Pies but lighter. They're giving us the chocolate pies because they're sending us somewhere horrible.

I am a soldier.

—

We go to a room with a bunch of computers and old women working them. We hand them our ID cards and they type in the info and they print out little receipts that tells us our assignment for training schools. I get assigned to the 123 Reinforcements.

One-two-three?

To the woman, I point to the receipt and say, "Nong-dam?" Joke?

She waves me off.

총 준호, Chong Junho, is Sa's real name. He says that the 123 Reinforcement Battalion is where they keep us until it is time for us to be eaten by bears.

"Do you have bad luck or something?" I ask him. "Why are you so miserable?"

"I was Four," he says, and stops.

Some guys are cheering when they get their receipts, guys from other squads. They get to be truck drivers or stock boys in warehouses or something. Our squad lost the game. So far everyone has gotten 보병, bo beyeong, infantryman destined for the DMZ.

"I was four years old once too," I say to Junho. "And five. And fifteen."

"Four is death number."

"Well, that's great. But I'm the one going to 123."

Junho shows me his receipt. He's going there too. But no one else from our troop is going there. Only us.

—

Junho scribbles in his little journal that he keeps in his back pocket. It's leather and folds up and over like one of those notebooks newspapermen use in black-and-white movies. Junho is from Mia-dong, Seoul. I asked Lieutenant Shotgun once about it and he just said it was a neighborhood for Korean chavs.

"What's a chav?"

"If you spoke proper English, you'd know."

"So, if you're English, how you end up here, anyway?"

He just tapped on the book of substitution drills.

This is what I know about Junho:

—He's from Seoul.

—He likes computer games.

—He translates for me, sits with me, and is comfortable enough to pick out the little fishbones from in between his teeth in front of me.

Does he have brothers or sisters? Does he like shooting games or building games? Does he want to travel, be a pro gamer?

I know next to nothing about him.

—

Last mail call. Only new banks saying that there are new loans. From what I can tell, one is either for a car or for tea.

Back in Tibicut, these kinds of letters came before guys came knocking. All you needed to do was not answer the door. Until they start shutting things off. Then you negotiated. But that would only happen if you really racked up some serious debt.

So, that's my plan. Ignore. The Army is sending me places. Banks will lose track of me.

But then how will Sheryl know how to find me? Write to me?

It hits me: It's been six weeks since I didn't arrive in America. Five since I sent my letter with the two stamps I stole from Thirty-Five. I'm on my own.

—

On buses, subways, and trains, by foot, escalator, and stairs, from early in the morning, through the day, and into the night, Junho and I go until we reach a small building on the outskirts of Seoul where two soldiers meet us, check our IDs, laugh, and then walk us in. Inside, a lieutenant holding a cigarette in one hand and an instant coffee in the other says, "Welcome. From now on I am your father."

—

Five hours a day, I do Korean substitution drills:

3. Substitution Drill

1. 준급해으른 대전까지 얼마나 걸티나요?       How long does it take [to go] to
                                            Taejon by Semi-Express?

2. 완해으른 목포까지 얼마나 걸티나요?        How long does it take [to go] to Mokpo
                                            by local?

3. 특급으른 쾅주까지 얼마나 걸티나요?        How long does it take [to go] to
                                            Kwangju by Special Express?

4. 급해으른 인천까지 얼마나 걸티나요?        How long does it take [to go] to
                                            Inchon by express?

5. 객선으른 부산까지 얼마나 걸티나요?        How long does it take [to go] to
                                            Pusan by passenger ship?

6. 배튼 제주까지 얼마나 걸티나요?           How long does it take [to go] to
                                            Cheju by ship?

7. 비행기른 강능까지 얼마나 걸티나요?        How long does it take [to go] to
                                            Kangnŭng by airplane?

8. 나룻 배튼 강화도까지 얼마나 걸티나요?      How long does it take [to go] to
                                            Kanghwado by ferry(boat)?

9. 전차른 영등포까지 얼마나 걸티나요?        How long does it take [to go] to
                                            Yongdungpo by streetcar?

10. 자전거른 용산까지 얼마나 걸티나요?       How long does it take [to go] to
                                            Yongsan by bicycle?

4. Response Drill (based on Grammar Note 1)

선생: 한국 말이 일본 말만큼 어렵습니까?       Is Korean as difficult as Japanese?

학생: 에, 한국 말이 일본 말만큼 어려워요.     Yes, Korean is as difficult as Japanese,

1. 완해차가 급해만큼 자주 섭니까?          Does a local train stop as frequently
                                            as a Regular Express?

   에, 완해차가 급해만큼 자주 서요.        Yes, a local train stops as frequently
                                            as a Regular Express.

2. 서울의 교통이 뉴-욕만큼 번잡합니까?       Is the traffic in Seoul as crowded as
                                            that of New York?

   에, 서울의 교통이 뉴-욕만큼 번잡해요.     Yes, the traffic in Seoul is as
                                            crowded as it is in New York.

9

Then I read flash cards. This is my job: learning Korean. A weird thing happens, meanings of words and phrases sometimes pop out without me having to think about it. I guess I'm learning.

The 123 Battalion is for misfits who need to learn languages. Usually it's for people they think will be translators, like Junho, to learn English. For me, they have me continuing with the same book that I was using with Lieutenant Shotgun: the 1968 Foreign Service Institute manual from the U.S. government. My guess is that they haven't had many Korean soldiers that couldn't speak Korean and if this book was good enough for the Americans in the sixties, it's good enough for me.

—

Junho sleeps in the bunk above me. Anytime I wake up in the middle of the night, he's awake, scribbling in his notebook.

—

Learning Korean is like having to say good game to a team that whipped you so bad no one can even look up at the scoreboard. Lieutenant Father, who gets off on making everyone who's a lower rank than him call him *father*, doesn't do any of the normal teacher things that teachers do to make you feel shitty, like slowly shake their heads, or sigh when they hand things back. But just being in class with a pair of Ukrainians and a guy from Albania who all work for embassies is bad enough. They're learning quickly. They speak English and five other languages. They're already joking with Lieutenant Father, calling him *old father*, while I'm still making sentences about playing American foot and ball.

Where is Albania anyway?

—

Payday comes and goes and I still get nothing. I ask to borrow some cash so I can get a phone card. Talk to Sheryl. Talk to Dick the lawyer.

Lieutenant Father tells me in English, "You get nothing." Then, in Korean, he says something like, "You, money, no have." Then he laughs.

—

*Jeong*, 정, means connection, the heart and bond of the Korean people. *Han*, 한, means connection, the sorrow and bond of the Korean people.

—

On weekends, we go to war camp. We shoot targets that look like Mr. Kim. North Koreans look like South Koreans because they're all Koreans. Lieutenant Father tells us we're going to join our company on the DMZ after we're done here.

—

More bills find me. I translate one as a loan for industrial equipment. So far my bio-douche-nugget-father has gotten loans for equipment, land, cars (or tea?), and industrial stuff all for a company called Korea Fresh One Renewal. It's like he's starting a factory or something.

—

Korean changes depending on who you talk to.

In America, if you talk to Coach, you use different words. Like, "Yes, Coach," not "Yeah, Coach." But you don't start speaking Shakespeare-like English. If you talk to the captain of the team, you don't talk like you're on the news.

But here, in Korean, you talk to Coach with proper Shakespeare-like English. You talk to the Captain like he's a somebody that went to knife-and-fork school. You talk to your friends and those younger than you like they're dirt, that's the same.

I recite the drills while we toothbrush the grout in the bathrooms.

—

If I see Chantal again, I'd tell her how I really am sorry because we never really talked, just fought.

—

Bunk rooms on floors three, four—which is marked with an English letter
F because Koreans don't use the number 4 because that's the death number—and five. The second floor has bare-walled classrooms that always
smell of chalk, and an office with desks in tidy cubicles for scowling officers like Lieutenant Father. Floor five also has a meeting room with racks
of dictionaries. We come here for mail call.

Today is payday. Every time, I hope that I'll get a letter from Sheryl. Or
Bobby. Or Haesoo. Or anybody. Not sure how they'd get anything to me.
But there's this sump pump in me somewhere deep down that keeps draw-
ing out hope.

This time I get a pay stub for the pay I don't get. It's got a bunch
of formal, heavy-duty verb endings, imnidas, 입니다's. That means it's
official. Each letter of the official verbs looks to stab, gouge, plow bodies into the ground.

Lieutenant Father snatches my pay stub out of my hand, then snickers.
"K-k-k," he laughs in Korean. "Ha! Ha! Ha!" he laughs in English, just to
make sure that I understand that he's mocking me.

"What is so funny?" I say, in Korean, all respectful, a heavy-duty formal
verb ending for a question, imnikka, 입니까?

He taps his single bar on his lapel.

"What is funny, Lieutenant Father, sir?"

"Kojangi," he says, "*something-something* translate *something* or you will
clean shit bucket *something* for—until?—next payday."

"I understand," I lie, in Korean. Lying in another language is easier, I think.

"K-Ha!" the Lieutenant laughs. "K-ha-k-ha-k-ha!" everyone looks up
from their envelopes and watches Lieutenant Father point to an ancient
Korean-English dictionary with a broken spine on the rack. "Two hours, or
you die, in bathroom smell. Kuku! Ha ha!"

Two hours later, I figure out that I have military life insurance. Also,
that I have two beneficiaries. One is the bank. The other, some guy named
Jun-dong, who just got added.

Since I did translate the letter in two hours, Lieutenant Father goes easy on my and Junho's nightly chores. Instead of the bathrooms we get the mess hall.

Who the hell is Jun-dong?

"Name very weird," Junho tells me as we scrub pots. "Very strange. Kojangi family is very strange."

"My family is missing or dead."

"Jun-Dong not missing or dead. Must be family."

A brother I never heard of? An aunt? An uncle? A Korean version of Uncle Rick drinking soju and eating roots? A sister who looks a bit like me—or maybe like Haesoo or Chantal?

It isn't until after we toothbrush the corner grout in the kitchen that it finally clicks into place; if you reverse Jun-dong, you get Dong-jun. JD for DJ. Bio-Asshat-Father is Dong-jun.

Motherfucker.

That asshat has taken out a life insurance policy on me.

Later, I figure out that he's taken a loan against the life insurance. Like taking out a loan on the bet I'm going to go to the DMZ and get eaten by bears.

—

When I'm shining Lieutenant Father's boots, he asks why I got so much debt, being a big rich American. It's not mine, I tell him. I say it won't matter as soon as I'm done and take the first flight out of here.

He laughs so hard he snorts.

"What?" Mwo? I say, forgetting all the respect.

He starts patting my cheek like a dumb child. "You must pay debt," he says in English. "Then can go America. But how you do that when in Army?"

It finally sinks in: they won't let me on the plane even after all of this, not unless the debt is paid.

I talk to Junho. I talk to the Albanian and Ukrainians. I talk to the guards. They all say the same thing. The only ways to get out of debt is to pay it, go to jail, become a Buddhist monk, or work it off in the Army. I'm already in the Army. I'm not getting out until it's paid.

—

By the time Sheryl gets on the phone, I'm hysterical. There are cats meowing in the background and all I hear is her "Hello?" before I just unload: They took me into the Army. They call me big-nose foreign fucker. Bio-Asshat-Father is alive and trying to get me killed to pay for his loans.

I stop in order to gasp and say "fuck" a few times. Junho is making all sorts of gestures of *shhh* and he's stopped picking through the colonel's filing cabinet to do it. The colonel's office is the only one with a normal phone that doesn't get routed through something-something tracking-something tech. It's the only phone for which we wouldn't need a phone card to make an international call. I got no money for a phone card and no one to help me except for Junho. Picking the lock was easy because we didn't have to. For some reason they put the door hinges facing out so all you got to do is tap out the pin with a screwdriver and a rubber mallet. I wish I could say any of this was my idea, but this was all Junho.

"Are you okay?" Sheryl says.

"Is that a joke? No, they're trying to make me pay for Bio-Asshat debts," I say. "They're keeping me here until they do, in the Army, in Korea. I'm sick of eating rice and soup, Sheryl. I need to get out of here, get a protein shake, kill Bio-Asshat. And where the fuck were you? Didn't you get my letter? Didn't you think it was fucked up that I never got off the plane?"

"Bucky, stop. Breathe," she says.

"I'm breathing," I say. "Why the hell aren't you fucking helping?"

"I don't hear you breathing," she says.

"Goddammit, Sheryl!"

Junho shushes me again, but I'm livid.

"Fucking just do what I say," she shouts. Then I hear her breathe. It's shaky and choppy. "Let me hear you breathe, please."

I put the talky bit of the phone up to my nose.

"Okay," she says, "okay. I want you to repeat after me."

"This isn't the time for motivation," I say.

Junho kicks my shin. I nod, take a deep breath. Then he puts his small flashlight in his mouth and pulls out files from the cabinet.

"Bucky?" Sheryl says, and sniffs. "This is exactly the time. Repeat after me. Every day . . ."

"Every day . . ."

"And every way . . ."

"And every way . . ."

"Life is getting . . ."

"Life is getting . . ."

"Better and better."

"Better and better."

"Say it again like you mean it."

"Every day and every way life is getting better and better," I say. Then I sniff. I feel the heat behind my eyes and cheeks and throat, and the hot ball of snot and shame and hurt and loneliness and fear and sickness cool a bit. Drop a bit. I swallow really hard and stab my tongue up to the roof of my mouth to keep myself together.

"We need to tell ourselves that, to keep ourselves together," Sheryl says. "To keep hoping."

"Hope? I don't need hope. I need help."

"I had to tell the same thing to Bobby. He's in boot camp now too."

"Are you hearing me, Sheryl? I'm in deep. I'm going to die here."

"They're feeding you? Are they keeping you dry, right?" she says. "We'll figure this out. You'll be okay. I'll talk to Graham—"

"You're not hearing me," I say.

"Bucky!" she screams. I can see her in my head by the towers of bills and coupons, in her pajamas, a Mustang Cool burning in the tray, bracing herself against the kitchen wall. She's teary, flushed. "I'm hearing you, Bucky, and I don't know what to do. Richard said there's nothing we can do."

Worse and worser. "Tell me, *Mom*, would you let Graham's kids rot in jail? Would you let them get fucking deported? Would you lie to them? Do you get them to call you Mom? Did your *DJ* ever meow? Pay you money to take me? Lie to me? Fucking tell Uncle Rick to tie this fucking gook to a tire? Huh?"

There is a long pause before Sheryl says, "That's not fair."

"Fair?"

Junho is waving. He's motioning that we need to go. Our time's up. Outside, I hear the garbagemen driving up to the dumpsters beside the building. After they leave is when the next guard rotations start.

"You're not my mother," I say, and hang up the phone. Junho's already closed the filing cabinet and, in just a minute, we hang the door back up and it's like it never happened.

Then I think I hear Sheryl crying into the phone. Did the phone not set on the cradle?

Junho jerks me along down the hall. I hung up the phone. Of course I did. And by the time we are back in our bunks, I feel nothing. Absolutely nothing. No hurt or anger or hope or concern or fear or anything. I don't feel the cracks in my hands from the bleach we use to clean the floors or the cold blowing off the window onto my buzz cut.

Like a black hole where a body is supposed to be, hollowed and invisible. Just a uniform over air.

I feel like a lie.

Two weeks from now will be my hundredth day in the Army. That's when I'll get my first furlough. Five days and four nights. Maybe go to Communes and apologize to Chantal. But all I can think of as I touch myself is British girl, only her body, her face gone behind all that red hair, her breasts everywhere.

—

The colonel's door falls off while he's yelling at Lieutenant Father and slamming and opening the door to punctuate every insult. It makes a ping and a pop and tips over, one corner right into the tile. That makes him angrier. He tosses the door onto the floor and gets Lieutenant Father into a wonsan right there on top of the fallen door.

The colonel calls him gay-se-ki and kicks him. Repeatedly. Not hard enough to hurt him, but just hard enough to bring a big smile on his face for the rest of the day.

I have no idea what set the colonel off.

—

How long does it take for the phone company to charge an international call to the Army?

How long will it take before Junho finally tells me what he was looking for in those filing cabinets?

Does the colonel know that I screwed up the pin on the top hinge and that's why it broke and tipped and dug the door's corner into the floor?

Is there a serious punishment for making long-distance phone calls?

Does anyone else hate the gold cat on Lieutenant Father's desk, the one with the paw always rocking, always waving?

—

Dreams come now in between blinks. Eyelids close, then it's like this:

Eyelids open. The clock says it's been five minutes. Days pass on the calendar and I'm not even sure how.

Digging my fingers into the bunk helps. Picking at scabs and calluses is better when they bleed.

When did I sleep a whole night?

Who was I when I could sleep a whole night?

—

The weapons locker is on the first floor. I know where the key is. There are five grenades in the back corner box with the thin skin of dust.

—

In two days I'll go on furlough. A vacation without a dollar. Maybe I can hitchhike. Maybe track Bio-Father. End him.

—

어이없다, o-iee-op-da, means "without a handle."

It's like trying to grind rice into flour between two millstones, but you don't have a handle to grab on to.

Whenever you can't do what you're supposed to do, or if you do, then it will undo what you want to do, that's "without a handle."

Whenever something is supposed to make sense but can't because if it did then it wouldn't make sense, that's o-iee-op-da.

Junho says I'm here because I'm o-iee-op-da.

—

Lieutenant Father sends me out alone to get ten boxes of Choco Pies. At the supermarket checkout I hear an old woman complain about soft spots in the watermelon she's trying to buy and ask for a discount. A man in a suit with a glittery tie argues on the phone that he isn't done and has to work all night. He's got a box of energy drinks in one hand and asks the teller for three packs of THIS cigarettes. On the street, by a bus stop, two women talk about how the bus shelter's bench is heated. And the guards at the box in front of our building complain about the cold and wish they had girlfriends to warm them.

They're all speaking Korean, and now, like a light switch, I'm understanding them.

I'm already through the door when I realize that I could have made a run for it. Didn't even cross my mind. I'm just a thing that goes through the motions.

## 39

A LONG TIME AGO, IN THE WEEK BEFORE UNC RICK TRIED TO HANG HIM-self off the backyard cedar and Fontinot was supposed to come and sweep me away to a better place after seeing me tear up the practice field, Bobby and I got so drunk that Sheryl woke us up by swinging two pans together. You'd think they'd make a gong sound. Instead they screech. Squeal so loud the gunk in your lungs loosens and you wake up with your chest crackling and burning like a road flare in a pond.

"Wake up!" Sheryl yelled. She scratched the pans together in the hall-way. "Family breakfast!"

Family breakfast used to be on Sunday mornings with toasted waffles, fried Lit'l Smokies, and Sheryl telling Bobby and me to clear the junk mail from the table where we'd eat. No radio. No TV. She'd pray, secret and hum-like, until she came to *Amen* and smiled. Uncle Rick always timed it so he'd arrive after *Amen* and would go directly to the coffee maker and pour himself a cup.

Sometimes we'd go to McDonald's. If it wasn't too cold we'd take the McDonald's to the park by the bridge and eat at the picnic tables, tossing crumbs out for the birds. Uncle Rick would show up with a cooler full of freezer-burned, multicolored bricks of leftovers. We'd chuck the bricks as far as we could into the water, even Sheryl. "If we had goggles," Uncle Rick would say, "we'd see those fish on it like hogs in shit."

What did we learn that week? Who did we meet? Why did I throw my Matchbox car at Bobby? Why did Bobby sand down a leg of my chair? These things Sheryl would ask between munches. "Family stuff for family breakfast," she'd say. "Isn't this great?" But that was before Bobby said he was going to join the Army, before Sheryl started dating Graham. And I started eating clean to get that extra second on my forty-yard dash.

At the table Bobby was staring at his coffee. It looked like he hadn't moved it since Sheryl set the cup in a dale between the coupons and credit card offers. Fat crackled in the kitchen.

"You two, clear that table," Sheryl hollered from the kitchen.

I leaned against the wall. Bobby didn't flinch.

"Clear it now!" Sheryl shouted. That rattled in my head. "Now!"

Sheryl's shouts are huge for a woman her size. But that angry biting tone all moms seem to use on their kids, Sheryl never had. Her voice has the boom of books dropping. When she's mad, she hollers, "Assholes!" A couple of times when we were little she chased us around with a wooden spoon or a metal spatula, and she could keep it up for a good long while. She had always gone running and did crunches on an inflatable ball in her room. But she never hit us hard or anything. Once broke a big wooden spoon on Bobby's ass. But that one was already cracked. When she shouted we listened, because we didn't want her to get all quiet and teary-eyed. That was the worst.

"NOW, ASSHOLES!" She stomped in the kitchen and some of the credit card offers fell off the dining table.

Clear the junk mail. Pile them in the cardboard box by the trash can. Wipe the table off. Set the paper tablecloth. Set the forks and knives. We did these things, then Bobby and I sat in our spots.

"No, no, no. You two get the plates."

We got our plates, our SunnyD, and sat around the table like old times, only the syrup was in a glass bottle in the shape of a maple leaf.

"What's that?" Bobby said.

"Hush," Sheryl said, closing her eyes, her arms on the table like she was holding it down.

"Seriously," Bobby said.

"Sy-rup," I said.

"No shit. Did you get it?" Bobby asked.

I shrugged.

With her eyes closed Sheryl snatched both our hands, tight, like we were thinking of running out the door or falling out of our chairs. "What we've got won't get us to God," she said, " 'Cause what we've got is only from our efforts before. The only thing that saves us is the work we do now."

Bobby was pie-eyed. I think I was too.

"The only thing that saves us are"—she opened her eyes, looked at me with this slight smile and then she looked at Bobby—"the deeds we do and the family we keep. Amen."

She let go. She grabbed the bottle and dripped lines of syrup along the waffle ridges, north and south, south and north. She set the bottle closer to me and started sawing her waffle with the gritty edge of her butter knife.

"Bobby, close your mouth before it catches flies," she said.

Bobby closed his mouth. I poured an X of syrup on my waffles and a bit off to the side to make a dipping pool for the Lit'l Smokies. Bobby just stared at the syrup bottle when I put it back in the middle.

My stomach twitched. I cut a nub of sausage and dipped it in the syrup. Syrup and Lit'l Smokies were the best, simply the best. Thousands of times better than four boiled eggs and three handfuls of carrots and celery and SolidCoreBullet Creatine. I swallowed. I waited for my stomach to kick me out to the bathroom. The nub dropped into the fire and calmed it. I tried to say, *Mmm*, but I think it came out like I was being kicked on the ground.

"Sheryl," Bobby said.

"Mom," Sheryl said.

"What?" Bobby said.

"I'm your mother," Sheryl said. "Call me Mom from now on."

"Okay, *Mom*," he said.

"Say it nice," she said.

"What's this about?" he said. "Fucking leaf glass syrup and you waking us up banging pans, talking God and Mom?"

"Don't you use bad words with me," Sheryl said. "Talk to me nice."

"Buck?" Bobby said. "Help me out here."

The waffle was crumbling with little puffs of waffle dust and gravel in my mouth. I shook my head no. I might've been groaning again, but the waffle crunched loudly.

"Bobby?" she said.

"The fuck is going on?" Bobby said.

She dropped her utensils on her plate, clanging with all the power of all the death metal that ever has, or will be, made. "I used to think that *fuck* was just a word," she said. "I thought that because I wasn't around enough, what right do I have to come down on you kids? What right? And this morning, first long night of sleep in a long time, and I wake up and . . ." She stopped. Shooed a bad thought away from her with hands like it was a horsefly. Breathed deep. Gave out an *ahh*, then slurped a bit of coffee. We listened to the oven hood wheeze.

"I'm so thankful you're alive," she finally said, holding on to her coffee cup with both hands, prayer-like. She set the coffee down and grabbed our hands. "Both of you. I was so thankful." She let go of our hands. "Then I thought about strangling both of you in your sleep. Hit you two with the pans, but then I thought, waffles. Nice bottle of maple syrup. Because how do you two drink two bottles of liquor and not be dead? There's a bullet hole in your windshield, Bobby. I've raised two boys so stupid that they shot a gun through their own windshield. Their own fucking windshield! And God knows what else . . . And drunk! Driving drunk! And puking! And, and, probably knocking up one of those Bennet girls . . . Shooting guns and drunk and sex? What kind of mother have I been? What have I done?"

They were both looking at me.

"What?" I said.

"You're drooling," Bobby said.

Sheryl sniffed. "Drooling, shooting, drinking my cleaning gin? I know we're crummy, but this? What is this?"

What this was, was Bobby and me drinking so much because Bobby got a call from his bio-father from the pen. A message I caught on the machine saying that Bobby's bio-father was dying and that he wanted Bobby to come and see him before he died. What this was, was Bobby needing a drinking buddy and me being so wound up like one of those clocks and deciding that I needed to blow off steam. We drank. We drove the Yota while slinging my .22 out the window and taking potshots at stop signs, and bear-crossing signs, and one time Bobby forgetting to lean the barrel out the window and shooting through the windshield, caking everything in the cab with the smell of gunfire.

I wiped my mouth with the leftover paper napkins from McDonald's. Bobby had that dumb look on his face like he shat himself. He couldn't think of anything to say. I couldn't think of something to say. Sheryl buried her face in her hands. Bobby kicked my shin but it didn't hurt like it should. Maybe it did but my body didn't seem to care like it should.

"Um," I said, and nothing else came out.

"Sheryl?" Bobby said.

"Mother," she said from behind her hands, "I'm your fucking mom, goddammit!" She dropped her hands, eyes all teary, and said, "Graham gave me the syrup after he asked me to move in with him. It's Canadian. Cost twenty bucks. He forgot to take off the sticker."

"They used to make molasses from maple syrup," Bobby said. "That's what a teacher told me. I've never had molasses."

I swallowed. The waffle slid down.

"Are you going to do it?" Bobby said. "Move in with him?"

"Do you two think I don't love you?" Sheryl said.

I stopped sawing on the waffle.

"Is all of this," she said, "because you two think I don't love you?"

"No," Bobby said.

I nodded, then shook my head. I was lost. I didn't drink often and didn't know how to handle hangovers. I wanted more Lit'l Smokies, but now was not the time to go for them.

"Since when does Bucky drink?" Sheryl was looking at Bobby. "Was that your doing?"

"No, no," Bobby said.

"You two don't like it that I'm trying to move on, be happy, with Graham, so you just drink and get stupid? Treat me like some foster mom?"

"It ain't that," Bobby said.

I shook my head.

"Then what is it? What is it?" Sheryl said.

I didn't know what to say. Bobby neither.

They were looking at me again. I swallowed and wiped again.

"I've got two stupid scared boys," Sheryl said. "We're a family. Maybe we haven't done a good enough job at that, but I'm going to try. I'm going to leave work on time. We're going to have family breakfast. I'm going to do what I can before you two go out on your own. We're family. I'm your mother. I'm going to see you two into adulthood."

The cordless rang. Sheryl went to grab it in the kitchen.

"I bet it's Daddy," Bobby said.

"Clean your plates, assholes!" Sheryl said. "Hello?"

"No prob, *Mommy*," Bobby said.

"Who's Daddy?" I said.

"Who do you think?" Bobby said. He put his last two Lit'l Smokies on top of his waffle and folded it like a hot dog.

# 40

MY TRAINING ENDS WHEN A WOMAN IN A SUIT COMES IN WITH A PAIR of stout, grim-faced MPs. She looks familiar in the way people in suits all seem familiar. In front of the colonel's office, a sergeant has to grab and move the door off to the side for them like a boulder that plugs a cave. It isn't fixed yet. He places it back after the woman and the MPs go inside.

The door to our classroom has a view to the colonel's door. Every few minutes we hear the colonel shout without the formality of imbnida, 입니다. He's lobbing "half-speak," which you use for people you don't need to respect, like family and douche-nuggets.

Lieutenant Father keeps looking out our door and at the colonel's. Finally, the Albanian asks if the lieutenant is okay. He tells us to do the substitution drills from the beginning of the book to the end of the book and then he steps out and closes the door behind him.

When the door opens again, the two MPs walk in and say my name. I raise my hand.

They must know about the phone call. Or maybe they're letting me go on furlough early.

They drive me in a loud jeep to a building a few blocks away I would never even peg for an Army building. Inside are soldiers and the building is laid out the same as ours. The woman and the MPs bring me to the mess hall. She sits me at a table and tells me in English, "We just need to record this while it's fresh."

The privates assigned to the kitchen keep looking our way from their stoves and giant pots.

"While what's fresh?" I say.

There's a recorder on the tabletop. The fluorescent lights above crackle and flicker, and metal keeps striking metal in the kitchen. The folding chair wobbles. She's looking at me and leaning on her elbows.

"You don't remember me, do you?" She's smiling. She takes out a pack of cigarettes.

It's Janie. The woman who got me out of jail. The woman who sat next to me on the flight over. I should've recognized her, but I don't see people anymore, just uniforms, like our green fatigues, or football jerseys.

"What are you doing here?" I say.

"My job. You have a way of turning up, causing grief."

"Who do you work for? You a spy or something?"

She shoots a laugh. "Tell me about Colonel Kim. Does he seem very American to you?"

"The colonel, American?"

"Yes," she says. "Does he put ice in his drinks? Does he talk to you in English, maybe about American football, or maybe he speaks English on the phone?"

"What does that even mean, *American*?" I laugh. American. *American?* Try to imagine the colonel in a helmet and shoulder pads. "You know, there are many countries in the Americas. In fact, you are the one that told me that. You're the one that speaks with the L.A. accent and likes UCLA football. Aren't you the one with Americanisms?"

"You"—she draws a line across the tabletop with her finger, starting at the recorder—"are on that side of the table. I'm on this side. I ask questions. You answer them, got it? Just because we've met before doesn't mean this isn't an interview, Mr. Nose-aholic. Does he give you preferential treatment?"

This is about the phone call. I should be feeling worried, but I just laugh again. "What do you want? I don't talk to the colonel. I'm a fucking kojangi private that doesn't give a shit."

She's going to throw me into prison, one of those horrible foreign prisons where the inmates shank each other over pudding.

"I hit a nerve," she says.

I give her the middle finger. I give her my thumb between my index and ring finger. That's when the MPs start shouting, and I'm ready for a brawl. But she stops all that with a calm hand raised up for them not to move.

"Is this about the phone?" I say.

"Yes," she says.

"All me," I say.

"Is that so," she says.

"Fine me. Throw me in prison. I don't care."

"Who helped you?"

I think for a moment. No sense in burying Junho in this. "Fuckhead Lieutenant Lee. *Lieutenant Father.*"

She laughs. "And I thought we were being honest because you don't care."

I give her the thumb again.

"You don't seem to realize that this is a serious infraction. Breaking into a superior's office, then lying about who helped you, but that's not really the reason I'm here."

"Then why? Your Bruins not make a bowl game?"

"You were done wrong."

My mouth drops.

She nods for the MPs to grab my arms. But she tells them in Korean that we're going out the back door. We go down a hallway and there are these big windows on one side, interrogation rooms. In the last one, she says stop to the MPs and bends down to tie her shoe. Through the window, in the room, I hear voices speaking what sounds like English. I see a white guy in a suit. Next to him is Sheryl.

Her hair is frazzled in a way that she never allowed. There are white streaks in her hair that are new. There are wrinkles cutting out from her eyes. It's like she aged twenty years.

Across from her are a pair of Korean guys in suits, not Army, from the looks of them.

"Here's what we're going to do for you," Janie says. "You're going to get two minutes with her. You're going to tell her you're fine, and healthy. You must tell her to stop her actions. If you do this, and don't cause a scene in front of these gentlemen, I promise you that when you finish your service you'll go home."

Sheryl's voice is getting louder. She smacks the table and the white guy next to her is telling her to calm down, I think. She's pleading. She's been crying and wailing and now she's using all the motivational tape knowledge she's ever had to try and force a smile, force a phrase to make something that isn't real, materialize.

Sheryl came for me. She came to save me.

"Beyonghak, if you want to talk to her, you must agree to do this," Janie says.

I nod.

"I need to hear it. *I will tell her to stop. I will not cause a scene.*"

"I will tell her to stop. No scene."

"Okay." Janie knocks on the door, then goes in and closes the door behind her. The MPs grip tighter. Janie tells them all a bunch of stuff I can't hear, but it all means that I'm here, right out the window. Sheryl looks at the window, her mouth says, *Bucky?* All the suits stand up and they walk out the door. The MPs let go and I'm through the door and around the table and Sheryl's squealing and I'm hugging Sheryl and she's crying and I can't breathe, she's holding me so tight.

"Two minutes," Janie says. "Remember, Private, the agreement." Then she's out and I'm just there in Sheryl's arms.

"It's okay, Bucky," she tells me. "It's okay. Sheryl's here. Sheryl's here."

She pulls back from me to look at my face. Her face doesn't look like it aged twenty years now.

"You lost so much weight," she says.

"I'm eating. Food sucks. I miss Lit'l Smokies."

"God, I can't even remember the last time you ate them."

"How did you—" I say, but can't finish.

"Oh, I've got friends," she says, "in low places."

"Where whiskey drowns and beer chases?" I say.

She laughs. I laugh. She used to sing that at karaoke night at the Tibicut Bar and Grill. She loves Garth Brooks.

"You're coming home with me," she says.

I nod. I shake my head. I want it to be true. I want to be so small that she could hide me in her jean jacket and take me out of here. For a split second I even believe it. Sheryl can peroxide this wound.

Then I see the two holes they have for the wall sockets. Snakebites.

"They're not going to allow that," I say.

"For now," she says.

"They want you to stop whatever you're doing," I say.

"Well, they can go to hell."

"Can we just be honest? Not wishing, just honest and right now? I'm surviving. I'll get through this."

"Okay," she says.

Then we just stand there, hugging each other like nothing I can remember since I was a little kid and got stung by a bee.

The door opens. Janie says, "Time's up."

We don't let go.

"Time's up," Janie says.

"Miss Monroe," says the white guy in the suit.

"You all go to hell," Sheryl says.

"Please," Janie says, "don't make this more difficult than it needs to be."

I let go. Sheryl doesn't. "It's okay," I say.

"No, it's not," she says.

"Miss Monroe," the white guy says, "this will not help."

Sheryl finally lets go. She's not teary. She looks fierce. I think she's about to hit somebody. She's dead-eyed on the MPs at the door with Janie. She's looking at a pistol on one MP's hip.

"Don't, Mom," I say. "Please, we'll figure something out."

She looks at me, sees something different, smiles. "You're right, son," she says. "We will."

"I'll be okay," I say.

"I know," she says. Now she's teary.

The MPs take me out, each holding on to an arm, Janie leading us down the hall, which echoes our steps. I think I can hear Sheryl asking them, "When you sonsabitches letting him go?" but I can't be sure, because as soon as Janie opens the door it's a blast of cold air and loud honks and a jeep's diesel engine needing a new timing belt.

# 41

I'M JUST A POOR BOY FROM THE WOODS. NOT THE SMARTEST, I KNOW. Spent too much time banging my head in football, I know. But seeing Sheryl, being in her arms, made everything okay for a minute. Calling Sheryl Mom felt right this time. Sheryl must've borrowed a ton of money from Graham to come. That would've hurt her so bad. She'd hates owing anybody anything.

We're in the parking lot, in a jeep. One MP, a sergeant, is in the driver's seat, Janie is sitting shotgun and talking something about accomplices, and I'm in the back with the other MP. The sergeant revs and jerks us out of the spot with the clutch. Janie keeps talking. The MP next to me keeps staring at a Caddy in the parking lot. The sergeant starts the jeep again, revs too much, and eases too quickly, and we jerk and stall. Nobody says anything. Nobody even looks at the sergeant driving. It's like I'm the only one even notices that our driver can't drive.

"Sarge," I say in Korean, "quit fast lifting foot."

The MP keeps vigil on the Caddy. Janie is talking about consequences. The sergeant pops the clutch.

"Sarge," I say, "do you know driving?"

Janie talks. MP stares. Sergeant pops the clutch.

Everyone is pretending this isn't happening. Nobody even winces with the grind of the clutch that rattles the windows.

"What the fuck is going on here?" I shout in English.

The MP is looking at me now. So is Janie. The sergeant says to Janie in Korean, "Sorry, but this jeep has broken down."

"That's a fucking lie," I say in English.

"What did you say, Private?" he says in Korean.

"Kwa-ji-mal," I say, slow and deliberate, to be crystal-clear. It means "lie."

Everything next happens so fast. He slaps me. I lean back and kick him out of the jeep and then the MP beside me whacks me and I kick him out of the jeep, and the next thing I know I'm in the driver's seat, starting the jeep and pulling right up to the road. Then I stop.

I stop because Janie is laughing. That brings me back, that I ought not to take the jeep, that I'm no longer angry, that I'm satisfied in showing that this poor boy from the woods knows how to drive a stick shift on a shit jeep with a spongy clutch and somewhere nearby I've got Sheryl, who's trying to save me, but now I've done a stupid thing like this.

"Beyonghak," Janie says.

"Yes," I say.

"Put it in neutral," she says.

I say sorry to the MPs but they make sure to cuff me tight. The sergeant rides in the back with me while the other MP who had been watching the Caddy drives us all to a small park next to my building, then they take me out and drop me in the grass while Janie sits on a park bench and lights a cigarette.

"Do you promise to be calm," Janie says, "like a person, not some unruly animal?

"Yeah," I say.

"Sometimes good people attract troublesome things," she says. "I don't know if you're good, but let's assume so. Let's assume that you're a hot-headed boy that hasn't grown up, hasn't learned that violence isn't the first solution to everything."

It occurs to me, if I got these cuffs off and got back into my building, I could get into the weapons locker and shoot her, these MPs, and post up on the roof and keep shooting until someone finally lets me go or snipes me from way out. Sheryl wouldn't like that. Definitely not good.

"Let's assume that all of this isn't some sort of well-deserved circumstance for the crimes of your ancestors," she says. "You know, karmic justice."

"You met Sheryl, you think she did some crime I deserve to pay for?"

"Maybe, maybe not. But she isn't your mother. And I am trying to say that maybe this isn't about you or karma from your ancestors." She coughs. "Did you end up finding your father?"

"What do you think?" I say.

"My heart goes out to you. But let's be clear on a few things," she says. "We didn't do this to you."

I raise up my handcuffs.

"That, you did. Your parents, the USA, paperwork, history, did the rest to you," she says. "Your duty as a citizen, here, is to serve. Do you know why? Because there are people, a lot of bad people, who want to take everything from us."

Five grenades. I know where the key is.

"I don't think anyone would serve if they didn't have to," she says. "They look at the North and think that they're still Korean. Like us. But they're not. Perhaps if history had been kinder and all these foreigners hadn't invaded, raided, stolen, then none of this would be necessary, including your predicament."

She lights another cigarette. I'm on the ground and the two MPs are staring through me like they've already dug the hole and tossed me down it and just need to set a headstone.

"You're too angry," she says, "to listen."

"All I ever wanted was to go home."

"Rules say that you can't, because this"—she waves her arms—"is your home. And you are needed to protect it. Maybe you're an exception. You don't know anything. Probably can't stomach kimchi. But the fact is that two systems believe this to be true, so that is reality. You don't matter. Exceptions can't be made. We suffered for this, and just because you didn't grow up here doesn't mean that this isn't your duty. Exceptions might happen later, but not right now."

"What do you even mean? What do you want from me?"

"Quit plotting to get out of here. When you've fulfilled your duty, you'll be able to go anywhere you want."

My duty, she says. My obligations, she means. My ancestors she calls on like they're people I ought to know.

"You," she says, "screwed up with this whole breaking-into-the-colonel's-office thing. Your American mother made it worse by coming here and getting embassies and newspapers involved. We can't even get out of the parking lot without you assaulting a superior. Americans are so violent. But you know what? I sympathize. Like many of us, you too have been done wrong."

"I'm going to die in Korea, aren't I?"

"So dramatic," she says. "Fulfill your duty. Quit trying to make this something more than what it is: two years in the country whose blood you share. If by the end of it you're still so ignorant as to think that they who sent you here are your people, then go back. Many gyopos come here to learn. You just act like a common prisoner."

I hold up the cuffs.

She laughs. "Do your duty. Quit causing trouble. Take your punishments, whether deserved or not, and deal with it. It's your palcha. Maybe learn to say a few things, eat a few things, then leave and tell everyone about how big and bad your blood is."

She takes a silver case out of her purse, takes out a card, and with a pen writes something on the card and hands it to me with both hands. It says only, *Kim Young-eun*, in Korean. No organization, nothing except for *Janie Rocket* on the back side of the card and a number: 010-3348-6969. She smiles. "That number there might be useful someday, since trouble seems to find you."

"My father is alive and taking out loans in my name. Everyone tells me that unless I pay the loans, I can't leave the Army."

"One thing at a time. That's how you deal with your palcha."

"The fuck is palcha?"

"Your lot in life," she says. "If you get lemons, lemonade."

"You know more than you're saying."

"I know that every time I hear about some gyopo getting into trouble, it's bound to be you. I also know that you're not going to the DMZ."

"Where am I going?"

She gets up to leave.

"Where are you sending me?"

She gets behind the wheel of the jeep. "Keep that card."

"How can I stop the loans? How can I find my bio-father?"

"One thing at a time." She starts the jeep and tells the MPs to walk me to my building. "Mind the card," she says to me, then wheels out.

Both of the MPs give me a kick to the ass before saying, "Asshole." Then they take me to my building, uncuff me, and tell me to get my kit. I've got five minutes. I won't be coming back.

—

We take old roads. They curve with the hills and the mountains rather than plowing through them with tunnels. In the valleys there are creeks and trees that look so fresh. It's pretty. There are no towns here, or if there are, the MPs avoid them.

What if Janie is right? Chantal wants to be here. Other people want to be here. Those *others* like me are here. The MPs are talking about baseball. Some team called the Bears and another called the Lions. They're speaking Korean, yet, I can understand them.

We're heading south, away from the DMZ.

*Every day and in every way, life is getting better and better.*

The jeep stops at a railroad yard next to an old bridge crossing a valley. There's a big barn with a few cows sticking their heads out between the slats, chewing and watching us. There's a stopped train of flatbeds with jeeps and artillery, all chained down. Then tankers and containers. An MP walks me to the very back, a car with brown wooden slats and the smell of a silo-sized pile of shit. It looks like a cattle car. It is a cattle car. There are frayed boards with clumps of shit and grass sticking out like thorns. The MP opens the door.

"Get in," he says.

"Joking?" I say.

"No joke," calls a voice from inside.

Junho steps into the light. His cheek is red and there is the beginning of a black eye. "No joke."

The MP shrugs. "Get in."

"Where are you sending us?" I say.

"Orders say put you on the train. So I put you on the train," the MP says, and tosses my bag into the car.

—

Oh-my-god-oh-my-god-oh-my-god: they used trains like these for the Holocaust. Coach Shaw showed us the movies in history class. I clench the card Janie gave me and start memorizing the number. First, a dive right up behind center. Next play, trap play, two times, to the left to the three hole . . .

After dark, when the train slows to where we could count the leaves and hear owl hoots, Junho shouts in English, "You fuck, shit, fuck!" then goes quiet again. I think I can hear him muttering in Korean, in half speak, angry. But it's loud in here.

—

In the morning the train stops and a couple of MPs tell us, "Get the fuck off the train," in Korean. We change to a cheap commuter train named after a flower. It's nice to be in a seat and to look out the windows that give everything a blurry undersea look.

If they were going to Holocaust us, I think, they wouldn't put us on a normal train.

The other passengers move rows away or to different cars. We reek. Junho takes a lone seat right near the door to the toilet. I sit behind him.

The MPs had given us envelopes. When I open mine, it looks like orders. Without a Korean-English dictionary, the only two words that I can make out are written in English: *Love Island.*

"What does it say?" I ask Junho.

"Go away," Junho says.

"Look, Junho—"

"Just go away."

"I'm going to keep asking until—"

"It says we join police on Love Island."

"Love Island? Sounds like a porno," I say, trying to sound cheery and forgetful and apologetic.

Junho keep staring out the window and says nothing.

"Is it like a code?" I say, beginning to feel a little desperate.

"Fuck," he says, "away."

—

What were the files Junho was looking at in the colonel's office? Did he see something he shouldn't have? How did they know about Junho anyway?

—

It's flat out here. Everything looks old, faded blue-and-green-tiled roofs, cracked gray buildings, and wooden frames.

In a town called Mokpo, we switch to a ferry that makes a circuit to a bunch of small islands. Behind all the cars, in the back of the boat, we sit on benches bolted down inside a clear vinyl tent with some farmers passing green bottles of soju. They eye us until finally one comes and sits across from us. He gives one of those concentrated looks like he's trying to read in a foreign language.

"You're going to Love Island, right?" the farmer says.

"Yes," I say.

"Good. We need you," the farmer says. "They call me Rabbit Man." He lights a cigarette.

"Rabbit, Man?" I say.

"I raise rabbits," Rabbit Man says. "Stews. Medicine. Pets." He takes a long thoughtful drag on his cigarette. "Yes, he will use you to solve our dokkaebi problem." He spits.

Junho chuckles.

"Yes, dokkaebis are funny," Rabbit Man says. "Of course, it is a fairy tale, a lie. I know because a dokkaebi would never make one thieving son of a bitch so much money, that's why. If they ever existed, the Japanese would've taken them, like every other thing."

From one of the benches a farmer hollers, "Don't listen to him. He's old, drunk, and crazy."

"You go to hell. He's been stealing your gas from the generator, and you know it," Rabbit Man says. He leans back toward me and Junho. "It's all made up by that thieving, lying sack of shit Cabbage Man. He's trying to con people into dokkaebi insurance and little necklaces that his daughter makes at some useless college. That's why you're here on this ferry. Chung Hee will have you investigate these dokkaebi crimes, and now you will know where to look."

My Korean is good enough to understand push-up. Disassemble your weapon. But Rabbit Man? Cabbage Man? Dokkaebi?

"Hey!" Rabbit Man barks. "Don't look so down, you two. You're going to do the first useful thing done by the government since, well, since they stopped building that gray thing."

For hours the ferry stops at little islands with a few desperate-looking houses and ragged shores. Rabbit Man talks and talks. About how we ought to learn how to scrape seaweed off rocks and how computers will give us cancer. About how the government guys with white hard hats and businessmen in glittering suits came and changed the name of the island from Seaweed Rocks to Love Island. The suits tried to build a travel paradise complete with an information kiosk and hotels looking out onto the sea. They failed. All that remains of that dream are a few concrete hulks and a dome karaoke bar. When the island comes into view, Rabbit Man takes a deep gulp of ocean air, stands, points at Love Island, and says that it is an island of proud fishermen, farmers, and one thieving sack of shit: Cabbage Man.

We are the only two to walk off the ferry; everyone else drives off in their trucks. This doesn't look like a proud island of anything. Directly in front of us is a small convenience store with a large sitting platform covered in yellow linoleum. Standing on it is a man watching us with binoculars. He stands military-straight.

"I don't like this," I say.

Junho spits. "Your fault."

"I said nothing about you," I say.

The man with the binoculars waves us over.

"Liar," Junho says.

Behind the convenience store is a hill with an uneven canopy. Uneven logging. There's trash on the beach, on the pier, and around the convenience store where seagulls circle above. It's cold. When I look behind us there is a straight line where the sky meets the water. Wherever this is, is the end of the country, the farthest away from home I could ever be.

# PART FOUR

## GHOSTS

# 42

"CALL ME SARGE. DON'T CALL ME CHUNG HEE. WE'RE NOT FRIENDS AND I'm not Army, I'm Angibu. Which means you should call me God, but dumb Army chicken heads can't think that big, so call me Sarge. Call me Chung Hee, and I'll drown you both out there by the crab pots."

Sarge says this without looking down at the orders or even taking the binoculars away from his eyes. He keeps scanning the water for something. When he puts his binoculars down he looks at us, Junho first, and then me, and shakes his head.

"I'm sorry." Sarge takes a deep breath. "I'm just surprised you're already here. Seoul usually takes its time, finds ways to make life harder. You're here to make my life harder, correct?"

After a long dumb moment Junho and I say, "No, sir."

"The Army has you guys trained, don't they?" he says.

"Yes, sir," we say.

"You two always respond in stereo?"

"Yes, sir?" we stammer.

"Well, gentlemen, I'm here to let you know that you're going to do something more important than anything you did in the Army," he says, looking out toward the horizon.

Some broken seashells crunch under my shoes. I don't know what an Angibu is and I couldn't point out where we are on a map. I do know this much: this place is going to suck.

"You can see Japanese islands from Busan," Sarge says, "but from here all you can see is the blue. That's why you're here." Sarge looks at us directly. "What were you two doing before you got here?"

"We—" Junho starts, but Sarge shakes his head and points at me.

"We were learning languages, sir," I say.

"Did he just say learning language?" Sarge asks Junho.

"Yes, sir."

"You are not even grunts?" Sarge asks me.

"No, sir," Junho says.

"You don't like letting him talk, do you?" Sarge says to Junho. "I'm guessing it's because nobody can understand him." He looks at me and asks in English, "Do you have a third nipple?"

"What?" I say.

"You heard me. A third nipple," Sarge yells, "do you have one?"

"No, I don't think—no," I say.

"Good. If you did, that truly would be a bad omen," Sarge says. "Do you drink?"

"A little," I say.

"Good." Sarge steps off the platform, then smiles and gives me a friendly punch on the arm. He's my size. But where I'm built to lift heavy things and break them, he's lean yet solid. Like a truck axle.

"Can't trust a man that doesn't drink," he says, then starts fitting caps onto the binoculars. "So," he says in Korean to Junho, "what did you guys do to end up here?"

Junho looks down at the ground and doesn't say anything. I don't say anything.

"Excellent. Just my type," Sarge says. "Seoul has its ways, doesn't it? Well, let me give you guys the tour. This is HQ." He slides open the door to the convenience store. It's small. We've dug holes bigger than this. Everything is dusty except for the bottles of beer and soju.

"There are a couple of futons in the closet behind the register," Sarge says. "Lay them out when you're not on watch."

"Watch, sir?" Junho says.

"Did I ask you a question?" Sarge says.

"No, sir," we say.

"When you're not on watch, sleep," Sarge says. "You two think you've come to a vacation spot where you'll be able to sit around and drink and fish. Nope. We've got a real mission. It will change everything." Then Sarge laughs. "We'll find the dokkaebis." He steps off the platform onto the road and points up to the hill. "That's our hill. Since you Army guys just love calling everything by a body part, let's call it Pepper Mountain." Pepper, gochu, also means dick. "Yes, I like that. Big Pepper Mountain." Then he points to a dark path that cuts between the shrubs. "That's the trail. Run all the way up to the top. Take two minutes to view the island and then get your worthless bodies back. Bring a white rock from the top."

I'm about to ask where to put our stuff when Sarge hollers, "Go!"

—

From the top of the hill you can see the old houses with blue-tiled roofs, green fields hugging the sides of the low hills, and concrete hulks of buildings started and never finished close to the sea. Everything looks old, tired, kept together with Bondo. There's a sandy beach. It's shaped in a boomerang, a cove. I've never seen a cove. I've never seen a sandy beach. On television there were always girls in bikinis on the beach but the only thing on this beach is what looks like fishing net. South, there's stretching blue-green ocean that looks like it cuts off in the distance, falling off the edge of a blue-green paper plate. North there are more islands and at the far edge is this haze, the mainland, I think.

Something small and quick flies past my head. At first I think it's a bug.

"I hate you," Junho says, then throws another rock at me. "You are going on the list, you gaeseki." Son of a bitch. He throws another rock—the size of a fist—and I have to duck.

"Relax, breathe," I say. "Everything is okay," I lie.

He throws another rock. This one hits me in the arm, and it stings.

"Junho, relax," I say. "What's wrong with you?"

"You," he says. "You. You now on list."

"Oh, come on, Junho, what did I do?"

Junho wrestles a long straight branch from some bushes. He tugs. When he tries to free it, he tumbles backward to the ground and his glasses pop off his head. He groans.

I step over and give him his glasses.

"Stupid gaeseki," he says.

I look at Junho. He looks at me.

"What was I supposed to do?" I say in Korean and again in English.

"What was I supposed to do?" he mocks in Korean. He groans as he gets up. He tries shaking off his coat. A pen falls out. He looks down at it and then out at the blue-tiled roofs, the empty hulks of buildings, the cove, and finally out to the flat ocean. He sniffs. "I thought we were friends. I thought . . . Beyonghak, if I have to explain, then you just don't understand."

He reaches down and grabs his pen and a whitish rock on the ground and stomps down the trail.

"Understand what?" I yell, but he just keeps going. I reach for a whitish rock and think of pegging his big head with it.

What don't I understand? These unspoken things you're just supposed to get, like TV shows that everyone else gets to watch because they have cable. People hang it over you. Like I need a reminder that I was ditched and raised poor in a trailer. Saddled with debt from a ghost. Life always pulling trick plays on me.

Chantal said I didn't get it too.

I'm about to run after Junho, tackle him. Beat him until he starts telling me exactly what I don't get. But then I notice something as the breeze comes in and the tree branches creak.

Silence.

I don't hear any birds. No squirrel chatter. No buzz of bugs. Down the road, the beach, the water, I don't see anyone. No cars. No boats. Nobody. The woods smell musky. And there's the ocean going so far it out it splits at a sharp line. It's so much bigger than anything I've ever seen and these woods smell like nothing I've ever known, yet like something I ought to, like a cellar. This is the first time since I've gotten to Korea I'm alone.

—

The Happyway convenience store is the only one on the island, and it's owned by the government. Sarge was the only government employee on the island, so running the store was part of his job. Now it's part of ours. Also, it's where we sleep and live. Sarge lives in a shed behind the store. There's a public outhouse and a second shed that serves as a jail, but its only inmates right now are a bunch of boxes of ramen.

After we find corners for our packs, Sarge tells us to change and we start running the island's ring road. He points out the boat launch with the island's police boat. We run by the karaoke bar and restaurant and the home-stays that Sarge says in English are "bed-and-breakfasts." To me they just look like sad houses that need their gutters cleaned. We do wind sprints in the sand of the cove and it's a new feeling for me, spongy. I like it. By sunset we're running paths along the houses and farm plots. When we get to Cabbage Man's house we stop and Sarge tells us to do a hundred push-ups.

"Tomorrow," Sarge tells us as we struggle on the ground, "you're going to meet these people. And right here is where you'll likely spend most of your time. Everyone just calls him Cabbage Man. There"—Sarge points to the loose rock wall built along the path between houses—"is where you'll have to deal with the most trouble."

Back at the convenience store, Sarge watches us cook ramen. We toss cans of tuna in the pot and he tells us to taste it first. We do. Then we eat from it and pick at kimchi from silver bags. Sarge paces the chip aisle and loops around the beer refrigerators for a long while without saying anything, but his feet, his slurping, his open-mouth chomping are loud enough.

"You two will begin training tomorrow," Sarge says, then tosses the left-overs in the trash. "You aren't Angibu, but when I'm done, you'll be trained like some." He smiles and steps out the sliding door.

"Angibu?" I say. "Sounds like a cut of meat."

Junho doesn't say anything. He unrolls his sleeping mat in the aisle between the chips and the tuna. I take the space by the refrigerators. I'm about to ask Junho again about the Angibu when he turns off the lights, leaving me kneeling on the sleeping mat in the dark. Then he's snoring. I wonder how he could sleep so quickly, but as soon as I lie down, sleep comes like a switch.

An air horn—I think it's an air horn—wakes us up early, still dark, and the next thing I know I'm thrown out of the convenience store out onto the gravelly beach in just my underwear. Sarge is yelling at us to start digging and hands us shovels. We are ankle-deep in the incoming tide. Junho and I shovel and shake. It's cold. It's hard to see. The porch light from the store isn't strong out here but as far as I can tell the mud and gravel we're shoveling out of the hole is just being washed back in with the tide.

Suddenly there's a gunshot. We drop into the water and mud. I look up and see Sarge's silhouette holding a pistol up to the sky. He holsters it. He laughs. "I think I can work with you two. Get up and take the shovels over to the bathroom and rinse them off. Then get changed. We're running."

# 43

*The convenience store's door
squeals from rusted wheels.
No one cares.*

—

Nobody on the island seems to have names, only jobs for names. Tangerine Man, Carrot Woman, the Owner—the owner of the dome karaoke bar and restaurant—Clam Happy, and on and on. Most names make sense. But Four Fingers doesn't make sense. She has all of her fingers. She is a fisherwoman with a scar splitting her eyebrow down to a milky right eye that doesn't blink at the same time as her left.

"So Chung Hee sent you to meet me?" Four Fingers says as she checks her cooler, then tosses it into the small fishing boat.

"Well, he sent us to meet everybody," I say. Which is true. Sarge told us to talk to everyone on the island. Get to know them. Find the odd things. I wanted to ask Sarge what was an odd thing but that pistol on his hip and the way he gritted his teeth stopped me.

Four Fingers's good eye looks at me hard. "What?"

Junho hands Four Fingers another cooler from the small dock. He says nothing while he does it. We've been meeting-and-greeting all morning. No one on this island understands my Korean. They give me this look, like Four Fingers does, long and unblinking, then down at the road or the grass or the water as they figure whether that was Korean or not. Then they smile like passing a fart and Junho takes over the conversation. This time he doesn't bother.

"Sarge sent us to meet everybody," I say again, speaking slower, more carefully. Enunciating.

"What?" Four Fingers says to Junho. "What is wrong with him?"

"Learning disability," Junho says.

"Ah," Four Fingers says. "I saw you three running earlier. I knew there was something odd with this one."

"I'm not odd. I'm American," I say. "My Korean isn't very good."

Four Fingers looks over to Junho. "What does Chung Hee have you doing?"

"Exercising," Junho says. "We're new and supposed to introduce ourselves and learn about the island."

"Well, Chung Hee is the kindest man I've ever met," Four Fingers says and then blinks and rubs her good eye. The bad eye closes slower than the good one. She's got big hands from lifting things out of the sea. "When he first got here he wandered and drank a lot. Nice guy, though, even then."

"Is that so?" Junho says.

"Hard to believe," I say.

"Something clicked, and next thing we know is he's fit. Never see him on that rock anymore." Four Fingers points out to tiny Star Island. "They named it something stupid, I forget."

"Star Island," I say.

"He used to sit out on the beach over there and drink on whatever they call that rock now," she says. "The beach looked green on the far side and so I go out there thinking maybe there was some seaweed, but instead I just find a lot of broken soju bottles. I'm surprised he's alive, honestly. Real nice, though."

"Star Island," I say. "Star Island."

"What is he saying?" Four Fingers says to Junho.

"He likes seaweed from islands," Junho says, and shrugs. "I think."

"Oh come on," I say in English.

Four Fingers nods, then makes a broad smile and gives me two thumbs up. "*Seaweed*," she says.

We help Four Fingers with the rest of her coolers and nets. She's stocky, stout, and strong enough to not need our help. She lets us help anyway, and when we finish, she looks back at the empty dock and sighs. She tells us how the island wasn't always empty. They used to fish a lot. There used to be kids. Young people who flirted and married. But they're all off to the cities for schooling, college, jobs that require test scores instead of callused hands. Now it's just this and the dokkaebis.

"What exactly are the dokkaebis?" Junho says.

"Are you kidding?" Four Fingers says. "You know, the little magical people with the big mallets always stealing stuff?" Four Fingers makes a clubbing motion with a fishing pole.

"Yes," Junho says, "but that's a children's story."

"Oh no, no, no. I'm not getting involved. As long as they, whatever they are, don't take my bait or my fish or . . ." Four Fingers laughs. "Look at me, talking about fishing like it isn't gone already. You can tell Chung Hee that I have nothing to do with it, don't care about it, leave me out of it. If those two grandpas finally convince him to investigate whatever it is, tell him I don't know anything."

There's a long awkward silence.

"We met Rabbit Man," I say. "We haven't heard anything else."

"Those two are old men hating each other like young men. They're from families that have been hating each other for a long time. I'm not sure if anyone is stealing anything. All I know is that only old people live on this island, a bunch of lonely people, like me, who keep going out hoping to catch something different but just come home with less of the same we used to get. Go talk to Cabbage Man if you want. You'll hear as much as you'll ever want to hear about it, especially if you've already talked to Rabbit Man."

Four Fingers starts the motor. "I need to push off," she says. "Nice to meet you two." She turns to me and says very loudly and slowly, "Nice. To. Meet. You."

When we first see Cabbage Man, he is stacking loose rocks that have fallen from a collapsed wall in front of his house. All the walls lining the paths and the farms are just stacked rocks. You can see through them in places and I wonder what's the point of stacking a bunch of rocks as a wall if they're going to tumble over into your cabbage patch every time the wind blows or the crows land. I tell Junho that these kinds of walls wouldn't last for a second in America. We'd just knock them over for kicks at night.

"Do they have walls like this where you grew up?" I ask Junho.

He just keeps his eyes on Cabbage Man, who notices us coming up the drive and waves us over.

"I want you two to go and kick down that son of a bitch's door and tell him to come out here right now," Cabbage Man says.

"Hello, sir," Junho says. "My name is Private Chong Junho and this is—"

"Yes, yes, you're helping Chung Hee. Now, I tell you that this is a crime." Cabbage Man holds up a rock and starts shaking it toward the house across the road. "Look, he's over there laughing at me right now! Do you know how many times he's done this? Do you?"

"No, sir," we say.

"If he wants to knock over my wall I might as well give it to him through his window." He hands me a rock. He hands Junho a rock. "Now go get some justice and throw these rocks through his window, please."

The rocks are heavy and rough. Junho says, "Uh—"

"How old are you?" Cabbage Man says to Junho. "What, nineteen? Listen to an old man and go throw this through that son of a bitch's window."

"Mr. Cabbage Man, I don't think we can do that," I say.

"What?" Cabbage Man says.

"Junho, translate for me, please," I say.

"What? Translate?" Cabbage Man says.

"He's gyopo. Learning disabilities," Junho says.

"You say that again, I'll beat you with one of these rocks," I say.

"I understood that," Cabbage Man says, then something catches his eye and he points again at the house across the road. "I just saw him, laughing. If you're not going to break his window—"

"Sir, please, we'll talk to Sarge about this," Junho says suddenly with a calm tone and then puts the rock down on the ground. "Just tell us what happened."

"You're joking," Cabbage Man says. "What do you think happened? That asshole came over last night and knocked over my wall."

"Which asshole?" I say.

"Which asshole?" Cabbage Man says.

"Which asshole," Junho says.

"Don't repeat to me like I'm deaf," Cabbage Man says. "Rabbit Man.

Without me he has nothing. No grass, no cabbage, no markets in Mokpo. I got him that. I help people, even that asshole. He's mad at me because dokkaebis steal stuff. What do you do when dokkaebis steal? What can you do? I've been very fortunate in my life, so I figure I can help people. So, I sell insurance. My daughter"—Cabbage Man shows us a bracelet on his wrist made of soda can tabs—"she makes these so that the dokkaebis will steal them instead of something valuable. That's what you do, give the dokkaebis something shiny, distracting, and just in case it doesn't work, get insurance."

"We will talk to Sarge," Junho says.

"Good. Who's Sarge?" Cabbage Man says.

"Um, Chung Hee?" Junho says.

"Ah," Cabbage Man says. "And when he tells you to sit on your ass and do nothing but exercise, what are you going to do then?"

I pick up a few rocks and fit them on the wall. "We'll fix your wall," I say.

After fixing Cabbage Man's wall, we finish our rounds meeting the island folk. From what people tell Junho, the dokkaebis have been stealing anything not tied down. Cans of beer left outside to chill in the night air, kimchi out of big jars buried in the backyard, moldy rice left out for the stray dogs, old batteries, rags, gasoline, socks and towels left out on clotheslines. Nothing all that valuable, just the kind of stuff left out by the carport.

"Any thoughts on who's stealing stuff?" I ask Junho.

We're on the ring road. It's dark and it's hard to see with all the trees and bushes hanging over the road and the few flickering streetlights.

"Yeah," Junho says.

"Yeah, what?"

"Yeah."

"How long are you going to keep this up? I get you're angry, but it's you and me and I didn't do anything wrong. I mean, come on."

Something hits me, and I'm on the ground and it feels like there's firewood clamping my neck.

Someone is choking me.

I try pulling on the forearms, but they don't budge, and I can hear someone yelp as things start getting fuzzy.

When things clear up, I see Sarge. First I think I fell down. Then Sarge says you have to go under the forearm, in English. "Leverage," he says. "You have none when you try pulling on an arm that's choking you and you'll just end up gurgling on the pavement."

Junho and I are coughing. The two of us just got our asses kicked. How does that even happen? Sarge must have been waiting for us by the road for the last few hours, squatting in the bushes.

"Americans talk too loud," Sarge says in Korean, "in every language. So, two lessons: the first about leverage and the second about volume. The third, watch out for areas in your track without good light coverage. Let's go."

"Leverage?" Junho says in between coughs as we walk back to the convenience store. "What's leverage?"

"It's what you two need to learn to survive a choke," says Sarge. "To finish this mission we need practice."

"Sarge," I say, "what mission?"

"The mission." Sarge laughs. "The dokkaebis, of course."

At the convenience store we report to Sarge everything we can remember about the islanders we spoke to. We tell him about Cabbage Man and Rabbit Man. We tell him how Four Fingers wasn't sure about the dokkaebis. When we try to move on without mentioning what she told us about Sarge in the beginning, he gives us this look.

"Report everything," he says. "You will report everything."

So we tell him everything. The green glass on Star Island and Sarge being a nice guy. He smiles at that.

Then we eat a generic kind of Spam and rice and kimchi out of a bag for dinner. Sarge tells us to "sleep well to train well." He turns off the lights and steps out.

I wait a long time in the dark for Junho to say something like, *I think we're going to die here*, but he doesn't say anything, his breathing sounding wet and heavy like, *Your fault, your fault*. God knows what mine sounds like.

I don't see any mission. All I see is a place without work where everyone that could get out, did. Two old men, wives gone, feuding like people in worn-out towns everywhere. In Tibicut, Unc and Jerry, his neighbor, used to get drunk and roll around in the grass fighting about who was the greatest quarterback ever. Then there were the Smiths and the Hogarts. They used to cut down each other's lumber when that still mattered, and each other's mailboxes when it didn't. Here they push over walls and talk about how the fishing's gone and dokkaebis. Like a Sasquatch.

Mission? The only mission is to be bored and get crazy.

Junho snores.

—

I've learned that a dokkaebi is a like a leprechaun with a big mallet. It's greedy and not too bright. Eats meat and steals.

—

Sarge orders us to pull a sappy stump out of Carrot Woman's yard. Some neighbors come by to watch us and sip drinks from Carrot Woman's fridge. They talk about the weather and how the fishing dried up, as if they didn't already know. Carrot Woman gives us small juice boxes of soy milk as we dig and chop.

When we're done, we all sit cross-legged on Carrot Woman's porch around a couple of low tables. The food laid out there is some kind of fish stew and rice and all of these little bowls with vegetable sides and shellfish sides in sweet hot paste and dried seaweed. The Army didn't give us anything like this. I didn't even know there were so many vegetables that you wouldn't just throw in a salad. They all have taste too: salt, spicy, vinegary, and other flavors with smells that make me think of mushrooms gone bad, but taste meaty and nutty. By smell alone, I ought to be sick, but I'm not. I kind of like it. A better way to get veggies than just blending them up with protein powder.

Carrot Woman just smiles and says the food is nothing when the other people compliment her. Then, as we're finishing up, she looks over at me and Junho, in our fatigues, and says, "The last soldiers that ate with me shot my dog. Then they shot my husband."

Chatter dies. One of the old men, Clam Happy, sucks air through his teeth. "The enemy was cruel. Heartless."

She picks up our plates. Her joints pop.

"But you're too young," Clam Happy says, rubbing his stubble, "to remember six-two-five."

Six-two-five means June 25, the day the Korean War began.

"My husband wrote for newspapers. He was too tough to die that way," she says. "But he wasn't tough enough to keep us in Gwangju. He never wrote again. I never owned a restaurant again." Then everyone looks down at their fishbones and empty plates like she just said we all were going to hell for those things we didn't get caught for. She looks at the dent of ground where the stump was. "He always hated that tree." Then she goes back into the house.

We hear her run the water, clank some plates.

"I've known her for fifteen years," Clam Happy starts, then stops.

Carrot Woman comes back and gives us more soy milk. "Weather is nice today. The air is nice today. And you boys helped out an old woman. Life is nice."

On the road back I ask Junho what the hell was that all about. I have to keep asking for him to finally say, "Riot against bad government," as we get to the Happyway convenience store.

—

A letter comes from a different bank. A new loan, but this time there's a full letter that takes me a couple of nights with my pocket dictionary to decode:

Apparently they are going to notify the authorities if I, as the owner of Korea Fresh One Renewal, don't pay more of the loan or return the KM 70 mobile crusher.

Is Bio-Douche-Nugget-Father operating some kind of demolition crew or junkyard?

—

*The ocean is deep.*
*The current is strong*
*leading away from Love Island.*

—

There's a skinny book holding up one corner of the chest freezer. It's swollen and faded brown and its name is in Chinese. Inside, in Korean, it says it's poetry by someone called Yi Sang.

The first poem is really weird. *Thirteen kids go down a street. A dead end alley is just fine.* Then it just counts them off, *First kid says it's frightening. / Second kid says it's frightening. / Third kid says it's frightening.* And so on.

I don't feel right. I stuff it back under the foot of the freezer.

# 44

WE TRAIN LIKE WE'RE GETTING READY FOR FOOTBALL SEASON. NO TIRES but lots of hills, lots of push-ups. Sarge also makes us do gymnastic stuff: climb trees. Jump, duck, and roll. Trot along the tops of walls.

Then we learn to hot-wire a tractor, a pickup truck. We learn to pick locks with tools and where to kick on the door to open it without tools.

We sneak. We lurk. When we aren't paying attention Sarge tackles us from the bushes, knocks us to the ground, and puts a stick to our throats and says, "Pay attention or you gurgle-gurgle."

We are not soldiers. We are not policemen. We are something that Sarge has decided, and I'm not sure what that is.

—

When the buds start blooming, Junho starts talking to me again. We're cleaning the jail. The ramen boxes and propane cans are out on the grass and we're bleaching the mold. My eyes burn.

"This is shit-terrible," he says.

"Yes, it is," I say.

"Kojangi, I need help. Teach me how to shoot."

Sarge thinks that scrubbing with bleach will steady Junho's hands. When we shoot, my groupings are tight. Junho rarely hits the target.

I want to tell him to eat shit and for me to shit in the toilet water tank the next time he is on bathroom duty. But I cool and say, "Sure."

—

Our duties besides training and running the store also include breaking up fights between Rabbit Man and Cabbage Man in the space in front of the abandoned post office. Islanders gather, the two cuss, shove, and yell, and we come and break them up. They always look too clean for guys fighting in the street.

This time they roll in the dirt. We can't stop them. Sarge has to come and put a hold on their shoulders like Spock, the pointy-eared guy from *Star Trek*, to get them to stop. One of Rabbit Man's rabbits has gone missing. Some of Cabbage Man's kimchi has been taken.

Cabbage Man blames dokkaebis for the rabbit and Rabbit Man for the kimchi.

Rabbit Man blames Cabbage Man for the rabbit, and Cabbage Man for forgetting where he put his kimchi.

When Junho and I go to their fields we find tracks of little feet. Hard to notice, always along tuffs of grass, but there.

We tell Sarge this. He beams.

He tells us, "Good job."

I can't help but smile back.

—

"Do you enjoy being on this island with the Sarge?" Sarge asks. That night we're frying the fake Spam and wrapping it in cabbage. After a few bites, Sarge takes a bottle of soju from the refrigerator, shakes it, and thumps the bottom of it against his elbow. He pours a shot for each of us. He has never been this nice. "Be honest, now," he says.

"No, sir," we say.

"Neither do I. But when I look at you two, and I consider the little bit of improvement that you've made in the brief time I've had you, it makes me proud. But this is not where good operatives belong. Not at all. Even you two don't belong here. Some old retired policeman who likes to swim and farm belongs here. Not us. Would you two agree with that?"

We nod. We drink.

"Now, I've been here longer than the two of you. I had done a lot of good for our country. And then, after doing good, I was sent here. And for the longest time I thought, Why, why, why?" Sarge pours soju on the ground, then another for himself.

"And then it came to me: Sometimes you need a break. Sometimes you need to go somewhere that is neglected, the kind of place where only the incompetent are sent to realize that the enemy is more clever than you expected. I think fate has brought us here. And the time is fast approaching when we will be asked to save the country."

I nod. Junho nods. The only thing that makes sense is that Sarge can't hold his liquor and is getting drunk too quickly. But he isn't slurring.

"The time is here, the enemy is approaching. And I was sent here to stop it. You two were sent here to help me stop it. And by doing so, we will be able to leave the island with a greater glory than we could have hoped for if we had stayed at our old posts. It may have seemed like a punishment but what we do here shall define a lifetime."

Sarge pours another drink and raises his glass for the three of us to toast. We look away from Sarge to drink because he's older and is our superior and we respect him because he taught us things that make us feel tougher than before.

"When we capture these spies . . ." Sarge stares off, lips smacking, savoring some phantom steak.

"Sir?" Junho says.

"Yes?" Sarge says.

"Spies?" Junho says.

"Yes," Sarge says.

"Spies?" I say.

"I already said yes," Sarge says. "Those tracks you found, the stolen food, it's the work of spies."

Junho nods. I nod. Sarge has lost his fucking mind. I worry that I'll give this thought away, so I make sure to look down at the fold-out table.

"You idiots don't get it," says Sarge calmly, in an almost motherly tone. "The North Koreans are here. On this island. Why do you think they even bother stationing people like us on these islands? They station us here because North Koreans used to infiltrate the country from here. Now they are doing it again."

We nod.

"They thought they could banish us here, and be forgotten," Sarge says. "But I've taught you well, and when the time comes we'll make them take us back. Make them see who we really are. True Angibu. Understand?"

"Yes, sir," we say.

After finishing a couple more bottles, Sarge sends us off to walk the island ring road and look for anything suspicious. Sarge is probably going to take a nap but we can't be sure. So we walk the ring road.

When we get back to the convenience store, Sarge is gone.

"Junho, is Sarge serious?"

We clear the table. "Yes."

"How can you be so sure?"

"He's Angibu."

"What exactly is Angibu?"

Junho checks the corners. Peers out the window to Sarge's shack. "Korean CIA. Very scary. You know Gwangju? You remember Carrot Woman's story? That's Gwangju. That's Angibu."

We unroll our mats. We turn off the lights.

"Junho, I'll teach you how to shoot," I say in the dark.

"I will take Kojangi off the list," Junho says. "But this is all your fault."

"List?"

"Many people wrong me. I keep list in notebook."

"Why do you want to remember that?"

"Revenge. Worse than death, revenge."

I smirk. I'm glad he can't see me.

"Some people," he says in English flat and serious, "never get punishment. But I patient. I dedicated. Someday I hurt them. Burn their houses down. Send photos of cheating wife. Punish wrong."

That night I listen to the water beat the beach outside, rough and busy. I stare up at the water spots on the ceiling, waiting for a door to creak or a round to chamber.

# 45

IT'S SUMMER. LEAVES WILT. JOGGING ALONG THE PEBBLE BEACH OR THE cove is hot and I've got rashes under my pits. There are no air conditioners. Everyone just hangs out under shade in thin clothes. You can see the outlines of the old women's breasts hanging like dough. At night everything sighs with the cool breeze coming off the water. But it's still sticky-hot. I like patrolling along the beach at night. The crunch of rocks under boots is soothing.

We jog the trails. We watch the water. We check clumps of bushes and find nothing but mounds—burial mounds, I find out—overgrown and unvisited. Some of them have little stone posts with old Chinese writing on them that Junho can't even read.

But no dokkaebis. No spies.

—

This morning, the ferry brings in a tour group. When this happens, the tourists march off the boat, eyes down on their tourist pamphlets, then stop right on the pier when their eyes rise and see the island. They smirk and follow the guide, a guy who lives back on Mokpo who takes them on a tour up the hill, past the ruins of collapsed farmhouses and half-built hotels. Most go back on the evening ferry.

—

I write Haesoo. I write her to forward letters to Chantal, long apologetic letters without an apology but a summary about what I'm doing, asking what she's doing. I write Sheryl. No responses. I keep writing and each time the guy brings the mail bag to the store I keep looking for an answer but I get nothing, except for notices from banks and credit companies and a lawyer representing somebody saying that they have to freeze my bank accounts. I've never even had a bank account.

There's a pay phone. But whenever I try calling the U.S. with one of the phone cards we have in the shop, it says in Korean, *Sorry, call cannot be completed as dialed*, and in English it says, *Call does not complete.*

—

One evening, we're sweating on the porch and watching Sarge bob on the water in the dinghy just outside the cove. He's patrolling, scanning the water with a fish finder or something. Then we get a call from Rabbit Man.

"It's too noisy," Rabbit Man says.

"What is?" I say.

"Will you all just shut up? Some of us have to work tomorrow," he says.

"Who is too noisy?"

"My God, a Tuesday? All of you on that dock, singing on a Tuesday?"

"The dock?"

"Who gets drunk on a Tuesday?"

"The north dock? The one by your house?"

"If you don't stop it, I'll go out there and break a bottle on your head. Good night."

I hang up the phone beside a golden cat with a rocking arm. Junho is out on the porch smoking a cigarette. He has a flashlight that he occasionally turns off and on to let Sarge know that we are still awake. We have a cell phone but Sarge says we got to save our minutes.

"I think that group of tourists that came in today are being loud on the north dock," I say. "Rabbit Man just called. We should tell Sarge."

"You should tell Sarge."

"You've got the light."

Junho starts tapping the flashlight against his leg. Sarge calls on the cell phone and Junho tells him the situation and after a long hiss Sarge orders us to go to the dock and let no one escape.

Who could they be other than tourists? Spies? Murderers? An invading army of couples who don't read up on where they're going so they end up here?

"Bring your pistols," he says, loud enough that I can hear it.

The dome restaurant is at the end of the north floating dock. I don't think the dome restaurant has a name, the sign just says FOOD, BEER, AND SINGING ROOM. Rabbit Man was right, you can hear the singing for miles. One woman's voice eagle-screeches through the night. A man's voice grates the air with sinus problems. They are all there, out by the front door of the restaurant, on the dock, smoking and drinking and dancing just beyond the dock light. It sounds like they took a portable karaoke machine out from the restaurant.

When we emerge from around the bend, they see us. Immediately there is a crash of glass and screams and yells and giggles as the big pale spotlight from Sarge's boat reveals them in the broken window from the restaurant. They're old. The men with white hair and jumpsuits and the women with perms. They power-walk off toward the woods.

"Should we chase them?" Junho asks.

"I don't know," I say.

Sarge shouts from the water, "Get them!"

They are fast. At the trailhead leading up the hill, they've already ducked into the woods and we don't see them at all. This is going to be an all-night thing. I get quick shivers from the breeze on my sweat-drenched shirt. We turn on our headlamps and go in.

For hours we search. We catch a couple who giggle and stumble out onto the trail. "You got us. We surrender." We take their photos with the cell phone and take their ID info and tell them to expect a call the next day.

"You're not going to arrest us and throw us in jail?"

"No." It isn't like they're going anywhere.

Up the hill we catch a few more, one snoring in the bushes beside the trail, another perched on a boulder smoking a cigarette that, from a distance, looked like a red firefly. The next we catch by his loud voice drunkenly whispering into his phone, saying things like, "win-win" and "government must protect investors."

From the summit we gaze down the slopes, looking for light, for movement. It seems like the rest made it back to their rooms. Moonlight strips and softens the color from everything, the dark veins of trails, the sweeping light from Sarge's boat on the north beach, the brush and canopy all the way down to the shore and the moon-lacquered ocean. Really cool. Really peaceful.

South past the cove there is something on the beach. Something shaped like a Twinkie. It doesn't glisten in the moonlight.

"What's that?" I ask.

Even though I can't see Junho's face, I know he's squinting. "I can't see anything."

"You think those old people are making a run for a boat?"

"They're drunk."

Junho tries to call Sarge but there's no signal.

"Well?" I say. "Let's go and check it out."

"We should talk to Sarge."

He's got a point, we should wait for instructions. What Sarge wants us to do changes with the twitch of his eyes. But if the tourists make a run for the boat and we just watch from above, dicking around with the cell phone as some of those drunks fall out of the boat and drown, zoomed out with the riptide, that would be very bad.

Junho is still trying to call.

"Junho?"

He doesn't look over at me. Just keeps dialing and listening to the phone.

"Think about what happens if we don't go down there and check that thing out. What do you think Sarge would do to us?"

He nods. He puts the phone in his pocket and starts for the beach.

At the beach we turn off our headlamps. If it is a group from the bar, we want to get close without alerting them. But as we get closer we can tell this Twinkie-looking thing isn't a boat. It's the length of a pair of pickups and about as wide as one. It's beached about twenty feet from shore in shallow water and must have gotten stuck as the tide went out. The water is only shoelace-deep. There are no marks. The whole thing is painted sea-green.

My first thought is it's a buoy or a gas tank fallen from a fighter jet.

Then we hear it, like the slam of a baseball bat against the side of a car door. Then a wail.

There are people inside.

It's a submarine.

Junho and I both unholster our pistols and point them at the submarine, not sure exactly what to point at. As we get closer we hear more yelling. There is a struggle happening inside. Bangs of metal. Groans of pain.

Thunks of bodies. Junho bends a knee and I step onto it and hoist myself up on a handhold on its side. Suddenly it's quiet inside. I put my hand up to my mouth for Junho to keep silent and I keep my pistol pointed at what I think is the main hatch.

I'm not sure how long I wait there pointing at the hatch, at this cockpit-looking thing, with Junho in the water pointing up with his pistol. It occurs to me that he might shoot me.

We wait for a long while. We are silent outside, and whoever is inside is quiet too. We wait until the hum of Sarge's dinghy chops through the night toward us. The hatch begins to squeak and my heart pounds so hard I swear that whoever is in there can hear it. The hatch opens and a man's face looks up and I look down with my pistol pointed at him.

"Get out," I say in English.

He keeps looking up at me as if he's drunk. Then he looks at the dinghy approaching. Sarge has the big light on us and everything is bright.

"Get out!" I say in Korean.

"Get out," Junho says, along with a bunch of stuff that I don't catch. I think it is that formal stuff we are supposed to say to North Koreans, that thing that I never learned but I figure goes along the lines of, *We got good food, so be cool.*

The man looks back at me, his face glistening in the light with sweat. He's steady, waiting for me to do something. There's a terrible diesel smell along with something else coming from inside. Finally the man looks down, as if he is going and closing the hatch like I'm selling Tupperware for a Pee Wee team.

"Get the fuck out!" I shout in English. I kick the hatch and it startles him and me, and I guess Junho too, since he fires a shot in the air. The guy in the hatch throws up a hand in surrender.

"O-iee-op-da," I think I hear someone say inside the sub. *Without a handle.*

—

By the time we get all four men out of the sub and out on the beach, Sarge has shot his rifle twice in the air. We lay them in a row with their hands zip-tied. When Sarge talked about the ways of spies, the way of the Angibu, and the way of the North Koreans, I didn't imagine who these people were supposed to be. I thought he was nuts. Another person on this shitty island thinking about dokkaebis lurking in the bushes. But here they are: North Koreans. Somehow I imagined that people who go on tiny submarines and do spy stuff would look like James Bond. These guys don't look like Bond. They don't even look like Mr. Kim. These guys are wiry, short, and smelling of diesel and piss. They cough a lot.

Inside, the sub is dark. I go in with my headlamp on and look to make sure there aren't any more on board. It's foul. Paint and body stank and that sanitizer used in porta-potties. I find a fifth guy with a bit of blood coming from his forehead in the corner. His eyes are open but he doesn't say anything. I tap his cheek and he mumbles.

I think he says, "Clean floors. Why doesn't he clean floors?"

Junho and I manage to pull him out on the beach. And now we have five North Koreans. That we pulled off a mini-sub. Five spies.

Sarge grins.

This is the mission. Somehow he knew: It wasn't dokkaebis, or old people screwing with each other. It was actually North Koreans.

The prisoners see Sarge but they don't seem to be all that excited or confused or anything. They breathe calmly and don't squirm in the zip ties. It is eerie, because no matter what you catch that's living, they're supposed to have that fear. These guys don't have it. I figure that if it were me, I would be a mess of temper and panic.

We hurry them to the convenience store. It is going to be another warm day and the adrenaline is gone and my eyes are heavy. We take the long way of small trails in the woods just beyond the road and the cabbage patches. Sarge wants to avoid the eyes of the farmers out in the fields.

We lock the North Koreans up in the jail. It still smells of bleach. We padlock the door. Then Sarge's smile grows and he is all red and looking like he's about to cry. Sarge grips us on the shoulders. He squeezes. "Good job," he whispers. "Good job."

I feel a tug in my cheeks too. We did something. We really did something. For once in my life, something I was trying to do, or at least trained to do, is paying off.

He clears his throat and says, "The clock is ticking."

I want to ask him what clock. But when I look over at Junho, he's got this steady face like he knows what needs to be done.

Sarge looks up into the sky as if in prayer. "We are Angibu and nothing else." After a moment he raises an I've-got-your-nose fist to the sky.

We look up and I see a couple of shooting stars. One of them not burning up, just moving across the sky.

"The only things above are satellites," Sarge says. "American satellites."

# 46

SARGE TELLS US TO GET THE SUBMARINE OFF THE BEACH AND HIDDEN somewhere before sunrise. "This must be kept a secret for now," he says. Then he goes in the jail and all we hear is whispering.

Junho and I think. We need a winch and a boat carrier. We've got a broken-down tractor with flat tires.

"Four Fingers has a tractor," Junho says. My first thought is, Yes, she has a tractor, but she might say no. And to keep it a secret we can't tell her about it.

"You mean steal it?" I say.

Junho shrugs.

The tractor is parked inside a carport surrounded by tall grass. Grasshoppers are chirping and jumping. It's a bit away from the house, maybe far enough not to wake Four Fingers.

"Wait until I give you the signal," I say, then walk over to the windows of the house for a look. It's hard to tell through the frosted glass, but there's a long lump of a body sleeping on a mat in the middle of the floor. I wave toward the carport and suddenly the tractor starts and jerks forward.

Junho is better at hot-wiring than I am, but that was fast. Four Finger's outline shifts position but she doesn't get up. When I catch up to the tractor I'm about to ask how Junho did it so quickly—but the key is in the ignition.

The tide comes in fast. By the time we chain the submarine, the tide is already frothing and the holes in the mud give off sucking sounds. We drag the sub all the way to this abandoned-barn-looking building that we use to hold extra police boats. Next to it is a big vinyl-covered carport. We clear out the canoes, kayaks, and rowboats and stack them in the carport and pull the sub into the barn. We cover the sub with spare tarps.

It's morning by the time we finish, and when we step outside Four Fingers is waiting.

"Why do you have my tractor?" Four Fingers says.

"Well," Junho says, "we needed it." Which is probably the most honest answer we could give. Four Fingers's good eye looks down at the long gash in the ground from the carport all the way back to the beach.

"There was a gas tank from a jet that was floating in the water," I say. "Could've caused problems."

She looks at me, and then at Junho for translation. "We had to clear some big trash, immediately."

"Why didn't you just ask?" she says.

"We didn't want to wake you," Junho says.

"Chung Hee knows about this?" she says.

"Yeah," I say.

"Definitely," says Junho. "His orders."

We all look at the gash. Then she looks at us. It doesn't feel good at all.

"Well, okay," Four Fingers says, then she gets on her tractor and starts it. "Tell Chung Hee that I want a full tank of gas. And the next time you two take it without talking to me first, I'll feed you to the crabs."

Maybe she let us off with it because we help her with fishing nets. Because that's the thing you do in small country towns, you help and you trust. You even trust when you know you're being lied to, because you'll get to hear the story later.

But she also has to. We have orders. We are Angibu.

—

We don't sleep. All day Sarge questions the prisoners while we cut the phone lines and shut down the transmitting towers. We siphon gas from boats. We cancel the ferry service by lying about a broken-down truck on the dock that will take a couple days to clear. We go door-to-door and tell islanders as they cook their stews in black pots or as they shovel for clams on the beach that the island is on lockdown. No one and nothing can come or go.

They ask why. We say we don't know. Which is true. Why Sarge doesn't want to call the mainland and get the prisoners out of here is beyond me. People believe us. People trust us. Most don't have people to call and places to be off the island, so a few days of lockdown won't change a thing.

From the jail come whispers and what sound like moans. In the evening, Sarge comes out and locks the jail door behind him. He takes a few steps and then digs a pack of cigarettes from his pocket. He taps it and a cigarette, tobacco side up, comes out, and he laughs.

"I'm not lucky," he says. "An American showed me this."

Sarge holds out a cigarette.

"I don't smoke," I say.

"No, no, a lucky cigarette," he says, and lights it. "You take one cigarette and flip it around upside down and put it back in the pack. When you get it, you're lucky. But we're not lucky, are we?"

Sarge cracks his knuckles. He cranes his neck side to side. Junho is cooking some ramen inside and it's just me and him in the purplish evening. "There are six. I know it," he says. "If we're ever going to get off this rock, we need the sixth." He squints at me as the smoke trails out the side of his mouth. He grins at me. "You are ready," he says. "We're going to take one out. Just you and me. We're going to take him out and let him know that we're worse than anything he has met before."

I nod. I take deep breaths and blink a lot, trying not to look tired.

"Get a shovel," he says.

—

That night Sarge and I take one of the prisoners out, hood him with a pillowcase, and take him up the hill. Just looking at this guy makes me angry.

Having them isn't enough. Turning them over isn't enough, Seoul will only change its mind about us if we bring them something so great they have to say, *Yes, you did well.* This is what Sarge tells me before we go in to grab the prisoner. "You want to be done with military service, pay your debts, and go home. I want to go back and work in Seoul. The only way home is by getting them to talk."

So, we take one out and start going up the trail.

"Where's the sixth?" Sarge asks.

"There are only five," the prisoner says.

"Where's the sixth?" Sarge repeats.

"Only five," the prisoner says.

Sarge and the prisoner keep this up until we get to a glade with a lot of uneven ground, where the trees have fallen and ripped their roots from the dirt. There's also the hole Sarge had me dig.

The prisoner trips on a rut and falls to the ground.

"Where's the sixth?" Sarge says.

The prisoner coughs. His head whips one way and another under the pillowcase as if looking in the right direction is what's keeping him from seeing. Suddenly I feel scared.

"Five," he says.

Sarge kicks him. He groans. Sarge looks at me and motions me to kick him. I shake my head. Sarge grabs my arm and hisses, "Kick this guy for the hell he's putting us through. For us being tossed here to wait for trash—like him—to wash ashore. For being the enemy."

I kick the guy in the ass. I feel the thud of bones.

We get him up and walking a few more steps before he steps in a rut again and falls.

"Where's the sixth?" Sarge says.

"Five," he says.

Kick.

"Where's the sixth?"

"Five."

Kick.

We keep this up for a long time. He doesn't struggle against the zip tie. He moans, he growls, but he doesn't resist. The taste of dust is in the air every time we kick him.

Six.

Five.

It's as if he wants us to kick him.

There's a bite to his groans. A slow suction of air that has no panic. I don't know why, but I keep thinking this is the sound of pride. This was the way Mr. Kim dragged on his cigarette, the way Uncle Rick sniffed when he shot a deer through the eye.

What do they do to these guys? Is this brainwashing? Is this what it means to belong to something: being willing to take an ass-kicking?

Maybe it's the lack of sleep or the island. I don't know. But every time he says five, every moment he keeps us out here in the dark, I enjoy kicking this guy more and more. But nothing we do gets this man to talk.

—

The next morning, I see Junho by the shed. I bring him some instant coffee. He is sitting at the plastic table smoking a cigarette. His hands are trembling. He is grinding his boots against the dry dirt. "Kojangi?" he says, and then goes very quiet. "What did you do?"

The cicadas rev like chain saws.

"We worked," I say in English.

He stands up, straight, and I see how different he looks now, the purple fade under his eyes thick as shadow. But there's another difference I didn't notice all this time, balls of muscles in his arms, his neck thicker and stronger—almost matching his big head. Solid, he looks solid. And exhausted.

"Rabbit Man came by complaining about the phone. We can't keep this up," he says. "This isn't right."

"What's *right*?" I say. I'm angry. I knock the cigarette out of his mouth. "What's right?"

Junho looks down at his shoes.

"Sarge knows what he's doing. He knew they were here," I say. "He'll get us off this rock."

Junho keeps looking down at his shoes. They have red splatters. The smoke from the cigarette rises between them.

"These people aren't supposed to have anything. No food. No computer games. Just lies," he says. "I gave a cigarette to one. He spat it out. He gave me one of his, it smelled like diesel. But he smoked and I smoked and it was really good. Really good, the best I've ever had."

"So?" I say.

"He said he grew it." He points down at the splatters on his shoes. "That's blood, Kojangi. "They're spitting blood."

I have to look away.

"Someone will get killed." Junho points at his shoe. "Blood, Beyonghak. That's blood. Why doesn't Sarge contact the mainland?"

"They wouldn't talk," I say. "We're doing what we're supposed to do. We're Angibu."

"Angibu? They're in jail, bleeding. We have a submarine and guys who run it. Guys like us. Do we know anything? Why would they know anything? We should contact mainland."

"They'll talk," I say. "Sarge knows what he's doing. He's Angibu. He knows how to get us home."

"Angibu did Gwangju," Junho says. "They shot Carrot Woman's husband. They shot students in the streets. They trucked a thousand people to the hills, men and women, girls and boys. They lined them by a ditch and shot them all." Junho fumbles with his cigarette pack. "One of them looks like my older cousin. Maybe he is some cousin."

Someone clears his throat and spits. Sarge is stretching in his doorway, far enough so maybe he didn't hear us. "Beautiful morning. Come with me, Junho."

—

I stand by the jail. Sarge and Junho have gone up the hill. No villagers, only Four Fingers out on her boat, way out, fishing. Everyone is staying away from the store, like we've got a disease.

Maybe Sarge is going to convince Junho that we're doing the right thing. Maybe Junho is explaining to him why this is all wrong. I'm not sure what is right anymore.

They're gone awhile, and then it's time to feed the prisoners. After putting together the pot of mush and bags of kimchi, I remember that in the back of the chest freezer, locked in a corner of frost and ice, is a box of mini shrimp burgers. It's got buns and all.

I bring it all to the jail, start handing bowls and spoons and bags of kimchi, and then after they've all got their hands full I say, "I have a special."

They eat quietly. They're looking at me but still shoveling mush into their mouths.

I show them the plate of microwaved shrimp burgers. "These are called burgers."

"We know burgers," says one. He's the tired one, the one we beat last night. "We also know Nike and Adidas and Pepsi and Ford. And we know that you're Yankee."

"Good," I say. "So how about I give you burgers, and you tell me about the sixth guy? Then, after that, we'll get you off the island and to freedom. In South Korea, you can eat burgers and kimbap and drink Pepsi. Maybe watch TV and someday be free?"

They keep slurping their mush. One says, "Your Korean is shit."

"Do you want Sarge to kill you guys?"

"No," says the tired one. He puts his hand out. "We'll eat burgers."

They take the burgers and take a bite of them in between mush and kimchi. A couple of them dip it in the kimchi bag. My plan is working. It's a motivation factor: like helmet stickers, nice uniforms, a jersey number matching your favorite player. These little things can motivate a player to try a little harder, work a bit differently, do what is needed.

"So, what about the sixth?" I say.

"Five," says the tired-looking one. "One"—he points to himself, and then to the others as he counts—"two-three-four-five." The ones that finish their bowls start pushing bowls forward toward the bars.

"Why do you look at us like that?" the tired one says.

"Don't you want to get out of here?" I say.

"Of course," another one says.

"Then why won't you tell me what we need to know?" I say.

They laugh. One takes out a cigarette and lights it with a match.

"The same reason why you haven't taken our dog tags," the tired one says. "We're not dead. This is war. And we're sailors. Defenders."

"War? Defenders? Look at you guys," I say. "Starving, in rags, what are you fighting for?"

"Our people," the tired one says. "Our families. Our land. We fight the most powerful Army in the world for fifty years and haven't been defeated. Yankee, don't give us burgers. Just let us go home. And you go home too."

The other four all look down at their feet and the cracks in the concrete. They nod.

I wait outside. I don't know what to do. When I see Sarge and Junho come back down the trail, I'm relieved. Then my stomach churns.

—

That night Sarge takes another captive. I can't tell if it's the tired one or not. He's hooded. Sarge and Junho take the prisoner out to the glassy mud-flats and dull moonlight. Sarge brings a shovel and a cooler. They follow a rope that leads from shore to a block of concrete that holds a length of buoys. I can hear the mud clasping their boots as they go.

They get far enough out to be the size of my thumbs and I can't hear much. Just murmurs. And a laugh.

Watching them, I try to match their nodding heads to what I think they're saying:

Five.

Six.

Five.

But Sarge doesn't kick. I think he's the one laughing. Or maybe it's the prisoner laughing. Then everyone gets really quiet while Junho starts shoveling in the mud.

When he finishes, I think Sarge asks the prisoner the question, the only question he seems to have, one last time. I don't think the prisoner says anything, because the next thing I know, they've tripped him and tied him to the concrete block. He is half in the hole. They're pouring the stuff from the cooler on him.

Then they leave the prisoner there in a hole in the mud, and walk back.

Sarge lights a cigarette and sits on the patio. Junho puts away the shovel and rinses out the cooler. He's wide-eyed. I want to ask, but I don't.

We sit. Me by the jail, Sarge and Junho smoking on the patio while the black tide comes in popping little bubbles in the mud.

The man lets out a shout. Then something that sounds like whistling.

"Get the dinghy," Sarge says.

The water is up to the man's face by the time we get to him. I can just make out the crabs pecking at chum on his clothes and the little trails of blood coming from him. The crabs are crawling over each other.

We take off the hood. It's the look of waking in a nightmare.

"Tell me where he is," Sarge says.

The guy looks at the water surrounding him, at the crabs on him and under the water.

"Here or there, I'll die," he says. "I'm not afraid of you."

I don't believe him. The dinghy is vibrating.

"Tell me," Sarge says.

"The tide will come and you will either save me or leave me to die. Both are fine. There will be others—luckier than me—to come. We will not abandon the mission."

Sarge laughs. "Of course. Of course! I had it backwards all along."

The guy looks confused. I bet I do too. The guy slumps to the side of the dinghy when we pull him over, and by the time we're at the launch Junho and I have plucked all the crabs off him. No one says anything all the way back or when we throw him in the shack. We're out front of the convenience store when Sarge finally says, "They didn't bring anyone; they're waiting for someone. That's why they came with five instead of six. The real spy is around, nearby, now. That's all they know."

I look at Junho for answers. He says nothing.

"They're picking up, not dropping off!" Sarge says. "They've never met the spy. They only know that they were supposed to meet someone on that beach." Sarge takes out his gun and sets it on a pile of crates we sometimes use as tables. "Someone so important to get a submarine for a taxi." Then he laughs. "We catch the spy, then we are heroes."

# 47

*The second child says it's frightening.*
*The third child says it's frightening.*
*The fourth child says it's frightening.*

—

Thunder and rain. Humidity glues everything together. I must've fallen asleep. Someone is banging on the sliding door and I peel off the mat. Outside there's a crowd in rain boots, holding umbrellas.

"I haven't been able to call my daughter for three days," says Cabbage Man.

"Where is my gasoline?" Four Fingers says.

"I need to go back to work. I need off this island immediately!" says a tourist.

Three days. How has it been three days already?

I have no words for them. There's not really a why anymore. It's our mission. Not that they would understand what I say. When I open my mouth, I hear Junho coming around the corner looking miserable in his raincoat. His glasses are beaded with water. He puts up his hands in that surrendering way.

"Calm down. Calm down," Junho says.

"Calm down?" Rabbit Man says. "Calm down? Why are you two carrying guns around all the time on your belts? Huh? Why are the phones out, and the gasoline gone out of her boat?" He points at Four Fingers.

"The gasoline is gone," she confirms.

"I want to go to the market," Owner says. "And I need a new window."

The tourists seems to shrink a little.

"Calm down?" says Rabbit Man.

Then we hear a gunshot. I reach for my pistol but it's in the store by the golden cat and the gum. Junho has his out and people are shrieking and checking themselves for blood. Everyone except for Carrot Woman. She's got a machete in one hand and a flare gun in the other. And she's walking straight toward us until Sarge, now beside me, shouts for her to stop and points his pistol at her.

"Hear me out, Myeongseong," he says. Then lifts his pistol up to the sky. "There's a serious criminal on the island." Sarge's voice can be heard over the rain patter. "We are very sorry, but we were not sure if he was on this island or another. We now know he's here. We will remain on lockdown until he's caught. That means no communication, no ferries, nothing."

Slowly, it passes over everyone's faces that no one is hurt. They're about to get really mad for feeling helpless, but then Sarge continues.

"And I appreciate your concern and desire to help. I'm sorry for having to keep this away from you, but it has been for your protection. The best way for you to help is not to search the island but to search your homes and outbuildings. Remain at home. If you do see him please use the police phones. You know me. I ask you to trust me. Thank you."

"Lies," Carrot Woman says. "Angibu only lie."

"It's true," Junho says.

Everyone looks back at him like he had just appeared.

"Don't lie to me, young man," Carrot Woman says.

"On my ancestors," Junho says. "There are communists here. We found their submarine."

The rain is loud and heavy. Carrot Woman lowers her machete, but keeps her flare gun pointed at Sarge.

"Is that true, Chung Hee?" Four Fingers finally asks.

He nods. He somehow seems shorter now.

"Prove it," Carrot Woman says.

We lead the crowd to the boat building. We lift the tarp and everyone gasps at the submarine.

"I thought they were done with that kind of thing," Clam Happy says. "Why would they come here?"

Nobody answers. Just stares. Then finally Rabbit Man says with disgust to Cabbage Man, "Dokkaebis, right?"

Cabbage Man says nothing.

Carrot Woman touches the submarine. Then she puts the flare gun in her purse and walks away, toward home, while everyone else walks the length of the submarine, then starts to disperse like Carrot Woman. Everyone except Four Fingers.

"Chung Hee, we're friends, right?" she says.

"Yes," Sarge says.

"Why is this still here?"

"Listen—" Sarge says walking up to Four Fingers.

"No, don't come near me," she says. "I don't know what this is but I know this shouldn't still be here."

"We need to find them all."

"Get the phones working. Get the proper people here."

"I am the proper person. This is why I'm here. Don't worry, we'll get the phones working soon."

Four Fingers looks at me. "None of this is right and you know it."

"We are doing our jobs," Sarge says.

She looks back at the shack where Junho is leaning against the wall. "Get the phones working," she says, and starts for the ring road. I think she's going for her boat, but instead she stops, as if remembering something, and goes home.

Sarge motions for Junho to come over. "If I didn't need you, I'd kill you," he says.

Junho bows his head.

"We need to find him," Sarge says, "before word gets out."

He looks out at the water as if waiting for a whale to pop up and breathe. "Start with the hill and work your way down. Don't stop until you find him." Then he walks off toward the boat launch.

We're doing something important. We caught North Koreans. I am doing something important.

—

For hours Junho and I plod through the brambles of the woods. We look behind moss-furred trees and rocks and we stop and listen to the rain. By lunchtime we make it up to the summit again and look down from the peak. There isn't a place to hide and survive for days unnoticed on this island. There's nothing on this hill.

"Why did you tell them about the submarine?" I ask Junho.

He's quiet, frozen. We're at the small clearing with the holes we dug. All around here on this hill are grown-over graves. Everywhere here in Korea must be graves. Marked and unmarked, grown over or paved, and forgotten. This is the difference between home and here. History is everywhere, here. War has been everywhere, even now. We're soldiers looking to make war on someone we can't find and throw them into one of these fresh holes, right here.

But that isn't true either, Tibicut has had people forever. Tibicut is probably all graves too.

Everywhere, graves.

Some fog, like cotton ripped from a stuffed animal, stretches from the side of the hill toward Star Island. Out by the rock the fog is heavy. Very heavy.

Without a boat, getting to Star Island is possible but hard. The best time to do it would be around noon when the tide is really strong with the moon and goes out far enough to reveal a spit of quicksand-like mud. At night the spit might be there too, but only a couple of yards wide, and brief. The riptide strips everything from the mud and flings it far out into the ocean, never to be seen again.

"Star Island," Junho says.

"Yeah," I say.

"Hard without a boat," he says.

"If you were a spy, maybe not," I say. "If we do find him?"

"He talks."

"If he doesn't?"

"He will."

"I thought you were against all of this."

Junho stares down at the rocks at his feet, taps on the button of his holster.

"Maybe this is how we lose shame," Junho says. "We are soldiers."

Sarge never showed us how to reconnect the phone lines.

The dock isn't far from here and there are boats. Junho probably put the gasoline in the boat shack. We could go back to the mainland. Over there we could report everything that has happened and . . . I don't know. I guess they would throw us in prison. They might call it abandoning my post, they might say I'm a torturer.

Bad debt and a torturer. A criminal.

One moment I feel this purpose driving me forward, then the next is this itch that doesn't want to go away. Star Island has the shape of a pilgrim's hat. A big hat floating in the water.

Junho kicks some rocks.

"We've done too much to stop," he says. "We can't go back without Sarge." Then he says in English, "North Koreans are brainwash. Crazy. Want to kill us. We are right wrong."

He's lying to himself.

"We'll get through this," I say. "I promise."

"You promise?"

"Yes."

He laughs and I laugh. I don't know why we're laughing. He pats me on the back, one of those solid pats that turns into a solid grip of the shoulder.

"Okay," he says. "Let's go."

By the time we get back to the store, Sarge has got a boat on the beach. He's already loading it. "Must be Star Island, right?" We don't say anything. "I didn't want it to come to this," Sarge says, then he breathes in deep and puts his boot on a pylon as if he's a general posing for a painting. "Let's get them."

"Get who?"

"The prisoners, we're taking them for a ride."

Wind pelts us with rain as we get the prisoners out of the shed. They cough under their pillowcases as we take them to the boat. "You can drown us but we won't talk," one of them says.

Sarge smiles. The swells on the ocean are bigger than I've ever seen and the sky is nothing but dark gutted clouds.

"Perfect weather," Sarge says.

It's hard to get the boat into the water. Junho and I slosh alongside until Sarge starts motoring and we both jump on and cling to the sides. We are not sailors. We have three life vests, eight people. I cannot swim well.

The island isn't far but it sure feels far. Everyone holds on to the ropes on the sides of the boat. If I believed in God, then I would say a very deep prayer to him now, something meaningful. Looking back at Love Island where the little streams are rivers, I can see the streetlights dim behind the rain until they flicker, then all go out. The generator must've flooded. It's our job to keep that running. Everything is dark.

# 48

THE BOAT SHUDDERS AND GROANS WHEN WE HIT STAR ISLAND'S BEACH. It's covered in green broken bottles. We bring the prisoners up to the tree line. The tide is still coming in, so we tie off the boat to a tree. Then Sarge tells us to tie the prisoners up to their own trees.

Wet, zip-tied, and shaking, they say nothing. They just cough. Their hoods are soaked. Could they drown in wet hoods?

With a stick, Sarge draws the island in a patch of mud. He tells us that we will do a parallel zigzag to find the spy. He'll hunt him behind us. It seems to me he's letting us walk ahead to be the bait. I don't like it—we don't know the island. Stomping around blindly seems like a good way to get shot. But I'm not the master spy. Maybe I'm missing something in the roar of rain and wind slapping the loose threads of my jacket at my face.

I keep looking back at the five men in black hoods and the boat we have tied up to the trees. The boat, the only way off this island, off any island, the only way to the mainland. The men squirm.

"Hey," Sarge barks, and I look up, "did you see something?"

"No, sir, I was just thinking—"

"No thinking. Only spy."

He points toward the woods.

"Back there about a hundred meters is a shack. Both of you start there. That'll get him moving and I'll do the rest."

We go into the woods and stomp through bushes. All I want to do is get back in the boat and go to an airport and fly back to the States and lie on an old beat-up couch with a Shasta cola and a plate of Lit'l Smokies and waffles and stare at the TV with an audience booing a guy who wants to marry his horse. I want to think, Wow, that's nuts, while I'm warmed by a dusty electric blanket. That's what I want.

I hear a crack. I've got my pistol out and beaded on a loose branch crashing down from a pine. There's another rustle and I turn and I see Junho poking at something in a bush with a stick. He looks back at me and shakes his head. Everywhere rain is plunking on leaves.

When we do find the shack, it looks like an abandoned chicken coop without any wiring. We take a peek inside and there's nothing but some old dry grass. It doesn't look lived in to me. The whole island looks abandoned. The ground cover of leaves and needles is soft and mushy, and there are a few cuts of runoff but no trails. Walking is hard. Back and forth, slowly zigzagging, our headlamps glistening off the leaves and the worms and bugs coming up from the ground for air. Is there a spy at all? Is this all just in Sarge's head?

Maybe all of this is in *my* head and I'm in bed at home under a dusty blanket.

I hate Sarge. I hate these dark, wet, shitty woods that smell like mold. I hate this island. I hate the ground littered with bottles.

As soon as Junho and I approach the rocky beach, the prisoners start coughing. A lot. Like they're choking. But what is weirder than that is the sudden thud. I turn with my pistol and I see Junho drop like something pulled the plug on him. Something knocks my gun out of my hands and there is someone holding something sharp, glassy, tight up against my throat.

"Where is the other one?" a voice hisses into my ear.

"Let me go," I say.

"The other one." He presses the broken glass against the soft skin of my neck. All the sweat and rain on my skin feels warm like blood. "Where is he?"

The prisoners tied to the trees start coughing again. This time louder, almost in rhythm. With the rain beating the ground and the leaves and the wind whistling, all of it sounds musical. Beats. The glass presses harder, and I can feel each jagged crevice in the glass's edge cutting into my skin. In the bushes there's no movement. The spy looks back toward where Junho fell. He's still there on the ground, groaning.

The coughing stops. Or maybe the thumping of my heart gets louder. I'm not really sure.

"Where is he?"

"I don't know," I say. There's a lot more warmth on my skin now.

He breathes deeply, calmly. This man is strong. Fit, He's the Bond-type I had always imagined. But even in summer the rains come in cold, and he's shivering. "Move," he says, and I do.

We take a couple steps and I can tell he's watching the shadows, all the movement. But that's impossible. Every leaf and branch is moving. Everything is drooping under the weight of rain. He hasn't pointed a gun. Maybe he doesn't have one. If he does, he wouldn't stick it to my throat anyway. A sharp bottle is silent.

He leads me tree trunk to tree trunk. I can hear Junho moaning, cussing, throwing up.

There is no sign of Sarge. I wonder if he's just watching to see what I'm going to do. Like this is another test.

We move to the boat. It would take two hands to untie the knot unless he decides to cut the rope. He would have to let go, even if only for a second. If he tries to cut the rope, then I'd have a chance to fight and yell and hope Sarge is close enough. I consider my options, I think of *The Matrix*, deep thumping music and me flipping him over and landing with my boot on his neck, the audiences in dark theaters cheering. I'd get to say something witty. Be a hero. Be somebody.

The other possibility: I'll end up gurgling on the ground with a fountain springing from my neck.

And then it happens. He looks around, maybe at the rope, maybe at the bushes, at something moving, he gives me slack. I take my chance, go under with my arms, drop and tumble and forward-roll onto my feet. This is my moment.

But it was only me that tumbled. From the ground I look up and see him pointing my gun at me. And he isn't smiling like a villain. No, he just looks down at me and then he's back to scanning the bushes.

"Grab that bottle," he says, nodding toward the broken bottle on the ground. Along the break I can see my own blood. "Grab it."

"If I grab the bottle—"

"Grab the bottle," he says.

I reach for it, shaking. The ocean is dark and miserable and gray, a shitty last thing to see. I grab the bottle and think of lunging at him. The pistol could jam, could backfire. It had dropped on the ground and it is raining hard.

But I cleaned that gun. It won't jam, won't backfire.

I carefully stand up.

"Toss it in the water," he says.

I toss it into the water.

"Untie the line," he says.

I look at the boat. I look at the line. I look back to the woods.

"Untie it," he says.

I take a couple of steps toward the tree, his gun trained on me. Suddenly there's a shot. And I drop to the ground. So this is how it ends, I think. On a shitty beach on Star Island next to Love Island.

The spy drops to the ground. Shooting his gun but not at me. I clamber over the glass and the rocks and pounce on the spy and struggle for the gun. Just as quick, Sarge is there kicking him. In moments, I'm up, pointing my gun at the spy, and Sarge has his boot on the spy's neck.

"Zip-tie him," Sarge says.

And I do.

# 49

THE SUN IS GOING DOWN BEHIND NORMAL CLOUDS AND NORMAL RAIN.
It is going to be a normal miserable rainy night. It could be a normal miserable rainy night anywhere. But this normal rain comes down on this not-normal beach with its broken bottles and plastic cups and five drooping prisoners tied to trees and one spy with a bloody hole in his pants.

Junho isn't stable on his feet. My hands shake. I keep my eyes steady on the spy who glassed my neck. He isn't as big as I imagined. He's lanky. Short. Every part of him seems to have that runner look—fit but two meals from starved. Sarge has got the first-aid kit out of the boat and is working on the spy's leg. He says it's a scratch. He says the same about my neck, which I guess is right, since it isn't bleeding anymore.

The tide is going out and the boat is completely out of the water. When Sarge finishes with the spy he tells us we'll have to stay the night on the island. We take the hoods off the prisoners, rope them in a chain, and we all march together into the woods. We leave the boat tied to a tree like a dog in a backyard.

When we reach the small clearing with the chicken house, Sarge asks the spy, "Is it okay to use your camp?"

The spy coughs.

We find a tarp buried under the grass beside the shack. We skin up a roof from the side of the shack and tie it to some trees to make some cover. And after an hour shaving and cutting some kindling Junho and I get a fire going. The prisoners seem relieved to be on the ground again instead of being tied to the trees. But that might be just me; they all have the same blank look of boredom. Maybe it's relief, like we're camping after a long hike. Even the spy, who is lying closest to the fire and biting his lip trying not to show pain, seems a bit relieved. Everyone except Sarge. He sits by the fire with his pistol in his hand and a cigarette stuck in his grin. But he doesn't say anything, just keeps grinning and blowing smoke out the side of his mouth and gazing squarely on the spy. For a long time the two of them just watch each other.

"There are some bottles of water and some cabbage under a board in the shack," the spy says. "Under that, some snake soju. You know, for health."

"Is that so?" says Sarge.

Then all the rain dropping on the tarp seems deafening.

"You wouldn't want me to die, would you?" the spy says. "After all of this work."

"What should I call you?" Sarge says.

"Jin-wook."

"Ah," Sarge says, then tosses his cigarette into the fire. Then he takes a stick we've been using as a poker from the fire and taps it against one of the exposed rocks on the ground. The tip is ashy. When the breeze blows you can see the glow of charcoal. "You know, Jin-wook, I've been doing this for a long time."

"Is that so?" Jin-wook says.

"Jin-wook, what a lovely name for a fisherman off course," says Sarge.

"How did you know? It's true. We're fishermen following schools of fish. We got lost and afraid that we'd get shot," says Jin-wook with a smirk.

"Such a shame that lost fishermen are treated so poorly on our island," Sarge says, poking the fire. "And to lose your submarine, hmm."

I look at Junho and he's looking at me. Sarge's voice sounds so tender, so normal.

"Fish live underwater," says Jin-wook. "To find them quicker and better, you too have to go underwater. But that's not important. These are things for me to tell your superiors. Assuming that I don't die from an infected wound."

"You know," Sarge says, "I really would like to know your name. The real one. Then I might consider getting you that soju."

"Snake soju. And the name is Jin-wook," he says.

"You're sure?" Sarge says.

"Very."

Taking the poker from the fire, Sarge steps over to Jin-wook and presses the hot end of the poker against his shoulder. I swear I smell it before I hear him yelp. Then I realize it wasn't the spy yelping but Junho. The spy just groans.

"The thing is," Sarge says, taking back the poker, "you think that I have superiors, that someone knows you're here, that I have patience." He points the poker at the other prisoners. "I asked questions and I got nothing. My patience is all gone. If I had superiors would we camp out here? Would I start feeding each of you to the crabs?"

"You don't want to do this, Chung Hee," Jin-wook says.

He knows Sarge's name.

"That's right," Jin-wook says. "I hear what you say to yourself when no one is looking. I know you want to go back. I know what you did that got you sent here. I want to go back too. Call your people and let's all go back together."

Sarge jabs the poker against the spy's other shoulder. This time the spy squirms and wails.

"What's your name?" Sarge says.

The prisoners look straight up to the tarp. A couple of them move their mouths, but mostly they seem calm, ready.

I think I hear Junho groan. Maybe it's me.

———

*A dead end alley is just fine*
*The first child says it is frightening.*

———

At dawn Sarge shouts my name.

"Grab tape from the boat," Sarge says.

It's still dark and for a moment I'm a little lost. I can make out the spy curled by the fire. Four prisoners are seated, looking at me, while the fifth digs a hole a little ways off, Junho standing guard with his gun. Junho looks bewildered.

"Move, sleepy beauty," Sarge says. "We are going to do some early morning good."

*Sleeping Beauty*, I want to correct, but I am struck by the air smelling like scorched ants under a summer magnifying glass.

It isn't ants.

"Go already!" Sarge shouts.

I nod and start toward the beach.

It started with the fire poker and got worse and worse until I got goose bumps and all I could hear was, "Your name. Your name. Where did you go? Why are you here? Your name? Your real name?"

I closed my eyes from the smoke of the fire. And then, dawn.

All the way to the beach my skin feels sticky and dirty. I go through the lockers on the boat and find tape. My fingers have dirt and blood stuck in the ridges. I start washing my hands in the seawater and feel the mud suck on my shoes. Out on the ocean, I can see the top of some big ship on its way to the mainland. It might be from America. I'm right next to a boat; I can get the hell out of here, tell them what's going on, then hide out in one of those closets on that big ship.

But I don't. I give up washing my hands and grab the tape and walk back. At the camp all the prisoners are sitting in front of the hole.

Sarge tells me to tape up the mouths of the prisoners, then he turns to the spy, who is sitting up now.

"I keep having this dream of Mongols burning towns to the ground," Sarge says. "All that's left is charred bones that they put in buckets like fried chicken. That Mongol blood inside me is in you too. No one will talk about it, but it's true. And you are trying to harm us, your own blood. For what?"

The spy coughs, gurgles what sounds like a laugh.

"Funny?" Sarge says. "I guess this whole mess is funny."

"I told you everything you wanted to know," the spy says. "I'm a spy! My name is Jin-wook. I was a fisherman, then I became a spy, and then I came here to look. That's it." The spy clears his throat and laughs again. "You are a mean bastard. There's nothing I can say that you'd believe."

Sarge rubs his stubble. "What were you sent to take?"

"Nothing to take, just look."

"At what?"

"I didn't make it," Jin-wook says. "Got stuck here. Incomplete."

"At what?"

"Nikes. Adidas. Bean Pole."

Sarge gets up and tells Junho and me to stand the prisoners up by the hole.

As a kid, when I got up to the top of a tree, high enough to see beyond the canopy, there would be this moment when the trees swayed with the breeze and you would feel like you'd gone too far and you'd look down and all those branches below you looked cracked and dead and you just knew you were going to fall. I feel that now as Junho and I force the prisoners to stand.

"Step back," Sarge tells us, and he points his pistol at the first prisoner. Jin-wook mumbles something I can't hear. "Why do you lie to me?" Sarge says. "You know what I am, what I must do."

"You are just another traitor trying be something you're not," Jin-wook says. "Act like Angibu all you want, but really you're just another drunk who can't keep his life together, another betrayer to your blood."

Sarge isn't going to shoot. This is all just a game to get the spy to talk. His threats are not promises.

Kojangi is lying to himself. Just like he called kicking a man when he's down *work*.

Sarge thinks his Fontinot will bring him home only if his stats are perfect. But how are a submarine, a crew, and a spy not perfect?

Sarge is lying to himself. He will kill these guys and Kojangi will watch, and shovel dirt on the bodies and say it was all for getting home.

I'm done lying. I don't know what I am, but I am not Angibu. I am not Kojangi. I am not going to be a spectator to these guys getting blasted.

I tackle Sarge with perfect form: square hips, arms wrapping, legs pushing up, and we drop like timber. Then there's little grace. We're rolling and punch at any soft parts we can. It isn't like the movies, no one is struggling for guns, because we've already lost them. This is like elementary school kids who've thrown their backpacks to the ground—pouncing and pounding each other on the playground.

The prisoners are yelling, and there's another scuffle, something else happening beyond our little rumble. But we don't stop until we hear a gunshot.

We look over at Junho. He's got his pistol pointed at the prisoners. They all check their bodies for the wound, but there isn't one. Then Junho points the pistol at us.

"I'll shoot both of you if you don't stop right now," he says.

Then he fires the gun.

There's an echo of the bullet hitting a trunk. Junho never could get the feel for it, even with all the help I gave him. I'm not sure if he tried to miss or tried to hit.

"Give me that gun," Sarge says. "Or shoot one of the prisoners."

"This is all way too . . ." Junho says, "without a handle."

"Shoot them," says the spy, pointing at Sarge and me. "They're nuts. You can blame it on me."

Sarge stands up and takes a step toward Junho. Junho shoots again and Sarge drops to the ground. He's searching his body, but blood isn't leaking from him.

One of the prisoners is sobbing, another is laughing.

"What is wrong with you, soldier?" Sarge says.

"You said we'd be heroes. You said we were righting wrongs. You said we were getting justice and when we were finished we'd get to go home."

"Junho, give me the gun," Sarge says, "or shoot one of the prisoners."

"I have the gun," Junho says. "I do the telling."

"Fucking without a handle," Sarge says.

"No kidding," says the spy.

"Shut up!" Junho says.

"What do you want us to do, Junho?" I say.

"This is war, Junho," Sarge says. "Don't let your soft heart fail us now. Do your duty. I believe in you. Shoot them."

"Hurting people is okay," Junho says, "bad people deserve bad things. But this makes no sense. This isn't going to get us home. We want them in hell, not us."

"They are going to kill us, Junho," Sarge says. "That is their job. Our job is to stop them. Kill them."

"Ha!" the spy says, then coughs.

"I just want to go home," one of the prisoners by the hole says. They're now all sitting on the ground.

"What do you want us to do?" I say.

"I want to go home," Junho says.

"And you will, when we're done," Sarge says. "After we kill enough of these assholes to get the intel we need for Seoul to be happy."

"You lie," Junho says. "You enjoy this, even when they did nothing to you. Kojangi, I want you to tie Sarge up."

Sarge yells, starts to get up, when Junho fires again. A clump of bark drops on Sarge and he drops right back down to the ground.

"They're trying to kill us!" Sarge yells. "For all you know, there's a bomb and it will go off any minute. Your duty is to protect. To serve!"

Slowly and cautiously I get up and zip-tie Sarge.

"Take him"—Junho nods toward the spy—"to the mainland. Get him there quickly. Get help."

Sarge is shouting as I take the spy through the woods to the beach, where the tide has come in. Behind us Sarge keeps yelling. The spy tumbles into the boat and I follow. I get the motor started and we round the corner and we keep going. I don't look back at the island. I just keep looking forward to where the compass says is north, toward the mainland.

I don't know what came over Junho. But I'm glad whatever it was did.

I keep listening for gunshots. But there's only the motor and seagulls.

# 50

BY THE TIME WE ARE FAR ENOUGH AWAY FROM THE ISLAND FOR THE swells to really rise and fall, I hear Sarge's voice in my head. "You doomed us all, *traitor*."

The motor sounds a bit tinny, like it's a lot lighter than it ought to be. I wonder if we have enough gas to get to the mainland.

The boat lands hard on a swell and water sprays all over us. Jin-wook, or whatever his name is, laughs.

"It feels good one second, then it stings like hell the next," he says in good English.

He looks bad. Swollen eyes. Busted lip. Scabs and blisters showing through burned holes in his shirt and a bandage around his leg from the gunshot.

"Life is good, then stinging like hell," he says. "When I told my father I wasn't going to be some government bureaucrat, always smiling and filling out papers, waiting to have a heart attack at my desk, he took me to the docks—"

"Shut up," I say. "Just shut up."

Another spray comes over the side. He laughs again and spits some blood into the boat. I worry about what happens when we get to port and I pull out this guy all mangled like the Toxic Avenger to hand over to the police. What will they say?

"Where are you from?" the spy says. He keeps using English.

I keep my eyes forward trying to see land, but there's only haze. Fog, maybe, or just more rain. What if I miss the port completely and have to clamber up rocks with this guy on my back?

"Don't pretend you don't understand English," he says. "Your Korean is terrible."

"Shut up," I say in Korean. "Shut up or I'll throw you over the side," I say in English. I keep the boat pointed north, turn to meet the waves head-on as I'd seen Four Fingers do.

"Canadian? You must be Canadian," the spy says.

Maple syrup. Molasses, Bobby said at breakfast, was made from the same sap. That was forever ago.

"CSIS, right?" the spy says. "Never met any of you guys before. Always figured you all would just let the CIA do everything. Are you a CIA? What is your story, gyopo?"

"For a spy, you talk a lot," I say.

"You assume I'm a spy because Chung Hee said so."

"You said so."

"Why would I tell the truth? From one operative to another, would you tell the truth?"

"I'm not a spy. I'm taking you to the authorities and you should be thankful your brains aren't poured out on those rocks back on the beach. So, shut up," I say.

"Not a spy. I forget that too sometimes." He gets off the bench and sits on the floor with the sloshing water. "So, hockey is soccer on ice, with a puck and sticks, right?"

"I'm not Canadian," I say.

"Neither am I. So, we got something we can agree on."

"Good. Now shut up."

"What exactly are you going to tell them?"

"Shut up already."

"Shut-up. Shut, up? Shut. Up. Shu-tup!" the spy says, and laughs.

The waves settle a bit and I feel hungry. The spy coughs. He's shivering. I dig out some ramen and a blanket out of the locker and toss it to him. He sits back on the bench and I break off a chunk of dried ramen and feed it to him.

After he swallows, he puckers his busted lips. "I look beautiful, right?" he says.

"Gorgeous," I say.

I give him more. He winces as he chews. "What are you going to say?"

"Eat," I say, and try to keep my eyes forward for waves and the land that is somewhere out there. I have no idea what I'm going to say. I have no idea where I'm going.

"When I was a kid, my father would always tell me, 'Never miss the boat.' He would walk me to school sometimes and we would pass this small—what do you call it?—port for small boats? Marina? One time there was this guy in a cheap suit sitting on a box crying into his hands with everyone walking by pretending he wasn't crying. He missed the boat, my father said. Years later when I told him I wasn't going to be a government paper-worker like him, he pointed out to the horizon and asked, Do you see that boat? No, I said. Because you missed it, he said."

"I'll tell them that. We caught you because . . ." I say, feeling very witty, "you missed your boat."

"Ha! That sounds poetic," he says.

"It's the truth," I say.

"Gyopos," he scoffs. "Truth," he spits. "Here's some truth: Canadians, or Americans, some country takes you and recycles you back here as an operative because you look the part. But you're not. The costume is all they see. And I know about costumes."

Ahead, the haze thickens. I should grab the duct tape from the locker, mummify this guy's head with it so he shuts up.

"The worst thing you can do," he says, "is tell the truth. Thought experiment: Let's say we don't drown and you do get me to a town. Who would understand your Korean? If they did, who wouldn't think that you just beat me up over money or a girl? Would you be *honest* and tell them how prisoners in your custody dug their own grave? Please."

"If you don't shut up, I'll shut you up."

The spy laughs. "You know you're acting, right? Do you feel the costume?"

We motor. Waves rock the boat. Water sprays.

Why didn't Junho take him? What am I going to say?

"I want to show you something," he says. "It's in my shirt pocket."

"What is it?" I say.

"My girlfriend," he says. "Want to see?"

He's mangled and zip-tied. So I go over and tear the Velcro off of his jacket pocket and there it is, a photo of a pretty woman in the spotlight of a stage play.

"She's an actress. In Seoul," he says. "Do you have a girlfriend?"

The motor hums and boat grates over whitecaps. I say nothing.

"Come on, now," he says, "I showed you mine."

"Yeah," I say. "A cheerleader."

"Ah," he says. "You played American football, didn't you? What position?"

"Running back."

"Tell me, in American football, are you playing for your own benefit or the team?"

"What do you mean?"

"You can't win as a running back while your team loses, right?"

"Why the stupid question?"

"I don't know anything about American football," he says.

I put the photo back in his pocket.

"Her name is Sue," he says. "She's gyopo, like you, but from Brazil. What's your girlfriend's name?"

"What do you want?"

"I want you to let me go."

I laugh.

"But," he says, "I'd settle for passing the time as I bleed on this terrible boat. So, what's her name?"

"Chantal," I say.

"Chantal," he says. "Chantal and Kojangi sitting in a tree."

"It's Beyonghak."

He bows his head. "Nice to meet you, Beyonghak."

"I don't think so," I say.

"Well, my name is truly Jin-wook."

I don't say anything. There's thunder out there and the motor isn't sounding right.

"And I'm sorry," he says.

"For what?"

He looks up at the sky, exposing his neck. I can barely feel the sting on the spot where he held the glass to my neck.

"You had the right idea," he says, "and you're strong. Smart. With the right practice—"

"Why lie to me?" I say.

"There are no lies when there's no truth, Beyonghak."

I laugh.

"You'll agree when you realize what you are."

"I know I'm not a shifty asshat bleeding on a boat."

"Oh? Tell me, what else am I?"

"A commie spy who got caught waiting for his submarine."

He coughs. "So what?"

"So what?" I say. "You're the enemy, a commie, an asshole who believes the Kims are gods and that it's better to live without power while the rest of the world has Nintendo."

"And freedom?"

"Yeah, douche nugget."

"In football, which is more important, the running back or the team?"

*The team*, I almost say, but stop.

"Beyonghak, what decisions do you get to make?" he says. "Really. You would never go backwards in a football game. An actress wouldn't invent a new play right there or decide to play football onstage. Freedom is a myth. It's merely packaged decisions being fed to you as freedom and truth by those with money and power.

"We true Koreans seek balance. Self-reliance. Juche. In your Nintendo world, you're blinded into thinking you're special and separate from every other person. You think you have nothing to do with the homeless man peeing on the street and envy the man driving the Lamborghini who enslaves you. Realize that your culture treats you as merely an enslaved body that worships money that isn't real."

He starts coughing hard.

"Well," I say, "this body will be playing football again while your body is getting shanked in jail."

"You idiot," he says. "You can't get me sent to jail. They'll ignore you. And I'll just go away. I'm trying to explain something to you because there might be hope for you. You don't understand what it means to be Korean. Seek balance, harmony, know that some notes on the scale are lower and higher, yet when they work together it's a symphony."

"Shut up already."

"If we survive this, the worst thing you can do to yourself is tell *the truth* and bring me in. You're not part of this orchestra, this play, this football game. They will punish you terribly, again and again."

What if bringing this spy does nothing but cause me more problems? It should've been Junho here.

Asshole is grinning.

It would be easier to let this guy go when we get to land. Let him crawl off to a bush and die.

One of the clouds looks like a cat's paw reaching down from the clouds. And to the east there's a storm bank that's all shades of black and bad. Lightning. That's the way to America.

"Do you even know why they sent you to capture me?" he says.

"Shut up," I say.

Off in the distance, emerging from the fog, I can see the mainland, a town. I raise the throttle and the motor coughs.

Then we run out of gas.

"For lies," the spy says.

We begin to drift.

# 51

We drift so long that whatever-his-name-is stops talking and just hangs over the side to look in the water and spit and lean back as it sprays back.

Part of me hopes he just falls over, tries to swim for it.

Under the life jackets and the last bottle of water is a shoebox. In it are all the letters I ever tried to send to Haesoo and Chantal and Sheryl. There are even a few from Junho. Sarge hid them here. I don't know how or why. They aren't even opened.

There are boats on the water, small boats far off going farther out to fish. Big boats going here and there but nowhere near us. I stand and wave my arms. I shout. I try jumping and the boat rocks and the spy stops staring and spitting in the water and sits back inside. Still, nobody comes to rescue us.

"It's lunchtime," the spy says, pointing at the ball of sun hidden up in the clouds. "I guess it's about one, maybe two."

"They must be able to see us?"

"They're eating lunch. They're not looking."

The weather calms. The tide shifts and we drift away from shore out toward the empty ocean. The sun drops lower and lower behind the clouds and they darken, threatening to rain again. The spy just closes his eyes and reclines back. I don't know how he can be so calm. Maybe it is fatigue. I'm tired too. So tired I give up jumping and waving. All I can do is lie down to get a little bit of rest.

We hear a horn. At first I think I'm back on the ground of the convenience store, but then I see the fishing boat heading right for us. I get up and start waving my arms. A voice cries out from the fishing boat, "Get out of the way, you idiot."

"We can't. Motor's dead," I say.

"What?" the voice calls out, and then I can see a couple of fishermen with faded baseball caps over the gunwale. The boat slows.

"We can't move. Can you help us?" I say louder, clearer.

They nod their faded baseball caps as they talk to each other. One looks back and says, "Do you speak Korean?"

I wish I had a gun.

"Help! We! Need! Help!" I say.

The two fishermen look bewildered. Then the spy calls out, "Our boat is dead. We need help. Help us, please."

The boat pulls up beside us and throws us a line. A fisherman calls out, "Why is that man tied up?"

The spy smiles at me. "Here's your chance."

"Shut up," I say. "He is a North Korean spy," I say to the fishermen, very slowly and very calmly. "I am a soldier from Love Island. I'm transporting him back to Mokpo. I need your help."

"Speak better. We can't understand you."

It washes over me so quickly I'm not sure if it's just in my head or if I'm actually screaming and kicking the side of the boat, the box, the outboard motor. A moment later my foot hurts, the boat is rocking, and everyone is looking at me shake and swear at the plastic top of the motor that's now cracked and depressed.

"He said that I'm a spy," the spy says calmly and clearly. "He's a soldier and he needs your help."

"Get them up now," says a voice that's much deeper, older, weather-beaten.

"You need to cut him free if we're going to get you on board," a fisherman says to me.

The spy smiles at me—with a wince—and holds out his hands.

"I can't do that," I say to the fishermen.

Up on the rail is an old man with a white beard, bald, in overalls. He looks like a man on a frozen-fish-sticks box.

"Cut him and get on board or we leave you," he says.

"Yeah," the spy says.

"Shut up," I say, and cut him loose.

After we get on board the captain points a flare gun at us. "I have no idea who or what you two are. But you're going to be very calm as we tie you up. Understood?"

The spy laughs.

They give us water. They give us crackers. I tell them to call the Army. They tell me to be quiet. I'm not quiet. So they duct-tape my mouth. They put us against the gunwale and we just watch them there as they prepare their fish for the docks.

—

It's dark. Under the lights men wait for the fish on the docks. We stink of fish. I'm sick of fish eyes staring from the few they don't throw down the hold. Some policemen are waiting too, sitting on crates smoking cigarettes, watching us as we glide over the water toward the dock. They meet us on the pier with pursed lips when they see us duct-taped and tied up.

"When you radioed that you secured them," one of the policeman says to the fisherman, "I thought you gave them soup, a blanket."

Another policeman radios for a pickup truck. "They'll stink up a car too much."

—

They separate us at the station. The spy goes to an office with an open door and they sit me out in a cubicle behind the front desk. An old guy with lots of bars on his shoulders stares at me for a long time before ripping off the duct tape. It hurts, a lot.

"Calmly, tell me what your name is," he says.

"That man that came in with me is a North Korean spy," I say.

The old man squints at his computer. "Let's just start with your name, young man."

"But that man—"

The old man sighs. "Please, your name?"

I can hear the spy's voice from the office down the hall. The old man snaps his fingers in front of me. "Yi Beyonghak," I say.

"We're getting somewhere now," he says. "Why were you out there on that boat?"

"I'm in the Army," I tell him, "stationed on Love Island. We found a submarine and a North Korean spy, that guy back there, and he needs to be put in jail, and someone needs to go back to the island because the crew is still there and my friend needs help and our commander went nuts. You need to go and help them!"

From down the hall I can hear people laughing. The spy is making them laugh. What could a guy like that, looking like that, say to make them all laugh? I'm a psychopath who had assaulted him and kidnapped him while he was on vacation? Could he just be telling them the truth?

"Why were you out on the boat?" the old man asks again.

"I told you. That man back there—"

The old man raises his hand. He dials a number. "Get Bora here, now." He hangs up and says, "Let's wait, okay?"

Bora. That's Chantal's Korean name. My heart jumps and I feel alive and I'm talking, trying to explain, but the guy shakes his head and motions to an officer to take me away. I hear another roar of laughter. By the doorway to the office where they took the spy there's a group gathered as if watching a game on television. I don't know what he's doing but I know if he keeps doing it, he will walk out that front door, never to be seen again.

The officer leads me toward a hallway. We pass a bunch of empty cubicles, no doubt people who joined the crowd being entertained by the spy. The officer's phones rings and he stops to answer it. It's his wife. She's loud. And I'm next to another empty cubicle. There's a cell phone on the desk, really small, the size of a pack of gum. I grab it and stash it in my pocket while the officer tells his wife that no, he doesn't know who that is and that he's got to go.

The officer leaves me in an interrogation room with the door open and walks back to the office. The smooth concrete floor and the white walls are all stained and cracked. The big black box with a mirror in the corner with the camera is all scratched up. Interrogation rooms all look the same.

There's another roar of laughter from down the hall.

The spy is going to joke his way out. He was so calm ever since we left the island. He knew this was going to happen, that I wouldn't hurt him and that he could escape. I didn't even get anything from him, not even a name, nothing. I just ferried him. I got duped.

On TV there are stories of good guys and bad guys and moments when heroes go do the right thing because that's the right thing and everything works out.

Maybe that's what everyone is laughing about. Maybe he told them I'm Canadian.

Canadian? Weak-ass, three-down, bullshit football?

The cell phone is in my hand. I run the plays in my head. I still know Janie's number.

She answers on the first ring, and I tell her as quickly as I can about the sub on Love Island and the spy here with me in the police station. "You need to get the police to hold him," I say.

Before she can say anything I have to hang up and pocket the phone again. The officer from before takes me back to the old man. There is a young woman with him now. Not Chantal.

"You speak English, correct?" she asks in English.

"You need to stop that man who came in with me," I say, in English. "He's a spy, a North Korean spy."

She takes a deep breath. "Please, not so fast. My name is Bora."

"That asshole." I start pointing back to the office where they had kept the spy. "Commie, enemy, North Korean."

"I'm sorry, please, I don't understand."

I tell the woman, "North Korean," in English. "Book-han-salam," I say in Korean, "북한," and point back toward the office where the spy is. Why isn't Janie calling?

She turns to the older man and whispers to him.

"Why are you in Korea?" she asks.

There is a commotion. The spy is limping to the front double doors and stops. "Chantal's my girl now," he shouts in Korean. "Plenty of fish in the sea," he says in English. "Got a boat to catch."

Then there is a jingle, like the theme song for a kid's cartoon like *Captain Planet*. Another phone rings, a bird chirping. Suddenly all the policemen's phones are wailing sirens, ringing xylophone jingles, and screeching lame guitar riffs. The policemen are answering. Then they grab him. And for the first time, the asshole is speechless.

## 52

FOR THE NEXT THREE DAYS I'M IN AN ARMY HOTEL IN TOWN. I DIDN'T know the Army had hotels, but here it is: A tiny room with linoleum floors bumpy with cigarette burns, a television on a dresser, and a futon on the floor. Downstairs is a cafeteria that serves roots and soup. It even smells like a barracks in the hallways but it looks like Haesoo's hostel. The television only has the golf channel. I didn't know there was a golf channel.

When Janie finally appeared at the station all she told me was that "they're all fine."

"Did you get them, the sub, the crew, Sarge? Is Junho okay?"

Janie looks at me with a pursed-lip seriousness I didn't think she had. "Everything is fine, you need to rest." Then she was gone.

I try to sleep. Getting only what feels like blinks, but hours pass. No dreams. Or maybe dreams that I forget and that leave me feeling woozy. Wandering the streets of Mokpo helps, even with the Army MP who has to go with me everywhere I go. He's good. I forget about him until he hocks a loogie into a street grate.

You're not arrested, they tell me. But it feels like I am, even if I can wander.

I sleep a lot.

The ocean isn't far away. But when I get close, the line of the ocean just seems so big and sharp, I got to turn around and head back. There is a trail behind the hotel that rises up into the hills. I run up the trail with the MP behind me first thing in the morning. Everything aches more once I get into the smell of trees.

There are cats everywhere. Paw prints are on everything, in the mud, on the hoods of parked cars. At night you hear them wailing and hissing in the alleys, but every time you turn to catch one cutting through a beam of light, nothing.

On the fourth day, an officer comes, and I, the guard, and the officer all drive a road along the ocean. I wonder if there's a shovel in the trunk.

We drive out to a small concrete building with lots of cracked paint and a couple of windows filled in with particleboard. It's right next to the beach. Out front of the bottom-floor café is a big plastic teddy bear in a bib.

I meet a stern guy in an officer's uniform in an empty office on an upper floor. His uniform is loose and the creases are wrong. He's no officer. The door is missing the doorknob. There's a couple of plastic chairs and a fold-out table, where Janie sits looking pissed, arms crossed.

"Well, Beyonghak, feeling refreshed?" the fake officer says in English.

"Did you all break in here?"

"Break in?" he says. And forces a laugh that sounds like a villain's. We sit. He gives me a folder. "These are your statements about your time on the island, any particular people you may have met, and so on. Sign them and it's all done."

There's a lot of paperwork, and I'm still tired. I try reading a few paragraphs but he starts tapping his fingers against the table. I'm about to sign when Janie clears her throat.

"You have a choice," she says.

The man in the crumpled officer's uniform clears his throat.

"What choice?" I say.

"What she means is, on when to leave," he says. "To go back to America."

"I don't understand," I say.

"You sign those and then you are done with your service," he says. "It is over. You go back to your country. Discharged."

"Dishonorably," she says.

The man in the crumpled officer's uniform takes her arm and they get up and go to a corner and start arguing in whispers. I start flipping through the paperwork. In the back on the second-to-last page, after some stuff about a man gone crazy and threatening the locals and how I'd never talk about what happened, there is a little clause saying that I'll be dishonorably discharged, my citizenship revoked, and deported.

"What's going on here?" I shout over to them, holding up the papers.

"Your discharge," he says.

"You're deporting me?" I say.

"You see?" Janie says to the man. "No idiot."

"Fine," he says. "Do it your way." He leaves, bringing with him the MP. Then Janie sits at the table and lights a cigarette.

"You have a choice," she says after a thoughtful moment. "We discharge you like this, and you leave now and never come back to Korea. This is the easiest way."

"How is this easy?"

"Less paperwork. We worry less about you talking about what happened and it is really easy to dishonorably discharge you and throw you on a plane for the U.S. to deal with. However, you're not a citizen there either. You'd be without a country."

"You guys took me off the plane—"

"True, but to them, you never showed up for your citizenship hearing. We don't know what they'll do with you now, being dishonorably discharged. They aren't friendly to foreigners these days, especially with any kind of negative record."

She ashes her cigarette on the floor.

"Always a foreigner," I say. "What's my other option?"

"You stay. Finish your service. But in recognition of . . ."—she sighs—"of the good you did, we transfer you out of the Army and to us for the remainder of your service. You'll have to stay in Korea and have to do some simple things, but you'll essentially be free to do as you please as long as you stay in-country."

"Who is *us*?"

"Who do you think?"

"Angibu."

"You're sharper than you let on."

"If I leave, will the collection agency follow me? You know, all the debts my bio-father racked up in my name?"

She laughs. "Yes, I forgot about that." She takes a long thoughtful drag.

"Well?"

"In my experience, private organizations that want their money will do everything they can to get it. Nothing we do here can change that."

"If I stay, I want help to find him, my bio-father. And I want a paycheck. And I want to see Junho and for you to tell me what the hell happened to that spy who cut my neck." I point at the scar on my neck. "And I want a phone card that works so that I can call Sheryl."

She laughs.

"Don't tell me that me bringing that spy back here wasn't important," I say. "There's no way a country sends a submarine to pick up a bum."

"Okay, okay," she says. "Look at you, all grown up. Negotiating. We'll provide you time and a paycheck. If you choose to pay the loan or not, that'll be your choice. But that's it. Remember, you'll be working for us."

"Answers. What happened on the island?"

"Go downstairs."

"Is this a riddle or something?"

"No, those answers are downstairs. When you're done, come back up and we'll get you sorted."

Downstairs is a teddy bear café with teddy bears suction-cupped to the windows and a giant teddy bear with a party hat on a chair just inside the door. Junho is by a window staring out at the ocean.

He's cleaned up. His fatigues are pressed with corners and his little notebook looks less faded. When I sit he says that he's got more names for the list. Guys in the Coast Guard, guys in the police, the teddy bears in this café.

"What happened?" I say.

Outside, the sky is gray and the ocean is green and the beach is littered. An old man pushes an old cart along the road. It's full of cardboard.

"You know," he says in English, "Beyonghak, you can order steak here."

"You called me Beyonghak."

He's smiling. Like everything is okay. Like nothing happened. Like he has already moved on and nothing can touch him.

There's a tableful of women at the end of the café, maybe office workers. They chat and sound happy.

"Are you out of the Army now?" I say.

"No. But I go to Seoul. Computers. For traffic lights."

There's a crash of breaking plates. We both reach for pistols we don't have. The table of office workers giggle and apologize to the barista, and a couple of MPs who were keeping an eye on us are now over there helping them clean up.

"What happened?" I say.

"We survived." He leans in. "It is okay, we all survived. All." Then he leans back. "Maybe I'll get started on this." He holds up his notebook.

I reach for it and he pulls it away. "Secret," he says.

"What happened?" I ask.

"We waited in misery," Junho says. "We were too tired to do anything else."

"Tell me why you did it. Why did you point the gun at Sarge?" I say.

"I was not alone," he says. "You changed your mind. Didn't want to be a bad guy. You wanted to send spies to mainland. I did too. We did the right thing. We're good people."

"Good?"

"In good computer games, good people sometimes do bad things. Bad people do mostly bad things. In the end there is balance."

*Balance.* I think of the spy. "Why have me take the spy to the mainland, not you?"

"The spy was more dangerous," he says. Then he laughs and holds up the notebook. "You're forever off the list."

The old man pushes his cart into the street. He stops and grabs a squished box from the road. He raises his hand to stop cars in both directions until he's stuffed the box in his cart and continues across the median toward the café.

"I never knew why old people do recycling," Junho says. "But it's a job. A simple job. Before IMF crash, he might have been a stockbroker. Crazy days. Businessmen jumped out of windows so they wouldn't have to do that." Junho taps the glass toward the old man. "That. But look, he can stop cars because he's old. One time I saw an old woman, in a white hanbok and with a cane going so slow across a highway. She was so old, you worry that she would die right there in the street. Traffic for blocks. No one honked. No one yelled. She earned the right to make everyone wait for her to cross the road."

We're silent for a while. I take a napkin and the pen on the table and tell him to write down his address.

"What does *Bucky* mean?" Junho asks.

"It's just my nickname," I say.

"But what does it mean?"

"It's just a name. Doesn't mean anything."

"Korean names always mean something. Girls: precious, pretty things. Men, everything else."

I nudge the napkin closer to him. "Give me your address, so that we can hang out. I don't know where I'll be, but I should have time."

There's a long moment when he stares at the napkin. "Sarge cried for a long time," Junho says. "Everyone did. Then we drank snake soju until the boat came." He looks me in the eye. "No one died."

He pushes back the napkin. "I do not want to hang out," he says. "I don't want to remember this. Any of it."

"Not even me?" I say.

"Not even Kojangi."

"But we're friends."

"When people go, they are gone. Like completed game. They are only past. I don't want to replay this past. I want to play with traffic lights. I want to stay in PC rooms all day. My father jumped out of window. I want to die old and quiet, complete. That's what I want."

Junho gets up.

"I never told anyone about you helping me into the colonel's office," I say. "I'm not the reason you got sent to Love Island."

"I know," he says. "I told them we did it together. And you lied. We were a team, I thought." He looks out the window. "Ocean looks smaller from here."

Junho walks toward the door. He's limping, one shoulder drooping. Whatever happened there had been terrible. But he survived. I think of going after him, but I don't. An MP runs out after him, but he's just limping along toward the ocean and then gets into a jeep parked beside the beach. He doesn't look at me, or the ocean, just down at his little black notebook. Then my friend is gone.

On that side of the road, one of the old man's bags of bottles drops to the pavement and spills out. People walk by as he collects them. After he gets the bag back on the cart, he leans back against a phone booth and lights a skinny cigarette. He and I both look out on a view of an ocean as big and endless and surrounding as it always has been.

# 53

I FIND MY BIO-FATHER WATERING A PEPPER PLANT GROWING FROM A paint bucket at the gate of a junkyard. Behind him a crusher is scrunching Kias, Daewoos, and Hyundais into fridge-sized squares. The junkyard is at the end of an abandoned neighborhood where grass grows between the roof tiles and a field of junk surrounds a tall rusted slide.

Janie gave me a wad of cash and two weeks to go find him. She said to figure it out, then be back in time to get settled in my first job with the Angibu.

It wasn't hard. I wish it had been some kind of great puzzle to unravel, a trick play to expose. But all it took was taking the letters to the different banks, asking for addresses of where the paperwork was filed. A few blocks away from the banks was the return address bio-father used. That address was a vacant bar. But then I heard the machinery—the loans were for heavy machinery, crushers. Around the corner, at the end of the road that marked the end of the town, was a recycling center: KOREA FRESH ONE RENEWAL was the name on the sign.

Giwon, the place with the hill and the crumbling house when I thought he was dead, is only two towns over. He was in this shit town rather than that one. Here and there and Tibicut are all the same.

I walk up to him. He stops watering. I try to say something but can't. I go completely blank. No *motherfucker*. No *gaeseki*.

He clears his throat, spits. "I've got nothing. Just a couple hundred thousand won in the trailer. Tell whoever that I just need a bit more time. I've got a lot of steel I'm going to sell. Got a new crusher."

"Dad," I say in English. "아버지?"

"Oh," he says. Then spits again this long stringy glob where the drop doesn't separate right and leaves a rope from his lip he swipes with his hand. "Oh?" he says again. Then he looks at me, really looks at me. "Oh."

There's boiling in my stomach, aches in my bones. A tide of long nights staring out the window, the paperwork, the debt, the gone mom, the cuts that never scabbed, and everything else that had ever gone wrong—it all storms ashore in my chest and slings boats of pain and hate through the rooftops. I'm going to kill this man.

"Beyonghak-i?" he says. He uses the -i ending. The one of affection. The one for children. Your children. But to me it's the sound of something old and tired, breaking.

—

The trailer has two rooms. Unopened letters and paper cups of ramen bury the desk, and a leather chair opposite looks like the most expensive thing in the building. He's got a pillow on it. My guess is the chair's cushion is cracked. The light bulb hangs naked from a string, the TV has only one antenna. There's a sleeping mat on the floor. Empty soju bottles on the floor line the walls. The wall has a dusty Jesus hanging off a cross with painted blood tricking from his ribs and the thorns on his head. When Bio-Father runs the water in the sink, it coughs.

He hands me a paper cup with a stick of mix coffee. We sit on the floor and stir with the wrappers. The crusher crackles outside and there's a cricket trapped in the other room, chirping. I don't know what to say. Here is Bio-Father. And all I do is stir.

He puts an ashtray in front of him and lights a cig. He puts the pack facing me and points to it. I can have one if I want. "You looked for me," he says, finally, in Korean. His voice is heavy, cigarette-and-booze-laden. He stares at the curl of smoke coming off his cigarette.

"Yes," I say in English. "I got deported. I'm here in Korea now, doing my military service. Your check bounced."

"Which check no good?" he says in English.

"Immigration paperwork. So I got deported."

"De-port-ed," he says, working out the word. He's clean-shaven. His shirt, even though sticking to him, looks like something made to fit. His hair is a shock of white but his face doesn't wear the scars of wrinkles to match. He looks exhausted.

"Told to leave," I say in Korean.

"You speak Korean?" he says.

"Learning. Military service," I say in Korean.

"Oh," he says. "You shouldn't have come back."

"America told me to leave."

"But Sheryl?"

"Your check was no good. She couldn't do anything."

He drags on his cigarette. He coughs and says everything is without a handle. "How did you find me?"

*You took a policy on my life*, I want to say. But all I do is shrug.

"Well, it doesn't matter. You look healthy. Fit. Our sacrifice for the country turns boys into men. What do you do? Driver for the Army? I drove trucks."

"Angibu," I say.

He nods, puts out his cigarette, and goes behind the TV and gets two bottles of soju and puts one in front of me and sits back down behind his ashtray, unscrews the top, and drinks straight out of the bottle. Gulps it like water. Doesn't shudder or anything. "Angibu," he says. He shudders.

"But you knew I was here."

"How would I know that?"

I dig out a debt letter from my pocket and put it on the floor between us. In my backpack I got hundreds more. I also have a special folder from the banks with paperwork to say that the loans were signed in bad faith and that they're actually the responsibility of the person who signed them, Yi Dong-jun, also known as Yi Jun-dong.

He doesn't pick up the letter from the floor, just takes another drink.

"That's one of the loans you took in my name. That's how I was able to find you."

It's a long moment before he takes the letter out from the envelope, skims it. "어이없다," O-iee-op-da, he says. "I haven't been any kind of father to you. But this"—he shakes the letter—"has nothing to do with you."

I open my backpack, and stack the bounded envelopes like bricks. There are three bricks, fifty in a bundle.

"I'm sorry for everything, but I never wanted"—he picks up a brick of envelopes—"this. This is about me, not you."

He takes a drink. He wipes his mouth with his sleeve. He takes another drink. Lights another cigarette and stays silent.

"That's it?" I say.

"What kind of name is Jun-dong?" he says. "Did you ever think of that?"

"I did," I say. "So much that here I am."

"Look," he says, and points to a filing cabinet in the corner. He gets up and goes to it and unearths a shoebox under a bunch of files and an old Ford emblem. He opens it up and rummages through photos. He mutters. He drags on his cigarette. Closes the shoebox and tosses it aside and opens up another drawer and pulls out another couple of shoeboxes.

"What are you looking for?"

"Just wait," he says.

It's from the fourth shoebox that he says, "Ah!" and carries it back to me and the ashtray. It's filled with Polaroids of people and places and cars. But from under all of that he pulls out a photo of a young man and a young woman, and a baby dressed in a tiger-striped onesie and sucking on a pacifier. The young man is wearing a Members Only jacket and the young woman has a fluffy sweater and fluffy hair. The baby in the onesie is me.

"That was a good day," he says. "Your mother won tickets to Woobang Towerland for us." He taps the photo. There's a Space-Needle-type thing. "I loved your mother and you more than anything. I loved you enough to leave you. Give you a chance at a good life if I failed, or a better life until I succeeded. I failed." Then he straightens up and looks me in the eye. The smoke from his new cigarette is really close to his eyes, and they look glassy.

"Do you have other photos?"

"Yes." He starts digging in the box.

I unscrew a bottle of soju and take a swig. My hand is white-knuckled around the neck.

"Here's one of your mother," he says. This time, she's got straight hair and is giving a peace sign to the camera with a big beaming smile. She's behind the register of a 7-Eleven. She's got the orange uniform on. The back of the photo has got what looks like coffee stains or mildew. "She worked because I failed." His eyes are glassy. "But I tried, I tried so hard because I loved you two so much." He takes a long shuddering breath in. "I," he says in English, "fucked . . . off."

My blood's boiling. Knuckles and fingers are so white that the blood gathers in the gaps. He's trying to juke out of it. He's trying to sorry his way out. Lie.

But I'm not braining him with the bottle. I'm not even shouting. Aside from my hands, everything is level and tense. "Stop lying," I hear myself saying. "I'm here because I want three things. I want you to hear exactly what happened to me. Then, when I say I'm done, and only when I say I'm done, you're going to tell me what I don't know. Got it?"

He sniffs and lights another cigarette. His hands shake, but they stop when the flame touches the cigarette's end. He looks me dead in the eye. He's decided something. "What's the third?"

"We'll see when we get there," I say.

"Okay." He looks to the TV. "There's plenty to drink."

—

I tell him. He listens. I drink. He drinks. I mix my English and Korean. I tell him about the time I had forgotten, but now remember, when I wished upon a shooting star for my parents to come and get me, and how I wrote the same to Santa Claus. I tell him about how kids jumped out from the aisles shouting, "Karate Kid," and how at night I can still feel the harness and the tire digging in around my shoulders and how the same rope snapped for me but brought down a big tree branch on the only man that had ever mattered to me. I told him how I got no college scholarships. I tell him how even I couldn't say my own name right. I tell him what it was like to be deported and conscripted. I tell him how I beat a man. I talk calmly like I know what I'm saying, but really I'm spilling, emptying. Just facts. Bullet points. Events. I lie and say that the Angibu taught me how to kill and live with it. Then I'm spent.

My stomach burns, my burps burn, and I'm drunk because I haven't eaten anything in god knows how long. When I'm done and he goes behind the TV for another bottle to add to the line of bottles we've built between us, he grabs a fresh pack of cigarettes. Outside, the crusher has stopped and the cricket gave up in the other room and someone is banging on the trailer door. Bio-Father goes to the door and I'm ready to tackle him if he tries to run for it. But he just opens the door and says, "Good work today," and that he and whoever is at the door will talk tomorrow. Then he closes the door and comes right back and sits and says, "Are you done?"

"Did I say I was?" I say, but I am.

"Show some respect," he says.

I scoff. Next he's going to tell me to bow. He's going to tell me to use highbrow Korean.

"I might be a shit father," he says, "but I'm still your elder."

"Only actions matter."

"Angibu," he says, nodding, "might say that because they don't believe in mistakes. But every pencil has an eraser."

We drink. We've got too many bottles in front of us. My eyes feel droopy.

"If you want, you can sleep here," he says.

"You think what you did was just a mistake?" I say.

"Oh, so it's my turn?"

I drink. I nod.

"None of this was about you," he says, and I scoff. "Do you want to hear it?"

"Yes," I say.

"I fell in love with a woman who had a respectable name, would inherit land, beautiful, but money-poor," he says. "That's the truth. It's also the truth I still wake up reaching for her. And for you. Also true is that she was a swindler. Back then I bought clothes on the docks and sold them in the cities. All over the country. Good money. Then, after we got married, I found out about the debt against the land by her father and that's why she had to work even though she was an only child, and what made it worse was that her father was a gambler. Then you came along."

He's flipping a corner of a blurry photo of us posing on a scooter. "I couldn't make enough money selling clothes, so I tried real estate. That didn't work. Then buying and selling at auctions of abandoned shipping containers. I hustled pool tables, worked two jobs, and your mother worked one and raised you. We kept getting more debt. Even the hospital was after us to pay for you getting born.

"One day, she walked to work, a day I was watching you, crossed the middle of the street, and got killed. The driver kept driving and it was never solved. At the time we rented a room from a family that would sometimes watch you when we were working. They were good people, but I had to do something big. Then I met Sheryl. I was in love again. She was American and sweet and smart. I didn't think of going, taking you there. But I was working in two kitchens and a bar. I couldn't raise you alone, I didn't want to tell Sheryl. But when I did, when she played with you, I thought, This is what I should do.

"She wanted to go back. No one knew that Korea would develop like this. First world. I thought, In America, I can start over. With a good woman I love. We go. It's shit. Nothing there. My English is poor. There were no jobs for me that were any better than I was already doing, just trees and country bumpkins. I hated it. Rice even tasted wrong. But you were happy. I think, maybe better fate. American fate. Not our palcha. You could do better. So, I came back to work hard. To pay off debts. Once I made enough money, I'd be able to offer you a nice life here if you wanted."

"Tell me about my mother."

"Sohee? Well, she loved you. Was terrible with money, you know, a woman." He takes a drink like he forgot something at the bottom of the bottle. "I came back to fix all the problems she left for me, and I swear that this will pay." He bangs on the floor of the trailer. "In a few more years, I'll be free. We can be free."

"Free?" I say.

"Yes," he says, and rubs his stomach. "Excuse me." He goes to the toilet.

Most of the photos inside the shoebox are of products: bicycles, shirts on sale, a building for sale. But after a little digging I find more pictures of my bio-mother. In most of them she's smiling and giving one or two peace signs. Usually, when she gives only one, it's because she has a hand around me, or around my stroller, or around her belly. She poses for all the photos in shops or in front of restaurants. They're always outside, never at home. Was she as bubbly at home?

Sheryl wasn't so bubbly at home. Usually she was tired. Looking at the photos makes me feel the warmth of alcohol coming off my cheeks. I feel hot. I have to get up.

Outside I hear a pair of cats fighting. Out the window it's so late that the sun is threatening to come up. The window is above the desk and a mound of unopened letters piling out of an ancient black briefcase. It's got gold tumble locks all on zeroes.

The letters are from banks. They're from payday loans. They're from sports books and from credit cards and real estate agents, and government advisory offices and lawyers and . . . I stop looking.

Bio-Father grunts in the bathroom. Shits firing out of him.

I go for the drawer in the desk. There's a stamp pad and his seal. Like a seal of a country, a personal seal in Korea is as good as a signature. I grab it. I go into the living room and grab the shoebox of photos. I see the lighter next to the ashtray. I smell all the alcohol we drank and spilled. I hold the lighter in my hand and for the first time in a long time I feel calm and in control. My skin is hot and sweaty, as the air conditioner only seems to sweep brief moments of cool.

In the hundreds of pictures in the shoebox, there's only a handful of us. There are three other boxes. I think of opening them up, burning the photos of whatever and whoever else I find there. The fire could start there, sweep through the alcohol and the letters, and torch it all.

He fires another shot on the toilet. He groans. He's not going anywhere for a very long time. I fumble with a photo of him leaning up against a Porsche, lighting a cigarette like in some old-time movie poster. The colors are faded, sun-exposed, sun-beaten. This is the most true thing about him: a wish, a fraud, a ghost.

I bang on the bathroom door.

"I'll be out in a minute," he says.

"Was it worth it leaving me?"

"What? You expect me to shit on my own floor?"

I should make him apologize. I should make him grovel. I should tell him, *If you put anything else in my name I'll kill you,* as I throttle him. But somehow, I only feel drunk, and relaxed, and settled that I've got a shoebox under one arm, his seal in my pocket, and a lighter in my hand.

I take the lighter. He'll have to search through piles of old photos and hills of bills for it. Outside is the so-early morning. Everything feels wet even without rain.

## 54

THERE ARE TWO KINDS OF DARK IN FOOTBALL. THE FIRST IS THE TUN-
nel: the tunnel of the stadium where everything on that end of the light is
louder and brighter and more important than you've ever known. Then
there's the tunnel when you're running, you only see the hole in the line,
the wavy path you need to take on the return. Tunnels are a good form of
dark because everything else disappears except for your next step and the
obstacles to it.

The second kind of dark is being buried in the bodies of a dogpile. Buried so deep in a losing hole you can't even look at the bright lights of the
scoreboard. The bottoms of dogpiles are the worst places to be in football
because every moment is foul with groping and kicking and grunting and
spitting and cussing and gouging. These are the moments you only think of
after: after I get the ball, after I cup-check this motherfucker, after.

There's a third kind too, concussions. But that's self-explanatory. There's
before and after, but when it happens everything just skips like a CD and
you come to, unsure of everything. But that's not unique to football.

After I stamped all the paperwork for the loans to be returned to Bio-
Father, and after I stamped a statement of fraud that I wrote for my bio-
father and handed that to the police in Giwon, I have this tunnel moment.
The next steps are clear. Simple. I have one year of military service to complete for Janie and the Angibu.

They decide that the best place for me would be at Yonsei University.
*Yawn-say University?* I didn't even graduate high school.

"We need eyes there," Janie says. "Just in case." We're meeting at a café
right beside the train station. She's drinking an espresso and she bought
me something fancy with chocolate and whipped cream. I don't like it.

"In case of what?"

"What does it matter? You're going to go to college for free for a year."

College. Free. For a year.

"What do I have to do there?" I say. "Do I have to kidnap people or something?"

"Beyonghak," Janie says, and drags on the cigarette. "You're not a real spy," she says. "Your job is simple. Go to class. Study and put something in that thick head of yours. There may come a time when we need small things, like information on someone or maybe a door left unlocked. But mostly, we only expect you to behave. Got it?"

"Janie, do you have a name? Like a real one, not bullshit on a card?"

"My name is Jihyeong, if you must know."

"Jihyeong," I say. "Well, that's nice."

"We all have many names."

"I guess."

"Names define you. If you change them, it's supposed to change everything, at least that's what they say. There was this pitcher for the Samsung Lions in a terrible slump. He goes and talks to one of the fortune-tellers who looks at your face, birthday, and all of that. He tells the pitcher his name is bad luck. The guy changes his name to Seok. Means something like stone or metal for knives. Pissed his parents off, but now he's an all-star."

"Good for him," I say.

"It doesn't always work that way, but it was good for him. Gives him a rough edge, I think. You and I have rough edges, don't we?"

"If you people are worried about me talking, I won't. Who could I even tell that would care?"

"Tell me"—Janie leans in—"when was it that you really decided to go to the mainland? When you were beating on those guys with their hoods?"

Blood drains from my face.

"Oh, don't worry. Nobody cares. It wasn't public. Besides, I'm pretty sure that was Chung Hee going on and on about his Mongol fantasies. However, we won't tolerate that kind of behavior while you're at university. All you will need to do is find out all the little things we wouldn't know from paperwork. Does this person smoke? If so, what brand? Does that person seem to be political? Which bars they hang out in, and with whom—that kind of thing. After you finish military service, you can get in as much trouble as you want, but not under our watch. Got it?"

I swallow like I'm afraid, like I'm actually going to be their lackey. "Tell me which people to find out about, which doors to leave open," I say with as much of a tone of fear and duty as I can muster, "and I'll be right on it," I lie.

She eyes me for a long moment and then drops her cigarette into her coffee as if a great thought has struck her, and laughs. "Ah, Beyonghak! You're a hoot! And all grown up! You really had me going! Just remember who the bad guys are if the time comes for it. You met enough of them."

So that's how I end up at a great big university where all the buildings are white as chalk and have ivy growing on them. A dorm room all to myself. A meal card for the cafeteria, which I have all to myself because I'm here way before school starts and everything is just empty. But even now there's a few people around and the cafeteria is open. Seoul never sleeps.

When I dropped into Communes, Haesoo hugged me so hard I thought my eyes would pop. She's got an engagement ring from GI Dan. She tells me this even as her breasts are smashed into my ribs and I'm thinking I lost a chance—that I never had—to see them. Simon and the rest are still there and I tell them that I went to the Army, that I'm in college, and everyone nods and says that's nice and then shouts out names of musicians to Hyun-shik, and even though I'm there the whole night, no one mentions Chantal, or British girl, or Mr. Kim. None of them show up either.

Janie picked my classes. I've got three of them. Korean Language 3, Intro to American Culture, and Eastern Philosophy. I'm in the bookstore, look-ing at more books than I think I've ever seen, when I see Chantal, flipping through the American Culture textbook I need. She's got on a dress with a frilly skirt. She dyed her hair orange. She looks like Kim Tae-hee from the billboards, like she's really from here. Yet, somehow it's still her.

She looks up. Closes the book. "You got to be fucking kidding me," she says in English. "What the fuck are you doing here?" she says in Korean.

I pick up a textbook. "Buying books for class," I say in Korean. "You tak-ing American class with Milan?"

"It's Dr. Jo. Mi-lan is a woman's given name, like Bora," she says. "And it's American Culture, not American class, you meathead," she says in English.

"Whatever," I say. "You taking it?"

"You seriously want me to believe that you got into this college? Is the football team that desperate?"

"Chantal—"

"Bora," she says.

"Bora, can we, like, you know, start over?"

"Start what over?" she says. "As I recall, you just wanted to get out of here, yet here you are. You following me? You're following me, aren't you?"

"O-iee-op-da," I say.

"What did you say?"

"어이없다," I say. "You're without a handle. Nothing I say makes sense to you because you won't listen. Look, I'm sorry for all the meathead stuff I ever said. I was being stupid and scared. I want to talk and hang out, start over. But right now you're freaking out. Let's talk later."

I grab a book off the shelf. The other people in the bookstore are looking at us but trying not to.

"What?" she says.

I walk down the aisle. I stop, turn, and flip her an I've-got-your-nose fist. She laughs.

"There's football here?" I say.

There is football. In fact, it's so new that the tackling dummies on the sleds don't even squeal when you hit them. There's a league too. Tryouts start on the running track, which is a first for me. But I run. I run faster than I ever have before. I've lost weight, and it seems that muscle power can also really slow you down. I'm not only faster, I'm the fastest. In the other drills, I'm the only one that can high-step the tires, the only one that can pull a sled and double up the cradle on the ball without the coach shouting at me.

These other guys try to hurdle, one-hand grab, and Heisman their way around with the ball. They've never played real ball. They've never been knocked so hard they slobber.

By the end of the first practice, the coach pulls me aside and says, "You're on our scholarship from here on out. Now, who do you think would be a good fullback to follow?"

When I get Sheryl on the phone I tell her all about this, college, football, the debt taken care of. There's a long moment when in the background Graham's two little girls scream.

"But Bucky, what did you have to do to get all of this? You haven't said why all of these good things are happening. Nothing is free."

"I can't say. But you just need to know that everything is fine."

"Bucky, you're there. You're not here. How are things fine?"

"Fine for right now."

"Are you okay? I mean, really?"

"I'm okay, Mom."

"It doesn't sound okay to me. Are you coming back for Christmas? Bobby is getting leave and I'm thinking of cooking a big dinner. You know, like they do on TV, with a ham and potatoes."

"Since when do you cook?"

"Since I've had a chance. I'd really like us all together, you and Bobby getting along with Graham. Maybe we all call Uncle Rick together, a real family thing. Are you coming?"

"I'm staying here this winter. There might be a championship game for us to play."

"Bucky, you're not a liar. Don't start now."

"I want to play. I want to stay."

"After everything? I mean, what—" She stops. I try to picture her out on a balcony of an apartment I've never seen, putting out her cigarette in a crystal ashtray. "I'm not asking you to tell me everything, but, Bucky— come home."

The phone beeps. It's got a low battery. This is my first cell phone, and I still can't remember to plug it in to charge.

"I chose to stay."

"Prisons have sports and libraries too. But they're still prisons."

"My battery is dying. I've got to go. Love you, Mom."

There's a long silence and I hear one of Graham's girls say it's their turn to pick the channel.

"Love you too, Bucky," she says. "Come home soon."

—

When I run, my legs move so fast they're like wheels. The drums rolled, the band squealed, and the team from Daegu kicked off and I caught it in the end zone and now I'm moving. I'm at the fifteen, the twenty, and there is still green turf in front of me. I'm going up the gut, right dead-center between the hash marks. It's dangerous because it's like going straight in the gullet of the net. But what I see right now are gaps. Players overthinking their coverages, anticipating me to bounce out to the left or to the right. It's the first game of the season. They don't have this in their bones yet. And right now the thing I know is that five yards in front of me I will be able to cut and juke back.

Cut and juke. Put in the extra huff, and I'm out and around the kicker. Here's something else I know: No one is going to catch me now. I'm the only one amped and ready to run to the end zone. I know this to be true. I know that Chantal is somewhere in the stands watching, maybe flipping me off. I know that next week when classes start, I'm going to show up, and it's going to be the hardest thing I've ever done because there will be all these things I don't know.

I know football. I know I'm going to score on this kickoff return. Just like how I'm going to change my name to something that sounds, feels, right. I don't know what just yet, but that's for later. I'll figure it out.

Right now I'm at the twenty, the fifteen, the ten, the five . . .

# ACKNOWLEDGMENTS

Thank you to those early teachers at the Vermont College of Fine Arts: Rigoberto González, Domenic Stansberry, Jess Row, Doug Glover, and Xu Xi.

A special thanks to the mentors and teachers who have guided and supported me at the University of Nevada Las Vegas and the Black Mountain Institute. I am eternally grateful to Douglas Unger and Maile Chapman, who convinced me that this book from the folder of abandoned children was worth raising and maturing.

Thank you, Jon Cook and all those at the David T. K. Wong Fellowship at the University of East Anglia and the Barrick Graduate Fellowship at UNLV for getting me to the end.

Thanks to Lorinda Toledo, Oscar Oswald, Kate Shapiro, Kelly Elcock, Dan Hernandez, Tim Buchanan, Brittany Bronson, Timea Sipos, Meagan Poland, Gord Sellar, Will Wickham, Dod Granville, Richard Cook, and Graham Winning.

Thank you, Justin Brouckaert, for taking a chance on me.

Thank you, Alane Mason, at Norton, for your sharp editing eye.

Thank you, Mom and Dad, for everything.

Most of all, thank you, Jumi Kim: my love, my bedrock of courage and strength who gets me to sit down day after day at the workbench of words and write and who gets me to leave and see that there is a world outside.

Source for Korean language learning: B. Nam Park, *Korean Basic Course*, Vol. 1 (Washington, DC: U.S. Department of State's Foreign Service Institute, 1968); *Korean Basic Course*, Vol. 2 (Washington, DC: U.S. Department of State's Foreign Service Institute, 1969).